Five Days in Venice

ALSO BY FIONA COLLINS

The Hours of You

Spring, Summer, Autumn, Us

Summer in the City

You, Me and the Movies

The Sister Swap

Four Bridesmaids and a White Wedding

Cloudy with a Chance of Love

A Year of Being Single

Five Days in Venice

FIONA COLLINS

LAKE UNION PUBLISHING

This is a work of fiction. Names, characters, organizations, places, events, and incidents are either products of the author's imagination or are used fictitiously. Any resemblance to actual persons, living or dead, or actual events is purely coincidental.

Published by Lake Union Publishing, Seattle

www.apub.com

EU Product Safety Contact:
Amazon Media EU S.à r.l.
38, avenue John F. Kennedy, L-1855 Luxembourg
amazonpublishing-gpsr@amazon.com

ISBN-13: 9781662531149
eISBN: 9781662531132

Cover design by Emma Rogers
Cover image: © Adisa © Maksym Fesenko / Shutterstock;
© Vera_Petrunina / Getty

Printed in the United States of America

Five Days in Venice

Chapter One

Venice

Tuesday 9 January 2018

Leo Greene walked into the frescoed lobby of Palazzo Tesoro on the Grand Canal in Venice, on the first day of the book festival. The milling throng – readers, authors, publicists and the odd curious tourist – watched him with the usual pleasure and admiration. People were always pleased to see Leo Greene. He was one of *those* men – good-looking, clever, successful – for whom the crowds and the gods smiled, and more than once upon a time, Olivia Sackville had almost been in love with him.

Of course, she had to be standing right at the edge of the bookish crowd as he strode through the lobby, wavy hair pushed back from his face, hazel eyes sparkling, vintage leather satchel slung from his shoulder. Of course, she happened to be holding a copy of his bestselling novel, *Midnight Echoes*, down by her hip – one that she was now quietly edging behind the canvas of her tote bag.

'Olivia!' Leo stopped right by her, his eyes wide in surprise, his smile confirming what she knew she'd feel if she were to ever see him again. 'You still have great taste in books, then?'

'*Leo*,' she replied, trying to make his name not sound like an accusation or an entreaty. She stopped trying to hide the book that three seconds before the catastrophe of his entrance, Olivia's publicist, Meryn, had handed her, saying rather too casually, 'Leo Greene is also going to be on the panel, too, did anyone mention . . . ?'

Olivia's thumb was over Leo's name. All Leo Greene's books had a similar cover: dark background, neon font, this one with a fleeing figure in shabby overcoat and chef's trousers disappearing around a damp-bricked corner. She felt her pulse in that thumb.

'It's nice to see you again,' Leo said. He was wearing black jeans, a dark wool pea coat, a striped scarf he was spooling off. 'How have you been?'

'Great thanks, you?' Olivia replied robotically. *How have you been?* was a simple question, a light exchange between some, but between a man and a woman who had not seen each other for three years, and had left on less than friendly – some might say disastrous – terms, it was not.

'I've been OK. What are you promoting?' Leo asked. He was five inches taller than her. His eyes were the rich green and brown and gold kaleidoscope she had so often tried to avoid. '*The Curator on Church Street*? Another big hit, I bet.'

'*The Curator*, yes,' she replied. With her free hand, she adjusted the waistband of her oxblood leather midi skirt; her silk blouse had become a little untucked. She unnecessarily handed his book to him, like it was a grenade, making sure their fingers didn't touch.

'I was only invited yesterday.' Leo shrugged at the book, opened the flap of his leather satchel and slipped it inside. No wedding ring, she noticed. 'I'm a stand-in. Louise Welland-Phillips broke her leg.'

'Shame,' Olivia said coolly, although her heart was a jumping jackrabbit under the silk of her blouse. She flattened her arm against her bag for the reassuring feel of her neatly lined A5 notebooks, her rainbow set of pens, her pencils. 'I was looking forward to seeing Louise.'

There was a twitch of another smile at the corner of Leo's lips, then his eyes turned serious. 'It really *is* great to see you again,' he said, his gaze set fast on her face. 'It's been . . . well, it's been a while. How are you, Olivia – really?'

She couldn't bear the sudden warmth in his voice, the richness of his enquiry, the history of the two of them lurking right behind it. He had no right to be looking at her this way. With friendliness. With curiosity.

'I—' she started.

'Leo Greene, goddamn it!' boomed a voice. It belonged to Anthony Beau, porcine author of the brilliant contemporary Jeeves and Wooster-esque books, *The Edwin Hurley Chronicles*. He had been behind Olivia, holding court with some young Italian book bloggers and the fourth attending author, Frances Holland, but stepped forward and thrust out his pallid hand. 'Nice to see you, my lad.'

'And you, mate,' said Leo heartily, that curious expression leaving his face as the one of professional author snapped back on.

Olivia stepped away, relieved, making a final adjustment to her blouse and skirt. She didn't want to listen to Anthony, in tweedy suit and flat cap, grumbling on again about yesterday's flight from London City airport. She didn't want to look at Leo – how unsettling that he was here! – or think about the last time they'd been together in Italy. She took a further step back, seizing gratefully on an adjacent fresco: a pastoral scene – maiden, milk jug, lamb.

'Glorious, isn't it?' Meryn came to stand next to her. 'Of course, all the buildings in Venice are glorious, but this is something else. I think the organisers of *An English Writer in Venice* may have found the prettiest palazzo in the city.'

Palazzo Tesoro was a faded old lady of Gothic beauty; a three-storey slab of Venetian wedding-cake in weather-blanched plum, studded with narrow arched windows and ornate balconies. A water taxi had dropped them off this morning at its rickety wooden jetty with mooring poles like giraffes' legs, and, inside, they had climbed two floors of the old stone staircase in awe, to reach the lobby of the *Sala Grande*.

'It's stunning,' agreed Olivia. Meryn, in her red, snappy wool skirt suit and her leather knee-high boots, had knocked for Olivia at the hotel at 10 a.m. sharp, armed with coffee and Italian cookies. In the water taxi, in the splash and morning steam of the Grand Canal, Olivia's publicist had marvelled at the splendid, toppling skyline of the city, as she had never been to Venice before. Olivia had, but not to Palazzo Tesoro. She admired its intricately painted walls and ceilings in muted shades of dusky peach and gilded rose, its cool, marble floor the colour of linen. 'Oh look, they're opening up!'

She kept her sights on two members of the palazzo staff – black skirts, white shirts, neat high ponytails, who were easing open the two huge gilded doors at the rear of the lobby – and nowhere near Leo Greene, somewhere behind her, talking to Anthony, Frances and a gaggle of admirers. She could hear laughter, mostly female. Anthony's bluster. Leo's seductive rumble. Olivia smiled tightly at one of the ponytails. She had to keep a hold of herself. She had to batten down any part of her that might flap open and betray the effect Leo Greene was having on her, but she also wondered how he was feeling about seeing *her*. She had known Leo. She had witnessed the masks he liked to wear with peppy lightness and cheery concealment.

The staff members were being instructed by the British organiser of *An English Writer in Venice*, Felicity Dunn, and the Italian co-organiser, Valentina Cavilleri. The doors, once opened, revealed a room longer than it was wide, its floor pearly in weak sunlight from three tall arched windows at its far end. Huge paintings and a sentry of grand walnut doors galleried the walls, and in front of the windows was a long table covered in a generous white cloth – with four seats.

'I haven't been put next to Leo, have I?' Olivia whispered to Meryn as they walked in with the other attendees. Gilt chairs, laid out in rows and dissected by a central aisle, like at a wedding, filled the elegant room that smelled of beeswax and history. An enormous unlit chandelier lorded above, prettily catching the pale winter light.

'Erm, I'm not sure.' Meryn's blank look told Olivia she was fibbing. Olivia Sackville and Leo Greene were both big-hitters. Having them on a panel together – the crime writer, the romance doyenne – was quite the coup.

'Hi, Olivia!'

A middle-aged woman in a green anorak and big owl-like glasses had tapped Olivia on the shoulder. She smiled at one of her favourite authors from under a silvery-blonde fringe, her hair short and flyaway.

'Beth! You came.'

'Of course I did! I saved all my pennies and told my husband to fend for himself. He'll be living on baked beans and cheese sandwiches all week, but never mind!'

Beth was a book blogger from Warrington (@bookWireGirlie68), with quite a big following on most of the social media channels and a talent for writing expansive and thoughtful reviews.

'Where are you staying?'

'A little guest house behind St Mark's Square. It's gorgeous. I see Leo Greene is here,' Beth whispered, lobbing a thrilled look in his direction. Leo was taking his seat at the table, two chairs in, and still talking animatedly to Anthony Beau. 'What an addition!'

Leo laughed at something Anthony said, before reaching across the table to shake him by the hand. Leo's eyes briefly flicked over to Beth and Olivia, and Olivia quickly looked away.

'Have you been to Venice before?' she asked Beth.

'No, never. It's amazing! I'm sure it's quite different now to how it is in the summer, but it's really atmospheric, isn't it?'

It was January, and yes, there was definitely something magical about Venice in winter, Olivia thought – a season in which the city was washed in quite a different palette. Its summer hues – terracottas, plums and yellows – were tempered by the watercolour brush of winter to elegantly faded pastels or, when fog crouched low over the canals, to a pencil sketch of black and grey, the coats and hats of tourists in St Mark's Square flicks and dashes in inky olive.

Olivia had written about Venice in winter in her notebook last night at the hotel. Just a few lines of prose, some observations. She liked to capture people and moments in her lined books with the plain covers. It was something she'd always done: a pretty scene glimpsed on a foreign shore, the play of light on a morning church steeple, the way a parent looked at their baby.

'I love your new hair,' Beth added. 'It suits you.'

Olivia smiled her thanks. Most of her life she'd had a neat blonde bob, dead straight, but now she had let her hair grow to her shoulders and embrace its natural wave. She was almost forty, after all; why not change a little something?

'It's a thing I'm trying. So, have you got some good questions lined up for me?' she asked Beth. Felicity and Valentina were ushering the last people to their seats. There was a faint clatter to their left from an open walnut door, and through it Olivia spied two elderly ladies bent over a gilt trolley, orchestrating rows of upturned cups on saucers.

'Of course,' Beth answered. 'Especially now.'

'Now?'

'Olivia? Could you please take your seat?'

Felicity, calling over, was a volume of burgundy cord. A rather doughy woman, of schoolteacher haircut and Alice band, she gestured to the author's table.

'Sorry. Of course,' Olivia replied. 'What do you mean, "now"?' she enquired of Beth, as she moved from her side.

'I read crime and romance,' Beth responded, a cheeky look on her face. 'You'll see, pet.'

As she reached the table, Olivia heard, 'I believe you're next to me. I hope that's OK.'

Leo was boyishly patting the seat of her waiting chair.

'I guess so,' she said, reluctantly sitting down. She could smell Leo's familiar aftershave and that putty-type product he raked into his hair with his fingers. She could hear the echo of his voice, the one she had once hoped might tell her that he loved her. She could taste her own regret. And she could reach out and touch him, if she wanted to. And she had often really, really wanted to.

'You sure you're OK?' He had that look again, warmth and curiosity. She didn't know what to do with it.

'Yes, fine, thank you.'

She glanced out to the audience, twenty to thirty people, some smartly dressed, some casual. She caught Beth's eye and accepted a small wink. Then she took a deep breath and tried to still herself, to keep herself contained, but she imagined she might fail.

She was not fine. How on earth was she going to survive this week in Venice with Leo Greene?

Chapter Two

'Your hair's longer.'

Leo was staring at her. He had taken his coat off to reveal a moleskin shirt: dark khaki, undone more than was necessary. The panel hadn't started yet. Felicity and Valentina were hiss-whispering to each other at the lectern to the left of the table.

'So is yours, a little.'

His arm was on the table, cuff risen to reveal his wrist. He was clean-shaven, a little tanned; his hair longer and wavier than would look right on any other man. Olivia's heart stepped into the front carriage of the familiar rollercoaster that was Leo Greene and strapped itself in, but how was his? she wondered. How had *he* been, really?

'Can you even remember what your book is about?' He smiled genially at her. It was standard fare that once an author finished writing a book and it was published, they promptly forgot everything about it – character names, who said what to who, the plot . . . 'I can't recall a thing, but I've made a list.'

He dived into his satchel and whipped out an A4 notebook she knew would be unlined inside. He placed it on the white tablecloth and tapped the matt orange cover. It had a hessian spine that was peeling off a little at the top, and a narrow press of graduated loose pages peeking out at the bottom.

'You love a list,' she said, foolishly divoting a piece of turf from the lawn of their past.

'I do.'

He flicked it open, and there was his familiar handwriting, sprawling, leaning backwards on itself, as though trying to catch what had gone before. The page it had fallen to was a list of character names and occupations, some scruffily underlined.

'And I guess you've done a mind map?' he queried.

She nodded, compelled to pull a neat piece of paper from an orderly folder in her immaculate tote: colour-coded bubbles and arrows, zealous use of highlighters.

'Very *you*,' Leo commented, looking at her quizzically. The soft light from the window behind him rendered his hazel eyes almost a nutty brown and a distant, unbuttoned version of herself wanted to weep.

She nodded again. She leaned down to return the mind map to the folder in her bag. He crossed his legs under the table, one foot kicking up the tablecloth.

'Cowboy boots,' she observed, probably unwisely, but she hadn't noticed them when he came in.

'Impulse souvenir.' He grinned at her. 'I was at a book event in Texas recently. I'm quite attached to them, really.'

'They're not very author-y,' she commented mischievously. 'Surely a jacket with suede patches on the elbow wouldn't have been too much of a stretch?'

'I'm a crime writer, not a geography teacher.' Leo's eyes were dancing. The rollercoaster lurched forward and started rumbling up the track. What were they doing? Why were they falling back into this teasing and banter? Had they forgotten?

'Or someone about to go to a dodgy nightclub.' Clearly, she couldn't help herself.

'Would you *like* to go to a nightclub?' he asked her, with one raised eyebrow.

'No, thank you,' she said archly. 'I've seen your dancing.'

Leo's face broke into the widest grin. They *had* forgotten, hadn't they? They'd forgotten how it had ended, and instead were blindly going back to the beginning. The chemistry. The witty words. The high-flying delight in each other. But no, they couldn't go back. However tempting it was to return to their version of autopilot, familiar and heady; at some point they had to land the plane.

She thought of all the times she would have to see him this week – today's panel, the signing at the bookstore tomorrow, the readings at the Guggenheim on Thursday, the Final Dinner on Friday night. Until this moment, they had been mere events in the diary; now each was a bout of turbulence to be buckled in for.

'So, how are you finding the hotel?' he asked. 'The converted monastery?' Safer ground. Small talk.

'You're staying at the Figo, too?' The rollercoaster, hesitating on the track, came to a stop.

'Yes. We all are, aren't we?'

If she were to turn in her seat and look out of the tall windows, she would be able to make out the hotel's bell tower, the green of its shrubbery and manicured fig trees, the faded dollhouse pink of its stonework. The Figo was on its own island, a few minutes by boat from St Mark's Square – a seventeenth-century Augustinian monastery that had been converted into a hotel in 1985. It had wide, carpeted corridors and sumptuously decorated rooms. A feeling of quiet elegance and history. The hotel was beautiful, and it was *huge*, which could now only be a good thing.

This trip had, up until about ten minutes ago, been perfect for Olivia. She had just finished her latest novel, which was currently with her agent, and she needed a break. She was more than happy to fulfil her obligations here in Venice, but in her downtime she wanted to lie in her hotel room and think about nothing.

No chance of that now. Charming Leo Greene was here. Bright, lively and funny Leo Greene. Often kind, occasionally arrogant, sometimes unreadable Leo Greene. But still she remembered how he had once peeled back his skin and revealed his heart to her. How much of hers did he remember?

'That's good,' he said, and she didn't know why.

'Good morning, everyone!'

'Buongiorno!'

Felicity and Valentina were all smiles at the lectern: Felicity's bland, pulpy face eager; Valentina's set and schoolmistressy above an aggressively pink trouser suit.

'Welcome to *An English Writer in Venice*, Day One,' said Felicity, smiling sweetly.

'Thank you to everyone for coming along to today's Q&A panel,' said Valentina in terse, excellent English.

'Hopefully it will be a lovely event for you all, in the beautiful surroundings of Venice's Palazzo Tesoro,' continued Felicity, gripping the edge of the lectern. 'We will enjoy a lively panel session for one hour, then take a twenty-minute break for coffee out on the balcony.'

'Yes.' Valentia took up the baton vigorously. 'Wrap up and the view will be worth it, I promise, then you will re-enter for a further hour of discussion. So, without further ado' – she flapped her left hand, almost clipping Felicity on the cheek – 'let's welcome our four esteemed English authors today: Anthony Beau, Frances Holland . . .'

'. . . Leo Greene and Olivia Sackville,' Felicity completed.

There was a ripple of applause. Meryn gave Olivia an encouraging nod from the end of the front row. At the back, a woman

Olivia recognised as Leo's publicist, Tanya, slipped into a seat. She was late twenties, with a big, equestrian laugh.

'Anthony Beau,' read Felicity from the lectern, 'as we know, writes humorous novels set in the world of the idle and rich. Frances Holland: family sagas from contemporary London. Leo Greene: crime novels featuring the insomniac chef detective, Ben Midnight . . .'

There was a grin from Leo, mirrored by several rapt faces in the crowd.

'. . . and Olivia Sackville,' projected Valentina, 'her wonderful love stories. Let's have another round of applause.' The attending obliged. 'And now let's go straight to the floor with some questions!'

Felicity and Valentina waited. A few rays of weak sunlight fanned on to the marble. There was a cough. A male tourist took an apple from a rucksack and bit into it quietly. Then a hand went up: a middle-aged man with a foxy face and red woollen scarf wrapped tightly around his throat.

'Please tell us about your new book,' he said, in a London accent that almost made Olivia start, for it caused her to think of Charlie, her father. 'That's a question for Leo Greene.'

'Thank you,' said Leo, full of customary author charm. He sat back in his seat, crossed his legs, flashed the cowboy boots. 'What's your name?'

'It's Sam.' Sam was nothing like her father physically; he didn't resemble Charlie Sackville at all – his face, or his hair, or his clothes – but something about his manner, and the way he sat in his seat, reminded her of home. Working-class Pimlico. Chip butties and tinned rice pudding and love.

'Pleased to meet you, Sam.'

Leo flashed one of his stage persona smiles: personable, approachable, supersonic, and Sam beamed back at him. Leo had the room in his hand already. Women were leaning forward. Men were wondering how he did it. Olivia was wishing she was at the other end of the table, while her body did not. Her heart did not. Because she knew. She knew who lay behind the stage persona. The man within. It had been bittersweet when he had stepped out from himself and taken her hand, whispered her name; incredibly sad that she would never know that man again.

'Well, this book has been a slight departure for me in that the hero, Ben Midnight, our furious chef' – he gave another grin, bounced back by his audience – 'discovers a murder himself whilst out on one of his nightly walks along the canal. A murder that both returns him to his past and threatens his future. I bring back the police constable who had been transferred out of the area and, oh, there's a new addition: a scruffy mongrel called Peaches.'

'It sounds fantastic.' Sam's foxy features were animated. 'I can't wait to read it.'

'Thank you, Sam,' Leo replied engagingly. 'I'll be signing a few copies at the Acqua Alta bookstore tomorrow, if you want to come along.'

Sam nodded his assent. 'Yes, I might do.'

'Great!'

Another hand went up, pale and slim.

'I also have a question for Leo.' The woman was in her early twenties, pretty under a 1970s curtain fringe. 'When are you coming to Verona?'

Leo laughed. 'Well, thanks,' he said. 'I do hope to get to Verona at some point, but I'm here now, aren't I?' A froth of laughter spun around the audience like candyfloss. 'And so are you. Anything else you'd like to know?'

'When are you getting married?' asked the woman coquettishly. 'You are forty, now, right? Are you thinking about settling down?'

Leo feigned wiping an exasperated hand across his forehead. 'OK,' he said, 'yes, I do think about settling down all the time, but no, I have no plans to get married. Thanks very much for asking.' The candyfloss hurtled to the top of the drum. Olivia couldn't look at Leo. She knew he *had* almost been married – once. 'Do you have any questions about my book?' His tone was pretend-serious.

'No, but I really enjoyed it,' said the woman, flicking her fringe out of her eye. 'I really love your writing.'

'Thank you.' Leo kicked back further in his chair. Cool, calm, devastating. A publisher's dream.

Leo Greene was an excellent writer, but everyone in the literary world knew his handsome face and relaxed sex appeal garnered him thousands more readers: the way he carried himself when interviewed on television; that look in his eye in publicity photos that had everyone running to the nearest bookshops to buy one of his novels. Leo was a sexy bachelor of crime fiction, not to be harnessed, not to be snared, but Olivia knew he had come close.

'Next question?' said Felicity pleasantly.

A woman stood up. 'I have a question for Olivia Sackville,' she said. Beautiful tumbling hair. Italian accent. 'Where did you get the idea for that scene in the Scottish lavender fields?' she asked. 'I really loved that part of the book. Especially the kiss.'

Olivia smiled. 'Thank you,' she said, 'and thank you for asking.' She kept her eyes straight ahead. 'I visited them,' she fibbed, 'a few summers ago, and thought it was just the most gorgeous spot.'

'Lucky you,' said the woman. Olivia could feel Leo's eyes boring into the side of her head. The woman sat down.

Another stood up.

'Hello to Frances Holland,' she said, rather bluntly. She was also Italian. Deep voice. Red coat. 'I admire your latest heroine, Betty Brown, so much. Is she based on you?'

Frances laughed. 'No, not at all,' she replied. 'In fact . . .'

The smell of coffee from the anteroom was strong. There was the faint chime of a teaspoon landing on marble. Frances finished talking about her heroine's love of the royal family. A man asked Anthony if he laughed while he was writing, and did it distract him? Anthony answered yes and no, while laughing heartily. Then Beth stood up.

'I have a question for both Olivia Sackville and Leo Greene,' she said. 'If that's OK?'

'I'm sure that's absolutely fine,' said Valentina sternly. 'Please go ahead.'

Beth looked from Olivia to Leo, then back again. 'This is a bit out there,' she said, raising a hand to wiggle her glasses on her nose, 'but I hope you'll bear with me . . .'

'Go on . . .' nudged Felicity, her blank look expectant with an edge of anxiety.

'Is it, how many times do we go to the fridge for snacks when we're writing?' chucked in Leo, 'because I can tell you, I go quite a lot – about once every forty-five minutes. How about you, Olivia? Could it be a Snickers on the half hour?'

'It's nothing about snacks,' Beth interjected, as Olivia threw Leo a horrified look. They were playing roles here, she thought. Eloquent authors. Teasing panellists. This was a game, and nothing like the reality she and Leo had once known together.

'*What?*' he mouthed back at her, his eyes twinkling.

The diminutive Beth took a deep breath. 'It's more to do with your books. *Both* of your books. Together.'

'I don't get you,' said Leo amicably.

'*Together?*' Olivia queried.

'Yes,' said Beth. 'My question is actually quite simple. Why did you both write the same scene in your latest books?'

Leo tilted his head to one side, looking puzzled.

'What on earth do you mean?' Olivia sat up straighter in her seat.

'Yes, what do you mean by this question?' echoed Valentina. 'Olivia writes romance and Leo writes crime, no?'

'Yes, absolutely they do,' said Beth, her face beginning to flush. 'But I was sent both books and I read both of them, one after the other, last week – studied them, if you will – and I noticed something very odd.'

'Which is?' asked Leo. His chin was now resting on his fist, *the amused*, but his eyes told Olivia he might be as unsettled as she was.

'That the plots may be really different' – Beth blushed further – 'Leo's the cat and mouse of the street detective and the serial criminal, Olivia's the story of the museum curator and the tycoon' – she sounded like she was reading the blurbs from the back of their books – 'but, somewhere towards the middle, you've both written the same scene.'

'Scene?' prompted Valentina.

'*Scene?*' questioned Leo and Olivia in unison.

'Yes,' said Beth, looking triumphant. 'You've both written the same scene in a restaurant. You've described the same meal.' Her eyes flicked between the two of them. She pulled a pocket notebook from somewhere inside her anorak, flipped it open and read. 'Italian restaurant. Burrata. *Bistecca alla Fiorentina*, sautéed cabbage and anchovies in garlic and olive oil. Chocolate gelato with an amaretti biscuit. Candles burned down to the nub . . .' She looked back up at them both, Leo Greene and Olivia Sackville, authors and one-time lovers. 'And I just wondered why that was.'

Chapter Three

The room was silent, except for the clangs and tinkles from the anteroom, a muffled Italian exclamation, the rustle of a bread bag.

'Well,' repeated Beth, mischief now transforming her flushed features. 'How did you come to write the same scene?'

Olivia finally exhaled, then attempted a high kind of laugh.

'Yes,' she said, 'I wrote a restaurant scene with some – all – of that food. It was between Kath and Justice, after Justice's overseas position had kept them apart for so long, and, of course, there's the whole business with the artwork conspiracy, and the injury, and Kath's baby . . . not to give too much away, of course . . .' She was trying to deflect. It hadn't worked. The audience was rapt. '. . . and I can't comment on Leo's book because I haven't read it.'

'You've never read *any* of my books,' Leo said slowly, to a rippling quill of laughter in the crowd. 'Not since the first one.' He trained his eyes on her, steady and unblinking.

'No,' Olivia agreed. 'And you, none of mine, not since the first one, either.'

The audience looked at each other, bemused.

'Maybe I could start *The Curator* tonight?' he added. 'I'm overdue a little romance in my life.'

'I don't believe that!' Olivia's return was quick-fire, but her shot almost went off target. She was distracted by his eyes, his lips, that warm skin at the base of his throat . . . and by all of their shared memories. For she had once revealed herself to him, too; had stepped forward, for him to embrace her, to know her heart and be its salve. She didn't like this showman version of Leo. She remembered it only too well. And she didn't like the quick-fire side of her, either. Once upon a time, they had been real with each other.

'Well, you've written the same scene,' said Beth conclusively. 'Anyone who happens to read both books would say that as well.'

Lit in pale winter sunlight from the window, there was a certain obstinacy about Beth, Olivia thought. She imagined that Beth had been a very forthright little girl, one who always had her hand up at school, who read and read, and wrote lists of the books she wanted for Christmas, presenting them to her father in September, along with the things she wanted from the Grattan catalogue. A little girl very similar to the one Olivia Sackville had been.

'Well,' Leo said generously, his voice like maple syrup, 'it happens. It's just a coincidence,' he added. '*Really*.'

'So, you've never shared a meal like that together?' Beth pressed.

'Us?' Leo looked at Olivia and smiled confidently, but there was a note of something else in that look, she thought. Melancholy? Reproach? Or was that just her? 'No, of course we haven't.'

Olivia's heart still thudded. Were they done with this now? What on earth had just happened? Where were Beth's usual questions about writing processes and how an author ordered their desk?

'Of course we haven't,' she echoed. 'Who on earth would want to go for dinner with Leo Greene?'

The members of the audience laughed. Somewhere in the anteroom, a coffee cup fell to the floor and smashed. Leo muttered, 'Bloody hell!' – either to the cup, or Olivia's put-down, it was hard to tell – to much amusement. They were still showboating, Olivia thought, her and Leo. They were sparring like actors in a sparky comedy, not acting like two people who had laden each other with guilt and anger before disappearing from each other's lives for three years.

Except, that wasn't quite true, was it? They *had* seen each other, eighteen months ago. Olivia had been escorting a rather worse for wear Maeve King, fantasy romance author, out of the London Reads summer party at the Victoria & Albert Museum in 2016. They had been clopping through the wide stone reception hall, past the gift shop – dimmed and closed for the night – Maeve hanging off Olivia's arm and chuntering on about something or other, when Olivia saw Leo standing by a low-lit alcove and a marble bust, in the company of two younger men.

He was in a suit, white shirt, wavy hair swept back like a Jane Austen hero. She hadn't seen him at the party, although she may have looked for him, like she always looked for him. They caught each other's eye across the expanse of cool stone and history. Leo's grin, at something one of the men had just said, eased into an uncertain smile, and she couldn't help but smile back at him. Smile at the still wonderful, intoxicating and welcome sight of him. A quiet smile, shy and full of sadness, for when they had last said goodbye. For when he had hurt her, and she had hurt him.

For Tuscany.

And then one of the young men said something else, and Maeve complained again about her feet, and they were out on the steps of the V&A, into the warm London night, and on to the Tube, with Maeve wittering on for eight whole stops – but the image of Leo's face stayed with Olivia long into the night, as did that awful feeling of having left something behind.

Leo was talking again. Olivia came back into the room at the Palazzo Tesoro. 'You have a wonderful skill for analysis, Beth,' he suggested cordially. 'Perhaps I should hire you as a detective consultant for my next book . . .'

The audience tittered. Beth looked proud.

'Well, I read it. You both wrote it. The end,' she added, in dour tones that made everyone laugh. 'Don't you find it interesting?'

'Not really,' said Leo lazily. The audience giggled. Some shifted in their seats. There was a short, sharp sneeze from the anteroom. 'As I said, there are a lot of coincidences in books.' He frowned now. 'Let's go back to talking about each author, in turn. There's no need to lump poor Olivia and I together.'

Poor Olivia pulled a face. Leo threw her a conciliatory heart-stopping grin, then the grin dropped and he looked a little sheepish. *Showboater*, she thought, as she told her over-beating heart to rein itself in. Surely he was a stranger to her; she no longer knew him. Their past was a drifting ship that had long sailed from shore. But somehow, in the last couple of years, they had both written the same scene about a meal they had once shared right here in Italy. They had described the same food, the same candles. As soon as she got back to the hotel, she was going to download a copy of his book.

'Alright,' said Beth, good-natured. 'I'll pretend I've got it all wrong.' And she sat down to a smattering of light applause, put her notebook back in her pocket and adjusted her glasses, but not before shooting Olivia another quick wink.

Olivia shook her head imperceptibly. *Book bloggers*, she thought. They were fantastic. Those who got behind your books could promote them online like nobody else. But this one had put a cat among the pigeons here in Venice, and that was a *lot* of pigeons for one cat. She could feel Frances Holland staring at her, eyes wide and amused. Anthony Beau had a silly look on his face. And Leo, sitting next to her, was Leo. He was always Leo. Complicated. Creative. Inescapable.

'OK, that was enlightening. Thank you very much,' said Valentina. She turned disapprovingly to the floor again, straightened the lapel of her jacket and consulted her notes, while Felicity looked on. 'Next question?'

Chapter Four

The rest of that first session belonged almost entirely to Leo. He was asked to detail his crime set-ups and settings. He talked hilariously about his infamous, occasional late-night roaming around the streets of London, hunting for characters, stories and situations. He was relaxed, charming, gregarious and his audience lapped up every word. The other authors sat back, mostly. Anthony Beau answered one question about the role of his hilarious narrator, Ignatius Mulch; Frances was asked about her South London settings and the rich St Lucian history weaved throughout her books.

Olivia answered two questions. One about where she liked to write (at her desk, at the window overlooking her garden in Marylebone – yes, she had 'really gone up in the world', as her father, Charlie, once liked to say), the other on who was her favourite romantic heroine from literature (Cathy from *Wuthering Heights*). The rest of the time, her scattering brain tapped at her about the restaurant scene in chapter twenty-five of *The Curator on Church Street*. Yes, it was in an Italian restaurant. In London, though, not Italy. Yes, the food had been as described. Yes, her two characters, Kath and Justice, had talked openly about parts of their pasts but not everything, and had looked into each other's eyes. Yes, it had been based on a real-life meal she had shared with Leo Greene.

Her cohort was now waxing coyly about his next work, kicking back in his chair again, like it was a deckchair on a beach.

'An idea in progress always sounds a bit lame when spoken out loud,' he told a glamorous, mid-life Italian woman with a huge coiffed hairstyle and hooded eyes winged with black eyeliner. She'd come with an equally glamorous friend. 'Telling anyone even a part of it makes me want to shoot it dead before it's even begun. Or myself!' he quipped wryly.

'So, no hints?' asked the woman. She had taken her coat off while he was replying to her, revealing a wine-red dress with a keyhole neckline.

'None whatsoever,' he replied with his trademark grin, and the woman flashed one back at him.

'Thank you very much, Leo Greene,' said Valentina decisively. She tapped twice on the lectern with her fingertips. 'And now we will have our interval with coffee and *bussolai* – Venetian butter biscuits – on the balcony.'

'Do put your coats back on,' Felicity urged, 'or you really will get cold – we don't want anyone suing us, ha ha – and make your way out.'

The same Palazzo staff members creaked open an arched grill to the balcony, immediately letting a blast of Grand Canal air into the room: brine, woodsmoke and the dank sluice of fog.

The patrons heaved on coats and hats and scarves and wandered out to take near-single-file places on the narrow balcony, like cut-outs in a paper theatre. Olivia hung back to fall in with Frances and they shuffled along to the left; Leo was far right, talking to Anthony.

'Beautiful venue.'

Frances was wearing a camel coat with a wide faux-fur collar and peeling on a pair of dove-grey sheepskin gloves.

'Beautiful city,' Olivia agreed.

Their vista was the green-black canal. The city's January coat of low, lazing fog. A lit brazier on the other side of the water a round thistle of orange burr-blaze from a small balcony. Winter gulls alighting on a copper roof. An arm raised in greeting from a vessel stitched to the water by an angled pole. And above the jumbled, majestic skyline, the shifting clouds, skulking through on their way to other cities. Yes, Olivia liked Venice in the winter very much. She liked the drained colours, the flashes of heat, the pause from the summer crowds.

There was a rolling clatter from behind them, and Olivia turned to see the two elderly ladies, carthorse-ing a trolley laden with a coffee urn, cups and saucers and an oval platter of pale gold biscuits. They parked the trolley in front of the open grill and made a two-woman chain to pass out steaming cups of coffee and plates of 's'-shaped, crumbly biscuits. Olivia received her coffee gratefully and her heart momentarily swelled at the scene in which she found herself: the grey plume of the morning, the literary minds, the readers. That somehow, she had made it here, all the way from a humble ground-floor flat in Pimlico with Charlie Sackville, to being an English author in Venice, standing on an ornate balcony overlooking the Grand Canal.

If only Leo Greene wasn't standing at the other end.

'I'm sorry we didn't have a chance to chat before the session started,' said Frances. She nudged her fur collar higher around her neck. 'You spoke wonderfully, by the way, and you look so well.'

'Thank you. So do you.'

Olivia had always admired Frances Holland, the fun and gossipy writer from Streatham in South London. She was also a little jealous of her sparse, incisive prose and pithy dialogue.

Frances stirred her coffee. She looked at Olivia through its steam. 'Fancy you and Leo Greene writing the same scene in your books!'

'Yes, fancy,' Olivia said airily. She glanced to the end of the balcony. Leo was sipping his coffee and staring out across the canal. Anthony was in deep, neck-forward conversation with Sophia Loren-lite and her friend, as they stood in a row. 'Although, have we *really*?'

'So, you've never had a meal like that with Leo?'

'No, no. Of course not. Like he said, it's just a coincidence. I've barely ever met the man.'

Frances nodded. 'Are you going to read his book?' she asked, setting her cup back into its saucer. A vessel on the canal clonked into another. There was a shout, an Italian hand gesture.

'Probably not. I don't like crime.' Always denial, when it came to Leo Greene, she thought. Always never quite telling the truth, or blurting out too much of it. It was what had brought them down. It was what had ground their story to its end.

'*I* might do,' said Frances. 'I've never read any of his. I sort of felt that a man that good-looking couldn't be any good.'

'Like it was his only talent? The bestseller charts might disagree with you!'

Frances laughed warmly. 'Yeah, I know. He's good-looking *and* brilliant. I *hate* people like that!'

They both looked from the brazier, that bright burr from the opposite balcony, to steal a glance at Leo Greene, collar up, game on. He caught them at it and gave them a bashful wave. Olivia frowned and turned back to Frances.

'Sometimes there's more to people than meets the eye,' she murmured, almost to herself. 'We write about characters like that often enough in our books.'

'We certainly do.' Frances had a warm but curious smile on her face. '*Onions*. Layers. They're our bread and butter. *So*,' she continued chattily, moving on, to Olivia's relief, 'are you at the London

Book Fair this year? Did you notice that Alistair Thomas, senior editor at Banks & Short . . .'

◆ ◆ ◆

Frances took centre stage for the second half of the panel. A man in a pale blue trench coat had several questions for her, including when did she first realise she wanted to be a writer, how long did it take her to get published, and did she like to do anything special on publication day? Frances was witty and indiscreet in reply, throwing in a few nuggets of candid publishing-world secrets that Olivia would have definitely left out. Then Sophia Loren stood up again and asked Leo another question.

'You're known for your lists, Leo,' she drawled. 'Do you always list the characteristics of your main characters before you start writing?' She had reapplied lipstick since the first session.

'Yes, I do.' Olivia glanced at him and he rewarded her with a flicker of a smile. She was convinced he had undone another button of his shirt. To her relief, they hadn't spoken when they had re-taken their seats for the second session, as Felicity and Valentina had launched into it straight away. 'But I add more as I go along. And sometimes I take some out, of course.'

'Can you give me some examples?' the woman asked with a toothy smile. 'Of some of those characteristics. I hope to become a writer. I am . . . I have started writing something. I need tips from the master.'

Olivia didn't think this woman looked like a writer. She looked like she spent her days idling on an eighth-floor Italian balcony in a slinky black slip, watering trailing plants and batting off wolf whistles from admiring men below.

'"Master" I'm not sure about,' Leo replied with a modest smile, 'but, examples, OK . . . For a male character, something like "opinionated, ambitious, gaberdine raincoat, fifties throwback" . . . so a mixture of physical and psychological characteristics. Sometimes totally random things that would make no sense to anybody else.'

'Do you ever lose your lists?' Slip Dress tilted her head and pouted. Olivia bet she couldn't wait for summer. She also thought of the lists Leo used to email her.

'Nope, they're vital to me. Everything important is in my notebook.' It was still in front of him. He tapped his fingers on the curl of its damaged spine. 'Someone once encouraged me to make lists, and I've never looked back.' He glanced tentatively at Olivia; she pitched him a tiny, self-conscious smile. 'Actually, my therapist has got me making gratitude lists,' he added. 'I have to write down all the things I am grateful for in life.'

The woman's eyebrows raised. 'What kind of things?' she asked.

Therapist? Leo was seeing a *therapist*? A rush of surprise and guilt pinned Olivia to her seat.

Leo grinned. 'Day to day stuff that makes me happy, like sunshine and cherry blossom. Freshly mown grass. The taste of sea bass in lemon butter. But also, bigger things out there in the world that I'm grateful for.'

Olivia stared at him.

'And is that easy or difficult?' asked the woman. 'Finding things to be grateful for?'

'It's easy,' said Leo good-humouredly. 'I'm grateful for a lot, just ask my accountant.'

The audience laughed.

'Is there anything you want that you haven't yet got?' the woman pressed.

'A couple of things,' Leo answered. 'A yacht, a Lamborghini . . . Some other things, maybe.'

He smiled coyly. The woman returned his smile like she was in love with him. She dropped back into her chair, her friend immediately offering her a boiled sweet from a rustling bag.

'And one last question from the floor, please.' Felicity looked at her watch, a little agitated.

A hand was raised. A querulous British voice: 'Yes, over here!' The owner of the hand was an elderly gentleman with a scholarly cotton wool ball of grey hair above each ear. 'Have you ever been on a writers' retreat?' he asked. 'And how useful do you find them? This question to Olivia Sackville, please.'

Olivia's heart took pause in her chest, and she quickly considered why he was asking. Was he a writer? Someone with a property in the Euganean hills, outside Venice, thinking of hosting a retreat for visiting authors? 'Yes,' she answered carefully. 'Just the once. Here in Italy, actually. In Tuscany.'

'Ah, Tuscany.' The old man looked pleased. His eyes twinkled in his face. 'I grew up near Volterra.'

'Oh, lovely.' Olivia remembered everything about Tuscany. She remembered its summer days and its evening glow and its outright trickery, fooling you into thinking you might be in love.

'Do you think they are useful for writers?' he continued. 'Get a lot of writing done?'

'Yes, I did, at first.' She avoided Leo's eye. 'Yes, it was very useful, indeed. All that space, the beautiful setting . . .'

'And did you travel around the area? Get to know Italy?'

'Yes, a little.' She definitely didn't look at Leo.

'And will you look around Venice while you are here? Go to Murano? To the Lido?' This man was *chatty*, she thought.

'I'm definitely going to the Lido,' Olivia volunteered. 'My godmother has a house on the island.'

'She does? Well, how wonderful!' The old man beamed. The puffs above his ears moved upwards. 'I expect she'll be so happy to see you there!'

'Well, she's actually in a hospice in Castello at the moment. But I'll be going to the house to do some packing up.'

'I'm so sorry.' The man looked downcast, and Olivia felt she had said too much.

'I'm sorry, too,' said Leo, turning to her with suddenly soft hazel eyes.

'Thank you. Both of you. And thank you for the question.' She smiled at the man. 'Really. That was a good question about a writers' retreat . . .' She looked down to her notes, gave them a quick shuffle, stacked them neatly again on the table.

There was a moment's silence, then, 'Well!' announced Valentina, clapping her hands. 'That concludes the morning! Thanks so much to our authors and all the attendees here at Palazzo Tesoro. I think we would all agree that it's been a really fabulous session!'

Olivia looked up. There was a small wave of applause.

'Thank you all for coming!' echoed Felicity politely. 'Please mind the stairs on your way out.'

Hands reached for bags, fastened coats and wedged on hats. Feet echoed on the marble floor to the open gilded doors, and through to the lobby.

Felicity and Valentina approached the authors' table, followed by Meryn and Tanya, Leo's publicist, who came up to Leo and bent down to give him a kiss on the cheek.

'Well done, Leo,' she said in her clipped tones. Tanya was the daughter of some marquis or other. 'You were great.'

'Thanks, Tanya!'

Leo stood up, packing his notebook into his satchel. The others stood, too, Olivia smoothing down her skirt and reaching for her tote bag.

'We will go into the palazzo garden now for more refreshments,' said Felicity.

'This way, please,' said Valentina, holding out her hand to one of the closed walnut doors.

'I thought that was it,' Olivia whispered to Meryn. 'I thought we were going back to the hotel.'

'I guess we're required to mingle,' said Meryn with a shrug. 'Sorry.'

'Damn,' Olivia whispered, and she stole another glance at dazzling, heart-breaking Leo Greene. *Damn it.*

Chapter Five

The 'secret garden' behind Palazzo Tesoro was pretty. A small square enclosed by the backs of the splendid buildings of Venice's plainer cousins, it had neat, biscuit-textured paths and a maze of semi-circular dwarf hedges around a central grassy disc. A small round table had been set up on the disc. The two catering ladies who had served coffee were now hovering over tall flutes of sparkling Prosecco and small platters of canapés as, behind them, a trio of patio heaters flared: orange flames and woody grey smoke licking up into the air.

Felicity and Valentia had herded the four authors and the two publicists down a narrow flight of stairs, through a ground-floor salon to the rear of the palazzo and out to the surprise of the garden. It was bitter out here, the January wind bothering the tops of the hedges and whipping up the corners of the ladies' black aprons, a low grey sky above. Olivia fastened the top button of her coat and pulled her cashmere scarf from her bag to wind around her neck. They stood in an awkward circle, the authors, the publicists, and Felicity and Valentina, both smiling rigidly.

Leo was to Olivia's right. She was trying to subtly move away from him – leaning her body to the left, towards Anthony, clamping her bag to her side again. The pens. The notepads – when Leo clinked his glass with hers.

'Well, that was lovely,' he said.

'Wasn't it?' She was forced to straighten her body. They weren't on stage any more. The show was over, she thought. The audience dispersed. They were left with only stilted words and the suspended chill of the past between them.

'I'm sorry to hear your godmother is in a hospice.'

'Thank you.'

She didn't want to look into his hazel eyes, but there they were looking into hers. She didn't know how to interact with him. Be with him. It had been three years since they had last said a word to each other. Three years since she'd disappeared into that car on a Tuscan lane, the cicadas chorusing in the night hedgerows as Leo stared at her from a softly lit farmhouse doorway, everything destroyed between them . . . 'And your parents?' she asked, as brightly as she could. 'Are they well?'

'Yes, very well.'

'How's Balth?'

Leo pulled a face. 'He's the same. How's Annabel? And Stella?'

'Both great, thanks. Stella's flying out here at the end of the week, actually. I've wangled her an invitation to the Final Dinner.'

'Sounds fun!'

Stella was on her way to meet a man in Verona she'd met online. She was stopping off in Venice for the free dinner and the chance to spend the evening with her friend, following an accounting conference in Rome.

'Things are always fun with Stella.'

They sipped their champagne. A bird flitted on to the hedge nearest them, looked around, then scuttered off, climbing into the bone-grey Venice skyline.

'So, we wrote the same scene,' he said. 'Apparently.'

'Well, I'm sure we didn't . . .'

'Interesting, though. All that food . . .'

'There's a lot of food in Italy. And in Italian restaurants. My scene was in London, by the way.'

He looked at her. 'So was mine.'

'Oh.'

They fell silent for a few seconds. Sipped a little more of their Prosecco.

'Not married then?' she asked him eventually. She couldn't help herself.

'No. You?'

She waggled her empty left hand at him. 'No.'

There was silence between them for a few seconds, then Leo asked, 'What are you doing now? Next? After this?'

'Now? Going back to the hotel for a lie down, I expect.'

He looked surprised, but she was tired. She wanted to lie on her bed and eat the contents of her mini bar. She wanted to digest Leo Greene being here in Venice, and what that might mean.

'Anthony mentioned the four of us going on to Harry's Bar. With Meryn and Tanya.'

'Harry's Bar?'

'For lunch, if you fancy it?'

'Oh, I'm not sure . . .' Her voice trailed off.

'Why not? It'll be great.' She realised he was standing too close to her. She could smell his aftershave again, the reminiscent scent of summer days and rainy afternoons. 'Unless you'd *really* rather go back to the hotel to start reading my book . . .' She chucked a look at him. 'I'm just kidding,' he added. 'You know I am. I know it's a long time since you've read anything of mine.'

He was looking serious again. This unnerved her, and she remembered something else about chapter twenty-five of *The Curator* (Leo was right, it was easy to forget certain details of her books, especially as, by the time they came out, she had usually written a whole new one and started another) – just after that restaurant scene, Justice and Kath had their huge row and tore their lives apart.

'Will you come?' He ran a hand through his hair. He was vintage Leo, *classic* Leo, she thought, the green and tiger brown of his eyes a hairpin trigger to many of her regrets. 'Everyone would love you to come.'

Now his tone was kind. This was what had always thrown her about Leo, had her feeling she might fall for him, time and time again. His ability, sometimes, to say just the right thing, at exactly the right time. 'No, I don't think so,' she replied, ignoring that tone. The side of Leo she had almost loved. 'Sorry.'

'OK. Totally your call.'

He looked down at his cowboy boots then back up at her with a resigned smile. She wanted to run. She wanted to flee from this place right now, and from that look in his eyes. She was lost here. She'd lost hold of herself the moment he'd breezed into the palazzo.

Meryn appeared, a glass of fizz in one hand and a mini mushroom bruschetta in the other. She rolled her eyes dramatically. 'Anthony's being a pain,' she said. 'He's panicking about bow ties and stuff for Friday. You don't happen to have a spare, do you?' she asked Leo.

'At the hotel. I'll go and talk to him,' Leo offered, and he moved away, Olivia's eyes trying not to follow him.

'Apparently, we're all going to Harry's Bar,' said Meryn, before popping the miniature bruschetta in her mouth.

Olivia shook her head. 'I'm not.'

'You *have* to!' Meryn was horrified. 'Anthony has promised to tell us what happened at his publisher's Christmas party!'

'No.' Olivia shook her head. 'I'm not going. I want to go back to the hotel.'

'That's disappointing. You'll be missing out.'

Olivia didn't answer. They both took sips of their Prosecco.

'That was interesting what Beth said, wasn't it?' Meryn ventured finally. 'About your books. You and Leo.'

'It was insane.'

'Fancy both doing the same thing!' Meryn's expression was that of an unrelenting ferret. She was never 'off', Meryn – her mind always whirring, plotting, shooting off at tangents. It was what made her such a good publicist.

'We didn't!' Olivia protested. 'It's just a coincidence.' That was becoming such a tired line already.

'Beth's put something about it on social media.'

Olivia nearly choked on her fizz. 'Really?'

'Yep! On Instagram. She's posted a photo from the panel and written about the two restaurant scenes in your books, giving page numbers. There's quite a lot of chatter online already.'

'Oh, God . . .'

'Chatter is good, Olivia, as we know. All publicity is fantastic publicity.'

'Hmm . . . well, I hope you're not looking to get some sort of *opportunity* out of it?' Olivia raised her eyebrows.

Meryn grinned. 'Of course not! But there is one right now, if I can change your mind. A chance to have your photograph taken at Harry's Bar with the other authors. It'll be great, we can put it everywhere, along with a big fat image of your book. And the food there is soooooo good! You can't be the only *English Writer in Venice* who doesn't go!'

'Now you're making me feel guilty!'

'Good. Please, say you'll come – please, for *meeeee*.'

'Oh God, Meryn, not the *face* . . .'

'Are you relenting?'

'Maybe.'

'So, you'll come?'

Olivia threaded her arm through Meryn's and dipped her head on to her shoulder. 'I'm only coming for *you*. And for the publisher. And my book sales.'

'Let's get a top-up,' Meryn said, thrilled, and, still arm in arm, they wandered over to the table, where the ladies refilled their glasses.

Leo and Anthony were standing by the fountain, talking earnestly. Anthony had his hand on his hip and was leaning in like a teapot. Leo's face was lit up in the receipt of Anthony's merry barbs.

'When did you first meet Leo Greene?' Meryn asked Olivia as they glanced over and sipped their fizz.

'A few years ago. On the circuit.' She could go to Harry's Bar, Olivia thought. She could go and talk to everyone, do the photo, fly the flag. She could survive the week, if she didn't have to look into his eyes.

'What, a book event or something?'

'Yes, must have been,' Olivia continued the lie. She had lied to Frances and now she was lying to Meryn. Sometimes, the wrong words just escaped her.

'I think most people would know exactly where they were when they met Leo Greene,' Meryn replied, with a quick smile. 'Don't you think so?'

Of course, Olivia knew. She knew exactly when, and where. It was 1998, in London, and she was nineteen. And she was never supposed to see him again, but she did.

Chapter Six

London

Thursday 20 August 1998

'Excuse me, my ticket's not working.'

Olivia Sackville, nineteen years old and fresh from a summer's day temping at possibly the most boring media agency in London, was standing at the barrier inside South Kensington Tube station, trying to get out. She'd tried four times but her ticket wouldn't let her through, and she had been asked to *Seek Assistance*.

'Mine's not, either,' piped up a male voice beside her. She glanced up at him. He was about her age: twice-unbuttoned denim shirt, brown wavy hair. She held out her ticket and the London Underground staff member gave it a cursory glance.

'Over here, please,' he grunted, and she and the man in the denim shirt followed him over to the right, to the wide barrier at the end of the row. 'Come on through, then, the pair of you,' he said after wearily tapping at something with a key fob.

'Oh, no!' Olivia laughed, hitching the straps of her tiny black backpack further up her shoulders. The guard's tired smile didn't quite reach his eyes as she busied through the barrier. 'We're not a *pair*.'

'Why not? What's wrong with me?'

She flicked her head around to the young man in the shirt moving through after her. He had unhurried hazel eyes, a slow but arresting smile. Posh voice.

She frowned at him. Her eyes told him, *Everything*.

'Have a good evening,' said the guard dryly.

Olivia stepped away into the crowd. 'You, too,' she batted back over her shoulder, ever polite.

'Yes, have a *good evening*.'

With one last repelling glance at him, the cocky voice of Denim Shirt Man was swallowed, too, into the rush of commuters, and Olivia rolled her eyes before heading as planned to The Cheshire Arms on Thurloe Place, where she was meeting her friend, David – 'Fellow Working-Class Stowaway', as he'd referred to himself at Canterbury University – for a Writer's Tipple Cocktail Night, inspired by the favourite alcoholic drinks of ten legendary writers.

'*Margarita – Jack Kerouac. Mojito – Ernest Hemingway* . . .' David was reading off one of the special menus littering the bar, while Olivia quickly defluffed his jacket with a mini lint roller from her backpack. *Ever-equipped* – that was how her friends described her. '. . . *Ramos Fizz – Tennessee Williams. Gin Rickey – F Scott Fitzgerald. Mint Julep – William Faulkner. Martini – Dorothy Parker. Boilermaker – Charles Bukowski*. I reckon we're in for a great night!' He checked out the lapel of his jacket. 'Thanks, Livs!'

'What's a boilermaker?' Olivia put the roller back in her pack, inside a sandwich bag, and peered at the menu. 'Oh, right. It's whiskey and beer mixed together, which sounds absolutely revolting. I'll have a mojito, please.'

‘I’m going to have a martini,’ said David, flicking his Jarvis Cocker fringe out of his eyes and exaggerating the flat tones of his Sheffield accent. ‘I’m ripe for channelling my inner Dorothy Parker.’

‘Oh no, you’re way too nice.’

‘I’m pithy, though?’

‘Always pithy.’

David was dry, funny, always up for a night out and the only other person who was still in London for the summer. Olivia’s uni friends, Stella and Annabel, were on a kibbutz in Israel and everyone else who’d just completed their second year at Canterbury seemed to be living it up in Greece or Italy or Spain. Not Olivia, who just before the start of the holidays had been offered a summer job working at Harrington Blunt, the media company, for six weeks and, needing the money as well as some media experience, she’d taken it, but she had regrets. The job was incredibly dull. It involved photocopying things and drinking weak hot chocolate at a desk empty except for an empty in-tray and an empty out-tray, trying to look efficient, and sighing a lot more than she wanted to.

David turned to the bar to order, whispering to her that the barman was ‘hot’.

‘Go for it!’ she whispered back to him. ‘He looks lovely.’

‘Do you think he’ll appreciate my down-to-earth northern charm and proletariat allegiances?’

‘Certain to.’

David leaned forward over the bar, giving his fringe another flick, and Olivia started investigating the ingredients in the Ramos Fizz.

‘I hope you’re not following me.’

Olivia looked up. Cocky Denim Shirt Man from the Tube was standing in front of her, holding a mojito.

‘I hope you’re not following *me*,’ she said, surprised.

'Well, I kinda did.' Denim Shirt Man shrugged theatrically. Slid his mouth into a hammy half-smile.

'You did? Should I be worried?'

'Yeah. No.' He attempted to look sheepish. She took in his hazel eyes, his mouth. He was very handsome, she supposed. 'We went the same way. I just happened to see you come in here. The girl who didn't want to be in a "pair" with me. I was curious. Who are you here with?'

'My friend.' She gestured to David, who was flirting intensely with the barman, not a drop of cocktail having been poured.

'Not a date?'

'No.'

'Are you looking for one?'

'No. But *you* clearly are. You followed a complete stranger to a pub. Are you a stalker?'

He laughed, and it was such a warm and disarming laugh. She noticed his eyes had several different shades radiating from the pupils. That his mouth relaxed into a smile so easily.

'Not at all,' he said. 'I promise. I was supposed to meet a mate tonight but he cried off. And I thought you looked nice, despite the faces you were pulling at me in the Tube. I'm Leo.'

She stared at him. He had long eyelashes. Velvety tanned skin between the unbuttoned 'v' of his shirt. 'I'm Olivia,' she said reluctantly, and then she thought, *Why not?* She could chat to this handsome, non-stalker bloke for a couple of minutes, seeing as David was otherwise engaged.

'I like your shirt.'

She looked down. 'It's a work blouse.' It had tiny figures on it – ironic tiny office workers sitting at tiny desks. It was kitschy. No one at Harrington Blunt had noticed her enough to notice it. Maybe they thought she was just a silly temp, with her neat blonde bob and her hot chocolate and her set of matching pens she lined up in front of her empty in-tray. 'I got it from a shop on the King's Road.'

'Where do you work?'

'Old Street. For a media company, summer job. How about you?' She glanced over to David and the cocktails; none were forthcoming.

'Mirror Group. Permanent job, my first after university. I work on reception.'

'Right.' She tried to take him in, all of him, without giving away that she was doing so. She decided he looked like the kind of boy who might pose with one leg on a fallen tree trunk in a catalogue photoshoot, in a nice jumper, then get off with the photographer's assistant later at a rave. 'So, you're a year older than me,' she observed.

'And you've just finished the second year? How old are you, twenty?'

'No, nineteen. I'm a late August baby. How about you?'

'Twenty-one. And I'm a lovely April fool.'

'Sounds about right,' she said, and he grinned. 'May I have some of that?' Olivia had been eyeing Leo's cocktail glass. She took it from him and slugged a big gulp. 'Sorry. I'm quite thirsty.'

'Can I get you one of those?' He looked highly entertained, and she liked that.

'No, I'll keep yours,' she said brightly. 'You can have mine' – she glanced over at the bar again. David's barman was finally performing with a stainless-steel cocktail shaker – 'when it comes. Shouldn't be too long.'

'Cheeky.'

'Sometimes.'

'I like cheeky.'

His smile felt just for her; like it had only ever been just for her. Now, she felt shy. She wanted to lower her eyes to the floor and look up at him through her eyelashes.

'Which university did you go to?' she asked. 'I'm at Canterbury Christ Church. Media studies.'

'Southampton,' Leo replied. 'Film and history. So, you're in London for the summer. Where are you from?'

'London,' she replied.

'Ah. Thought I could detect the accent.' She was disappointed. 'Your parents live here, then?'

'My dad does,' she said. 'Pimlico.' The thing about Pimlico was that it covered all bases. From the working man in the ex-council flat, to the toff in the ginormous house. Perhaps he would think the latter. People at Canterbury sometimes did, and she could pretend to be like everyone else.

'What about your mum?'

'No.'

'Divorced?'

'Dead.'

'Oh, I'm so sorry,' said Leo, and for the first time she saw something different in his face. Empathy. A kind of kindness.

'Thank you,' she replied, and she meant it. 'It was a long time ago. I was three.' The moment hung in the air, like mist on an autumn morning.

'I'm sorry,' Leo said again, like he really meant it. 'I live in London, too,' he added. 'I live with Royal Ben.' He said it like he said it a *lot* and he enjoyed saying it. The mist cleared, and she was glad of that.

'*Royal Ben?*'

'My mate, Ben, from Southampton. Well, he thinks he should be royal, and sometimes he pretends he's a member of the extended Lesotho royal family, to get lucky. It seems to work. Let's just say there's a lot of handsome boys traipsing through our flat in the mornings.'

'He sounds like fun.'

'He is. He wants to be a literary agent. He reads *everything*. He's an intern at Penguin – tea boy, really – but I know he's going to go far.'

'Good for Royal Ben,' she said. 'And what do you want to do when you grow up?'

He pulled a face like he was embarrassed. 'I want to be a writer. A bestselling novelist, preferably, one day. A journalist, first. To get some experience, and to be realistic. I can't just *become* a novelist, can I?'

'Maybe you could,' she suggested. 'And then Ben can represent you.'

'Maybe.' They smiled at each other. There was a nice attraction here, Olivia thought. It was bubbling up like champagne poured into a glass.

'You won't believe this, but I want to be a novelist, too,' she said. 'I have done since I was a kid.'

'Really? Well, actually, I'm sure there's a lot of us about. In life's strange corners. Did you grow up addicted to books?'

'Yes. I got it from my godmother, Gillian. Her house was full of books. And the library, of course.' Charlie had taken her every Saturday morning, loitering in the doorway, smoking a cigarette while she made her weekly selection of six.

'Great,' said Leo. 'I locked myself in the bathroom for hours, fleeing the tyranny of my childhood with other people's stories.'

'You're kidding?' He was *talking* like somebody in a book.

'Yes,' he replied, but she wasn't sure. He smiled at her. She was obsessed by his mouth, actually. She didn't think she'd ever been obsessed by a mouth before. Its shape, the frankness with which it curled into a smile, starting with a comma at one corner.

'Well, you never know,' she said, 'we both might end up writing books. What genre would you do?' She saw David turn from the bar, a mojito in his hand, clock her and Leo, and swiftly turn back again.

'Crime,' he said.

'I would write romance, I reckon.' Something about the love stories she'd read made her feel she could write her own.

He nodded. 'Then we could get married and have an office each, at opposite ends of the house.'

'You want to marry me? That was quick.'

He shrugged. Grinned at her. 'We could be the perfect match. We could both be exactly what the other never knew they needed.' It was her turn to grin. *Ridiculous*. She took another huge sip of his cocktail. 'What's your favourite Phil Collins song?' he asked her.

'Who?'

'Phil Collins, you must know who that is!'

'Someone that only deeply uncool people like . . . ?'

She wondered if she had spoken a little too far out of turn, but Leo laughed. 'My dad got me into him. He plays him in the kitchen of his restaurant. I love a bit of Phil Collins.'

'I like Britpop.'

'A rocker?'

'Occasionally,' Olivia quipped, facetious. Leo laughed. 'Your dad owns a restaurant?' she continued. 'Is he a chef?' Leo pulled up one of his sleeves and she noticed he had a freckle on the inside of his left wrist.

He nodded. 'Quite a famous one, actually.'

'Anyone I might know?'

'Yeah, probably. Isaac Feu.'

'Isaac Feu! You're joking?'

'Feu's not his real name, of course . . . *Feu*, fire, much more dramatic for a chef, don't you think?'

'Well, definitely. Confit, that's his restaurant, isn't it?' Leo nodded. 'So, you have a famous parent. Your mother's not famous, too, is she?' Olivia asked.

'No.' Leo shook his head. 'She's very much the wind beneath his wings. The silent partner. I can't see *you* being that . . .' he added.

'Being what?'

'Being underneath anyone's wings. What does your father do?'

'My dad?' Here she had a choice. Sometimes she played up her working-class roots, sometimes she didn't; she fudged them into something else. Little white lies. It depended on her audience. With Leo, she risked being honest. 'He's a carpenter. Fits out pubs and bars.' She realised she had announced it as a kind of challenge.

'Oh, fantastic,' he said. 'A man who is good with his hands should always be celebrated. *I'm* good with my hands, you know.' He gave her a cheeky wink.

It was Olivia's turn to laugh. 'Oh my God,' she said, shaking her head. 'Corny as hell.'

'So, I'm deeply uncool *and* I'm corny. I feel I'm on to a total winner tonight . . .'

Twenty-five minutes later, they were pressed into a hot corner of the pub, kissing and kissing and kissing. Her hand was in his hair; his was gently cupping the side of her face. Her work blouse had come a little untucked. His denim shirt was crumpled.

'You have to marry me now,' she joked, when they finally stopped.

'Absolutely,' he replied, his handsome face flushed. 'Just tell me when and where. Except . . .' He hesitated. 'Well, I kinda have a girlfriend,' he said, looking sheepish. 'I mean, she's only a new one, only about a week. I can get out of it . . .' His face reflected that he had caught the look on hers. 'Oh, God. I've blown it, haven't I?'

Olivia pressed her lips together, still tasting him. 'Are you a player, Leo?' she asked, her eyes narrowed.

'Yeah. Might be. A little bit. Sorry.' He shrugged. 'I'm young, what can I say?'

'No need,' she continued lightly, 'for any angst. I'm really not looking for anything right now,' she fibbed. 'Nothing serious, at least. Better to be upfront. If you have a girlfriend, you have a girlfriend.'

She was trying to quell the rise and fall of her chest. She was looking into those dazzling hazel eyes and trying not to show her disappointment. Wishing his lips were on hers again.

'So, what do we do now?' he asked. He attempted to put his hands in his pockets but missed one of them.

'I think we can leave it there,' she said. 'You've been straight with me, which I appreciate. You're a good kisser,' she added, 'but I guess that's it. I guess this is goodbye, Leo.'

Damn, she thought. The chemistry and the banter had been on *fire*. She turned from the hot corner, shifted her little backpack higher up her back, and started walking away.

'What if I never see you again?' Leo called after her. She looked back and he was both satisfyingly incredulous, and incredibly gorgeous. 'What if I never bump into you?'

'If we do, we do,' she called back. 'If we don't, we don't!'

'But it's such a big city!' he called out, already just a beautiful face in the crowd. 'What would be the chances?'

'Slim to none!' she called over her shoulder – grinning to herself and cursing inside that he'd been so delicious, but so very, very wrong for her – and she was gone.

Chapter Seven

Gatwick Airport

Monday 8 January 2001

The flight to Newquay was delayed. Annabel, Stella and Olivia – the three best friends who had met in the first year at Canterbury Uni and had been in each other's pockets ever since – were in The Beehive, a bar at Gatwick Airport's South Terminal, debating something of utmost importance: whether Carl Jeffries, a boy they had known at Canterbury University, deserved his success as an actor in top TV show, *The Cash*, a glamorous drama about a group of women working in the City.

'I mean, he's rubbish, isn't he?' Stella laughed. They were all nursing second glasses of white wine. They had been in The Beehive for a long time. 'And every time I see him in that bloody black trench coat, I just think of him in the union bar, up on the table.'

'Dancing to the Backstreet Boys,' giggled Annabel. She tucked her Joni Mitchell hair behind her ears and leaned back against her Afghan coat – long-since shrugged off to a 'Bloody hell, it's hot in here!' – that was draped over the back of her chair. 'Yes, I remember. Such a buffoon, and now he's in the *Daily Mail* showbiz pages nearly every day.'

'With all the housewives fancying him! Unbelievable! I could never be famous,' sniffed Stella, swivelling the stem of her wine glass between her fingers. She looked too chic for the airport in her after-work suit and her tan court shoes. 'All those kiss-and-tells coming out of the woodwork. Safer to be a boring accountant.' She grinned. 'Hey, didn't you have a brief thing with him, Olivia?'

'Who? Carl? And by "thing", do you mean a snog and a grapple on a building site over at Dovedale campus?' Olivia wrinkled her nose at the memory. 'And you're never boring,' she added. 'You're the most fun accountant on the planet.'

'All those numbers having a party in my brain . . .' Stella trilled. 'Yes, that's exactly what I mean. He asked you out afterwards, didn't he? Why didn't you go? Hold on . . . !' They all listened as the loudspeaker system announced the boarding of a flight that wasn't theirs, then sank back into their seats.

'Because Olivia never went out with anyone!' declared Annabel. 'Not seriously. No one ever met her high standards.' She winked at her friend.

'Well, at least I wasn't falling in love every five minutes.' Olivia counter-winked. They had this conversation a lot. They knew all its tracks and its grooves that they slid along like merry bob-sleighers. 'And getting my heart broken every five minutes after that.'

Annabel giggled. 'I did fall in love a lot,' she agreed. 'It was fun.'

'Fun is not cry-vomiting over some boy in the loos at the students' union,' said Stella. 'My policy was better. No romantic nonsense, plenty of sex, good laughs and lots of boys who remained friends. I still practise this philosophy today,' she added, 'unlike Ms Sackville who is holding out for her Perfect Love. Come on!' She slapped her thigh. 'Give us your earnest little speech about it.'

'I haven't got an earnest little speech!' Olivia protested.

'Yes, you have! The one about waiting for that special person you'll be with for the rest of your life. The one about emulating your parents' marriage. The one about knowing him when you see him.'

Annabel nodded. 'You've let a lot of good men go,' she agreed, looking kindly at her friend.

Olivia sighed, not unhappily. 'I *will* know him when I see him,' she insisted, 'and my heart is open and ready. For the right person, with all the right boxes ticked.'

'Boxes ticked with colour-coded pens,' suggested Stella. 'Meticulously plotted plans, followed to the letter. Maybe you want someone exactly like you . . .'

'No, not *exactly* like me,' Olivia objected. 'I'm too in my own head, often. Too . . . careful, and sometimes I say the wrong things or I don't say the right things. If only I could just write everything down . . .' She grinned. 'Although, yes, someone who could match my organisational skills would be quite good. Think how *streamlined* our life would be. But I do want the Perfect Love, the love that's just right for *me*. You were incredibly lucky, Bel,' Olivia added affectionately, 'with Andy.'

Annabel had met Andy in the very last week of university, at the Final Ball. He'd been there all along; she'd just somehow never spotted him and when she finally did, it turned out he was exactly the man she should marry, next year, in Kent.

'Love at first sight,' sighed Stella.

'Well, not really,' said Annabel. 'But when I talked to him, I knew.'

'That's what *I'm* talking about!' Olivia cried. 'Not love at first *sight*, but love at first chat, first connection . . . There's somebody out there who'll be able to give me everything I need.'

'But do you know what that is?' Stella asked.

'No!' Olivia laughed. 'Not all of it. But I want someone to miss me when I'm not there, and I want someone to be grateful for me, every day. I want someone to go on trips with. Someone who doesn't mind that I spend ages in the bath reading. Someone who listens and looks out for me. The rest, I'll know when I find it!'

'That's quite a list!' Stella commented drily. 'And Andy *is* a prize,' she agreed. 'So, do you think there'll be any contenders for you this weekend, Livs? Any bath-reading travellers with big ears?'

The friends all laughed. They were flying to a wedding in Penzance. The groom was Douglas Fitzpatrick, a boy from their halls. He had lots of floppy-haired, going-places, *from*-places rich friends.

'I doubt it,' Olivia said. 'And you're right, I *would* like something perfect like my parents had. The stuff of legend,' she added sadly, and her friends' eyes were full of sympathy, as they both knew the story of Olivia's mum and dad.

Charlie and Ann. Ann and Charlie. Destined to be together forever, if cancer had not prematurely wrenched them apart. Charlie and Ann had met at the bowling alley. They had got engaged after three months, married when they were both nineteen. Ann worked at the local newsagent's, Charlie built kitchens in endless rows of London terraced houses. Their evenings were spent in front of the television or at the local working men's club. A pint for Charlie, a brandy & Babycham for Ann, until she got pregnant with Olivia in 1978, a new baby appearing in a carry-cot on the sofa in the front room, between the cabinets and the shelves full of photos and Ann's trinkets, the crinoline ladies and the brown bone china horse pulling its cart that was still in situ on the mantelpiece over the gas fire. The painting on the front room wall of the dog with the big eyes looking up at the little boy – the one Ann had loved and Charlie had not cared for, but he had hung it up for her after they had moved to their little council place on Moore Street, the day after their wedding, and there it still hung.

Charlie and Ann had never been on an aeroplane, or gone abroad. They had only taken one holiday together, their honeymoon: a wet week in Camber Sands. And here was their daughter, Olivia, a university graduate with a 2:1 degree, a job in the media and lovely middle-class friends, flying off to Cornwall – instead of driving! – for the wedding of a boy who was the heir to a company that made the biscuits Charlie dunked in his tea every morning. That was how Charlie had summed up this adventure last night, when Olivia had phoned him from the flat in King's Cross she shared with Stella and Annabel, his voice incredulous and full of delighted laughter. He was so proud, and Ann would have been, too, he said. They never had anything like she had. But Olivia wanted what Charlie and Ann had shared: the Perfect Love that would give her everything she needed.

'I'm not a saint, though,' Olivia said, lifting her wine glass and finding it empty. 'Or a nun.' She'd had a couple of boyfriends at Canterbury, both fairly short-lived; she'd enjoyed one or two encounters in London that had also gone nowhere. She hadn't found him yet.

'We know,' said Stella. 'Every girl's got to kiss a few frogs before she meets her prince . . .'

'Right!' Olivia stood up, hoisting her cross-body bag back on to her shoulder. 'I'm going to Boots. I need to get some stuff – I didn't have time after work. Does anyone need anything?'

'No, I'm fine, thank you,' said Annabel. 'Oh, I forgot my hairbrush. Can you get me one, please? Just something cheap.'

'Sure.'

'And maybe a Twix?' said Stella. 'For the plane. We'll stay and keep the table.'

Boots was busy. People were trailing around wheeling their cases behind them for other people to trip over, killing time before their flights, staring at moisturisers and endless cans of hair mousse just for the sake of it. Olivia made her way to the first-aid section, consulted the list she had tucked into her bag, and got started.

'Stocking up?'

Olivia placed a second pack of plasters in her basket. You could never be too careful. 'Excuse me?'

She turned. A man was standing next to her. He had dark wavy hair and was wearing a ridiculous outfit: a thick and itchy-looking cream roll-neck jumper; shiny red ski salopettes, the straps dangling down at his hips like the handgrips that hung from buses; Timberland boots with walking socks. A man she vaguely recognised.

'You're buying a lot of supplies. Are you flying out to a war zone?'

She looked down at her basket full of deodorant, plasters, inner soles, paracetamol, ibuprofen, Vaseline, Savlon, baby wipes and two types of make-up remover.

'Er, no . . .' she said. 'And I really don't know what business it is of yours. Are *you* about to slalom down Mount Everest?'

He grinned. 'I *knew* I knew you. You don't remember me, do you?'

She looked at him again. The answer was yes, but she decided not to give him the satisfaction. 'Should I?'

'We met in a pub in Kensington. About three years ago. Well, we first encountered each other in the Tube, then we met again. Surely you remember? The work blouse, the cocktails. The kissing . . .'

Of course she did, particularly the kissing. She'd remembered it for quite a few weeks afterwards, actually. Due to both its duration and its high calibre.

'Oh! It's you . . .' she said. 'Sorry, I don't remember your name.' It was Leo, and, amazingly, he had been a little less handsome the last time she'd encountered him, as he was now – at what, twenty-three? – off the chart. Hazel eyes; cheeky smile; open, friendly face. That hair, the perfect length. Since that night, physically, he had become her type.

'*Leo*,' he filled in, 'and you're Olivia. I remember quite a few things about you, actually.'

Her basket was fairly heavy. She wanted to set it on the floor but she didn't. 'Oh, do you?'

'Yes. Pimlico. Canterbury. Britpop. Where are you off to?'

'Newquay, for a friend's wedding. How about you?' He was very attractive still, she thought. Those eyes. Even in his ski get-up there was something mesmerising about him, a glowing confidence and a self-assured vitality. Mesmerising, she thought, but not for her. Not what she needed at all.

'Your friends are getting married?' He looked fairly disgusted. 'Mine are way off that! I'm going to Méribel,' he continued. 'French Alps. Ski trip. I'm meeting my girlfriend there. She's working as a chalet girl.'

'Excuse me!' A large man with an enormous trolley-suitcase pushed past them, clutching three bottles of shampoo.

'Careful!' Leo gently pulled Olivia out of the way so she avoided being barged by the man's big shoulder. They moved over to the glass front of the shop and watched together as the man stomped to the checkout.

'Thank you,' she said.

'You're welcome,' he replied. They now watched each other for a couple of seconds. They were standing too close. Olivia subtly stepped back. Leo set down his bag on the floor. Olivia held on to her basket.

'Another girlfriend?' she commented finally. 'The terrible taste in music doesn't seem to be putting them off, then?'

'What terrible taste in music?'

'Two words. Phil. Collins.'

Leo tried to look affronted, but his dancing eyes gave him away. This is what it had been like in the pub, she remembered. Her and this man. The banter.

'How dare you!' he said. 'Are you travelling with your boyfriend?'

He swivelled around, pretending to look for one.

'No, I'm with my friends.'

'Haven't snared anyone recently, then?'

'In, what, three years? Yes, of course I have.'

'*Of course you have.*' His eyes were locked on hers. 'It's nice to see you, Olivia,' he said. 'You *look* nice.' His smile was warm. His face was curious, interested.

And so do you, she thought.

'My plane is delayed,' he added.

'Mine, too.'

'So, do you want to grab a quick drink? We could . . . ?'

'I'm with my friends,' she repeated. 'I'm halfway through a glass of white wine,' she fibbed. Neither of them made to move. 'Do you still live with Royal Ben?' she asked him.

'You didn't remember my name, but you remember Royal Ben?' Leo's face was quizzical, amused.

'He seemed like a memorable character.'

Leo tilted his head. 'He is. And yes, I am.'

'Is he a literary agent yet?'

'Not yet. Are you a writer yet?'

'Yes, actually. Film reviews.'

He grinned. 'I'm *restaurants*,' he said. 'I review for the *Evening Whisper*.'

'How funny, I review for the *Morning Shout*.'

'You're joking!' They smiled at each other, bemused. 'Sister publications . . . and ships that pass between the day and night,' Leo said. 'Ever been into that office?'

'No. Everything's email.'

'They don't want the likes of us in there. The small fry.' He grinned. 'Although I do slope in on the occasional Wednesday morning, unsolicited, just to remind them who I am.'

I could wander in sometime on a Wednesday morning, she thought. *If I wanted to.* Then she said, 'Hang on, please don't tell me you're LL Greene?'

'The very same.' Leo looked delighted. 'I thought LL Greene sounded distinguished, and like I was much older,' he confessed. She noted the boyish look on his face, a pass of ambition, sensitivity, perhaps. 'At least forty.'

'I've read you! Your pieces are funny. And brutal. But you're the only person to ever make me crave okra. You don't have your photo with your column?'

He shrugged. 'Never got around to it. So, you're Olivia Sackville?' he said. 'I've read your reviews, too. There's no photo for you, either.'

'No, they never asked me for one.' *What did you think?* she wanted to ask him, but she didn't. 'I enjoy it though, the reviewing. How long have you been at the *Whisper*?'

'About three months. I'll do it for as long as I need to, to move up the ladder.'

'Until the novel.'

'Until the novel. I don't want to be starving in a garret when I finally get around to it.'

'Are you still at the *Mirror*?'

'Yes. Are you still working in the media?'

'At Harrington Blunt? Yes.' She was in the press department now, in charge of filing, phone answering and mail.

'You've lost the accent.'

'Sorry?'

'The London accent, the nice touch of Cockney. It's not there any more. You sound posher.'

'Oh. So, I sound more like you,' she retorted, a hint of shame rising to her cheeks. She knew her accent had been planed away, erased finally by being with her friends at Canterbury for a further two years. It had happened naturally, accidentally, but she had not stopped its disintegration, and that was what gave her a customary flash of guilt now, about Charlie – as when she was with him, she let it slip back in.

'Posh? Hey, I'm just a country bumpkin. I'm originally from Wiltshire.' He pushed up the woolly sleeves of his jumper, revealing tanned forearms. She wondered if he'd been away for Christmas, and here he was, going away again. 'Cheese and cider running through my veins.'

'*Posh* Wiltshire,' observed Olivia, and Leo didn't deny it. 'Aren't you too hot in that jumper?' Leo looked down at himself and laughed. She remembered that laugh, and how much she had liked it. She should go, though, back to her friends. It had been nice seeing him, if totally pointless, but she ought to pay for this stuff in her basket. 'How's Isaac Feu?' she asked him, though.

'My dad?' He pulled a delighted face. 'Fiery. Cantankerous. Brilliant.'

'My friend went to his restaurant last week.' Stella had, on a date. 'She said it was amazing.'

He shrugged. 'It's amazing every night.'

There was a beat. They looked at each other. *Handsome*, thought Olivia again. 'Well, I'd better get back to my friends. Our flight could get called any hour now . . .'

He laughed again. 'Of course. Hope you don't have to wait too long,' he said. 'And have a great flight. It was good to see you again, Olivia.'

He held out his hand. She took it, with reluctance, but was greatly surprised to find the touch of his hand was strangely like coming home, if home was a log cabin with a roaring fire and a faux-fur rug, a table set with two glasses of deep red wine, for seduction. Things reserved for Chalet Girl, surely.

'Nice to see you again, too, Leo.' Why had he not let go of her hand?

'That was a great kiss,' he said, after too many seconds. '*Wow.*'

He winked at her. He finally let go. He picked up his bag and he bounded out of the shop.

'It wasn't *that* great!' she risked calling out after him, but he turned in the doorway, and he was laughing. She paid for her items and returned to Annabel and Stella and a further two-hour wait, but she saw him again, at their gate. He was at the next, in his preposterous ski gear, talking to a middle-aged couple who were laughing at something he said. He gave her a jaunty wave and she raised her hand in reply.

'Who's that?' asked Stella.

'Some bloke I kissed a few years ago,' Olivia replied, still looking at him. *Great chemistry, great banter* . . . she thought. *Shame about the girlfriend and the cockiness.*

'Really . . . ?'

But they were boarding. Their passports were in their hands, open at the right pages for inspection. She would tell this short story to her friends on the plane.

Chapter Eight

Venice

Tuesday 9 January 2018

The four authors and the two publicists were walking to Harry's Bar. It was busy, for a winter's day in Venice. Clusters of wandering tourists with the straps of their backpacks stretched over thick coats took photos of the scenery and each other on their phones. Gondoliers with roll-necks under monochrome-striped jumpers, and beanies stuffed beneath straw boaters, manoeuvred their vessels through the green-grey waters, their passengers huddled under blankets. And lunch, it seemed, was cooking in every restaurant. The smell of aromatic garlic and rosemary drifted through the streets and along the canals in a fug of expectation.

There had recently been an *acqua alta* – or high water – in the city, flooding it to several inches and briefly joining St Mark's Square to the lagoon. If Olivia and the walkers cared to look closely, the margins of the alleyways still hosted shallow puddles.

'Have you ever been in Venice during an *acqua alta*?' Meryn asked her author. They walked with Tanya; Leo, Frances and Anthony were behind.

'No,' Olivia replied, 'but I've read about it.' She had, in books and the occasional magazine article: tales of ubiquitous wellington boots, people wading calf-deep across St Mark's Square and the dining rooms of hotels being temporarily moved to the first floor. And she had occasionally wondered about her godmother, Gillian, in the high tides of the city, too. Had Gillian stridden purposefully through the puddles on her way to the Guggenheim, in a cape and galoshes, her face set? Did she witness children lifted high on shoulders, a teenager on a skateboard coursing through a flooded alleyway, like Olivia had once seen in a photograph? She had no idea. Olivia had not seen her godmother for many years.

'I'm glad we missed it. It would have played havoc with my new boots. When was the last time you were in Venice?' Meryn asked Olivia.

'About three years ago,' Olivia replied. She was aware of Leo walking behind. She could hear him laughing.

'To visit your godmother?'

'I planned to. But it didn't quite work out that time.'

'And did you go to Harry's Bar?'

'No, I haven't been. Oh, is this it?'

They had reached the double doors of the bar. They were glass-paned oak, bearing the legendary name below two Victorian wall lamps, and set into a white building with grilled windows. Inside were lemon walls, wood panelling, a white beamed ceiling, a bar to the left with a marble top, and a scattering of tables. Their party was directed to one at the back of the bar by a waiter with close-cropped salt-and-pepper hair and thick-rimmed glasses.

Meryn, Tanya and Olivia sat facing the room; Anthony, Frances and Leo were the other side of the table.

'You won't regret coming,' Leo said to Olivia, with a smile.

'No.' She returned one, but she did, already. She wished she wasn't in the corner. She wished Leo wasn't sitting opposite her. She glanced up at a painting on the wall to her left: a seated woman with a lute and a jaunty suitor standing over her. Perhaps she could stare at that the whole time she was imprisoned here and avoid Leo's eye.

They ordered Harry's famous bellinis, which came in short tumblers, and perused the menus, Leo excitedly reading out every dish. Leo had always lived for food – breakfast, lunch, dinner, afternoon snacks, late-night suppers – she thought, with a residue of bittersweet affection.

'We've also got a brunch tomorrow at Fellini's, before the signing,' said Tanya, after Leo had reeled off the last item on the menu and they'd ordered from the waiter. 'If you want to come.'

'Oh no, thank you,' said Olivia, looking back from the fascinating lute in the painting. 'I'm going to my godmother's house tomorrow morning.'

She knew she was being reserved, a little brusque. She knew she couldn't be expansive, or fun, or engaged here with Leo Greene. She knew it was for self-protection.

'Do you need a hand?' Meryn asked.

'No, it's just a few boxes to sort.' And a bench, she remembered, to move into the garden, but she could manage that on her own. She could manage it all on her own.

'You sure?' Frances chipped in, hovering over her bellini. 'We could all pitch up and get stuck in.' Although Anthony looked horrified at the thought, his mouth a dismayed *moue*.

'Of course, I'll be fine. There's really not much to do. Thanks for asking.'

'Leo?' prompted Tanya. 'Fellini's? You're coming, aren't you?'

'Yes.' Leo had looked momentarily distracted. Probably by a plate of grilled octopus sailing by to another table. 'Yeah, probably. Thank you. I've heard great things about that place.' He smiled genially, then he turned to Olivia. 'You ordered the risotto,' he said to her. 'Good choice. You like risotto.'

'That's why I ordered it.'

Her smile was terse. She could feel Meryn looking at her, probably wondering why she was being so aloof, and how Leo knew she liked risotto. But she didn't want Leo telling her what she had liked, what she had felt, what she had said. Tossing out memories like scallops from pan to plate, shaking them over an open flame, flambéing them with a dash of brandy, while she preferred her memories on ice.

He seemed to be waiting for some kind of further response from her, but when she didn't provide one, he turned away, and she returned to the painting. She didn't want to talk about food they had shared, or study the skin at his throat, which she had once smothered in kisses. Or consider his bottom lip, which she had once tugged at gently with her teeth. She didn't want to be tempted by memory.

Their starters arrived: king crab, baby spinach salad and carpaccio. They talked about Felicity and Valentina, about Palazzo Tesoro, the *bussolai*, the frescos. They discussed the current top five books in the *Sunday Times* Bestseller List, where Leo was hovering at a close sixth and Olivia at number five.

'Side by side, and both with the same scene in,' quipped Anthony. 'I'm surprised no one else has picked up on it.'

'Maybe no one else will,' mused Frances, spearing a last piece of mozzarella. 'If the crime and the romance readers keep themselves to themselves.'

'Let's hope they do,' said Olivia dryly, trying not to think about it already being on Instagram. 'It's such a lot of nonsense about nothing.' She dared a glance at Leo, who was now staring vaguely out of one of the intricately grilled windows. She didn't want to hear about that scene again, didn't want to think about it. She was two books on. A lifetime on. She didn't need to live in the past. She had her world, and Leo had his. She had never rightly been a part of his, and the one time she thought they could finally collide as equals, they had splintered away from each other like a satellite exploding.

'Oh, God, someone's just fallen over outside!' Leo cried. Olivia leaned forward to look out of the window and spied a figure on the ground outside Harry's, surrounded by shopping bags. 'I think it's Beth!'

Leo was up, and running to the door. Olivia watched through the window as he arrived at Beth's side, helped her to her feet, and seconds later, there she was, coming into Harry's Bar, Leo grappling with all her bags.

'Are you alright?' Anthony asked, making no move to get up.

'I tripped over,' Beth said, brushing down the front of her coat and straightening her glasses. 'Uneven slab. But I think I'm OK. Dodgy hip,' she grimaced. 'The joys of middle age.'

Leo pulled out a stool for her at their end of the table, helped Beth out of her coat, placed her bags carefully in the corner.

'Have a menu,' he said, handing one to her. 'Order what you like. Tanya's picking up the tab.'

'Am I?' Tanya looked amused above her designer scarf.

'Of course. Or Jones Hill can, all that money I've made for them this year.'

'Oh, well, yes. Fair do's,' Tanya said with a little pout.

Leo called the waiter back over. Beth ordered a Cipriani risotto and a sparkling water.

'Are you sure you're OK?' Olivia asked her. She reached over and touched Beth's wrist.

'Yes, I'm fine, honestly.' Beth smiled. 'Thanks to Leo. *My hero.*' She winked at him behind her owl glasses. Leo laughed.

'How did you enjoy the panel this morning?' he asked her. The others were embroiled in a conversation about an author who had replied to a negative book review on Goodreads, creating a trio of Beth, Leo and Olivia at this end of the table.

'I loved it,' she replied. 'Although, I hope I didn't embarrass you both. Making a scene about a *scene*.'

'Of course not!' Olivia jumped in far too quickly. 'It was interesting, really.' Leo looked at her; she looked away. 'Very incisive. You're a great member of the book community. What is it you do for a day job, though, Beth? I'm curious.'

'I'm a swimming teacher,' said Beth with a grin. 'At Swim! Warrington.'

'Oh, fantastic,' Leo said. 'That sounds great.'

Someone's phone started ringing. They all watched as Leo plucked his up from the table and pushed back his chair. 'Sorry!' he said. 'I forgot I was expecting a call. I'll just take this outside.'

He left the bar. Frances raised her eyebrows and mouthed, 'A woman,' to Olivia from across the table.

'So, yes,' Beth continued, 'my granddaughter's just started having lessons so I've been teaching her, too.'

'Your granddaughter? That's sweet. How old is she?' Olivia asked.

'Fourteen months.' Beth beamed. She extracted her own phone from her cross-body bag and showed them a photograph of a baby in a pink swimming costume, grinning with one top and one bottom tooth on proud display.

'Gorgeous!' declared Olivia. She absorbed her usual pang.

'She's the love of our lives, little Darcie,' said Beth. She proceeded to show Olivia dozens more photographs, all of which Olivia felt required to coo over.

'How did you get into reading, Beth?' she asked, once they came to the end of the photos. 'Did you start early?'

'Oh, yes,' Beth replied. 'I learned to read at age three, and I've never looked back.' They all leaned from the table as their main courses arrived, the waiter solicitous, and making two trips to bring everything. Amidst it all, Leo returned to the table, bringing the cold air in with him and a thoughtful, preoccupied expression that made Olivia wonder about that phone call. 'I started with Peter and Jane, graduated to Goldilocks, and after that there was no stopping me. I'm talking about my reading history,' she explained to Leo.

He nodded, phone back on the table, engaged once more. 'And which do you prefer?' he asked. 'Thrillers or romance?'

Beth looked thoughtful. 'Hard to say. I love a twist, but I also really love a happy ever after. Don't we all?'

There were smiles around the table.

'Ah, the HEA,' Leo mused. 'Olivia's department.' He looked at her kindly. 'Reading all of her books must have made you an expert on them.'

'Oh, I don't think anyone's read *all* of my books,' Olivia chipped in.

'Yes, I have,' said Beth proudly. 'Each and every one, from *The Stylist on Sydney Square* onwards.'

'Ah, but that wasn't my first book,' said Olivia. The waiter appeared again with more bellinis, and Leo turned to him and started asking about how Harry's mixed their drinks. 'The first was *The Florist on Fenton Street*. I mean, it wasn't that good. It just scraped by into being published.' She was glad Leo was preoccupied with the waiter.

'Well, in that case, I'm delighted I still have a book of yours to read!' said Beth.

They sipped their bellinis. Olivia could hear the others talking about negative reviews and how authors stopped themselves from reading them.

'Which was the first book you ever reviewed?' Leo asked Beth, the waiter now gone.

'*Romeo and Juliet*,' Beth replied. 'For school.'

'And what was your take on it?' He picked up his fork and eyed his steak. 'What did you say about it?'

'I can't remember, exactly. I'm sure I said I liked it.' Beth grinned, and they began to eat. 'These days I'm a bit more analytical. I like to think about arcs,' she said. 'The steps the characters need to take, and whether the author gets that right.'

'Oh, interesting.' Leo leaned forwards a little, and Olivia remembered all the times he had leaned across a table towards *her*. The times they had got close, the times they had nearly made it. Until they had both been too *Leo*, or too *Olivia*. Spoken so far out of turn they had wrenched themselves off the road.

'Yes, I've been thinking about the steps a lot lately,' said Beth. 'How a hero and a heroine get from the beginning of the story to where they are at the end, how they change. The steps they take to get back to each other again. Or in the case of Romeo and Juliet, the steps they take to destroy themselves.'

'Do you know all these steps to love, Olivia?' Leo asked her, and she could not read his face. Was he curious? Teasing? There was a warmth in his eyes she didn't trust.

'I've never really boiled them down,' she replied cautiously.

'Oh, I've studied them,' said Beth proudly. 'I know them all.'

'Should I make a list?' Leo made to get his notebook from his bag.

'No, I can tell you!' cried Beth, looking thrilled, her face lit up under her specs. 'So, in the case of a couple coming back to one another again, let me detail the steps. OK, what the hero – and the heroine, it works both ways – needs to do, if there's been a "rock bottom" or an "all hope is lost" scenario in their relationship, is several things. The first is to start talking, open up a dialogue, but don't chase, stay busy, be approachable. Listen, think about what needs to be done, what needs to be apologised for – and sometimes there are massive things that need apologising for, obviously.' She took a breath. Olivia didn't dare look at Leo. 'Show that you're a better person, that you're different now. Don't be jealous. Be confident, responsible, kind' – she counted these things off on her fingers – 'but also vulnerable. Dance a little.' She smiled. 'Dancing always helps. Then make a move, but the timing has to be spot on. If the move is made too soon, it can be disastrous. Suggest something romantic. *Take* them somewhere romantic, kiss in an unexpected, romantic place. And then, when the time is right, make that apology, put things right, declare your love. And the very last step is to promise to be with them forever, but this has to be *both* of them. A proper and lasting commitment.'

'Sounds complicated,' said Leo. He frowned, like he couldn't compute all of that, like his head was suddenly full of clouds. The clouds were behind Olivia's eyes, too. All hope had been lost between her and Leo three years ago. Surely there were no steps to bring it back? 'Does that tally with your books, Olivia?'

'I suppose it does,' she conceded. 'I suppose all those things are there somewhere in my books.'

'But the most important thing,' Beth continued, 'is that a character must be ready. Both of them must be ready to have the other person in their lives. That's the key. Whether that involves forgiving each other, or forgiving themselves for something . . . all of that stuff needs to be resolved.'

'They must be *ready* . . .' echoed Leo. 'Yes, I get that.'

Beth looked from Leo to Olivia and back again. 'Or maybe they could just reminisce about a meal they once shared . . .'

'You don't have all of this in your crime novels, Leo,' Olivia commented breezily, setting her tumbler down on the table. 'There's no real character arc, is there? Just a crime, the solving of it . . .' She was swerving on to safer ground, when there was no safer ground here. Just shifting earth and fractured memories.

'But there *is* an arc for Ben Midnight this time!' protested Beth. 'He really learns something by the end of the book. Yes, he loses Martha, but he gains such important knowledge about himself!'

'He loses Martha?' Olivia wrapped her fingers around her glass.

'Yes, he does,' Leo replied, looking straight at her, and there was a sudden note of sadness in his eyes, something she hadn't seen for a long time. 'But he hopes to get her back. And, wow, *Beth*, you should be a book reviewer or something . . .' The sadness from him gone, he turned and winked at Beth, making her blush.

'Ha. I just really get into this stuff,' she said, all proud. 'I love the arc, the set-up, the pay-off. The last-minute sting in the tail. But I guess I like the stuff in the middle the most. Especially with romances.'

They were interrupted then, by Anthony turning to Leo with a loud laugh and asking him about the best first sentence he'd ever written, and a lively conversation ensued, with everyone talking over everyone else and laughing together, and glass tumblers being clinked merrily in boisterous toasts.

Spirits were high, and they were kindred spirits, these members of the Book World, the secrets of reading and writing and publishing binding them together, cover to cover. The visitors to Harry's Bar, old-time regulars and puffa-coated wide-eyed tourists, coming through the legendary doors, must have stared over at the riotous table at the back and wondered who these people were having such a good time there in the heart of Venice on a cold winter's day. And they may have even noticed the woman in the corner, smiling and laughing, but with regret and longing in her eyes.

Chapter Nine

As they headed back to the water taxi pier at St Mark's Square, there was pale sunshine and a lull in the crowds. Perhaps, feeling the chill, the tourists had all wandered into bars and cafés for *caffè* and *cioccolata.* Perhaps they were all inside Doge's Palace or the Basilica, consulting their guidebooks. Perhaps they were peering out at Olivia and her merry band, from various Gothic arched windows, as they walked through the lovely grey and blush of Plaza San Marco.

They were all a little drunk, the four writers and Meryn and Tanya and Beth. More and more bellinis had come to the table, then martinis, then a few negronis. They had deliberated about gelato, they had ordered coffees and petits fours, they had taken that photo – leaning forwards, bringing their heads together as the waiter took it with Tanya's phone. And they had talked on and on of books and the classics they had adored and been inspired by.

Olivia spoke of Virginia Woolf and Edith Wharton. Leo spoke of Oscar Wilde and Jack London. It had been dangerous, drinking bellinis with Leo Greene, sharing passions and delights, but she had survived it, Harry's Bar, with Leo sitting opposite her. Now there were just four more days to go. Four days to be with Leo Greene and not do the catastrophic thing of nearly falling in love with him again, or risk getting anywhere close, because even the slide, the pitch, the prelude to the fall, was always laced with jagged glass.

It was 4 p.m. Anthony and Frances were arm in arm and weaving across the square. Meryn and Tanya were either side of Leo, that charming centrepiece, cracking up at his apparent mischief. Beth was walking with Olivia. Something made a noise within her bag, and Beth pulled her phone from it, opened the pink leather case, clicked and scrolled.

'Look!' she cried. 'Another of the book bloggers from this morning has posted about the panel – a very interesting tweet! *Nice to see Leo Greene and Olivia Sackville on this morning's book panel #AnEnglishWriterinVenice, denying that apparently they have written the same scene in each of their books. Intriguing!! Ciao!*'

'What's this?' Leo had obviously heard his name. He dropped back and asked Beth to read the tweet again.

'Oh, dear,' Olivia murmured. 'People are getting rather carried away.'

'People are *really* interested,' Leo echoed with a frown.

'Sorry!' said Beth. 'I expect Meryn will love this!' She stepped forward to tap Meryn on the shoulder, holding up her phone like a trophy.

'I guess we're being "lumped together" all over the internet,' Olivia said after a few moments, as she and Leo walked in tandem.

'"Lumped together"?'

'You said in the session you didn't want to be lumped with "poor Olivia". Oh!' She nearly tripped on an ancient paving slab; he grabbed her arm and steadied her, keeping her upright.

'You OK?' His eyes, on hers, were suddenly intense. His hand on her arm, in leather gloves, was warm through the wool of her coat, reminding her of another time, in London, when his hand had been on her arm in a similar manner, but not in similar circumstances.

'Yes,' she said weakly. 'Thanks.' It was the first time he had touched her in three years. The first time he had steadied her, made her feel better somehow in his own Leo way. And time seemed to stop, just for a moment. He was here again, and so was she. They were together in Venice. She could almost take pleasure in it, if she let herself. She could almost fall under the spell of this moment.

'I'm sorry,' he said. 'You're neither "poor" nor someone I wouldn't want to be lumped in with. I was just showing off. I'm trying to stop doing that.'

She was surprised. And *I used to be poor,* she thought. *I used to wear church project hand-me-downs and shower using a plastic tube attached to the bath taps. Bread and butter with every meal.* 'Then you don't mind being here? Or me being here?'

She wanted to know. Did he have a carousel of regret in his own mind, going around and around? Had he thought about their last night together like she had, over and over? Did the things that had happened, and that were said, still matter to him?

'I knew you were going to be here,' he replied steadily. 'So, no, I don't mind.'

'But *I* didn't,' she risked saying. 'I didn't know about you.'

His eyes were a rich hazel in the afternoon gloom. Hers could not stop looking at him. His face. The puzzle of him. The ways they had hurt each other. But moments always passed, and life took over.

'We didn't finish talking about the stuff in the middle.' Beth dropped back to them again. Leo let go of Olivia's arm. 'In Harry's Bar, when we were discussing the arc of a love story.'

'The stuff in the middle . . .' Leo thrust his hands in his coat pockets. Looked at Beth brightly. Looked curious.

'Yes, after the Meet Cute.' Olivia wondered if, like Meryn, Beth never switched off. If she had a little battery inside her causing her to look for meaning in everything, to be excited by it. 'The back and forth, the fun and games. Not the early days, or the coming back together – finally – but what's in between. Meeting again and again, being on and off, obstacles, misunderstandings, secrets . . .' She looked delighted. 'The stuff in the middle.'

Olivia didn't like this; the things being put out there into the atmosphere of Venice in January, to be sifted through, disturbing her objectives – her focus, her forbearance – with the fog of memory. All these moments with Leo in Venice, all this *talking*, this walking, were taking her straight back to moments with him in London and beyond, captive, and the past was a dangerous place that threatened the future. Everyone knew that.

She glanced across at Leo, but his hands were still in his pockets and he looked deep in thought. He executed a slow turn, scattering the curious birds of St Mark's Square, while she lamented every moment they had ever spent together.

They should only have had a beginning: the pub in Kensington, the encounter at the airport. Fate should have left it there, turned the pages, closed the book, abandoned it at a very short story and let them return to their lives, but there was a postscript. And another. *How easy it was to go back there*, she thought. To the past. And further back. To her father's house. And a date that never was.

Chapter Ten

London

Tuesday 28 September 2004

On Saturday mornings, Olivia would visit her father. She would stop off at the corner of Glebe Road, in the little convenience store, and buy a newspaper and two bacon rolls. She would go around the back, knock on the door, and she and Charlie would sit at the kitchen table, eat the rolls and drink giant mugs of tea, and catch up on their news. She would stay for a couple of hours and leave just before lunch. They would hug in the doorway and Charlie would tell her to 'be good', and she would tell him not to have another bacon roll until the following Saturday, as he had to keep an eye on his health. Today, though, she was going to her father's on a Tuesday evening, as it was his birthday.

Charlie Sackville's flat in Pimlico was on the ground floor of a three-storey low building, flanked by a brick wall with separate gateways; an ex-council property Charlie had bought with a mortgage back in the mid-eighties as part of the government's Right to Buy scheme. As he was often to be found, her father was out the back this evening, in the little covered yard, working on something at his bench, a cigarette sizzling in a seashell ashtray at one corner.

'Happy birthday, Dad!' Olivia waved with one hand, held up a gift bag with the other. 'What are you making?' she asked him, walking over to the bench. Charlie was wearing his old blue jeans with the scuffed knees. A navy V-neck jumper. His beloved, old blue and yellow Gola trainers.

'A skateboard deck,' he said, running his hand over the board's smooth flank. His sandy blond hair was sticking up, as usual. Charlie's hair had been doing its own thing all his life. 'I'm making it for one of the teenagers next door. They've got the wheels, I'm doing the board, then I'll put the two together for them, do the grip tape, and all that.'

'And then spend the rest of the year trying not to get run over by them on the front path,' said his daughter.

Charlie smiled. Gillian, her godmother, always said that he and Olivia had the same smile, that his daughter was a mini female version of him. 'Two peas in a pod,' Gillian always said. 'Two blond, blue-eyed peas.'

Charlie had been a carpenter since he was a teenager. At fifteen, he had asked his mother if he could go to art school, and she had apparently roared with laughter and answered, 'No.' Art school was for rich people, she'd told him; he better catch on to himself and learn a trade. So, he'd become a carpenter's apprentice when he left school and still worked, crafting bars and cabinetry for pubs, had done for twenty years. And in his spare time he enjoyed taking on small projects for members of the local community, like a skateboard for the neighbours, or a shelving unit or picture frame for a drop-in centre.

Charlie was a man of few words, with a daughter full of them. He was a man who could make anything with the right tools and the right wood.

'It looks really good,' said Olivia, about the skateboard.

'Yes, I'm pleased with it,' Charlie replied with obvious satisfaction. He stood back a little, studied the board from a different angle. 'Are we keeping you up?' he asked, as he caught Olivia suppressing a yawn.

'Sorry,' she said. 'I'm a bit tired. Been burning the candle at both ends.' And she had a deadline tomorrow morning for a film review that she had to do when she got back to King's Cross tonight. Still, that was no problem; they wouldn't be out late. 'And it's a bit chilly out here.' She gave an involuntary shiver. 'Shall we go in? What time is Gillian coming?'

'About half past.' Her godmother was taking Charlie and Olivia out for his birthday treat that evening – a behind-the-scenes visit to the Gielgud Theatre on Shaftesbury Avenue, to admire the craftmanship of a wooden set for an upcoming production of *The Merchant of Venice*, designed by leading set designer – and Gillian's old mate from university – Maxwell Holt. 'She said we're walking there. For the exercise. Not that I need any more after the day I've had.'

Charlie stifled a contented yawn; his days were long and physical. He covered the work bench with a familiar piece of old green tarpaulin, and father and daughter went inside.

'Would you like a drink? Lemon squash?'

'Yes, please, Dad.'

Charlie wandered into the kitchen. Olivia remained in the sitting room, looking around at all the trinkets and the photos, like she always did. There were photographs everywhere: on the mantelpiece of the fake coal gas fire, on top of the television, on occasional tables between the floral chenille three-piece suite. Photographs with thick gilt frames: Olivia as a baby, a toddler, a teenager. Olivia in her graduation gown in three different iterations: smiling at the camera in the professional close-up shot; outside Canterbury

Cathedral with her dad looking combed-down and trussed up in a suit; throwing the mortar board in the air with Annabel and Stella, their faces a blur of laughter.

Her parents' wedding photo. There they were, coming out of the church door, same height, same smile, doused in confetti and gratitude for one another. A picture of Charlie standing next to a cabinet he'd made for a pub, sleeves rolled up, cigarette dangling from one hand. And Ann Sackville perched on a stool at the local working men's club, singing her beloved country and western songs, for, yes, shy Ann had been a singer occasionally, and she'd been paid for it, too – a little pin money, when word got out. Charlie told his daughter that her shyness disappeared when she sat up on that stool and her voice rang out clear and true. He said she had sung while doing the ironing and when mopping the floor. She had even sung a little in the hospital, at the end, just to keep the nurses' spirits up.

'Want a custard cream, Livvy Mivvie?' Dad called from the kitchen.

'Yes, please!' Lemon squash and a custard cream biscuit, that was what Olivia had always had. She sat in one of the armchairs, everything facing the television, and fingered the doily on the arm she had once used as a lacey bed cover for her Sindy doll.

'You still like them?'

'Of course, Dad.'

'Thought you might just be eating posh biscuits these days,' he said, coming out from the kitchen with a plate and a glass. His mop of hair was smoothed down a little, from the tap. 'The ones from Prince Charles' shop.'

'Oh, stop it, Dad!' He was always teasing her about turning out posh. 'Here's your present.'

He sat on the armchair opposite. Olivia reached forward and gave him the gift bag. He pulled out the present in the racing car wrapping paper and opened it.

'What is it?' Charlie held the garment aloft. Red and navy stripes. Pure new wool. Tassels that dangled all the way to the floor.

'It's a scarf, Dad. You say your neck gets cold.'

'Well, it does. Thank you, Liv.'

He folded the scarf back up and placed it on the arm of the chair. Olivia's heart sank. She had gone wrong again. Her gift was too long, too preppy, too *Oxford and Cambridge*. He wasn't going to wear it; he had his tatty old West Ham scarf he wore in winter. She was buying things for her taste, not his.

'I'm pleased you like it, Dad,' she muttered, and he smiled brightly at her, put his hand in his hair and messed it up again.

'It's really great,' he said, and she worried a little about them growing apart. The university-educated daughter who spoke in a different voice now. Who worked in the media, wanted to become a writer one day, and who had ideals and ambitions. Her carpenter father, whose front room and outlook never changed, who still grieved for his wife and kept everything the same for her: the furniture, the photographs, the brown bone china horse, the print of the dog looking up at the boy that hung on the wall above the television.

Olivia barely remembered her mother, her recollections dreamlike, shot into fragments. A face, close to hers on Christmas morning, as she sat by the tree opening a Tiny Tears doll. The softness of a blouse against her cheek. A laugh on a summer's afternoon in the garden, for it was the sound of her mother that had seemingly stayed with her the most. On starting primary school, the songs they sang in assembly, cross-legged in class rows across the wooden floor – 'Lord of the Dance', and 'He's Got the Whole World in his Hands' – surprised Olivia by being strangely and comfortingly familiar. She had asked her father about them, and he told Olivia her mother had sung those songs softly to her daughter when she had put her to bed.

There was a knock at the window, behind the nets that still hung there. A cheerful face. Short, charcoal-grey hair, a little flicky over the ears. Tortoiseshell cats-eye glasses. Bright lively eyes.

'There she is!'

Charlie let Gillian in. She was a tall woman with broad shoulders, wearing jeans tucked into knee-high boots, an acorn-coloured cape and a big grin. She had her tapestry carpet bag over her shoulder.

'No sign of spring yet, then,' she announced, as the cold air from outside was shut out again by the closing of the front door. 'It's brassic out there tonight.'

Gillian was Charlie's best friend. They had gone to primary school together, bonding as Mary and Joseph in their first nativity play when Gillian had to say a terrified Charlie's lines for him, then secondary school, after which Charlie left at sixteen to become an apprentice carpenter, and Gillian stayed on to do A levels. By this time, their differences were apparent: Gillian was a determined character, academically smart and destined to go places. Charlie was good with his hands and destined to stay exactly where he was. But they remained good friends. When Charlie married Ann, Gillian was a bridesmaid, holding the bunch of sunflowers Ann had chosen for their heatwave summer wedding, then taking the train back to Sheffield after the front-room reception, to continue the second half of her first term at university.

Gillian became a well-paid art historian. She had got her first job at a gallery in Belgravia, as a researcher. Olivia was born and Gillian was proud to become her godmother. Charlie continued making kitchens in old Victorian houses. Ann gave up her job in the newsagent's. Charlie lost Ann to cancer when Olivia was three years old, and became a single father. *It was funny, really*, Olivia thought: Charlie was suspicious of rich people, believed most of them to be crooks, especially some of the property developers he came across, but Gillian was his exception. Gillian may have bought a house in the posh part of Pimlico when Olivia was six, but she never changed a jot. It was simple, really; they had always liked the same things, and they just got on together. That was the story Olivia had been told all her life.

'Here you are,' Gillian said, perching on the edge of the sofa and pulling two wrapped presents out of her big bag for Charlie – one small and tubular, one flat and square. 'Happy birthday, my old friend.'

Charlie's face lit up as he opened the first gift. A planing tool with a sleek black handle. 'Oh, great!' he exclaimed. 'Thanks! This looks good. Thanks so much.'

Gillian beamed. She shrugged off her cape muttering that it was like a 'furnace' in here. She watched Charlie open the second present.

It was a record. An album.

'Northern soul?' Olivia enquired.

'Yep!' said Gillian, beaming. 'Old habits die hard. And it's a limited edition. Digitally mastered.'

Charlie took the record to the ancient stereo system crouching on the sideboard in the corner of the room. He placed the record on the turntable, and he and Gillian grinned at each other.

'Shall we?' she said.

'Why not?' Charlie replied.

Gillian held out her hand, they rose from their seats and, to Olivia's delight, they started to dance, right there on the busy floral carpet, that bouncy northern soul style of shuffling and foot-crossing and spinning. Serious faces, but within seconds they were laughing like a couple of school children.

'You still can't beat it!' Gillian announced, as the record came to an end.

'No, you can't,' said Charlie, flushed and happy. Olivia felt sorry her present had not lived up to Gillian's, but that was OK, she thought; she would make it up to him next time.

'And we should get going,' Gillian said, looking at her watch. 'I said we'd be there by eight.'

'Alright,' said Charlie. He went to the small hall to get his coat.

'Oh, aren't you going to get changed?' Olivia asked.

'No. Should I?' He pulled a contrite face at her. 'We're only going to look at a set.' Apparently, Gillian had asked Charlie if he wanted to see the play, too, once it opened, but he had said no, visiting the set would be plenty enough and he wasn't a fan of Shakespeare.

'True,' said Olivia, and she felt ashamed of her question, but Gillian shook her head and said, 'You know what he's like. A right old scruff-bag,' with great affection, which made her feel better.

Charlie lit up a cigarette as they walked through the London streets. 'You still puffing on those things?' his best friend asked him.

Charlie looked unrepentant. 'You used to smoke.'

'I know.' Gillian shrugged. 'Then I read some stuff. Apparently, they're bad for you now . . .'

'They haven't killed me yet.'

'Well, you never know,' said Gillian, rolling her eyes at Charlie's daughter, 'there's still time.'

The streets were cold. The walk seemed quicker with the chat and the banter. Olivia checked her own watch. She was really looking forward to this evening. Celebrating her father's birthday. Being with him and Gillian, and going to Shaftesbury Avenue with them to admire some carpentry. And tomorrow night, she was going on a date. At twenty-six, Olivia had found herself having a bit of a wild summer, full of mischief, confidence and slightly lowered standards, followed by a wildish September. There had been lots of partying, mostly with Stella; quite a few dates. Plenty of kissing – yes, it seemed the nineteen-year-old version of herself had returned – and far too many frogs. There'd been no one she'd really liked. No one she'd particularly sparked with. Tomorrow night was going to be different, though, and the thought filled her with tiny bubbles of frothing, fizzy excitement that threatened to spill out of her in a shiver. The streets may have been cold but, inside her, Olivia was warm and lit up like a Christmas tree.

Tomorrow night she was going on a date with Leo Greene.

Chapter Eleven

On Tuesday of last week, Olivia had, in a rare occurrence, been asked to go into the offices of the *Morning Shout* to collect a payslip. The payslip had fallen foul of some consequential clerical error, had been amended, and needed to be signed for in person, and Olivia could go in to collect it anytime she chose.

She chose that past Wednesday morning, after momentary consideration, and for no particular reason, except that there was a slight possibility a man she had met three years ago at an airport, and who she had once kissed in a London pub, might be there.

It had been a few years, it was true, but she remembered how much she'd liked that man, that there had been a real attraction between them, as well as banter that had been sparky and fabulous, and she hadn't really experienced that with anyone since, and especially not in her wild summer and her wildish September of dating and of kissing, so why not?

The *Morning Shout* offices were near Green Park. The lobby area was busy. The steps up to the editorial office on the first floor were quiet. And there he was, that Wednesday morning, when she walked into the busy room with the people hammering away at their computers or dashing across the carpet clutching bits of paper, and he was standing at the huge grey photocopier in the corner of the room and swearing mightily at it.

'Doing battle?' she asked, behind his right shoulder and recalling what he'd once said to her about buying supplies for a war zone.

Leo turned, looked surprised, and then his face broke into a grin.

'Bloody things. The machines, I swear they conspire against us. What are you doing here?' He touched her lightly on the arm and she remembered how his touch had made her feel. She also remembered how much she'd liked his face; she felt giddy, breathless and discombobulated to see it again. 'Didn't you once tell me you never come in?'

'No, I don't, but I've come in today to pick up a payslip. Why are *you* here today?'

He was wearing a smart pair of grey trousers, with a pale pink shirt, no tie. The sleeves of the shirt were rolled up. He looked like a newspaper man, a finance guy, a really good-looking one with great hair. She was glad she'd worn her new autumn check mini dress with the black tights and cute lace-up boots. He was gorgeous and she had to compete. There were a lot of pretty women in this office.

'I'm here *every* day,' he replied. 'I work here full-time. For a sister magazine, *Money Talks*. Ugly stepsister, more like.' He pulled a face, glanced around him conspiratorially. 'Shh . . .' he whispered. 'Don't tell anyone, but it's *so* boring. And I'm writing for a financial magazine when I don't know anything about finance.'

'And I'm a press officer when I don't know much about the press . . .' she offered. 'I'm still at Harrington Blunt. But you're still reviewing, right?'

She knew he was. She read his reviews every week.

'Yep,' he said. 'And I know *you* are. Your writing is getting better and better.'

'Really?'

She had been doing that reviewing job for so long, she felt like she was almost dialling it in these days. Especially when she was running late on a deadline.

'Yes. Some of them have been truly beautiful. Particularly if you're reviewing a love story or something. What you said about *The Notebook* was really quite moving.'

'Oh!' She felt chuffed. It was lovely to hear that. And especially coming from him. He had written about a restaurant last week she was now desperate to go to with Stella and Annabel. 'Are you sure you're not just being kind?'

'No.' He shrugged. 'Couldn't be *less* kind. So, are you writing that novel yet?'

'No,' she said. 'You?'

'*No*. One day, though, I promise. I have been thinking about writing some short stories, though.'

'I've written a couple,' she confessed.

'You have? Can I read them?'

She shook her head. 'God, no! I don't think they're fit for anyone to read.'

'That's a shame. And I bet they *are*.'

She wasn't sure, and she wasn't being entirely truthful. She had recently sent one of her short stories off to a publication in Kent for a competition. Someone must have read it, but it clearly hadn't got anywhere. She had heard nothing. 'So, we're not bestselling novelists yet,' she commented. 'What else is new?' she asked him, as though she were asking it casually. She was dying to find out if he had a current girlfriend or not. 'Are you still living with Royal Ben?'

'Oh, good memory!' She was trying to gauge what he might be thinking about her. Whether he was pleased to see her. Whether he, too, remembered the kissing, the frisson in the airport. Whether he thought it lame she still remembered the nickname of his flatmate. 'He's good, he's good. He's an agent's assistant now. Doing really well.'

'That's great.' She wasn't sure what to say next. She had run out of questions, except the one she was beginning to think she really wanted to ask.

'Who've you come in to see? Harry?'

'Yes.' Harry was the editor of the *Morning Shout*.

'I don't think he's in until eleven. Want to come over to my desk and wait for a bit?'

She thought about it. She looked at Leo's face. His eyes. 'Yes, please.'

Leo's desk was by a sash window at the front of the building, overlooking Green Park. The chair was pulled back and at an angle, and the desk was a bit of a mess: pens and papers scattered everywhere, an upside-down stapler cruising down the centre, three coffee mugs with days' old dregs skulking around.

'Do sit down. 'Scuse the mess.'

'That's alright.'

She sat carefully on his chair and Leo pushed it forward for her, to its rightful place nudged up to the desk. It was way too low for her and she felt a bit silly, down there.

'Do you want a coffee or anything?'

'No, I'm OK.'

'Sure?'

'Well, OK. Yes, please. Coffee, milk and half a teaspoon of sugar, please. Quite milky. Not too full in the cup,' she added.

'Coming up,' he replied with a grin, and he headed off to the small kitchen at the side of the office.

While she waited, she flicked through a copy of *Money Talks*. Found his name inside several times. Lined up his old coffee mugs together. Peered into her bag and checked her pens, her notebook; ordered what was already in order.

'There you go.' He was back. 'Milky, half a sugar, a clear inch from the top.' He placed a mug in front of her which said, *Another 8 hours of pretending to work.* Then he pulled another swivel chair over from an empty desk behind them and sat right next to her. Put his elbows on the table and his chin on his hands.

'So?' he said. 'Why are you really here?'

'Why am I really here . . . ? I'm here to see Harry.'

'*Really?*' Leo looked amused, cheeky, delicious. 'Was it to see me? Do you want to ask me out?'

She took a chance. 'Would you *like* me to ask you out?'

'Turning it back on me, I like that! Well, I wouldn't mind,' he said. 'Seeing as you're here.'

'We haven't seen each other for years,' she said. 'I don't know why you think I might be interested.'

'I think this kind of chemistry is hard to deny, don't you?' Leo whispered close to her ear, and she felt herself blush.

'I might even be engaged or married,' she said. She surreptitiously hid her left hand under the desk.

'No rings,' Leo said. 'I already checked. And I'm not engaged or married either, so what's stopping us, Olivia? It's good to see you,' he added sincerely. 'I'm glad you came in. Where would you like to go on our date?'

'Well, when are you free?' she asked. She sounded more assured than she felt. She felt like he was a boss giving her an induction, sitting here next to him at his desk like this. Like he was her *mentor*. And the thought of that made her blush, too. 'Are you available next week sometime?'

'How about Tuesday?'

'Tuesday I'm out for my dad's birthday.'

'How about Wednesday?'

'Wednesday is good.' She was supposed to be meeting a man named Nick for drinks, but she could cancel that.

'Great. How about Swiss Cottage? I can book Nicoletti's, a little Italian I know. It's really fantastic. I think you'll love it.'

'Yes, Swiss Cottage is good.'

'Great. Seven o'clock?'

'Great.'

'Want to exchange mobile phone numbers?'

'No. I'll be there.'

She already felt brazen enough to have walked in here and approached him. She didn't want his number. That felt a step too invested. And she didn't want to give him the opportunity to cancel.

He held her gaze. He had a soft look in his eyes that made her feel like they were the only people in the room, that the hubbub around them, the industry, had faded to nothing.

'I've been cheeky,' he said finally. 'I know you didn't come here to ask me out. But as soon as I saw you by the photocopier I knew that's what I wanted to happen, and it was fun getting there, wasn't it?'

'Yes, it was fun,' she replied. 'And your desk is really messy,' she added. 'You really should do something about that. A tidy desk is a tidy mind.' He laughed. She remembered she had loved how he laughed. 'And I'll just go see Harry about my payslip.'

She knew he was watching her as she walked across the floor. She knew their encounter had once again been bouncy, effervescent, magical.

And she had walked out of that office with both a payslip and a date.

Chapter Twelve

Charlie, Gillian and Olivia arrived at the Gielgud Theatre just before eight thirty. A woman in a black dress opened the double doors to let them in and directed them from the lobby into the auditorium.

'Wow!' Olivia exclaimed. The theatre was already a gorgeous one, a baroque confection of red velvet, dazzling chandeliers and ornate, gold-embossed balconies, but the set onstage – ready for the play's opening the next week – was quite astonishing. Depicting a Byzantine building in Venice, it was a stage-wide, two-storey fretwork construction composed of a grand central plinth, with intricate 'windows' on each 'floor', and two sets of wooden steps up each side to the second level.

'See, Charlie?' Gillian cried as they all walked over to it. 'Look how wonderful the craftmanship is!' They wandered around, Charlie taking in every surface, every joint. 'Honestly, I could get you a gig like this! I have connections . . .' Gillian wiggled the fingers of both hands theatrically.

'I'm happy with my current employment,' said Charlie, but not morosely.

'Oh, Charlie, and this is why we love you so much,' said Gillian. 'You just never change.'

'And neither do you,' Charlie said to his friend. They gave each other a squeeze. Olivia loved their relationship. That never changed, either. 'But thank you for bringing me here, Gill,' he added. 'It's fascinating.'

Charlie peeled off for a closer look at the artistry of the flight of steps. Olivia and Gillian peered through a fretwork window at the scaffolding beyond.

'So, are we writing?' Gillian asked her.

'I'm reviewing,' Olivia replied. 'The film reviews, still, for the *Morning Shout*.'

'Well, good. Good girl.' Gillian fingered a trellis, lasered her eyes on her god-daughter's. Olivia's first memory of her godmother had been Gillian giving her a book wrapped in a brown paper bag for her fifth birthday: *Little Women*. 'Keep it somewhere safe for when you're older,' Gillian had told her disappointed and bewildered god-daughter. She'd been expecting a *Bunty* annual. 'What about something more, darling? What about a novel?'

'I'd like to, one day. It's just finding the time. My day job's pretty full-on at the moment. And the social life.' She grinned sheepishly.

'Been out enjoying yourself?' She couldn't tell if Gillian looked disapproving or not.

'A little bit.' Another sheepish grin. 'And I have to keep all the plates spinning, financially, you know?'

'But it's still a dream, right?'

'Yes, it's still a dream. I do have big dreams, and I'm thankful that you're always encouraging me. I want to be successful. I want to write things that people want to read. I want to make some money—'

'I get it,' said Gillian. 'You want more out of life. I did, too. Something creative *and* lucrative. But you also want to keep some of what you already have, right? Your working-class roots. Your feet on the ground. And there'll always be your dad.'

'Yes, there'll always be Dad,' Olivia said with a smile. They both looked over at him. He was running his hand along one of the wooden steps.

'Good girl. Well, I'd love to see your name in print. And not just in a newspaper. You'll get there, I'm sure you will, if you carry on doing the right things. And if you work hard.'

Charlie drifted back over.

'Look at these flats,' he said. Protruding from the side of the stage the technician had disappeared into, stage left, was a wide, thin stack of painted backdrops, fabric on MDF, set on to castors. The one facing them was a scene of the Grand Canal in Venice, pale eau de nil water, ghostly buildings. Gillian ran her hand over the St Mark's Basilica and they all walked into the wings to follow the skyline's progression.

It took a long while, examining all the flats. Gillian was quite enraptured by them. The scenes of Venice, a city she told them she'd always wanted to visit. The colours, the brushstrokes. Charlie liked the one that had been embossed in the corners with wooden frets and scrolls in pale oak. There was an extended chat with set designer, Max – Gillian's mate – who turned up with a tray of coffees and ready to give a sip-by-sip and piece-by-piece explanation of the craftsmanship of the entire set. Then there was a tour of backstage at the Gielgud, the green room, the stage door and the portraits of former players that lined the walls. Then they were back on the stage again, with Sam talking about dovetail joints and the contrasting merits of a scroll saw, a fretsaw and a coping saw. Charlie was rapt.

At ten thirty, Olivia checked her watch for the final time.

'Sorry,' she said, tapping Gillian on the arm. 'I have to go. I have a deadline.'

'You do? You not coming for something to eat with us?'

'No. I didn't know we were going to. I have to deliver a film review in the morning.' She frowned. 'I thought there was plenty of time. Dad usually likes to be in bed by half ten – I reckoned we'd have left by now.'

'You couldn't ask for an extension?' Gillian looked disappointed. 'Have a birthday supper with us instead? I thought we'd go to a steak house somewhere.'

'No, sorry, I really can't. You don't mind, do you, Dad?' She turned to him. 'I can pop over tomorrow, bring a cake?' She looked at her watch again.

'No, of course I don't mind! Go, go!' Charlie said, flicking both hands in her direction. 'Go and do what you need to. And cake tomorrow sounds good.'

'Thanks, Dad.' Olivia gave her father a big squeeze. 'See you tomorrow. Thanks, Gillian,' she said, giving her godmother a quick hug, too. 'It's been a lovely evening.'

Olivia waved to them as she turned and left the stage. Gillian and Charlie. Her little world. Gillian's face could not be read, but Charlie was smiling, his hand raised in goodbye, his hair a little messed up. Scruffy jeans. Navy V-neck jumper. Gola trainers.

Smiling and waving goodbye.

An image of her father she would keep in her heart forever.

Chapter Thirteen

Venice

Tuesday 9 January 2018

The past was a shallow puddle you could barely see your own face in, she thought. The past was the dark water of a canal you could stare down into for a lifetime and still not be able to rewrite or change.

The authors and the publicists had taken the river taxi back to the Figo, having said goodbye to Beth near the alleyway to her guest house, but Olivia hadn't gone with them. She needed to clear her head, she'd said. She had drunk a little too much. She wanted to walk around a little more.

'But it's freezing!' Frances had cried.

'I know. It's fine. I'll see you all later.'

Leo had tilted his head. 'You sure?' he'd asked, with too much unfathomable concern in his eyes.

'Yes!' and 'Go! Go!' she'd told them, and they'd peeled off in a bluster and a chatter into the crowds of Venice, the cold and the hint of afternoon fog.

Olivia had wandered through the alleyways of Venice for a while, alone. Among the damp walls and beside the canals – flat and still in some stretches, chopped up into devilish peaks by rocking boats in others. Among the people: the tourists, wandering or purposeful, wrapped up in coats and scarves, industrious with online maps on their phones, halting to gaze into unusual shop windows or to frown at the prices on a menu displayed under glass outside a bustling restaurant.

She grew tired of these streets – when, who, would ever grow tired of these streets? – as she reached yet another shop selling masks, overlapping on posts outside like molluscs on a ship's mast, so she turned back on herself, and headed to the Grand Canal, where she descended two damp steps, stared into the dank water for a while, and then hailed a gondola.

'Ninety euros, thirty minutes,' said her captain, a tall, skinny male of middle age and enthusiastic beard.

Olivia handed over the cash. It was extortionate, but everyone knew that on their visits to Venice, and, besides, most people had someone to share the fare and the journey with.

There was a heap of blankets where she took her seat, thick and grey like army surplus and smelling of wet dog. She pulled two gingerly over her for it was bitterly cold out there on the water, and sat back to take in the view.

Her gondolier was humming, right from the off. They headed down the canal, slow and undulating, the slap of the water against the side of the vessel, Olivia's future winding before her, the past lying behind, still but never silent. She gazed up at the buildings left and right, enjoying their dwindling colours, their pale, pretty details; the way everything was beautiful, but nothing quite perfect. The palazzos and basilicas and guild halls pressed together wonkily to keep themselves upright; the mooring poles creaked in the shallows; the eyes of a thousand windows looked sleepily on.

They passed under the Bridge of Sighs, and the gondolier started to softly sing. An Italian lullaby maybe, and she was cocooned in the red and black wood of the gondola, safe for now.

She didn't want to see Leo again today. She would order room service, take a long hot bath, hunker down at the hotel. She wished Stella would come early. She might phone Annabel tonight, at her big old ramshackle farmhouse in the country, her phone ringing under a pile of papers among the contented chaos of the evening, the school clubs, the running around – Andy asking where his shoes were, Annabel answering in a rush – harried, but pleased to hear her friend's voice. Olivia smiled at the thought of that. The thought, too, of Stella, with her man in Verona. Having drinks, dressing up, planning dinner. Feeling hopeful. Olivia needed these thoughts of her friends; she didn't need her memories, but they always came.

Of the people she had lost. Far too many. One of them right here in Venice – her godmother, Gillian, lying in a bed in a hospice until Olivia was brave enough to go and see her. Contact between them had been minimal for so many years now. A few postcards, including a new-address card sent from Venice, a couple of short letters, a piece of writing Olivia had posted to Gillian, in the hopes of what she didn't know. Maybe forgiveness, for something she could only guess at, for Gillian had never put it into words. Maybe understanding. Something. Gillian had never once mentioned that piece of writing she had mailed. Once upon a time, she had written her god-daughter long letters as meandering as the Venice canals, when she was out of the country, working abroad somewhere exciting on a secondment; Olivia had run to check the letterbox after school for Gillian's chatty news and views, for tales of other cities, for advice and encouragement.

Dear Olivia, it's sunny in Paris today and the new art pieces that have come into the gallery are astonishing. Lucky me! How is school? How did you get on with your book review of Great Expectations? I'm sure you got a really good mark for it . . .

Dear Olivia, there's a stiff breeze in Barcelona today, otherwise the city is lovely. Hope school is going well and you're looking after your father. Thank you for sending me that piece you wrote about the coffee shop. It was wonderful! Keep going, I really think you have a great talent . . .

Dear Olivia, it's busy, busy in the gallery at Lisbon today! I miss you both a lot, though. Did you write that short story for the Young Writers competition in the end? I think the deadline is the 24th . . . P.S. Sorry about the handwriting, I'm scribbling on my lap as I drink my tea . . . xx

The gondolier started humming 'That's Amore', really playing his part. A man at the canal edge called to his wife. A tourist dropped their old-fashioned camera into the water with a *plop*.

'*Disastro!*' muttered the gondolier, then resumed his song.

Venice, the watery city, continued on its day. The city held another person lost to Olivia – Leo Greene – and she didn't know what to do about that when seeing him always stirred so much within her. Their history, their mistakes, when at one time to see him had been to find solace, but it had been fleeting; time with Leo was a fleeting ride on the surface of deep, deep water.

Her gondola passed another. A wrapped-up young couple, sharing a kiss and a future. Olivia pulled one of the grey blankets further under her chin and looked the other way. Kisses and imagined futures were deceptive. Stolen nights could be crimes. And a rainy afternoon in London, far away, full of sadness and regret, could lead to both release and farewell.

Chapter Fourteen

London

Friday 22 October 2004

Olivia stopped in the drizzle, placed her right hand over one of the spikes to the railings bordering Green Park and pressed down hard. She kept her hand there until she became self-conscious that people might notice her doing it, almost piercing her palm with that spike, so she took it off and moved on, bumping straight into a man in a trench coat walking in the opposite direction.

'Oh, for God's sake!' he muttered from above her. He was tall and she was small. 'Why don't you look where you're going?'

She extracted her head from his chest. '*Sorry!*' she spat, angry and defensive, and already pushing past him. Her hand was smarting from the spike, and she welcomed it. She'd wanted that sharp pressure, to feel a different kind of pain – one that was searing and only temporary. The man grabbed her arm.

'Hey!' he said. 'Hey, it's you, isn't it?' She turned back, furious, hurting, and looked at his face. '*Olivia?*'

It was him. It was Leo Greene. Her pub snog. Her airport encounter. Her stood-up date from another lifetime ago, although it had been barely three weeks. Her eyes flicked over him, taking in his various elements: beige trench coat, umbrella, mock-croc briefcase, hazel eyes. He was just as handsome, just as devastating – why wouldn't he be? It was her world that had changed, and she was already devastated, so what did she care?

'Oh, hi,' she said. She didn't care how she sounded. She didn't care that she had stood him up. She didn't care about anything.

'Where are you going?' he asked her.

'Home,' she said.

'And where have you been?' He didn't add, 'Looking like that.' She was wearing a smart black wool coat, a black wool dress, black tights and black court shoes, and a broken heart.

'I left my umbrella,' she told him randomly, watching the rain drip from the edge of his. 'And the Tubes are up the spout, and I've just walked from Pimlico. I'm just walking around, really . . .' Green Park. She realised she was not far from the offices of the *Morning Shout*. '. . . and I feel like one of my heels is going to snap off and everyone will be staring at me when it does, and I can't do it any more, this day,' she concluded, and she didn't know why it was, whether it was because his was a face she wasn't expecting to see today, or because of the cold, or because of the rain, but she broke into sobs – big ones, loud ones, the kind to make the people walking past stare at her in horror.

Leo pulled her carefully back over to the railings, and she realised his hand was still on her arm, on the black wool, where raindrops stood proud on its furry surface.

'You're soaked,' he said. 'It's OK,' he added, and because his voice was kind, she collapsed against him, her head once again on the damp coolness of his trench coat, her tears soaking into the fabric as he steadied his arms around her. 'Funerals are really, really tough.'

She'd thought her crying had been done for the day. She'd been to the ladies just before she'd left the wake at the Boleyn Arms in Pimlico, and her eyes in the cracked mirror were red and her eyelids were swollen. She'd splashed them with cold water and had told herself, 'Enough now,' but here she was, crying right into LL Greene's mac.

'I'm sorry,' she said, finally pulling back from him. 'I have no idea what I'm doing.'

'It's OK,' he repeated. She could still feel his arms around her, his kind embrace, here on the street, that she knew she didn't deserve. He looked at her. 'What would you *like* to do? Would you like to go for a drink?'

She stared back at him. 'I stood you up three weeks ago,' she said. 'I didn't even try to contact you.'

'Don't worry about that,' he replied, and the tender look on his face wanted to make her burst into tears again. 'There's no need to explain.'

'And all I've had are endless cups of tea,' she continued. '*Dry bar*, because of bloody Aunt Amelie. The driest, most depressing bar I've known in my entire life.' She attempted a watery smile. 'I think I need whiskey.'

'I can find you whiskey.' Leo smiled gently at her. 'Let's go to the Ritz.'

Chapter Fifteen

All Olivia saw was gold and brown. All she felt was the kind of thick warmth that would make a person want to sit back in their finely upholstered, art deco armchair and sleep, if they weren't savouring their whiskey cocktail. She needed warmth; the church had been freezing and so had the wake, as a distant cousin had insisted on leaving the door open so they could chain-smoke selfishly on the threshold. Olivia had risen countless times from her chilly seat next to dry Auntie Amelie to close it, but had eventually given up.

'Had your father been ill?' Leo asked her.

Olivia blinked against the brown and gold opulence of her surroundings. The gilt domed ceilings. The lit-up Lalique panels. The gleaming camphor wood.

'No. No, he hadn't been ill. He'd been fine.' She flicked at the corner of her cocktail menu. 'He had an aneurysm.' She exhaled. Her father had died on leaving the Gielgud Theatre that night with Gillian. He had collapsed on the steps, falling to the street, dying instantly. While she was on the Underground dashing home to King's Cross to meet her deadline. 'It was his birthday.'

Her voice wavered. She took a sip of her Churchill's Courage – bourbon, maple syrup and white port – from a big fat tumbler. If ever she needed a good old dose of British stiff upper lip, it was then. A robust, ballasting drink to keep her upright and not spilling on to the carpet like rancid oil. There were nuts on the table, olives; they hadn't touched them.

'I'm so sorry,' Leo said tenderly. 'That's incredibly sad.'

She took another big sip, before setting down the glass. A waiter appeared to discreetly check for depletion of nuts or olives, then glided away. She stared at an illuminated panel of Lalique engraved glass above Leo's head. She didn't want to crumple in front of Leo Greene, but what did it matter if she did? What would it matter if she unspooled on the floor of the Ritz?

'Actually,' she said, 'my father passing away was why I stood you up. It happened the night before our date.'

'I'm so sorry, Olivia.'

'I'm sorry I didn't get in touch. I couldn't. I've just been a mess.'

'I understand.'

'I haven't been able to do anything. Nothing. I haven't even been to work. And then before I knew it, it was today. The funeral. I wasn't ready for it, ready to say goodbye, and I still don't want to say goodbye. I want to say hello as I go into his flat. I want to say hello and for him to make me a lemon squash, and I want us to tease each other and for Dad to call me Livvy Mivvie, after the lollies I liked as a little girl. I told my friends to get in a cab after the wake, that I would walk – walk it off in the rain, but I can't walk it off, can I? It's always there, this pain, and I don't know how to make it go away.' She was softly weeping at the table now. 'You know, some woman came up to me today and started blathering, "Oh, I know *exactly* how you feel. I lost my father two years ago, blah blah." I didn't behave well, Leo. I snapped at her, saying I'm sure she didn't, and she was so lucky not to be feeling like I did . . . I wasn't there,' she said. 'I left him and my godmother. We were at the Gielgud Theatre and I left them to go home and finish a film review. *I wasn't there.*'

She was sobbing. Leo let her. He was different today, she thought. He wasn't flirty, or full of banter and deliciousness. He was what she needed. After a few moments, he spoke.

'Was there anything you could have done?' he asked her gently. 'If you *had* been there.'

She shook her head, the tears still falling. 'No. It was instantaneous.'

'So, you couldn't have done anything, said anything . . .'

'No.' She had been through all this with Stella and Annabel; they had said the same, but still, the guilt remained. She should have been with him, with *them*, when it happened. She should have been there in her dad's last moments.

'You have to see it that way,' he said kindly. 'That you couldn't have done anything. It wasn't your fault, what happened. It was just one of those tragic things. You could never have known, and even if you had, there was nothing you could have said, not in that moment.'

Her eyes filled with tears again. 'You don't understand,' she said. 'I *never* said what I should have said. The things I should have said *before*, but I never did. There was so much time! I thought there was so much time! But there wasn't.' She took a deep, sobbing breath. 'I never told him how proud I was of him, like he always said he was of me. I never told him!' And this she had not said to Annabel and Stella. Not this part. It had stayed in her head. 'I didn't always show it, either, that I was proud of him, or where I'd come from. I got rid of my accent as soon as I could, when I went to uni. I told people I was from Pimlico, which was the truth, but I let them assume which side of the area, which *class*. I bought him stupid, snobbish presents he was bemused by. I wanted a lot of clichéd things: to better myself, to climb out of the gutter. But it wasn't a gutter.' She started to cry. 'It wasn't a gutter at all. It was my dad and me, and we always did just fine. I was moving away from that world, he knew that, but I didn't want him to think I wasn't proud of him! I never told him that I was proud of his creativity, and I was proud of how he brought me up on his own, and I should have done. I thought there was more time.'

As she'd spoken, Leo had sat there and soaked up all of her words. She appreciated his sympathetic face, the warm planes and consoling contours of it. Walking here, she had been trying to forget Gillian's at the funeral: tired and pinched and never looking directly at her.

'And my godmother, I think she blames me for not being there when it happened. For going off, for being late on my deadline. She's been distant with me, and I asked her today, the first time I could bear to, did she resent that I wasn't there? When he collapsed? That she had to deal with it on her own? And all she said was she had "no words". No words! And I never had the right ones for my dad. Not the ones I should have said. And now it's too late. Sorry,' she sniffed. 'You must think I'm being really irrational.'

'You're allowed to be irrational on the day of your father's funeral,' Leo said calmly. 'You're going to have a lot of complicated emotions for a while, and that's OK. You can do this, you can. You can get through this. I bet your father knew you were proud of him.' She shook her head. 'I'm sure he did. And I'm sure your godmother will come around, in time. What was his name?'

'Charlie,' she said miserably, and his name brought her to fresh tears. 'He was Charles Albert Sackville. Thank you for asking that.' Leo had the right words, she thought. His words were a soft balm to her, more than the whiskey, more than the cocoon-like warmth of the Ritz. He may not understand the working-class father, the roots of her past so thick and strong they buckled the pavement outside Charlie's flat, but he had the empathetic words she craved tonight.

'Then, cheers to Charlie,' said Leo, and he raised his tumbler.

They sat in silence for a few moments, Olivia absorbing the happier sounds around them. Refined chatter, coats slunk on and off. And the hush, in some places, of seduction. Stockinged toes climbing a leg under suit trousers. Whispers of later bedroom plans. Soft giggles and rumbles, married people up from the suburbs, celebrating, away from the children, role-playing, pretending they were someone else entirely.

She wished she were someone else entirely, but she was glad Leo was not. He was *here*. He had been gentle and solicitous. On the way here he had threaded his arm through hers like a ballast and had held her up as they'd headed through the streets.

'How's *your* dad?' she asked.

'You really want to change the subject?' Leo looked at her quizzically.

'I *need* to,' she said. 'Just for a minute. I need to talk about something else. I read something about Isaac Feu last week. Some big new venture he's undertaking – a chain of three restaurants.'

Leo sighed. 'If he gets the investment . . .' he said cautiously. 'There's been some premature reporting . . . But yes, he has big plans. Always big plans. Are you sure you want to change the subject?'

'How did your dad get famous?'

Olivia had seen Isaac Feu recently, scowling from the cover of a huge hardbacked cookery book. A stained apron, an untamed thatch of red hair, his arms folded high on his chest. Inside the book, that she'd picked up absent-mindedly in a bookshop, pretending she was still a normal member of the human race, were amazing-looking dishes displayed on rustic work benches, and slabs of butter were whisked into absolutely everything.

Leo frowned. 'Hold on,' he said. 'I'll order us two more drinks.'

He called over the waiter and it was only after they had two fresh cocktails sitting in front of them, and she asked him again, and insisted she wanted to talk about *him* now and not her, that he began.

'Isaac's first job was as a delivery driver's mate, delivering art supplies. His father told him at seventeen that he needed to get out there and work, that nothing was going to be handed to him. Isaac was from money, but he did badly at school – dyslexia, I think, although Isaac will deny it. He's not that good with money either, despite being born with plenty of the stuff.' Leo pulled a face. 'Anyway, he hated the greasy spoon cafés they had to keep stopping at, so he started making lunches, in the morning, for him and his driver. Healthier food – sandwiches, but on proper bread, with spiced meat, vegetables, salad. He'd never really cooked before, but he got into it. He tells it that at first his driver wasn't happy about it, called it "pretentious muck", but then he really began to enjoy Isaac's food. Isaac set up what I suppose would be the equivalent of a pop-up restaurant these days. A small tent in the car park of the supplies depot, serving upmarket burgers, fancy herby chips and all that. It all went down a treat. He gave the drivers what they wanted and what they didn't realise they liked. Eventually the bosses started coming down to eat from there, too, and Isaac left the delivery driving job when he was twenty to become a chef.'

'That's a great story.' Olivia took another sip of her Churchill. 'Why are you calling him Isaac and not Dad?'

'Because he's my stepfather.'

'Oh! You didn't tell me that before.'

'Yeah, since I was four years old.' Leo spoke proudly, but Olivia noticed something. A flicker of sadness, a shadow across his eyes, and suddenly he was not the man she'd met so far, but a little boy, revealed.

'Who's your real dad?'

He pulled another face. 'A loser called John-Timothy Greene.'

'And he's where?'

'In Africa, in India, in a church. Sailing up a lonely river on a driftwood raft . . .'

'That's a lot of different options . . .'

'He's a missionary. A charismatic one. The sort of charming do-gooder women like my mother, and others, swoon over, until they get to know him. Flaky as fuck. Far more interested in the souls of the good people of Ecuador than his own wife and son . . .'

Leo Greene, she thought, as he lowered his eyes momentarily to the table, then raised them to her, clear and unblinking. *You have a flush of vulnerability to your face.* She had the sudden urge to touch his mouth, his hair, the soft skin of his cheeks and the rough skin of his chin, creeping into five o'clock shadow territory.

'I'm sorry.'

'I'm not, not really. Good riddance to the sanctimonious prick. And in his meek, mild absence, I got the fantastic Mr Feu.'

Olivia sat back in her chair. The alcohol had oozed into all her bones. She looked at Leo curiously, trying to decide if he had just grinned or grimaced, trying to fathom how good or bad he was going to be for her. 'How did Isaac and your mum meet?' she asked.

'She was newly divorced and took a job as a waitress at one of his first restaurants, reading Erica Jong in the back room between shifts and not taking any shit from him, because she'd had so much from my dad. Isaac started wandering into the back room to watch old episodes of *Columbo* between the lunchtime and evening service. He pursued her until she gave in. Wore her down.' He smiled ruefully. 'Let's just say, she doesn't read Erica Jong any more,' he added.

'Does your mum cook, too?'

'Yeah. She's a fantastic home cook.' The smile returned to his face. 'Casseroles and cassoulets, huge steamed puddings, meringues. All the old family favourites, but done really, really well. She spends her days planning and shopping and cooking for these amazing dinner parties – lots of noisy guests; a big, long table that takes hours to set up. She does what she calls a Kitchen Supper most Wednesdays – an open house for whoever is around – and it's usually about fifteen people from the village all coming in the door and plonking bottles of wine on the table, talking their heads off.'

Another world, Olivia thought, to her own upbringing. It sounded absolutely fantastic. 'Was all this catering going on when you were a kid?'

'Yeah, I'd be told to play in my room. To come down later. But "later" was always everyone tanked up, flopping around the table, stuffed to the gills. Stevie Nicks on the stereo. Isaac barking out the most outrageous chef's kitchen anecdotes. My mother over-compensating and fluttering about . . . They're a bit much, my parents. But I guess they instilled in me a love of food,' he continued. 'But I didn't want to cook it, I wanted to write about it.'

Olivia nodded. They both sipped at their drinks. A dowager in a fluffy coat came into the bar, shaking her umbrella imperiously before handing it to a serf. A young couple followed, their body language rich and loving.

'How often do you see Isaac?' Olivia was interested in what their relationship was like, a living breathing relationship. One with a future. And a home.

'I see him every Friday at his restaurant. He lets me try something new,' Leo said absently. 'I get a free lunch.'

Leo scratched at his forearm. A small abrasion, a paler dash on his wrist. Maybe it was a burn, from taking one of Isaac's esteemed dishes out of the oven in the between-service kitchen. Olivia considered it poignant. She reached out and traced it with her finger. It was smooth and papery. Leo looked up in surprise.

'How are you feeling now?' he asked her huskily. She saw his Adam's apple move down his throat. 'A little better?'

'A little better,' she replied. Truthfully, though, she didn't want to talk much any more. She was tired. She wanted to get out of her funeral dress. But she didn't want to say goodbye to him just yet. 'I'm not normally this spontaneous, but my hot water will have just come on and I really want to go home and have a bath,' she said, gazing at him. 'Would you come with me?' She swallowed now, too. 'I mean, come home with me. Wait while I have a bath. Talk a little more. I have a bottle of limoncello in the fridge, if you need an incentive.'

'That's an unusual offer,' he said.

'I know. But I don't want to be on my own tonight. Would you please come home with me?' She swizzled her drink, but she was staring right into his hazel eyes.

'I don't know, Olivia, but I *am* spontaneous. Which can be dangerous . . .' He looked at her. Waited a long, slow beat. 'Is it real limoncello from Italy?'

'All limoncello is from Italy, isn't it? I mean, I got it from Tesco – special offer – but I don't think they make it in Basingstoke . . .'

He smiled a slow smile. 'Then I'll come home with you,' he said.

Chapter Sixteen

The bathroom was so steamy she couldn't see her face in the mirror any more, but the floor was a little cold. Olivia placed a fluffy bath mat down she'd brought from the flat in King's Cross. She added some L'Occitane bath gel to the deep, scalding-hot bubble bath, and a few drops of lavender oil.

Olivia had been staying in Charlie's flat since her father died, and in the run-up to the funeral. Taking long, hot baths she couldn't take in the flat share, as they didn't have one. Tidying things up; sorting things out. Crying into her pillow in the spare bedroom that used to be *her* bedroom and still had her old desk in it, the one her dad had made for her.

'Now I know everything I need to know about you,' Leo said from somewhere behind her. He was on the sofa in the living room. 'You like bubble baths and limoncello.'

Olivia and Leo had shared four glasses between them, drinking it on the sofa while the bath – old and deep and incredibly slow to fill – had run. They had not talked much. Leo had said, generously, that the place was 'nice'. Olivia had replied, 'Yeah. Not what you're used to, I expect, but yeah.'

'Yes,' she replied now with a soft smile. 'And I'm closing the door.'

She took off her funeral clothes, her black, functional funeral underwear; pulled off a scrunchie from her right wrist and used it to pile her hair on top of her head in a messy bun. She eased herself into the bath, sighing as her body slipped into the heat and steam of the water. She submerged herself in bubbles, leaned back against the hull of the tub, letting the memories of this awful day wash away, just for now. She tried not to think about Charlie's bath accessories which she had gradually replaced over the past three weeks. His soap bar for her bath gel. His flannel for her Korean exfoliating towel. His Vosene shampoo for her fancy oil. The bathroom smelled of sandalwood and lavender now, not Charlie's shaving foam and the bottle of Old Spice he had used for decades. Olivia closed her eyes, breathed in the scent, and focused on the moment. She needed to forget this day, the funeral, just for a little while. She needed to escape.

'You can come in,' she said after a while, to the closed door. 'If you want. Bring a kitchen chair.'

'If you're sure?' the door answered.

'I'm camouflaged by bubbles. It's perfectly safe.'

The door opened. Leo, in his office charcoal trousers and chambray shirt, with the sleeves rolled up, came in with a wooden chair and sat down, tugging up the knees of his trousers as he did so.

'Feeling a little better?' he asked her.

'Yes.' She had bubbles up to her chin. She liked him in here with her. She liked his voice.

'Relax,' he said, 'you've had a rough day.'

She closed her eyes. They had put the radio on next door, something soft and jazzy. The tap was softly dripping. Her mind quietened in the hot water and the steam and the oily, lavender bubbles.

'What's your favourite word?' he asked her, after a luxurious couple of minutes.

She smiled, opened her eyes. '*Vainglorious*,' she replied. 'What's yours?'

'*Garlic*.'

She smiled again. 'You like garlic?'

'I like the word garlic *and* I like garlic.'

'You're a strange creature.'

'Pride myself on it.'

She closed her eyes again. Let herself be lulled by the water and the soft music and his presence.

Eventually, without opening her eyes, she asked him, 'When did you first start writing?'

'When I was twelve,' he answered. She let his voice wash pleasurably over her. 'I stopped locking myself in the bathroom to read, and instead I started to write.' She looked at him; she'd thought he'd been joking about that. 'And I was always a critic, I suppose. I started writing up critiques of the school assemblies. Scathing put-downs of the headmaster. Just for myself. Then I got bored of that, so moved on to the lunches. Playing with the language of food. Finding exactly the right words to convey a chicken stew or a piece of sticky toffee pudding . . .'

'The language of food.' She smiled languidly. 'I like that.' And because of Isaac and his mother, she thought. It made sense.

'In sixth form,' he continued, 'I created the position of food critic for myself at the student newspaper. I would flounce around Salisbury in a big coat, sweeping into unsuspecting bistros. I started getting quite the reputation, you know, for trouncing places. I was really bloody obnoxious. What were *you* like as a teenager?'

'Oh.' She considered this. 'Determined. Really good at netball.'

'And as a child?'

'Determined. Really good at Fuzzy-felts.' She heard him laugh.

'What books did you like to read?'

She thought of the books at Gillian's house she'd read as a young girl, the books she had borrowed from Pimlico Library. '*Just William*, *Brock the Badger*, loads of Enid Blytons, *Swallows and Amazons*, *Black Beauty*.'

'At your godmother's house? Didn't you tell me something like that once?'

'I did. You remembered.'

'*I did.* Favourite Enid Blyton?'

'*Mr Meddle.*'

'Ha. Mine were the island adventures. Loved those, so exciting. And *Just William* . . .' he mused, 'a nod to the mischief in you.'

'Only occasionally,' she admitted with a smile. 'But, yes, I'm . . . careful. Except when it comes to you, it seems . . . and random bathroom invitations.' She covered her eyes with her hands in embarrassment, but she wasn't embarrassed. This felt right. She took them away again. 'Are you still a player?' she asked him seriously, but as soon as she'd said it, she wanted to take it back. Preserve the moment.

'Of Fuzzy-felts?' He looked curiously at her.

'No, of women.'

'I don't like to think so. I'd like to think I've grown up a bit. That I'm becoming a good man. I mean, I know I like to kid around a lot, but I'm trying to have a good heart.'

All she could hear now was the soft *drip, drip* of the tap.

'Good for you,' she said, and she meant it. 'The world needs more good men with good hearts.'

'I'm trying to not be like my father or my stepfather,' he said, and she was surprised by this. She'd had the impression he idolised Isaac. 'How have I been tonight?'

'Very good,' she replied. 'Very gentlemanly . . . so far.' She gave a soft smile. 'It's a shame you never met Charlie Sackville,' she added. 'He was one of the best.'

She closed her eyes again. Listened to the soft seeping of the tap, the rain now, at the window. Felt the nearness of Leo and wished they could stay in there forever.

'Hang on to the good things,' Leo said. 'Hang on to all the times that were really good with your dad. And there will be better times for you, I know there will. *I like you*,' he added. 'It may not be the day to say it, but I like you a lot.'

She opened her eyes. 'Then say it again tomorrow,' she said. 'I like you, too.' And she meant it. 'Will you stay tonight?' she asked him. 'Stay over? I don't want to be alone,' she repeated. 'I don't mean sleep together, as I don't think it's the day for that, either. But would you mind just being here with me?'

He took a beat before he answered. 'No, I don't mind.'

They stayed there in the bathroom for another twenty minutes or more, talking softly, Olivia eventually turfing Leo out so she could emerge from the bath. She dried herself quickly, with one of Charlie's comfortingly rough old towels; put on her pyjamas, a soft dressing gown of shell pink. They lay squished up on the single bed in her old room for a while, just talking, then, when she grew sleepy, he moved to the sofa, with a quilt and a pillow she'd fetched for him from a cupboard.

She didn't sleep well, knowing he was just in the next room. Early in the morning, she rose from her single bed and stole into the sitting room, where he was lying on his side, sleeping on the sofa, one flick of brown hair over an eye.

'It's tomorrow,' she whispered. He stirred, and opened his eyes. 'Will you come back to my bed?'

That morning, they stayed under the covers of the single bed for a long time, exploring, pleasuring, pleasing. His gentle eagerness was a delight and a fire, and her receiving of him a sweet, sweet release. He was a balm to her, a relief, a solace and a temporary healing. Temporary, yes, for after the tussled, tangled heat of it all, after the quiet and the stillness of the hours beyond, the fresh bout of tears that made him clasp her to him tightly, she understood somehow what would be. That she and this beautiful man had arrived somewhere, but only for now, and that they would be saying goodbye before the end of the day.

Chapter Seventeen

Venice

Wednesday 10 January 2018

Leo was standing at the end of the hotel jetty. It was a foggy morning, 8 a.m. The air was thick and languid, pricked by the shouts of boatmen and the slicing trajectory of low-slung birds, and pierced by the bronze spires of the skyline.

'Morning!' he called to her quite cheerfully, as Olivia approached.

She noted the slosh of water against the planks and the balustrades of the jetty. The teasing of the canal dank between the barbershop mooring poles. The fact that she and Leo were both dressed warmly – Leo in a great khaki padded coat and a furry trapper hat; Olivia in jeans and knee-high boots, her fluffy 'teddy' jacket, plus her tote bag over her shoulder stuffed with packing tape, bubble wrap and a large brass pair of scissors.

'Hello.' She hooked her bag further up her shoulder. 'What're you doing here?'

She hadn't expected to see Leo until the book signing at the Libreria Acqua Alta this afternoon. She had eaten alone in her room last night, a room service snack of antipasti and salad, before TV and bed. She'd spent several hours trying not to think about him.

'I know you said you didn't need any help, but I thought I'd come along.' Leo looked unrepentant. Far too cheerful. Far too handsome.

'Ah,' she said. 'Well, I did mean that. I really don't need you. It's just a few boxes.'

'I can come anyway, though? For moral support? Please don't send me away.' He pulled down the ears of the trapper. 'This hat is expecting an outing.'

'It's hardly an "outing" just to pack up a few boxes,' she replied. 'And that's a ridiculous hat,' she added.

He stroked one ear theatrically, like it was a pet, a silly look on his face.

She couldn't help but smile. 'Alright. The hat can come,' Olivia conceded, misgivings building as soon as she'd uttered those words. Why was he here? 'But only because there's a bench you can help me move.'

'Great,' said Leo. 'I can move a bench.'

They waited for the water taxi, which pulled up to the jetty with a gentle thud and a sluice of the Adriatic. Leo helped Olivia on board, and she baulked at his touch, although they were both wearing gloves; the leather on velvet a static charge. He settled opposite her, leaning back against the unglamorous plastic windbreaker.

'We should make the twenty past ferry,' she said.

She focused on the scenery. The morning. The majesty of the buildings they putted past. The slap of water at rickety jetties. The yells of tradesmen heaving boxes of produce off rocking vessels into the waiting arms of restaurant staff on narrow decks. The brisk call of the seabirds.

They spoke about breakfast, what time they'd had it and what they'd had. The decor of the bedrooms. The man on reception who attempted to tell jokes in English. They spoke of anything and nothing, without curiosity, and she was glad. She was scared to even look at him. Wary of what he might say, and what her heart might reply.

The ferry to the Lido was slower than the water taxi. Olivia ran out of nothing to say, and Leo got up to 'have a look' at the front of the ferry, and to get talking to a couple from the north of England. Olivia could see the three of them laughing at the rail, that he was asking them lots of questions, that the woman found Leo handsome.

'Nice people,' Leo remarked as they disembarked at the main pier of the Lido, just before nine o'clock, that long slip of an island shaped like an aardvark's snout which curled gently in the water parallel to Venice's main island. Leo talked to anyone; Olivia remembered that.

They walked along the wide, quiet streets to Gillian's house. Past the little bakery with the green awning, and the tiny dry-cleaners' where Olivia remembered a *nonna* sitting outside on a little chair in the summer, barking good-naturedly at people. The overhanging willow from a neat front garden that tickled at arms and shoulders like a child's fingers when you walked beneath it. She had walked this street once before.

'Are you OK?' Leo asked her.

'Perfectly.'

'Are you cold?'

'No, not at all.'

'You're hardly talking.'

'I'm OK.'

When she had last walked along this street, the pavements were busy and the velvet band above the skyline had been a bright blue, not a steel-wool grey. When the sun danced on the surface of the canals and crept down the alleyways, illuminating eager faces. Now, there was a man walking beside her in puffa coat and silly hat, his breath distilling into the air. Mystifying, irresistible Leo Greene.

'This is it,' she said, stopping on the pavement.

The house was the colour of washed spearmint. It sat back from the street behind a fretted ironwork fence and a gate heralded by two stone pillars, one with a letter box trapped inside. It had a huge, drooping monkey puzzle tree in the front garden. A striped awning proud over the front steps. A pretty stained-glass door, and cobalt-blue shutters at narrow arched windows that housed faded window boxes.

'Wow!' Leo exclaimed, followed by an appreciative whistle.

'Yes,' she responded.

'Have you been here a lot?'

'Just the once. But I didn't go in.'

Leo looked at her in puzzlement. She had a copy of the key in her bag, tied to a piece of pale blue velvet ribbon. The key struggled in the lock. The door swung open.

'Goodness!' Olivia cried.

She had tried to imagine this empty house on the Lido, free of Gillian's furniture and possessions, now sold at auction houses via a Venetian clearance company, but she was chilled by how bare and unwelcoming everything looked. The hall smelled musty. There was no console table, no squishy sofa, or plants, or paintings; no patter of excited dog paws, no swoosh of Gillian's very English slippers on the cool Venetian marble. All the things Olivia had envisaged inside.

Olivia had imagined Gillian often in her house in Venice, pottering around in the front garden, over-fussing her dogs. Touring about on the *vaporetti* with one of the smaller 'babies' in her arms, his snout curious over the water. Squeezing into one of those tiny, stand-up bars to have a shot of espresso with all the old boys who went there for breakfast. Wandering the alleyways of Venice with her famous carpet bag over her shoulder, certain she wouldn't get lost, but smiling to herself when she found another set of uneven steps heading straight down to the Grand Canal. Gillian had curated a whole new life for herself. An ornate and sweetly aesthetic one, full of art and beauty. Gillian, clever as clockwork and paid handsomely for that in her field, had created a world beyond what most people could dream of.

The house was cold. Leo's footsteps echoed behind hers up the empty hall with its faint, ghostly trace of coffee and lavender.

'What do you need to do first?' he asked her.

'Check for any remaining boxes or possessions,' she replied. 'There shouldn't be much to do. But I have to be at the hospice by twelve. Your phone's ringing,' she added.

'Is it?'

Leo pulled his phone from his coat pocket, frowned at its screen, saying, 'I thought that was later,' and clicked it off. 'Why is your godmother in the hospice?' he asked, peering into rooms off the hall. A sitting room. A dining room. 'What happened?'

'Complications following pancreatic surgery, just under a year ago,' Olivia said. There were boxes in the dining room, so they wandered in. 'A chronic infection. No hope.' She sighed. 'It's been difficult to accept, especially as she's only in her late sixties. And she could have come home, have nursing care here, but Gillian prefers to pay to be in the hospice, apparently.'

'Apparently?'

Olivia sighed. 'I haven't seen Gillian for quite a while,' she confessed. 'All we've had is some postal correspondence here and there. Then her solicitor got in touch, said I had been named next of kin – she has no family, no children – and would I be willing to oversee the final closing up of the house. I had the festival booked here, so I thought, yes, I could do that, and I'd like to visit her, too.'

'I see,' Leo said. They went to stand by the boxes in the corner of the room. 'And she must want you to visit, if she made you next of kin.' Olivia didn't reply. 'You said you came here once, but you didn't come in. Was that in 2015, when we were in Tuscany? You were due to come here after Santa Luce.'

At the mention of Santa Luce, Olivia's body became still. How could he mention it so casually, the site of their final stand-off? Their disintegration?

'Yes. She couldn't see me in the end,' she replied. 'It was complicated. Anyway, let's take a look at some of this stuff.'

The dining room was completely bare but for this one corner: three large cardboard boxes in a stack, two unassembled flat-pack boxes leaning against the wall, and a neat pile of items including a packet of Lavazza coffee and the detached tassel from a tapestry cushion. There was a handful of books piled up, too: a heavy hardback on botanical plants; Gillian's old, treasured, leather-bound compendium of Jane Austen novels that Olivia remembered from the house in Pimlico; an old Harvard prospectus; and two smart coffee table books on the Guggenheim Collection – the Venice art museum.

Olivia bent to pick up the top book and started flicking through it. The wan sun through the window created a square on the floor.

'Nice books,' Leo observed.

'Yes, Gillian always had lovely books.' They were her own route out, Olivia remembered. Gillian had been a voracious reader from about five, she had once told her, slipping extra books from the reading corner at school into her bag. Reading under her covers at night with a torch. Taking books to her father's allotment or on outings with her ma to the local 'medium' sessions, where she'd read while her ma drank weak tea and listened to a woman tell her audience that the dead were standing over their shoulders.

'How are you feeling about the reading at the Guggenheim tomorrow?' asked Leo. He had picked up the book on botanical plants and was perusing the back cover.

'Reluctant,' she replied. 'I don't like reading from my own books. I'm always frightened of discovering a mistake, or something I could have said better. I get nervous, too. You enjoy it,' she stated. He was too close, she thought. And she hated that she liked that.

'I do,' Leo admitted. 'I guess I like the sound of my own voice.' He flashed her a boyish grin.

'Typical of the privileged classes,' she responded.

'Of which you are now part,' he retorted.

'True.' They'd never got far when they'd moved on to class differences. 'But I have always enjoyed hearing you read.'

This was also true. Leo read his own words beautifully, having no such qualms about breathing new life into them. He really got into character as well, applying the right cadence and inflection to his cast's voices. Once upon a time he had read a chapter or two of her own work aloud. But that was when they were friends.

'She worked there,' Olivia said, 'at the Guggenheim. Gillian.' She paused at a photograph of an old Picasso in the book, and smoothed her hand over it.

'Oh?' Leo sat down on the floor. He made a good fist of crossing his legs, then took off his hat and placed it beside him. 'You never told me that.'

'Yes, she worked in the office there for quite a few years. I only knew about it from the postcards she sent me. She said she became a kind of mother figure to the interns there – the young girls who did the tours and took the covers off the exhibits in the morning, that sort of thing – American girls, English girls, French girls . . . She told me she used to organise a party for them on the last Friday of every month on the roof terrace, to say goodbye to those leaving and hello to those arriving. I guess she worked there until she got ill. But I think she loved the Guggenheim. And I loved that she wrote to me, telling me that.'

Olivia ran her finger down the spine of the book, then replaced it on the stack. She walked to the other window and peered out at a side passage, at peony bushes – big, blousy and blustery in the spring, no doubt; now dormant with their leaves furled. Gillian had intermittently sent her postcards from Venice. The first, when she'd newly arrived, a photo of the Grand Canal, writing on the back, *I have moved to Venice. Hope you are well,* and describing a little about how she had got the job at the Guggenheim, and that she now had three dogs she called her 'babies'. Gillian had never asked her to visit; Olivia had only asked that herself.

'She actually knew the Guggenheims, you know?' Olivia continued. 'Well, she met one of the grandchildren at Harvard – she was there in her third year at Sheffield University – so I think that's how she might have got the job. Or it helped. And she can speak Italian. She has great style, too.' She smiled. 'I think Peggy would have approved.'

'Peggy Guggenheim,' Leo commented from behind her. 'What a woman! Peggy liked a list, too.'

'How do you mean?' Olivia turned from the window. 'What do you know about Peggy Guggenheim?'

'Apparently, she had a shopping list of artworks for her collections when she first got started.'

'A kindred spirit, then . . .'

'You got me into them. The lists. Don't you remember?'

'Of course I do.'

They smiled at each other as weakly as the morning sun creating the square on the floor.

'So, you'll have mixed feelings when you step into the Guggenheim tomorrow.' Leo, cross-legged in his jeans and big coat, looked at her thoughtfully.

'Yeah, I will. I think, just like this house, traces of my godmother will be there.'

'You'll be with friends, though,' he said. 'We'll be there to support you when you do the reading. And if you can feel your godmother there, then all the better. Her traces might even shore you up.' He was rising to his feet. 'What about the two boxes?' he asked, retrieving his hat. 'Do you need to check what's in them?'

'I suppose I should.' She stepped over and used her scissors to knife through the brown packing tape on the first. 'Just old paperwork,' she said, rifling through its contents. 'The same for this one.' Her thoughts were not on the job in hand, they were on Leo. His kindness, so often what she needed. The way he calmed her, made her look at things a better way. But he had ceased to be her friend a long time ago.

'May I explore?'

'Of course.'

Even stripped bare of all Gillian's touches, the kitchen was wonderful. It had pale cream units, a milky marble floor and arched windows that overlooked the garden. Leo glanced around him admiringly. Olivia noticed a tea towel accidentally left on a hook, a print of the Mona Lisa. She plucked it up and tucked it into her coat pocket, where it trailed like a fox's tail.

'I barely saw Gillian at all after my father's funeral,' Olivia admitted. They were both at the windows. The garden's bare trees, the crouch of winter hedges and the smooth path flecked with old leaves made it look like a forgotten winter painting. 'She hardly came over, there was always some excuse. She was busy, she had plans. And then she moved to Venice. You remember when I was going to come here, after La Clementina?' She had said the word and it hadn't killed her. 'Well, she had friends over, I heard them in the background when I phoned her that time.' Did he remember? The morning in Bologna? 'And when I got here, I could hear them in the back garden. Music, laughter, lots of Italian accents, and I felt I didn't deserve to come in. I had invited myself, she never really wanted me here. She never really wanted to see me at all.' Olivia walked to the island and ran her hands over its surface. 'So I didn't go in. I turned away. I walked back to the ferry. I didn't explain to her and she never contacted me to find out. So, I'm really nervous about going to the hospice today. Maybe she wants me as next of kin to tie up the house and everything, but I don't think she wants to see me.'

She had felt tears coming into her eyes and she didn't want him to notice. Leo said, from behind her, his voice gentle, '*Next of kin.* She wants to see you.'

'I don't know.'

'Who wouldn't want to see *you*, Olivia?'

Olivia turned from the island, and Leo turned from the window. Why was his voice so gentle? The look in his eyes so soft? She felt suddenly that this moment might collapse in on itself, and she would end up in his arms by the window, but that was only a dream, surely, and the time for dreaming was past.

So she said, 'I think she still resents me for not being there when my father died. I think that must be it. Why she's been so distant with me all this time. I know people's lives move on, and we didn't have Dad to connect us any more, but I thought we would be connected, forever.' She shrugged. 'It hasn't worked out like that.'

'I'm sorry, if that's the case,' Leo said. And now there was something unspoken between them, she thought. They, too, might once have imagined they would be connected forever. And they, too, had failed to work out.

'I've lost a lot of people in my life,' she said. Did he know he was one of them? Her loss of him and how painful it was? Did he see it each time her eyes were reflected in his? The air stilled between them, then he spoke again, like a hand cupping through it.

'Then go *find* one of them,' he said. 'Go to the hospice. Talk. Make it right. You'll be able to do that, Olivia.'

He took a step towards her and she was terrified he was going to hug her, one of his special Leo Hugs, that always served to both make everything alright and to spark in her that terrible longing for him, and she didn't want to long for what she couldn't have, so she said, 'Thank you. Yes, I can try. Do you want to tour the garden?'

He let his hands fall to his sides. 'Yes. If you'd like to.'

'Oh, the bench! Can you help me bring it out?'

The bench was in a small back hall: pale oak with carved legs. Olivia was to leave it in the garden for the neighbours, who she'd been told had expressed an interest. They would collect it when they returned from an extended Christmas break in Naples.

Leo took most of its weight and she held the other end, and they moved it out of the double doors at the back of the house and into the garden, where they set it down under a spindly pine tree.

In the summer, they may have sat on it for a while, and they might have talked a little more; they may have even been brave enough to venture, tentatively, into talking about 'Us', and Italy, and La Clementina, but it was winter, and the air was still, and the ground was cold with hibernating bushes and empty planters. So, instead, they walked around the garden a little and Leo admired what it once must have been, and she knew, if she reached out to touch his hand, then she might not feel cold any more, but she didn't dare.

Back inside, they packed the books and the curtain tassel and the coffee into one of the flat-pack boxes, which Leo had assembled, and Olivia wrote a label in her navy-blue marker pen and placed the box for the removal company. Then she locked up the house with the little key on the slip of velvet ribbon and they walked back to the jetty to wait for the ferry.

'I'd like to come with you,' Leo said as they walked. 'To the hospice, to visit Gillian. Will you let me?' Olivia turned to look at him. His hands were in his pockets. His face open. 'Let me support you?'

They walked a few steps further. The sun slipped out from behind a cloud and presented itself again, a pale cascade over the tops of buildings. Olivia thrust her cold hands into her own pockets. 'I don't know,' she said. She really wasn't sure about anything. 'Can I think about it?'

Chapter Eighteen

From the outside, the Hospice Calma Bianca at Castello could have been one of Venice's less extravagant hotels: a pearl-white frontage studded with small windows – some circular, some oblong; four tiered storeys stacked neatly on one another; and a pale oak door with a honey-coloured portico.

Olivia and Leo went through the portico and into a glass-backed, simple lobby beyond it, the circular, herringbone path of a courtyard that showcased a modest fountain at its centre. The lobby was painted white and was very light; a nurse behind a marble desk, in pale blue starched uniform and old-fashioned white scrub cap, made no sound as she moved from computer console to digital pinboard, detailing the quiet schedule of today's doctors.

'I think we need to sign in,' Olivia commented to Leo, in a whisper – she felt that everyone must speak in whispers here – as they approached the desk.

They signed in, adding their plain-looking English names to the list of Italian ones, and, nodding at the nurse, made their way through the glass sliding doors to the courtyard, around the herringbone, and along a path to a two-storey building with awnings in dusty pink that reminded Olivia of an American road-trip motel.

Olivia led Leo to the second floor. She noticed how he still tugged at the knees of his trousers before he climbed a flight of stairs. How he kept his head down, concentrating. How he smiled gently at her when they reached the top. Who was he? she thought. Who was he in Venice?

They walked along a blank corridor, their footsteps echoing. A soft wail came from behind a distant closed door. They reached the door of Room 201, which opened, and a nurse carrying a jug of water glided out.

'Hello,' she said. 'Can I help you?'

'We're here to see Gillian Goddard,' said Olivia. 'I'm her goddaughter. And next of kin,' she added.

'Of course,' said the nurse. 'Please go in. I was just refreshing Gillian's water. I'm Piera.' She had excellent English, a round face and curly hair wrestled into a neat bun. She started walking away down the corridor. 'She's tired. But it's good you are here,' she said, over her shoulder. 'And you have brought a handsome man, so that's even better.'

The two visitors entered the room. Inside were crisp white sheets on a high motorised bed; a circular window behind with a view of a beautifully jumbled skyline; a vase of soft winter foliage on a bedside table; and Gillian Goddard in a very un-Gillian periwinkle woollen bed jacket, her once charcoal hair now a pale silver and combed off her face.

'Hello, Gillian.'

Gillian looked so different, Olivia thought, to the person she had known. That robust woman, full of steel and laughter, had paled to this frail woman in the bed, and she had brought none of the material manifestations of the past with her. There were no photographs in this room, no books, no art, no personal mementos. There was nothing from the house in Pimlico. Just Gillian, the bed, two chairs and a bedside table.

'It's Olivia.' Leo hung back. Olivia stepped towards the bed. 'Olivia Sackville.'

'Olivia. You came.'

Was she pleased? It was hard to tell. Gillian's face was softer than it had been years ago. There were fleshy domes under her eyes, lines at the side of her mouth. Was the mouth smiling? But her eyes looked bright.

'I've brought someone with me. Leo Greene. He's another writer. We're here at a book festival, and we've just come from the house. We've packed up the last of your belongings, got everything sorted.'

'How are you doing?' Leo asked. He approached the bed and took Gillian's hand. The Leo Greene charm saw Gillian's face momentarily brighten.

'Handsome,' she muttered. 'What do you write?'

'Crime,' Leo replied.

'Excellent,' she said. Gillian knew all about Olivia's career, she must do. She had sent a *Congratulations!* card in the post when Olivia's first book had been published. But that was all. Her scant correspondence never added up to much, and everything she had sent had read as so hollow. Olivia had no idea how to make amends with her own words, have them fill in all the gaps and make their relationship whole again. She had no idea what to say.

There was silence. Olivia waited. Gillian grimaced a little and shifted her body under the sheets – a shrouded leg pricked to the left, an elbow rising.

'How can I make you more comfortable, Gillian?' Olivia stepped closer to the bed. Gillian shook her head, and Leo said, 'Let me.'

He plumped up Gillian's pillow as she meekly lifted her head. He tucked the sheet firmly around her and gently stroked her elbow through it, until her body was peaceful and still. He then took the chair at the left-hand side of the bed, and Olivia sank into the other, opposite, shrugging her coat off.

'Thank you for making me next of kin,' Olivia said eventually. 'I didn't know whether that meant you actually wanted to see me, but—'

'You look so much like your father,' said Gillian. For the first time, she was looking directly at her god-daughter and she had tears in her eyes. 'I really miss him. Still.'

'Me, too,' Olivia replied, but so quietly. 'I'm sorry it's been so long since we've seen each other.' She thought about the time she had stood outside the house on the Lido and walked away. She thought about all the years, over thirteen of them, in which she had felt Gillian's cold shoulder and colder heart from a distance, always from a distance, and here they were, unsatisfactorily reunited at last. 'Are they looking after you well, here?'

Good start, she thought, to skirting all the way around. Her words were like Gillian's postcards, messages sent through the air, polite, signalling some small desire to make contact, but not a great deal of it. Not enough. Just enough to keep lines of communication open, not enough to have them singing.

'Yes, they do. It's calm. Tranquil. I even forgive it its uninventive food.'

'Forgiveness is a wonderful thing,' Leo commented. Olivia looked at him. Why had he said that? He and Olivia had not forgiven each other, how could they? And it would not happen here today with Gillian. She was certain of that already. 'And how bad can the food be? It's Italy! Can I fetch you some water, Gillian?'

Gillian nodded, then reached up a hand from under the sheet to touch her hair.

'I look a mess,' she said, only to Leo.

'You look lovely,' Leo replied. He poured Gillian some water from a fresh jug on the bedside table into a plastic tumbler, and helped hold it while she sipped from it gratefully. Olivia felt redundant. Leo's kindness was elbowing her out of the room. She knew why he was doing it, acting all solicitous; he was quilting over the painfully apparent void between godmother and god-daughter. Stitching together the awkwardness. 'Do they ever let you look out of the window at that magnificent view?' he asked.

'Seldom,' Gillian replied. 'Although occasionally they turn the bed around. Mostly, Piera describes it for me. Her English is so effective.'

'That's good,' Leo said. 'Sometimes you need someone else's words.' He stood up and peered through the window. 'Would you like me to describe the view for you today, Gillian?'

'Yes, please,' Gillian said with a smile, closing her eyes.

Olivia stood up. 'I'm going to get a coffee. Would you like one, Leo?'

'Oh, yes. Black, please.'

Olivia left the room and walked to the small vending machine at the end of the corridor. When she returned, Leo was back on his chair with his head bent towards Gillian's, and Gillian was softly laughing.

'You two look like you're up to no good,' Olivia commented, handing Leo his coffee.

Leo looked up at her. 'We're talking about you.'

'Me?'

'Yes. Gillian was asking me about your career recently. I was filling her in.'

Gillian could ask me herself, Olivia thought. *Why can't you bear to look at me?* she thought. *Why can't you?*

'Why did you make me next of kin?' Olivia asked. It just came out, and she could bear it no longer, this skirting around. They had skirted around each other for nearly fourteen years.

'I don't have anyone else,' Gillian responded. She coughed, then coughed again, giving a little splutter – her hand coming to her mouth. Olivia was already out of her seat.

‘More water, Gillian?’ She quickly refilled her godmother’s tumbler, raising it to her lips. ‘Not too much,’ she warned. ‘Careful.’

‘I’ll be quite alright,’ said Gillian briskly and, with that, the conversation was shut down and Olivia knew she couldn’t open it up and dig down deep.

There was a small knock at the door and a nurse appeared in the doorway: short, stocky and clean-cut, with floppy brown hair and a uniform of pale blue baggy trousers and a crackling cotton tunic.

‘How are we all getting on here?’ he asked, strong Italian accent. ‘Anything in the notebook for Damonte?’ He walked over to the bedside table. There was a small notebook there, behind the water jug, that he picked up. ‘Gillian and I play Dots and Boxes,’ he said, showing them the top lined page, and evidence of the game where players create a grid with dots and then compete with a partner to draw lines between them to make boxes. ‘Hangman, too. She always beats me.’ Damonte and Gillian shared a smile. ‘And sometimes she leaves me instructions that she writes to me when I’m not on shift.’ He turned to another page and read out affectionately, ‘*Please can you locate some elderflower cordial to put in my water jug, as water gets really boring. Thank you, Damonte. Oh, and please can you ask reception if they can find a book for me, an English edition of* The Thorn Birds, *somewhere in Venice, for I haven’t read it for a long time. Sorry to be so demanding.*’

Damonte grinned as he returned the notebook to the table.

‘He’s like putty in my hands,’ Gillian said, and everybody laughed, but still Gillian did not look at Olivia.

He turned out to be a chatty sort, Damonte, full of tales from outside the hospice and the streets of Venice that Gillian, from her bed, seemed to enjoy, and Olivia welcomed as a distraction. At a humorous junction about a gondolier and a chicken, Olivia caught

Gillian's eye, hoping they could share a smile too, but Gillian glanced away. Worse, Olvia happened to then catch Leo's.

'Perhaps we should go now,' said Olivia finally, once Damonte had slapped his thigh and insisted that he must get on, before leaving the room with a finger point and a whispered and rather unnecessary, 'You guys!'

'I like Damonte,' Gillian summed up from her bed, once Damonte's footsteps had died away down the corridor. 'He cheers me up. Can I have some more water, please?'

'I'll do it,' said Leo, rising from his chair. He went to the bedside table. 'I'm writing Damonte an instruction, too,' he said mischievously. Smiling, he picked up the pen next to the notepad and scribbled something on it. '*Bring Gillian better food . . .*' he read out, then he poured some more water into the tumbler and waited for Gillian to sip it. 'Thank you for letting me come. It's been lovely to meet you, Gillian.'

He bent and kissed Gillian on the cheek, and Olivia stood up and kissed her on the cheek, too, alert for bristling, but Gillian's face was impassive.

'I can be here on Saturday morning,' Olivia told her, but Gillian did not answer, and Olivia honestly did not know if she wanted her to show up here again.

'Yes, we'll come again on Saturday,' said Leo. 'Talk some more,' and Olivia shot him a look he pretended not to catch.

Outside, the door closed behind them and Leo said, 'Well, that wasn't easy,' and before Olivia could reply, he had enveloped her in a huge hug she immediately struggled to get free of. She couldn't bear his arms around her, the warmth of his chest, the smell of his aftershave. The chemistry. The memories. She wanted *out*.

'I probably deserved it to be,' she said, having finally extricated herself. She smoothed down her hair, tried to compose herself. She couldn't be hugged by him. She couldn't have that pull inside her to never let him go.

'Then you just need to talk some more,' Leo said. 'Both of you. Find the right words.'

'I don't know if I can.' He looked a little disappointed she had wriggled out of the hug. But he shouldn't have done it. He shouldn't have touched her. She had never expected him to touch her again. She had once said the wrong words to *him*, in a Tuscan lavender field, and what he'd told her there, too, had meant the end for them.

'OK,' he said measuredly. 'But you'll be here again on Saturday,' he said as they walked back down the corridor. 'She didn't say no to you about that. It might be better.'

'Maybe. You said you were coming with me.'

'I will, if you want me to. She's very important to you, isn't she?'

'She was my dad's best friend,' Olivia replied simply. 'And, you know, you're far too saintly,' she said to him flippantly as they descended the quiet stairs together. She wanted to change the mood, get out of her own head. 'Here in Venice. I'm slightly suspicious of it.'

Leo laughed. 'Saintly? That's a word that hasn't been used about me before. What do you mean?'

'The bedside manner. I was quite impressed.'

'You've *seen* my bedside manner.' Leo looked at her and she had to try hard not to blush. 'And no need to be suspicious. I'm just trying my best. Want to go for lunch? We don't have to be at the bookshop until three. And please don't say you'll think about it,' he added. 'Please say, yes. I think we've earned it, don't you?'

She thought about it. She was a little drained, and she was hungry. And he was right, they didn't have to be at the bookshop until three o'clock. 'Alright,' she replied. 'Where?'

Chapter Nineteen

The sign above the door said 'Casa Macellare' and the smell coming from behind it was a wonderful mix of garlic, hot charcoal and a spice she thought was cinnamon – or maybe nutmeg; Olivia always got those two confused.

Leo was right. This place, to a first glance, was a butcher's: white walls, sawdusty floor, spotlessly clean glass counters and display cases showcasing different cuts of meat – but the wonderful smell was coming from an ashy hole in the brick wall behind the servers and, beyond it, Olivia could glimpse a cavernous fire pit and chefs in thick aprons and woolly hats turning thick discs of meat with flashing silver tongs.

'It's very *rustic* in here,' Leo explained. 'Just choose your cut of meat and wait for the magic to happen.'

They both chose a rump steak. The steaks were expertly wrapped in paper and pushed through the hole in the wall to the waiting chefs who slapped them in their palms before unwrapping them and tonging them deep into the smouldering ash.

'Come on!' Leo said, and he led her past one of the glass counters and along a narrow passageway at the back, which opened on to a tiny courtyard. Three long wooden benches hosted people in big coats huddled over steaming plates of food, tumblers of red wine at their fists. There was a workbench at the end, set with a large bowl of crusty rolls, a dish of red cabbage and a pyramid of wrapped cutlery.

They dropped into seats at the end of one of the benches and ordered beer and wine from a simple handwritten menu. They helped themselves to salad and rolls at the workbench. Then, after ten minutes, two of the chefs lumbered out of the back of the restaurant and dropped discs of blackened meat on to their plates.

'Oh, you're right, delicious!' Olivia exclaimed, after taking a few mouthfuls.

'One of the best-kept secrets in Venice,' Leo boasted.

They ate and drank, and Olivia took it all in, this scene. The locals, tucking robustly into their lunch. The fire and coarse heat from the kitchen. The hulking chefs. The rough wood of the benches. Yet, something about this place was almost romantic, she thought, a place to hunker and whisper secrets over steam and smoke.

Olivia wasn't entirely sure what she and Leo were doing. How strange it was, she thought, to be in Venice with him, moving benches, and visiting her godmother and going to lunch. For them to be together, but not be together. For her heart to lurch every time she looked at him, but her head determined to remain sensible and unscathed.

'Have you brought women here before?' she asked him, attempting to sound casual. 'Girlfriends?' *Fiancées* . . .

'Here? No.' Leo laughed. 'Last time I came here, I brought Rowan.'

'Your hotshot agent?' Leo nodded. 'How is he?'

'He's great.'

'Because of you.'

Leo laughed again. 'He does have other authors on his books.'

'But you're the most successful.'

'Arguably. Aren't you Alice's most successful?'

'Arguably,' she echoed with a smile. The mood had definitely lightened. She felt relieved to be out of the hospice. 'So, thank you for coming with me today. Both to the house and to see Gillian.'

'My pleasure.'

'You were great with her.'

'Was I?'

'You always seem to know the right thing to say. Unlike me.' She suddenly wanted to change her own subject. 'So, no girlfriends?' she asked, immediately wishing she had chosen something else. Why had she brought that up again? Was she so relieved to be out of the hospice she was now self-sabotaging?

'I'm holding out,' said Leo. 'I don't want to make any more mistakes.' They watched as the hulking chef lobbed another piece of meat on to another customer's waiting plate. 'Well, my engagement obviously didn't work out, and I want to be really sure, if there is a next time.' She studied him, trying not to give herself away, more words from that night spitting out of her brain, just as they had catapulted from her mouth back then. 'You have to be sure, don't you?'

'Yes. I'm sorry the engagement didn't work out.' She had read an interview with Leo a year or so ago when he'd said he was currently single. She remembered feeling surprised, and something close to relief, though this news was nothing to do with her.

'You knew?'

'I read something. And you do have to be sure. James proposed to me,' she said. It felt strange saying his name again to Leo.

'He did?'

She nodded. 'I turned him down.'

'Why was that?'

'Because I didn't love him enough.'

'Oh.' Leo studied her. 'Well, you really have to love someone enough to marry them,' he said, and fragments of a lost conversation jabbed at her.

'I know. And I didn't. You saw him once,' she added tentatively. 'We never spoke about it.'

'No.'

After they'd been together about six months, James came straight from work to meet her and Annabel at the end of a book event at Waterstones Piccadilly – for David Nicholls – most of which they'd spent hiding in a corner as Leo was there, too, with his agent. Olivia had clocked her ex-friend early on, and had made an excellent stab at avoiding him, but as everyone had filed out, he and Rowan had been behind them.

'You were disdainful about his gilet.'

'I was *not*!'

He had been. Olivia had overheard Leo muttering something to Rowan about Olivia's 'finance bro' and commenting that James' gilet made him look like a jockey. She was telling it as though it had been a light-hearted encounter, but it had not.

'You didn't like it that you were no longer top dog in my life.'

'*Top dog?* I wasn't in your life at all.' They looked at each other. 'Anyway, this is the kind of thing I talk about with my therapist.'

'Top dogs? Gilets?' She was being far too light-hearted *now*.

'No. Loving people enough.'

'Is it?' She tried to sound objective. Not entirely interested. And also not guilty that it may have been her who had led him to the therapist's door in the first place.

'And other things. Settling down. *Babies* . . .' he whispered – his eyes wide – and her heart gave a lurch. She wondered exactly what else he'd been talking about in therapy, how many times he had lain on the couch and for how long, and if he was heading back there again after this trip, but she didn't dare enquire.

Instead, she asked, 'You're ready to have a baby now?'

'Yes. Are you?'

'Well, truthfully, yes, I am.' Maybe this was too much truth. She had not said this out loud to anyone before. It was the kind of thing one might reveal to their own therapist. 'But I think it might be too late.'

'You still have time.'

'I'm thirty-nine,' she responded. 'So only just.'

His eyes were unblinking. The irises magnetic. She had once thought she'd seen the future in the kaleidoscope of his hazel eyes, but that future had passed them by. Olivia lowered hers to her plate, a suddenly and particularly interesting piece of walnut in her red cabbage.

'Mum has left Isaac.'

'She has?' Olivia was astonished. 'I haven't seen anything about that. In the papers or anywhere.'

'It's very recent. They're keeping it hush-hush. Isaac is furious.'

Olivia chose her words with care. 'I hope Caroline finds happiness,' she said. 'I hope she finds . . . better.'

'She's happy,' Leo said. 'She feels free. Of him. She's told me so. Oh, another change,' he threw in, 'I no longer listen to Phil Collins.'

'Well, that's something,' she replied. 'I no longer lint-roller people.' Leo smiled. 'And with Isaac . . .' Olivia swallowed; she could barely look at him for worry and for guilt. 'Tell me, are you able to—'

'*Hello,* Leo Greene.'

Olivia immediately recognised the woman standing at their table. It was Slip Dress, from yesterday morning's panel at Palazzo Tesoro. She was wearing a glamorous fur-trimmed hooded coat, her hair in a chignon, those cats' eyes glinting.

'Oh, hello,' said Leo. 'Nice to see you again.'

The woman's mouth curled into a gratified smile. She placed one hand up to her cheek, blood-red nails on bronzer. 'I'm here for lunch with a friend,' she said in her rich Italian accent. She flicked her head to the end of one of the other benches, where a woman, turning up the collar of her jacket, gave them a timid little wave. 'I wanted to come over and ask you out for a drink tonight, if you're free? Unless you have to be with the other authors always . . .'

She flashed Olivia a condescending smile. Olivia granted her a tight one in return. She set her knife and fork neatly down on her plate.

'Ah, well, that's lovely. Thank you very much for the invitation. But I'm afraid I *do* have to be with the other authors while I'm in Venice,' said Leo beguilingly. 'At *all* times, so I won't be available.'

'You are not free tonight?' The woman glanced back over to her friend, fanning her fingers from her cheek in a small gesture of bewilderment.

'No, I'm afraid I'm not,' Leo said pleasantly.

'That is a shame,' said the woman with a seductive scowl. 'We could have had a nice time. I would have taken you to one of the best places in Venice.'

Your apartment? Olivia thought, and a bolt of unwanted jealousy reared up, threatening to throw her out of the saddle she'd been precariously perched on since day one of the book festival.

'Never mind,' said Leo chirpily. 'Thanks again for asking.'

The woman pouted, opened her mouth to say something, then closed it again, and walked back to her friend.

'Wow.' Olivia tilted her head at him and picked up her fork. 'You should have said yes. She's very attractive.' *Jealousy* – she thought – another reaction to Leo she had to dampen. This trip to Venice was proving to be very hard work.

'I didn't want to. I make it a practice not to date my readers.'

Olivia scoffed. 'Very funny!'

'*What?*' He held up his palms in protestation.

'You've never dated a reader?'

'No! And I don't know why you think I have!'

'I think you take opportunities,' she said. 'And you had an opportunity right in front of you there,' she added slowly, releasing each word methodically into the chill air. 'You should have taken it.'

'I told you, next time I want to be sure,' he said, looking at her closely. 'I need to.'

'Right,' she said, dropping her eyes to her plate again. 'Still,' she said, finally looking up. 'You've earned your success, you should be allowed to reap the benefits.' How had this happened? she thought. This lunch, this sparring between them, so familiar? They had been lovers, and they had been friends, and they had been enemies; is this what had grown between the cracks? 'You're a star of the literary world, Leo. A magnet, a firecracker, a force. You were, right from the start.'

'I was just lucky.'

'And supremely talented.'

'And so are you.'

'I was a few steps behind you, remember? And I have readers. You have *fans*.'

'I think you're being disingenuous. You have fans, too – ardent ones. Just look at the book panel!'

'My fans don't fancy me.'

'Are you saying my readers think my writing's rubbish and only follow me for a certain aesthetic, whatever that is?' He narrowed his beautiful eyes at her.

'I think your aesthetic is a lovely bonus.'

'Oh, you do?'

'For *them*,' she qualified. It had sounded like she was almost flirting with him, and she had never intended to flirt with him again. 'I don't think about your aesthetic at all. Unless I'm writing a cocky charmer, of course.'

He flung his head back and laughed. 'A cocky charmer, eh? Well, I'm glad I've still got it!' He grabbed his beer. Took a gulp. He forked up some red cabbage with a frown. Then he looked at her more seriously. 'But I've been single since Tuscany. Don't you believe me?'

'It doesn't matter what I believe,' she replied, and she wondered again about the call he'd taken at Harry's Bar. She didn't always believe he was a cocky charmer, of course. She knew he had much more to him than what he often presented to the world. But she wouldn't tell him that. 'Can I ask you something?'

'Sure.'

'Do you think we could ever be friends again?'

His fork halted in the air. His eyes took a long pause on her face.

'Why not?' he eventually replied.

Because we're both guilty. Because we were both so angry.

'I'm not sure if we can repair what happened,' she said.

'I'm not either.' The fork didn't move and neither did his gaze. 'Are you ready to talk about things? To get into it?'

'No,' she replied honestly.

'Then we won't.' She nodded, relieved and disappointed. They had a shared story, but in many of its chapters they had typed ways to hurt each other, pressing on the keys with speed and determination, watching the words appear with haunted eyes. She was frightened to leaf through their typed guilty pages, or to creep to the wastepaper basket to unfurl the screwed-up sheets of bitter paper they had chucked there in fury. 'But I guess one day we might be able to be friends again.'

'You do?'

He nodded. She watched as he thumbed the edge of his tumbler. She absorbed the husk of rigorous smoke from the kitchen, the grey cool of the air, the sight of huddled heads bent over plates of food. And she felt a sweet melancholy, a hankering, that only came with Leo Greene. A swirl of desire, regret and sorrow that this man alone could lay at her heart.

Theirs was a tale that bore reading, time and time again. It was a book she peeked at after lights out, under the covers, with the faint beam of a pen torch illuminating each line, like how she had read as a child, to wonder if she could have written her part differently.

'Now, then,' he said. 'Would you like something chocolatey? They do amazing gelato here.'

'With an amaretti biscuit?' she queried, regretting the words almost as soon as they left her mouth.

'Oh,' he said, surprised. 'Our scene.'

'Yes. *Apparently*.' She had not yet downloaded his book. Something within her was frightened to. Maybe she would read it when she got back to London; maybe not.

'Well, it was a great meal,' he said carefully, and she knew they were back on dangerous ground. They had kissed at the end of that meal. Both at the table and then out on the street, pressed into a damp wall at the edge of the dark water of a canal, everything that existed between them overtaking them, suffocating them, filling a need in them. That was why she had not yet downloaded his book. 'Shall we order some?'

She swallowed. She could easily imagine sharing a gelato with Leo, two spoons, but she didn't think they should.

'I'm quite stuffed,' she said.

'Is that a no?'

'It's a no.'

'OK.' He shrugged casually, sat back in his chair, smiled at her gently. '*Olivia, Olivia, Olivia*,' he murmured. 'What are we doing here?'

'We've come to a book festival in Venice,' she responded quietly, but she suddenly wanted to make a gesture that was loud, that spoke volumes. She wanted to lean across the table and kiss him, remind them both what that was like. But she wouldn't. She couldn't. They were better off as non-friends, fellow authors. They were better off consigning all of their memories to the past, where they belonged.

'OK,' he repeated, but he kept on looking at her, curious and with a soft note of affection, until she had to look away.

Chapter Twenty

London

Friday 16 November 2007

Outside on the street it was minus two, and the heating inside Parchment & Plots, bookshop of the moment in London's Piccadilly Circus, had been cranked up so high that those elbow to elbow inside had shed their winter coats like chrysalises and were balancing them over their arms or grasping them to their stomachs in resentful bundles.

'No cloakroom,' lamented Annabel, looking around her. 'I should have worn something I could shove in my bag.'

'Like a cagoule?' Olivia suggested, flashing a smile at her friend. 'But then you'll be freezing when we leave.'

They looked through the pretty Victorian-paned windows to the street: the streaking buses, the bundled-up office workers dashing to the Tube, the Christmas lights reflecting the gearing up of festive cheer, even though it was only mid-November. People were starting to get frenetic: to wear sequinned tops, to drink more than usual, to excuse all sorts of indulgences with 'It's Christmas!' while shoving sausage rolls in their mouths. The winter was about to be brightened by its annual consumption-fest and the masses were up for it.

'Maybe it'll be a white Christmas.' Annabel shifted her coat to the other arm.

'Maybe. The last one I remember was a grey-slush Christmas. Are you too hot? Do you need water?'

'No, I'm fine.' Annabel patted her seven-month pregnant bump through her cashmere jumper dress. 'I'll grab something when a tray next comes around. Oh, God, look at Simeon!'

Simeon Dunne, making his way through the room, was a hot young thing. A debut author who had written a terrible book set in 1950s London about a woman who runs away from everything – her husband, her family and the stifling, kitchen-sink-and-rollers social mores of the day – and moves to Florence, where she spends her days on the back of a Vespa and her nights on her back in a crumbly hotel, living out all her *belle de jour* fantasies with a series of young lovers bearing snake hips and prosciutto.

Not enough women were outraged he had written from a woman's perspective, in a woman's voice, writing about how this particular woman really loved sex, and how beautiful and sexy and amenable she was, and the book had risen to the bestseller lists, surprising everyone – especially its small Surrey publisher, who had arranged this signing belatedly.

Simeon Dunne was carousing through the assembled crowd like an eager starlet, grinning his head off and high-fiving people. He was dressed as a beatnik, Jack Kerouac style: black turtleneck, turned-up dark blue jeans, stompy baker-boy boots and, indeed, a beret. Olivia and Annabel followed his delighted form to the back of the bookstore, past Historical Fiction and Sagas, where he sat, a diminutive figure behind three huge stacks of his book, *Florence in Firenze*, and a long serpent of people waiting for him to sign one.

'How do you know him again?'

Olivia rolled her eyes. 'He used to work for the *Morning Shout*. He was Sports and Leisure before he was Anti-feminism and Male Pleasure. I lent him ten pounds once and he never gave it back.'

Annabel giggled. 'He looks preposterous – is he?'

'Totally,' confirmed Olivia. 'But we came for the snacks, right? I've heard rumours of crostini and cupcakes.'

'I came to see *you*.' Annabel shifted her coat over her bump again to the first arm. 'Because I haven't seen you for bloody ages.'

'I know, I'm sorry. I've been so busy. But at least this was close to both of our offices, and we can catch up, even if it is as hot as the Sahara in here. Where did Stella say she was again?'

'Second date. A surveyor from Shoreditch.'

'Second date sounds promising . . .'

'While *you've* given up . . .' Annabel tilted her head at her.

'Not this again! I haven't given up – I've just called off the search. For now.'

They watched as Simeon stood up to emphatically wave to someone he'd spotted in the crowd. Annabel held a hand to her stomach.

'Is she kicking?' Olivia asked with a smile.

'Protesting.' Annabel and Andy had found out at their latest scan that the baby was a girl. 'How are things with you?'

Simeon was now bowing from behind his stack of books in mock humility, as one of the women in the serpent blew kisses at him.

'I'm protesting, too,' Olivia replied.

'No, I meant life. Work.'

'Work is work. I've just had a promotion.'

A huge tray came past with Prosecco in flutes, water in tumblers and mini cupcakes with the cover of Simeon's book printed on top in sugar paper. Olivia grabbed a Prosecco and a water.

'Well done, you. Is it still . . . *interesting*?'

Olivia pulled a face. 'Yep. Still a total vanity project. But definitely more interesting than Harrison Blunt.'

Olivia now worked as a press officer for a small theatre company and its owner who starred in all of its plays. She enjoyed it, for all its quirkiness and slightly tyrannical boss. The salary wasn't great, but at least it was in a creative industry and was related to writing. She was still writing short stories. She may have left the *Morning Shout* after so long, as the film reviews were getting her nowhere, but she had won a short-story contest. A story of hers, called 'The Sunflowers', had won first prize in the annual Dublin Review Romantic Short Fiction Competition.

'Oh, look, here we go.'

Simeon had started signing, the queue was slowly moving forward, a delighted person already peeling off, his hardback in their hands. A very tall Black man was swishing through the crowd towards him in a smart suit and a natty green cravat. The man stopped at the table, towering above Simeon, and procured himself a microphone.

'Welcome, everyone,' he said, leaning against the front of the table. 'I'm Benjamin Moleko and I'm very proud to be Simeon Dunne's agent at Janko & Butler. Please join the queue if you'd like the author to sign a purchased copy of his book, *Florence in Firenze*. Otherwise, enjoy the cupcakes and bubbly. Oh, and don't forget, book two will be coming next summer – *Romilly in Roma*!'

Royal Ben . . . Olivia thought, but through the round of applause she had already spotted him. Leo Greene. Lounging against a pillar amidst a grapple of people trying to funnel into the signing queue. The hair, the looks. A black silk shirt. The last time she had seen him, he had been walking down the front path from her flat in Pimlico in his trench coat.

Olivia instantly turned to the window. Annabel, clearly sensing something was up, turned, too.

'Leo's here,' Olivia hissed to her. 'My famous one-night stand.'

A London bus sailed past. A woman trudged by with a Boots carrier bag dangling from her wrist. It was a crisp, very cold evening – different to the wet, windy weather of an October two years ago, but Olivia remembered her day and a half with Leo Greene, following her father's funeral, very well. Firstly because, as she'd told Stella and Annabel, it had been the best sex she'd ever had. *The* best. And secondly, because it had been poignant and emotional and almost cinematic, but, by sometime early in the evening in the flat in Pimlico, things had become a little . . . confusing. They had become awkward around each other, her grief looming too large, and her desire to be alone once again along with it – a painful pull.

Leo hadn't known when to take his leave, she could tell. He was polite, he was hesitant about looking like the bad guy. But, at about 6 p.m., he said he really should go, and she had let him. It had been amazing, but the time wasn't right for them. Leo was a bittersweet adjunct, a complication to her feelings and her grief. She needed space to grieve on her own. And, when Leo had gently kissed her goodbye on the doorstep, and had told her it had been wonderful, neither of them would deny he had looked a little relieved to be leaving.

She turned back from the window. Annabel followed suit. Another tray floated past them. Olivia gave her water to Annabel and grabbed two cupcakes. It was getting almost suffocatingly busy in here, the manufactured heat cloying. A lady in a huge hat was shoving through the crowds barking about needing a hardback and a cigarette. A group of middle-aged women hooted with laughter at something, each clutching a copy of Simeon's book.

He saw her. Leo looked over and caught her eye. Olivia worried how to arrange her face, but she decided to smile a little, to show him she was perfectly happy to see him again.

'Is he coming over?' Annabel whispered.

'Yes, I think so.' Olivia was looking good. She was wearing that new velvet pinafore dress with the cherry blossom print from Jigsaw she'd seen in the window and bought with her weird-theatre gains. Her hair had recently been highlighted to the blondest blonde imaginable. 'Brace yourself, my friend,' she said, with a jollity she didn't feel. She was nervous. She knew, at the very sight of him, the effect Leo was going to have on her.

'*Olivia.*'

He was in front of her.

'*Leo.*'

'How are you?'

'Really good, you?'

'I'm great, thanks. Long time, no see.'

'Indeed.' *Indeed? What kind of an answer was that?* His effect on her had been noted, with dismay. He was still gorgeous; he was still the kind of man whose shoulder you wanted to curl up on, like a dormouse, before you climbed him like a tree. 'This is my friend, Annabel.'

'Very pleased to meet you, Annabel. Do you know the author?' Leo asked them. He was wearing a green jumper, soft wool. His hair was cut a little shorter. His eyes were a little greener, in this light. *Beautiful.*

'Simeon? Yes, I used to work with him,' Olivia said casually. 'How do you know him?'

'Through his agent, Ben, of course. You know, *Royal Ben . . .*?'

'Ah, that's him, is it? Oh, right.' She recognised Leo would probably realise she was being disingenuous.

They stood staring at each other awkwardly. She felt exactly how she'd thought she'd feel when she saw Leo Greene again, apart from the obvious physical attraction. Sad, reflective. Swirling with thoughts of her father and his funeral. But she was better these days, much better. She could think of Charlie without crying, although she still had moments when she felt wretched for not saying the things she should have said to him. And Leo . . . actually, as she looked at him – his handsome face, a soft note of friendliness and warmth in his eyes – she realised she could handle seeing him again. *Just.*

'Oh, there you are!' Ben Moleko appeared behind them and clapped his hand on Leo's shoulder. 'How are you doing, mate? Fancy going for a curry after? We'll have to bring Simeon along, but we can ditch him before the dancing. Who's this?' he asked, looking at Olivia.

'Olivia,' said Leo, smiling at her, and she found herself smiling back. She forgave herself for letting him go, and she forgave him for giving her the space she needed.

'Hello,' she said. 'And this is Annabel. But we must move on,' she added politely. The smiling had been nice, but they *had* both moved on, hadn't they? Two years was a long time ago and her life was quite different now. She could almost feel embarrassed about the bathtub and the limoncello and inviting Leo into her bed in the early hours . . . 'We've got . . . some people we need to talk to. Shall we, Annabel?'

'Of course,' Annabel replied, looking bemused.

They sailed off like two ladies in a regency dance hall.

'You OK?' Annabel whispered, once Olivia had steered her friend and her bump carefully through the crowd.

'Of course. Never better!'

Olivia gave Annabel a grateful squeeze as they headed to the back of the bookstore.

◆ ◆ ◆

By 9 p.m., people were down to their shirtsleeves and, in some cases, lacey camisoles. It was so roasting, a layer-cake of coats and jumpers had formed underneath the Christmas tree in the back corner like a pile of really bad presents. Parchment & Plots had become a bookish nightclub – all naked arms and glistening brows – but with Simeon's droning voice instead of thumping music.

His long, rambling and self-indulgent speech, far grander than his book or his talent merited, Olivia thought, hilariously exaggerated his publication story, making out he had been squatting in a frozen garret before his book got plucked from obscurity to success, when she knew he had been living with his parents in a Mayfair townhouse. He pulled off his beret and flicked his curtained hair like a boyband member, before patting at the wrong side of his chest in humility and thankfulness.

'I'm thrilled to have just even *one* reader,' he sopped, a tiny tear in his eye. 'To make every single word I write worth all the pain.'

'I think I'm going to go,' Annabel said. 'It's too hot and I'm tired. You stay though, if you want to. Congratulate your old twit of a colleague. I'm going to get a cab.'

They still hadn't got near Simeon. The queue had been stalled by his interminable speech.

'You sure? I can come with you.'

'No, it's fine, stay, get your tenner back. I'll call you tomorrow.'

Annabel gave her a quick, sideways hug and moved off to the Christmas tree to retrieve her coat. Olivia waited, but ten minutes later Simeon had still not finished his speech – he was now thanking anyone who'd ever been in his life, even for five minutes – so she battled past all the bare shoulders to the Christmas tree, dug out her own coat from the toppling pile and made her way out.

Two things hit her as she went through the door. The first was freezing cold air, bracing and welcome. The second was the sight of Leo Greene, leaning against a wall.

'Hello again,' he said.

'Oh, hello,' she replied. He looked handsome, one foot up against the wall, staring at his phone. She'd never forgotten how handsome he was.

'Couldn't get a signal in there.'

'Right.'

'And it's baking.'

'Yes.'

The door of the bookshop closed behind her.

'You going home?'

'I am.' It was perishingly cold out here, she thought. If she started shaking, he really wouldn't notice.

'Want to talk for a bit, first?' He put his phone in his jacket pocket.

'I don't know.'

But she moved over to where he was, and then she was standing next to him, her back against the cold wall. Leo had the sleeves of his paisley shirt stoically rolled back, and Olivia felt a pang of recollection at his forearms, his hands, his fingers.

'I was pleased to see you again,' he said. 'Just thought I'd mention that, if that's OK.'

'That's OK,' she said.

'In fact, I have a confession.'

They had both been facing forward, watching the street, but she turned to look at him.

'A confession? What is it?'

'That I hoped you'd be here tonight, because of your Simeon connection. I wanted to see you, if you were. I still think about you, about that night, that morning. Do you still think about me?'

'No,' she lied.

'OK.' He grimaced a little, but he continued. 'I couldn't really read you at all, to be honest, by the time I left your flat that day. But I do still think about you. More than I should, actually. So, I managed to wangle tonight's guest list off of Ben, and you were on it. With a plus one, and I'm so glad it was your friend Annabel, and not some bloke.' Now he grinned, and she couldn't help but break into a smile, too. 'And, well, you look really pretty tonight, Olivia.' Leo's eyes were earnest, his mouth delicious.

'Thanks.' A bus went past, all lit up inside, wan pre-Christmas faces at the steamed-up windows. Olivia made an attempt at counting them. She was not certain around him. She felt like they'd been in a war together, and had both emerged not entirely unscathed. Why on earth would they return to the battlefield?

'And also . . .'

'Also?'

'That day. That night. The next day. Your *father*, how you felt about him, and how he clearly had felt about you. It was in that flat. It was everywhere. It stirred up things for me that I didn't want stirred up. I couldn't do it, and I'm sorry.'

'Oh.' This surprised her. 'What kind of things?' *His real father?* she thought. The missionary on the driftwood?

'Just stuff. Maybe I'll tell you one day.'

'But we're never going to see each other again.' He looked at her like he was looking at her for the first time. He raised his eyebrows; she raised hers back. 'I'm sorry, too,' she said. 'That it all went weird in the afternoon. But it *was* all weird. Emotions were too high. Mine, I mean. I was all over the place. It just wasn't right for something more to develop. So, you're off the hook,' she said. 'It wasn't you, it was *us*.'

Neither of them spoke for a while. They put their backs to the wall again and stared out into the night. They watched in silence as a band of taxis sailed by, their lights off, people inside, going home to husbands and wives and lovers, to flats, to houses, to bedsits. Listening to cab drivers talk about football and the famous people they'd had in the back.

'I passed your door,' he said. 'A couple of months or so ago. I thought about knocking.'

'Why were you in Pimlico?'

'I was just in the area. For work. How's everything going there?'

'Fine,' she replied. 'I've redecorated,' she added, unnecessarily. The flat had been left to her, of course. The flat and the mortgage. For a time, she had considered selling it. But Pimlico was central. Pimlico had been home. Her childhood had been in that house. Her father was in every room, every molecule. When she had officially moved back in, it had been so painful. Boxing up all her father's things. Replacing the net curtains with drapes. Collecting all his tools together in a cardboard box and donating them to a local handyman. When it was time to sort out his wardrobe, she had stood at the double doors and cried. When she had held his worn, navy-blue jumper to her chest, she had sobbed bitterly. But at least she was there. 'And I think I'm going to go home now. It's cold. I have a busy day tomorrow.'

There was nothing else to say. There had been a bittersweet coming together and it could only result in another bittersweet parting. She wasn't sure what they thought they were doing, out here at the wall. She wasn't sure why he had wanted to see her.

'OK. I guess I'll go back in. How are you getting home?'

'The night bus.'

'Right. So, take care of yourself.' He hesitated. 'I feel I want to kiss you on the cheek.'

'Don't do that.'

'Why?'

'Because I don't want you to. And why do people tell you to take care of yourself, anyway, when they don't really care either way?'

'I *would* like you to take care. I'd like to think you're at least alive, as I move through the world. That you're doing alright.' He gave a small frown. 'I like the way you challenge me,' he said. 'I've always liked that.' He hesitated. 'But, anyway, goodbye, Olivia.'

'Bye.'

She walked away from him, heading for the bus stop. Then, she heard footsteps behind her. A rush of cold air. A hand on her shoulder. *Leo.*

'Sorry, but I really want to see you again. I need to. Would that be OK? What are you doing tomorrow?' He was out of breath. His face was flushed. Tomorrow was Saturday.

'Going to the library,' she replied, taken aback.

'To take some books out?'

'No, actually, I'm attending a writing workshop. Islington Library. I'm trying to get serious about finally writing that novel.' What did it matter if she told him?

'Oh, great! Good for you! I've started . . . something,' he said. 'Just a couple of chapters. But it's going OK, you know?' He mussed up his hair above one ear. 'What time are you finishing?'

'Three o'clock. Why?'

'Can I pick you up? Can we go out? Do something?'

She looked at him. 'Why would you want to do that? Why would *I* want to do that?'

'I like you, Olivia. It's been great to see you. I'd like to see you again. We could do something, couldn't we? Start over? Can I please pick you up from the library?'

She considered him. She considered the fact she hadn't been attracted to anyone as much as him since their night together – not even close. She considered that, despite all her misgivings about him and the past, she liked talking to him, she liked the rhythm of their conversation and the things he said to her.

'OK,' she said. 'You can meet me after the library.'

He looked delighted at the plan. 'Great!' he said. 'That's fantastic. I'll see you tomorrow.' And he gave her that kiss on the cheek she had disallowed earlier and he was jogging away and waving at her over his shoulder.

She got the night bus back to Pimlico. She liked the rumble around the streets, the stopping and starting, the *whoosh* and *clunk* of the doors opening and shutting. She wanted to think. Think about Leo and the words they had spoken to each other outside the bookstore. That she would see him tomorrow.

She let herself into the flat on Moore Street.

'Hello, Dad,' she said into the empty air, as she opened the door. She always did.

Chapter Twenty-One

The parent-and-baby nursery rhyme session was overrunning. A circle of mums and one dad sitting on the carpet – some serene, with rapt small babies on their laps; others harried, with squirming infants grabbing at their hair – were gamely singing along to 'The Wheels on the Bus' as the session leader (curly hair, dungarees, a shirt with smiling leopards printed on it) over-enunciated and conducted them all with great zeal.

Those there for the writers' workshop were hovering over by Non-fiction. Olivia had perused the spines of several self-help books and a run of Italian cookery books, but was now transfixed by the only father and baby in the session. The father, joining in with 'The Wheels on the Bus' but intermittently kissing his plump baby on the top of her head, was holding one of her feet and gently stroking it with his thumb; the baby, wide-eyed and velvet-cheeked, was softly gumming on a cloth book and soaking up her father's smile. Olivia thought them a wonderful duo, both imagining her father and her like this back in the day – not that Charlie would have actually come *inside* a library – and wondered if she would know such a moment with a child of her own one day.

The song came to an end and the leader clapped, and the parents clapped, and they took their babies' hands and made them clap, too. Bags were reached into, and miniature coats were pulled out; chubby arms were bent into the sleeves of fleecy jackets; rigid knees and stubborn feet were gently stuffed into the legs of snowsuits. Pushchairs were retrieved from the corner of the library, one-handed, then blankets were tucked around little legs, and the parents and babies were ready to set off home to their milky evenings.

Into the space they had vacated, two library staff members made busy, moving in a table and some chairs, and calling over the workshop speaker – a moderately successful author from the Kent coast called Kitty Codwell, who shuffled over with her stack of notes and her white bob, and immediately picked up a muslin cloth from the carpet.

'Has anyone left this?' she called in a headmistress voice to the last of the departing parents. Olivia and the other workshop attendees were making their way over to the horseshoe of chairs the library staff had arranged. The dad with the wide-eyed baby turned in the doorway. His baby was now in a white fleecy snowsuit and a pink bobble hat.

'Oh, that's me!' the father said, and he swivelled buggy and baby and came to retrieve it. 'All this stuff when you have a baby, some of it invariably gets left behind!'

Kitty handed the muslin to the dad between finger and thumb. The dad thanked her with a smile and moved off again. The attendees took their seats and Kitty Codwell, shrugging off her coat to reveal a tent-like dress and a beaded necklace made of tiny wooden books, stood before them with a big smile.

'Shall we start?' she trilled.

Kitty had a thing for brown Labradors and men with long, striding legs and luscious forearms. She spent the first half an hour of the workshop talking about how she got into writing – not much use for anyone else, unless they too had come from a very posh boarding school in Dorset, and wanted to get back at the girl in their English lit class who was an 'absolute bitch' . . . but you know, 'sod her', as look at Kitty now!

The seated all laughed dutifully.

'And now I'm going to give you my Top Tips!'

Olivia suppressed a sigh. She suspected Kitty was all bluster and not much information.

'Write first, edit later,' Kitty puffed. 'Like most things in life, just do it, and you can always come back and make it perfect later on.'

This was not Olivia's way of writing. She wrote meticulously, planning everything to the nth degree before she even got started on a scene or a chapter: character arcs, plot points, back stories. She edited as she went along, trying to make everything perfect first time. Well, she'd only written three chapters so far, but that was the way she was doing it.

Olivia was writing romance. She had read many love stories at Gillian's Pimlico house in her teenage years, sitting cross-legged in the seat of one of the bay windows, and in occasional sunshine – including the entire Jane Austen oeuvre. Written into those books, time and time again, was the happy ever after she craved for herself, a Perfect Love like her parents had known, and she wanted to craft her own perfect love stories.

'Drink lots of tea,' was Kitty's next tip. That was greeted with another laugh. 'Also, research your subject thoroughly by travelling to your locations. This is, of course, not always possible,' she tittered, 'if your location is a makeshift surgery tent inside a Cornish WW1 hospital – or Mars.' Again, everyone sniggered charitably.

Olivia looked at her watch. In exactly forty-seven minutes, she would be meeting Leo outside. Kitty was talking about some of the settings in her latest novel, continually gesturing to a fresh pile of her own paperbacks, in a deft sales manoeuvre.

'Research, research, research,' she continued. 'As readers will sure as hell pull you up on something if you get a detail wrong, and so they should! Do you know, I once had a reader write to me to complain I had included the use of a parking meter on the coastal road at Deal, when in fact, there were none! So be alert, romance writers! And finally, everything you do, and everywhere you go, make mental – or, if possible, *physical* – notes. Any adventure you go on in life, however small, could be used as fodder for your writing.'

Olivia realised the other women and one man in the audience were taking notes now, so she tugged her notebook out of her bag. Kitty wanted to set an exercise. They were to write freeform for twenty minutes and have their work read aloud by the person on their left. The person on Olivia's left was the sole man, who had a beaky nose and a hard stare, and had complained about the overrunning nursery rhyme group when they'd come in. She didn't want *him* reading the best day she'd ever had out loud, as it was the special day, aged twelve, when her father had taken her on the train to Clacton-on-Sea and she'd been on all the rides and had an ice cream at the end of the pier, so instead she wrote about her second best day – the day she met Stella and Annabel in the queue for the Wine Society at Canterbury University.

Everyone else wrote something romantic, or about their wedding day, or the day they had given birth to their first child, and Olivia felt a little embarrassed when the beaky man read out her funny prose about meeting her friends and wished she had told the tale of the day out with her father instead. And that, at twenty-nine, her best days had been spent with her friends and her lovely father, and not with a romantic partner, her own family not yet created.

'And now I want you to write something else,' said Kitty, once the last of the attendees had read out their neighbour's best day. 'Just for you, just in the here and now, that you won't share.

Something about love, or something you feel in your heart, and I want you to take that piece of writing home and work on it, and improve it, and polish it until you think it's as perfect as it can be. And I shall do the same.'

Kitty had a soft look in her eyes. She sat at the desk and brought out a notebook. Popped the button at the end of a biro.

Olivia looked down at her own book and turned to a new page. She thought of the father and the baby she had witnessed in the singing session, and she began to write . . .

> *I saw a father and a baby today at a library. The baby was sitting on her father's lap, a muslin square caught in her fist and her father's attention equally captured . . .*

She glanced briefly around the circle, everyone quiet, everyone concentrating. She wrote about this father, this baby. She wrote about the love between them. Then she wrote about her own father, the feeling of how it had been between them, right from the beginning. All those memories, all that love. And she concluded with:

> *For fathers need daughters, and daughters need fathers. We need each other like the meadow in spring needs sunshine and rain. My father taught me it's good to be humble, but it's also great to create something long-lasting. My father often told me he was proud of me. I wish I had found the words to tell him I was proud of him, too.*

And as she wrote the final word, and set down her pen, she let the sadness wash over her.

'Well, I hope that was really useful!' said Kitty, looking at her watch and closing her notebook with such satisfaction that Olivia suspected she had set this exercise for her own benefit. 'I wish you all well in your publishing journeys, and if anyone would like a signed copy of *Love Comes to Dorset Bay*, here they are!' she added, slapping the top book on her stack.

A few of the crowd circled. Olivia grabbed her coat and scarf and made her way to the exit. Outside, the chilly air was a blast of goodwill after the stuffiness of the library.

She looked up and down the street. Leo wasn't there. The other attendees, and Kitty, came out of the door and disappeared one by one. She waited ten minutes. She waited a further five minutes, but just as she was telling herself that he wasn't coming and she shouldn't have expected him to, there was a honking of a horn to rival Mr Toad's in *Wind in the Willows*, and a navy-blue sports car steamed around the corner.

Leo stopped the car at the kerb and lowered down the window.

'Sorry I'm late! Get in, it's freezing!'

She hesitated for a moment, then opened the passenger door and climbed into a low bucket seat, upholstered in navy leather.

'I have an invitation for you,' he said. 'I've been thinking about it all the way here, and that was a lot of thinking as the traffic was awful.' He twitched the stereo down, which had been blaring the Arctic Monkeys. 'Would you like to come to Wiltshire with me?'

Chapter Twenty-Two

'*Wiltshire?*'

'Yeah, to the family pile.' Leo grinned at the wheel. 'I've been summoned. It'll be good,' he qualified. 'Mum and Isaac are holding a big dinner party – pre-Christmas bash. All the local characters will be there. Great food, lots of booze. It'll be very entertaining, and I have to be there. Please say you'll come with me,' he entreated. 'Please be my plus one.'

'Your plus one . . .' An entwined couple passed them on the pavement. The man's thick coat brushed against her window. 'This is a bit of a surprise,' she said.

'I know. Sorry. I know it's a bit of a punt, but I'd really like you to come. What do you think?'

'How long will it be for?' she asked. 'When will you bring me back?'

'We'll need to stay over. It's too far to go there and back in a day. But there's plenty of room.'

'I haven't got any stuff on me.' *Stay where?* she thought, but she was beginning to consider it. *Why not?* she thought, after the sadness she had felt in the library. *Why not?*

'We can stop at your place on the way to pick up whatever you like.'

She looked at his face, eager and handsome. She looked at the road ahead, November sun-washed and inviting. She had something new hanging in her wardrobe she'd been dying to wear. Could she be up for an adventure? She was writing a novel, perhaps this would be fodder for it, like Kitty had said. And she liked him. Despite herself, she liked him. He had wanted to see her again. He had tracked her down to Parchment & Plots. He had thought about her, in traffic, all the way here. And he was inviting her to Wiltshire and, despite herself, she wanted to go. What else did she have on but work and the flat in Pimlico and trying to write but not quite managing it? Who else had she felt any chemistry with in the past two years? And the chemistry was buzzing around the inside of the car like fireflies.

'OK,' she said. 'If we can stop off and pick up some of my things, I'll come with you.'

'Good,' Leo said, a wide grin on his face. 'I was so hoping you'd say yes. And I'll make sure you won't regret it.'

'You definitely have hideous taste in music.'

They had been on the road for thirty-five minutes. Leo had stopped outside Olivia's flat, and she had run in and grabbed a dress, underwear, her t-shirt nightie, wash bag and some party shoes and shoved everything into an overnight bag. She had also fetched a bottle of limoncello, still a staple in her fridge, as a contribution to the party, although she suspected it would be a token one now Leo had told her about the giant wine cellar in the basement. Everything was stashed in the boot along with Leo's bag and a six-pack of beer. She could hear the limoncello rolling around – they'd had to stop near Hammersmith Bridge so he could jump out and wrap it in a picnic blanket.

'I hope you're not referring to the mighty Phil Collins?' Leo said, his eyes on the road. 'I'll have you know that "A Groovy Kind of Love" is an absolute classic.'

'An *acquired* taste, then.'

'And do you think you might acquire it?'

'No. I'm still an Oasis girl and I'll continue to roll with it.'

Leo laughed. 'How was the workshop? I forgot to ask.'

'Good, thanks. The writer was a little bossy for me, but it was useful.'

'Were you inspired?'

'I suppose.'

'Have you written anything yet, for a novel?'

'Just a couple of chapters. Like you.'

'Have you told anyone?'

'No,' she laughed. 'I'll tell people if it gets published.'

'I made the mistake of telling Isaac,' Leo said.

'And?'

'Distinctly unimpressed.'

'Oh, sorry.'

'He's not big on encouragement – or praise. Thinks it's character building not to dish it out.'

'Some fathers are like that,' she replied, but hers hadn't been. Charlie had told all the lads at work when she had gone off to university. About her new friends. Her job in the media. He was a little bewildered by her ambition, but he had been all for it. This morning she had found a letter she'd written him from university. A bubbly, showing-off kind of letter, detailing all the fun things she'd been up to. It was inside a book about carpentry at the back of a kitchen cupboard, the pages well-thumbed, and when she'd found it, she'd cried.

'Yeah,' Leo said. 'It's OK. He's probably right. I like the thought of a character that's been built from solid, bruising bricks . . .' A pall briefly clouded his eyes, then disappeared.

Olivia couldn't talk about her father right now, so she said, 'My godmother was really big on encouragement. She's moved to Venice.'

'*Venice!* How come?'

'She's an art historian. She had an opportunity, I guess. She sent me a postcard, telling me she was there.'

'Well, that's wonderful. Maybe you'll go there for Christmas or something?'

'No, I don't think so. We're not that close now. I'll be spending Christmas with Annabel and her family.'

The postcard from Gillian was pinned to the fridge. Olivia looked at it sometimes and lamented what might have been. A close relationship with her godmother, her late father's best friend. Trips to see each other. Christmases. But, no, all she had received was a single postcard from Gillian, and Olivia suspected it might have been out of politeness.

Leo was frowning at the road, concentrating on a bank of cars slowing up ahead. He applied the brakes, and they came to a halt behind a people carrier, a line of traffic stopping either side of them.

'Uh-oh,' he said, 'looks like we're stuck here for a while. Change the CD if you like.' There was something so intimate about being in someone's car, Olivia thought, reaching for the glove box: the spare change in the well by the gearstick, old receipts and scuffed CD cases of beloved artists stuffed in the side pockets, a brown brushed cotton jacket flung like a sleeping beagle on the back seat. 'But I'm happy to be stuck with you,' he added. 'I like being on a road trip together. And I don't want to mess things up this time.'

'There's nothing to mess up,' she said. 'And you're lucky I got in the car.'

◆ ◆ ◆

Foxes, Isaac and Caroline's house, was huge. It lay in wait behind by a five-bar gate that Leo had to jump out of the car to open, and jump out again to close once they were through, and at the end of a gravel track that rumbled through unruly meadow grass and the arch of a manicured hedge. Lit by twinkly windows and fanning uplighters from rustling lavender beds, it was a beautiful Tudor-Gothic mish-mash of turrets and arches, pale-grey stone and black-beamed porticos, and climbing, clambering ivy. To its right, five or six classic cars were parked in front of a stone stable block. To its left, an elegant walled garden capped a sloping lawn.

Leo parked the old Porsche next to what Olivia guessed was a Bentley.

'Here we are.' He turned off the ignition.

'Bloody hell.' Olivia stared at the house from her seat. 'How the other half live, eh? Did you bring me here to try to impress me?'

'Might have done,' Leo admitted sheepishly.

'Well, I'm impressed.'

'That's because you haven't met anybody yet.'

As if on cue, a woman burst out of the grand front door with a tea towel over her arm. She had tumbling, dark brown hair with an eye-grazing fringe, wore a long jersey skirt she was almost tripping over, and a voluminous, cornflower-blue mohair jumper. After her came a rotund man and three – or was it four? – bouncing, marauding Labradors, brown and blond. The man had dishevelled red-squirrel hair. A striped blue shirt, rolled-up to the elbows. Baggy jeans, too long. Both were laughing hysterically. The woman turned and swiped the man with the tea towel; he stretched out fat fingers and tickled her at the waist.

'Let me introduce you to my parents,' said Leo drily. 'Caroline and Isaac. And welcome to the madhouse,' he added, undoing his seat belt. '*Buckle up*.'

'Leo!' shouted Caroline, batting her fringe out of her eyes as she caught sight of the car and bowled towards it. 'You made it!' As he and Olivia got out, she threw herself on her son. 'Isaac said you wouldn't show up, but I told him you would! Sorry,' she added, brushing flour off Leo's jumper. 'I've been cooking since three and I pong of wild garlic.'

'I *said* that I'd be surprised if that old rust bucket would get him beyond the A4.' Isaac's voice was a low growl. He folded his arms high on his chest like he had on his book cover, then approached the car and tapped at the bonnet suspiciously, before holding out an imperious hand to Leo.

'Isaac,' said Leo, shaking it.

'*Leo*,' said Isaac. A brown Labrador danced at his feet.

'Well, hug each other, then,' commanded Caroline, her hands on her hips and the checked tea towel dangling from her arm like a rustler's flag. 'Honestly, you boys!'

Leo stepped forward and Isaac placed one arm awkwardly around his back, then withdrew. 'Who do we have here, then?' he asked, looking at Olivia.

'I'm Olivia,' she said.

'Girlfriend?' barked Isaac, looking her up and down. Caroline was staring shrewdly at her, too, and Olivia wondered if she was one of those mums who believed no one was ever good enough for their son.

'*Friend*,' remarked Leo warmly, to her relief. '*Currently*, although I probably don't even deserve that. She's my plus one,' he said to his mother. 'Remember? You're always telling me to bring one.'

'Only because you refuse to avail yourself of all the fine fillies here in the village,' said Isaac gruffly. He had a strange way of standing, legs too wide apart, short arms down by his sides, like a stocky tripod. 'Are you one of us?' he asked Olivia, lasering in on her under bushy eyebrows.

'One of us . . . ?' Olivia looked helplessly towards Leo.

'Public school, two Volvos in the garage, Mummy goes to Peter Jones . . .' Isaac barked.

'Er, no . . .' said Olivia. 'Not really.'

Leo looked aghast. 'Ignore him,' he said. 'Sorry,' he mouthed.

'Oh, do!' echoed Caroline in jolly tones, but her smile didn't quite reach her eyes. 'Come back inside and finish helping me with the dessert,' she cajoled her husband. 'No one dusts a zabaglione like you, Issy.'

Issy harumphed. 'Very nice to meet you, Olivia,' he said begrudgingly, and bringing one leg of the tripod in, and then the other, he allowed himself to be led back into the house – followed by the high-spirited hounds. 'I hope you like lamb.'

'Love it,' said Olivia to his retreating back. 'Nice to meet you both.'

'Told you,' Leo said, after they had gone back in. 'Absolute nightmare.'

'They're . . . nice,' Olivia mustered. She already knew she was not one of "them" and probably never would be.

'If you like the ultimate good cop, bad cop double act. What Mum giveth, Isaac taketh away,' he said cheerfully. He took her hand and led her back to the car, where he opened the boot. 'Let's get this stuff in. We're in the Milking Shed, by the way. I hope you like it.'

'The Milking Shed? That sounds . . . homespun. Do I get a bed?'

'Absolutely.' And putting on what she suspected was his mother's voice, added, '*The Milking Shed has four well-appointed guest rooms all with a charming view.* It's beyond the walled garden,' he added. 'Come on.'

'Oh!' she exclaimed when they were standing in its doorway. It was indeed a shed, but a very big one, with cute cream shutters on its cute round windows and, inside, a wide hall with pale oak boards, whitewashed walls, sheepskin rugs and ditsy flower arrangements in vintage milk churns. It was warm, too. Toasty warm, after traipsing through cold wet grass in the dark to get here, Olivia's suede boots darkening at the toes. 'Well, this is the most glamourous milking shed I've ever seen!'

'It is pretty great. Sleeps eight. And I'm afraid we don't get the whole thing, as two of the other rooms will be occupied by Close Family Friends – but we do get the two nicest ones.'

Leo opened a door, revealing a room with two small double beds, a pressed giant wheatsheaf spanning the wall above both, a small tartan sofa, a country-chic en-suite bathroom and a floral window seat. Then, the one next door, almost identical. Leo walked into this one and drew the curtains at the four-paned round window.

'It's gorgeous,' she said, 'and there are even packets of biscuits on the pillows.'

'Home-made,' Leo confessed. 'Mum likes everyone to feel very welcome. Are you glad you came?'

'Yes,' she said, setting her bag down on one bed and sitting next to it. 'I am. Thank you for asking me. But was I always your first choice for this trip? I mean, you said you thought about it all the way to the library, but did you invite me because someone else couldn't make it? Am I here by accident?'

'*Olivia*,' he said, sitting down next to her. 'Nothing about this is accidental . . .'

He grinned at her. She grinned at him back.

'OK,' she said. 'I guess I can believe that.'

'Now, do you want to get changed?' he asked. 'I'll excuse myself to the house and bring us back a bottle of wine.'

'Yes, please.'

'Alright, I'll knock for you in about twenty minutes.'

He left the room. She looked through the round window up at the huge house, and Leo walking towards it.

A different world, she thought. He was like so many people she had met at university. From good families, *rich* families. And she, inserted among them, faking it until she made it. Playing the part. Walking the walk and talking the talk, in time. Yet, she had still gone home to the house in Pimlico. To live where she lived, and to walk those streets. She had been drawn back, like a dog pulled on a chain. To home. To history. She had written to Gillian to tell her she had not sold her father's house, but was living in it; she had received no reply. Only that postcard from Venice. Olivia also knew she was living in Charlie's house because she felt it was a way to make things up to him, to prove, 'Hey, Dad, I came home.' To be close to him. To talk to him in the still of a lonely night and tell him the things she didn't say when he was there.

She stood up. She was going to a dinner party and this was not the time for sad thoughts. She unpacked her new dress and hung it on the back of the door, smoothing a couple of light creases out with her hand. She could be in a different world for the night, she thought. She could be here with Leo Greene.

Chapter Twenty-Three

'Oops!'

Olivia's heels sank into the grass as she and Leo made their way to the house. She grabbed on to his arm, his sleeve silky to the touch in a navy paisley shirt.

'Are you alright?'

'Yes, my heels are like tees on a green, but, yes, I'm good.'

'Well, you look beautiful.'

'Thank you.' She did feel lovely, she had to admit. She had bought this dress – calf length, deep olive-green velvet, one shoulder, with one close-fitting sleeve – on a whim last week from Portobello Market.

Leo was wearing black jeans, slightly startling but incredibly sexy snakeskin boots. His hair smelled amazing as it had some kind of new product in it. She felt they were playing the role of an established couple, her hand on his arm, walking through the damp grass to a dinner party, not two people who had bumped into each other the night before in Piccadilly Circus, had got into a car together outside a library and had driven down the M4.

It was cold, but there was no wind. The flames from a line of tealights either side of the path to Foxes were steady. The trees at the edge of the property stood dense and motionless. And every star in the purple-black bruise of the sky stood out against its velvet backdrop.

The front door was wide open, revealing a hallway with red-and-gold chequered tiles, black-and-white prints on tropical-papered walls, and an aspidistra bowing its head from a black Chinoiserie console table. A mynah bird chirped in a blur of turquoise and gold from a gilt cage hanging from the high ceiling, and Stevie Nicks' 'Gypsy' rose to meet it. It was both lush and bohemian, Olivia thought – a magical stage set.

They walked through a door at the end to a living room, or it could have been a dining room, or a library, or study. Three walls were lined floor to ceiling with books and the fourth was painted a rich, dark green. Sumptuous, mismatched sofas competed with occasional tables and tall lamps, dripping with beaded fringes. Heavy velvet curtains in shocking pink, restrained by gold tassels, made theatre with two enormous chandeliers.

'Wow!' said Olivia.

'Yeah,' replied Leo, grabbing two glasses of champagne off a passing tray.

There were people everywhere. Whispering on the low, plump sofas; leaning on the edges of the bookcases, or against door frames; standing in clusters on the antique Chinese rug in the centre of the room. Glasses rested on palms, clutch bags were delved into for cigarettes, chunky whiskey tumblers were brought to lips. The men were in suits and smoking jackets. The women were in ball gowns or cashmere dresses, with skyscraper heels. A fabulous lady in a man's suit, thin as a rail and already smoking a cigar, had bent herself over the arm of a sofa like an Anglepoise lamp.

'Bubbly OK?' Leo asked her. Three young girls, dressed in black, were walking around the room, topping up drinks from long-necked bottles.

She nodded and took the glass gratefully. 'Where are your parents?'

'Still in the kitchen, I expect, either rowing over the lamb or snogging in the pantry – you never know with Isaac and Caroline. They'll emerge in a cloud of glory at some point, all rosy-cheeked.'

'Really?'

People were suddenly rising from sofas, and the clusters at the centre of the room morphed and started moving to a pair of double doors at the side of the room.

'I didn't hear the gong,' Leo said. 'But dinner must be served.'

This was the dining room. It was painted a vivid duck-egg blue, with gold cornicing. It had a rich teal carpet, soft underfoot. Two huge, leaded floor-to-ceiling windows, overlooking wide stone steps and a lit-up back garden. A long dining table, a stately candelabra at each end with wax stalactites and stalagmites. Huge gold plates and heavy-looking cutlery. Sideboards, either edge of the room, thick with framed family photos: Isaac, Caroline, Leo. Skiing. Wedding day. Disneyworld. There was another boy with them. Blond. Smiley.

'Who's that?' Olivia asked.

'Balth. My stepbrother. Don't worry, he's not coming tonight.'

'Why should I—'

'Good Lord, is that you, Leo?'

A man – loud floral shirt and red cord trousers, sitting side-saddle on one of the ornate dining chairs – beckoned them over. David Bowie was playing in here, 'Rebel Rebel'.

'Dominic,' said Leo politely, and he and the man shook hands.

'Dragged back from London, then, boy?' The man had ruddy cheeks, translucent teeth, button eyes.

'Thought it was time I showed my face.'

'How's it going up there?' He was one of those men who would completely ignore a plus one, Olivia realised.

'Good, good.'

'How's *Isaac*? I hear there's trouble at mill.'

'Not that I know of.'

'*I* know of investment troubles. Building regs. *Something*. Thank goodness for Caroline, eh? For putting up with it all.'

'Yes,' muttered Leo. 'Thank goodness for Caroline. Let's sit down,' he said to Olivia. 'I'll see you later, Dom.' He nodded at the man, pulled Olivia subtly away. 'It doesn't matter where . . . Mother doesn't do place cards . . .'

They sat halfway down the table, Leo to Olivia's right. To her left, the seat was quickly filled by a beautiful middle-aged woman – former model? – with a strapless black dress and a brass breastplate necklace. She smiled wanly at Olivia, then turned to the gentleman to her own left, a beaver of a man with a bristling hairline and a cravat.

'OK?' Leo asked her.

'Perfectly.' Olivia felt . . . starstruck, to be honest. Like she'd joined a whole new constellation.

Quickly, places were filled, clutch bags laid on the table, jackets on the back of chairs. Hands reaching for water glasses and wine bottles and into bowls of olives. Faces smiling, searching. An air of expectancy. Murmurs of 'Isaac' and shrugs of 'Caroline'. Where *were* they?

The music changed. It went from Bowie to Bach. There was a riptide of applause, a chiming of spoons on glass stems, a lusty holler of 'There you are, you old buggers!' and Caroline and Isaac walked into the room holding hands, like a bride and groom entering a wedding reception.

Caroline was in a column of a petrol-blue chiffon dress, her dark hair swept up into an elegant chignon, plus the fringe; Isaac had been cushioned into a white ruffle-yoke shirt and a black dinner suit, face scrubbed and eyebrows combed. He slipped his hand from Caroline's and held out his palms to the assembled.

'Welcome to Foxes!' he bellowed. 'Feast like it's your last night on this godforsaken earth!'

Caroline smiled accommodatingly and they took their seats at the head of the table. Immediately, three girls were bringing bowls in and setting them in front of guests – a fiery red pepper soup with a comma of crème fraiche and a sprinkle of toasted onions.

'Looks delicious,' Olivia remarked to Leo.

'So do you,' Leo replied.

She soaked up the atmosphere of the room, the zing of the wine and the piquancy of the soup. She was on a wild ride, an adventure. She felt like she had no idea what was going to happen.

'. . . aren't you, Leo?' Isaac was addressing him from the head of the table. Shouting down.

'Am I what?' Leo called up.

'Writing a book?' boomed Isaac.

'Maybe,' Leo responded sheepishly. 'Early days.'

Isaac roared with laughter as though Leo's words had constituted a joke. 'What's it about, lad?'

Leo looked mortified. 'Knock it off, Isaac,' he said confidently, but his fingers were tapping on the edge of the tablecloth. 'I'll tell you some other time.'

'Tell us now!' Isaac would not be satisfied.

Leo shook his head. He bent his head back over his soup. 'Idiot,' Leo muttered good-naturedly, but Olivia caught Caroline glancing down the table at her son – her eyes momentarily grave – before being re-engaged by a female guest with a chattering-joke-teeth smile, and the moment disappearing into the air with the last steam of the soup.

'I bet it's going to be a splendid book,' said an elderly lady across from them.

'Oh, it is,' fibbed Olivia effusively. 'I've read some of it. It's absolutely marvellous.'

Leo smiled at her gratefully. The soup dishes were taken away and the main course arrived: Moroccan lamb studded with sultanas, accompanied by pearly couscous and glistening vegetables. Isaac's voice was getting louder and louder. He was recounting endless stories about London restaurant kitchens, the useless underlings he had to order around, the wet-behind-the-ears, incompetent boys and girls who turned up not knowing a chicory from a chowder. Who he had nurtured, who he had fired.

His audience was eating up every word and Isaac was growing larger than life as a result, like a great slab of beef, rippled and bloody, soaking up all of life's good juices. He now had someone's arm pinned good-naturedly to the table with his beefy hand – a man who had just confessed he had been to Confit last week – and was growling throatily, 'Did you actually *eat* the *canard*?'

'Isaac believes that food is the one true art,' said Leo at her side. 'One that can be swallowed up and devoured in three seconds. He believes art should be bold, beautiful, and then gone. I want to create something a little longer lasting. With my writing. Does that sound like pretentious rubbish?'

'No, of course it doesn't. I feel the same way.'

'Why do you want to write?' he asked her. 'I know you said about your godmother's house and the books, but is it something more?'

'It's always something more, isn't it? Creative satisfaction, the joy of writing, getting things out of your head and on to the page. Money, success . . .'

'It's not the money for me.' He frowned.

'Of course it's not. Look around you . . .'

'I can make it on my own.'

'Of course you can.'

'I *will* make it on my own.'

She had touched a nerve. 'I know that, Leo.'

'Oh, look – cake!'

To a cry of delight around the table, a large zabaglione cake was being brought in on a huge silver platter, held aloft by two waitresses, with a third carrying a large jug of cream. Behind them, a young woman in a pale pink satin dress trailed in, a fur coat slipped over the shoulders. She had long straight-ironed hair, honey brown, ears peeking through. A pretty face, retroussé nose. And she walked right over to Leo.

'Surprise!' she said in a soft voice.

Leo's face broke into a smile. 'Cressie! I wasn't sure if you were going to be down!'

'The lure of lamb and good zabaglione . . .' Cressie had grey eyes the colour of huskies, and pale lips that had no edge.

'This is Cressie,' Leo said to Olivia. 'Cressida. She's the daughter of Dad's best friend, Robert. And we practically went to school together.'

'Well.' Cressie smiled, showing milky teeth. 'Different schools, same street. Leo was at the boys' school. I was at the girls'. Let's just say there were several explosive joint discos . . .'

Leo laughed. Cressie laughed. She was the kind of girl that the more casual she dressed, and the less make up she wore, the more beautiful she'd look. Like she should be on a hay bale in a checked shirt – and Olivia wondered if she ever had been with Leo. She suddenly felt wildly unsuitable, not quite pretty enough, no shared history with the son of this grand house except one night huddled together in a flat with some grief, two hundred balled-up tissues and an empty bottle of limoncello.

'And you are . . . ?' she asked of Olivia.

'This is my friend, Olivia,' said Leo. 'We drove down from London together.'

'Delighted to meet you.' Sweet, supercilious smile.

'How are Patricia and Robert?' Leo asked. 'Your dad's not here, is he?'

Cressie arranged her face into a pretty frown. 'Oh, he's in Dubai, looking at property. They've had one of their mild falling outs, I believe. He and Isaac. Something and nothing. I expect they'll be back on the golf course together next week.'

Cressie seemed shy in Leo's presence. Paper thin, like a coin of that plant, Honesty, in winter, stretched so delicately between its monocle frame a person could push their finger through.

'Where will you sit?' Leo asked her. 'We can make some room . . .' He grabbed either side of his seat and made to shuffle.

'No, I'm not sitting,' Cressie said, to Olivia's relief. 'Or eating. Despite the call of the lamb . . . I'm just here drinking with some friends in the salon.' Olivia wondered if the 'salon' was the first room they'd been in and how much of an open house this affair was tonight. 'I just thought I'd pop through and say hello.' She bent down and gave Leo a kiss on the cheek. 'See you soon.'

'She's lovely,' Olivia said, once she'd gone.

'Yeah. My dad's always trying to push the two of us together.' Leo chuckled. 'Cressie's old man is richer than God, and Isaac's always badgering him to invest. He thinks if I marry Cressie then it's a solid deal for life.'

'And do you think you *will* marry her?' Olivia pretended she was asking lightly.

'God, no. She's lovely, but she likes ponies.' He frowned. 'Oh, no,' he muttered. 'Balth's here.'

There had been a sudden shift in the room. A pulsing of new energy.

'*Balth!*' A cry from Caroline at the head of the table, rising from her seat. 'Our Balthazar! Welcome, welcome!'

Balth was blond, tow-headed, in faded jeans and a white cricket sweater. Olivia could already tell he had freckles and buckets of entitled charm. She watched as Caroline gave him an effusive hug.

'The prodigal.' Leo frowned. 'Don't run off with him!'

'Why on earth would I do that?' But Olivia had to admit he was quite arresting, in a completely different way to Leo. If Leo was a dark-haired prince of Sweden, Balthazar was a tousled, preppy golden boy of the meadows of New England. He was Ryan O'Neal in *Love Story*, Robert Redford in *Out of Africa* . . . Had he landed his biplane on the lawn?

'He's irritating.' Leo stood up, as a seat was found for Balthazar next to Caroline. 'Let's go to the kitchen and find something less *vintage* to drink.'

They took a circuitous route, Leo showing Olivia several more reception rooms and a peek inside a dimly lit and echoey orangery. By the time they got there, there were quite a few people in the kitchen. A rangy man with a hoodie under a blazer, a woman in a floor-length knitted column dress, a dramatic young couple in matching black tuxedos. And at the far end, Cressie was talking to Balth by the fridge, his hand casual on the freezer compartment above her head. She caught Olivia's glance, doe eyed, then looked away.

Leo was rummaging in a cupboard. 'Aha, here we have it. A fun drink.' He brought out a bottle of tequila. 'We just need some grapefruit juice . . . I'll go to the cellar. Wait here?'

Olivia nodded. When she looked up, Balth was next to her, his cricket jumper now over his shoulders. He had on a t-shirt that said *Scoundrel* in disco writing.

'Are you here with Leo?'

He did indeed have freckles, and eyes the colour of cornflowers.

'Yes, I am. I'm Olivia.'

'I'm Balth,' he said. He held out his hand for her to shake, and it was cool and dry. 'Did Leo find you in London?'

'Like a penny on the ground?' she queried. 'Well, yes, I suppose so. We've known each other for a while, then we bumped into each other yesterday at a book signing.' *Was it only yesterday?* she wondered. She felt like she'd been living a completely different life since then. 'We're only friends,' she said, but she didn't know what they were or what they might be. 'And you're his brother?'

'Stepbrother.' Balth looked her up and down. 'A book signing, eh? Are you a wannabe writer, too, like Leo? Dad told me all about it.'

'Trying to be,' she made the huge mistake of saying.

'It's not erotica, is it?'

'Er, no.'

He looked disappointed. 'Right. I knew a girl once who wrote erotica . . .' Balth's voice trailed off and he looked wistfully into the distance. 'And if it doesn't work out, will you get a real job?' he asked. 'I mean, it's a nice little hobby, but it doesn't pay the bills often, does it? Leo's lucky he's got the family dosh to fall back on if it all goes tits up and no one reads the thing. I mean,' he repeated, leaning down to her. He smelled like a sixth former: the inside of a pencil case, spearmint chewing gum and hair gel. 'I keep saying to him, you need to get a movie deal, that's what you need to do. That's where the big money is.'

'Yes, it's really easy to do that.' Olivia smiled at him beatifically.

Balth looked to the ceiling, flickering his eyelids.

'I've had an idea for a book for quite a while,' he said, 'about a cricketer who discovers a whole other world under Lord's, an allegorical one, set in the past, but I'm far too lazy to do it myself, so I need someone to write it for me. I've already asked Leo – you know, fifty-fifty profits and all that, if he can pull it off – but he said no, as he wants to do a different genre, but if you're not yet set on exactly what you're doing, maybe you could write it?'

'Thank you for asking,' she replied, 'but I'm sure if it's a really good idea then you could make the time to write it yourself. What do you do?' she asked him. 'Are you in the restaurant trade, too?'

Balth threw back his golden lion's head and laughed. 'God, no! You wouldn't get me inside one of those sweat holes! I do a bit of this and that, trading, commodities. I'm a qualified pilot so I fly whenever I can, as well.'

'Is your plane on the lawn?'

'What?' His gaze was wandering. He was already tiring of her, she could tell. 'What do you think of my dad and Caroline?' he asked her.

'Great,' said Olivia.

He narrowed his eyes. 'An acquired taste, I think. Although at least Caroline's an improvement on my own mother . . . You're quite pretty,' he observed. 'If you get bored of my stepbrother, give me a call. Although, I'd be careful with Leo, if I were you. I mean, always keep one hand on the door handle, because *he* certainly does.'

'Which *door*?' Olivia asked sweetly.

Balth had clearly had enough. 'Well, very nice to meet you, Olivia,' he said, bringing their lovely little chat to a close. '*Cressie!*' He yelled back over to her. Cressie waved merrily at him. 'Now, *she's* gorgeous,' Balth whispered to Olivia before he walked away. 'Total marriage material.'

She watched him go. The privileged boy swagger. The entitled hair flick. He passed Leo coming back with the grapefruit juice, but they barely acknowledged each other.

'So, you've met Balth?' Leo asked. 'Did you survive?'

'Only just. Quite the character, isn't he? You're not close?'

'No. He's hardly ever here, thank goodness. Too busy in the south of France with his mum or lording it up in the City.'

'He flies planes.'

'Yes. Right. Let's grab a couple of glasses.' Leo handed her a cocktail glass from a tray on the kitchen table and gave her a bright smile, 'and then we'll head back in for some of that cake.'

◆ ◆ ◆

They returned to the dining room for zabaglione and coffee served in thick smoked-glass coffee cups and saucers ('How delightfully retro!' a siren in silver satin observed), plus poppy seed crackers with slivers of blue cheese and fat black grapes. A slice of cake was passed down to Olivia on a bone china plate, its light cream filling a whisper on her tongue.

Isaac Feu was well oiled now, a collapsing joint of meat held together with string and red wine. He'd got to the 'And let me tell you this!' stage of the evening and was telling the assembled a lot of different things. How shifty his current sous chef was. What he thought of the current London Mayor. How he viewed the draconian health and safety measures in the capital's eateries.

Caroline sat beside him, a blank smile on her face. The table had been recently surrounded by extras, those from the salon, the kitchen. The music had been turned up and some of them had started to dance, silky hair shaken, velvet arms snaking. People began to stand up from the table, change places. Isaac got up unsteadily from his seat and, arm in arm with a tall man in a burgundy shirt – like a lanky schoolgirl and her short friend walking home from a school disco – left the room.

Olivia went to the bathroom, which was off another door from the vast hall. On her way back, she realised one of the buckles on her shoes was loose and stopped by the doorway to the salon to fasten it. She could hear voices – Isaac's and another man's, the man in the burgundy shirt. They were perched on low, elephant-leg stools either side of an occasional table made dollhouse small by the girth of Isaac, the big flank of his thigh, his Fabergé egg belly. One of his thick arms was fastened right over it, his fingers clamping its far edge like he was about to croupier the whole thing towards him.

'So, you said at the table your son's writing a book,' said the man in the burgundy shirt.

Olivia shifted herself nearer the doorframe.

'Who?' Isaac barked. Eyes bloodshot. Mouth slack.

'Leo,' slurred the man, his head drooping. 'Your son.'

'Leo's not my son,' Isaac replied, playing the table like a piano with his other hand. 'I *have* a son.'

Olivia placed the side of her wrist on the doorframe and leaned in.

'But you treat him like a son, don't you?' the man said. One of his arms dangled to the floor, his fingers grazing the carpet.

Isaac made a strange noise, a half-scoff, half-grunt. He rolled his bloodshot eyes. 'I treat him the bare minimum, for Caroline's sake,' he huffed, 'that is all. Balth's my son, I don't need another.'

'Alright,' the other man said vaguely. 'A bit harsh, Isaac.'

Isaac grunted again. 'What's harsh about it? There's no blood connection and blood's what matters, isn't it? I *tolerate* Leo. That's what I'm asked to do.'

There was silence but for a ticking clock and the swell of distant music and laughter from the dining room. Finally, Burgundy Shirt said, 'Alright. Got any more whiskey? I'm as dry as a dog in a dusty outhouse . . .'

Olivia moved on, buckle done up, heart unfastened and pulsing free of her chest. For one moment only she considered telling Leo, one moment in which she imagined recounting every cruel word Isaac had spoken, but in the next she knew she couldn't, and she also knew, from this moment, she would remain utterly heart-broken for him.

'There you are.'

He was waiting for her at the entrance to the dining room.

'Would you like to escape for a bit?' he asked her.

'Where to?' she replied, trying to still her heart, trying to forget what she had heard.

'The attic,' he said, and he took her hand. 'I was wondering if you'd like to come and see my Scalextric.'

Chapter Twenty-Four

The attic was accessed by a long pole which hooked open the hatch, and a concertinaed ladder which pulled down on to the landing at the top of the house.

'Alright?' Leo asked Olivia. 'Are you happy to go up first?' She nodded. 'I'm right behind you,' he said, as she climbed. 'Flick on the light switch when you get to the top.'

The attic had a vaulted roof, pale oak beams and was completely boarded out. Around the edge were mini cities of neatly stacked boxes; in the centre was a huge figure-of-eight Scalextric track, including bridges, what Olivia assumed to be a pit stop, and two controllers on the boards at a casual angle as though they had just been set down.

'Is it safe to tread everywhere?' she asked.

'Absolutely.'

She walked gingerly all the same. Leo sat down next to the track and crossed his legs, picking up one of the controllers. She came and sat down next to him.

'It's a bit dusty,' he said, as she tucked the skirt of her dress around her.

'It doesn't matter.'

'Do you want to be red or blue?' he asked.

'Red, please.'

He showed her how to operate her controller and soon her red car was whizzing around the track, flying off at the corners and being patiently put back on again.

'You need to slow down! Brake at the bends.'

'I'm trying!' she protested. The red car flew off the track again and Leo caught it expertly in one hand.

'I wish you'd been my girlfriend when I was a teenager,' he said. 'I would have had you up here all the time.' He winked at her.

'Is that so?' His *girlfriend*. Could she imagine that?

'Oh, God, yeah. You'd be an absolute expert at this.' He grinned at her. 'What do you think, then?' he added, more seriously. 'About Foxes?'

'Interesting,' Olivia said carefully. 'It must make my little place in Pimlico seem like an absolute hovel.'

'I liked your little place in Pimlico.'

'Really?'

'I liked the bath. And the bed, too.'

She pretended she hadn't heard him. 'Do you have many friends down here still?' she asked. She was fishing, dropping a baited line into water.

'Not really, not now. Everyone left.' He grinned. 'Apart from Cressie.'

He had taken the bait, but it was Olivia who felt the tight pull of jealousy. 'She never left Wiltshire?'

'No. Her degree was in theatre production and she's working at the Theatre Royal, Bath. Commutes there. Total daddy's girl, too.' His grin didn't falter. 'So, I guess she wants to stay close. Some people have no urge to flee where they were brought up,' he added. 'But I prefer London. I prefer *you*.'

The line twitched. 'She's really pretty. Have you ever dated her?'

Leo laughed. 'Cressie? No! I don't see her that way.'

'I think *she* does . . .'

'What do you mean?'

'I think she holds a candle for you. I think she's *that* girl, the one waiting in the wings.'

'Where do you get that from?' Leo's eyes had mirth written into them.

'The way she looks at you.'

'That's it?'

'Yes. She's really never made a move on you?'

'No, never.'

'Well, maybe she's been waiting for *you* to.'

'I don't think so. And I think you've got a very good imagination.' He set the red car back into the grooves of the track. 'I don't want to talk about Cressie. I want to talk about *us*,' he said, leaning closer to her. 'How we left things, how we could begin things again. Maybe.' The corner of his mouth rose into the comma of a smile, self-effacing, and the way he was leaning made his forearms look really good in his silky shirt, and Olivia thought Kitty Codwell was probably on to something, after all. He took her hand, across the corner of the track. She couldn't help but drink in the kaleidoscope of his hazel eyes. 'Shall we give it a proper go?' he asked. 'You and me?' His voice dropped to a whisper. 'I couldn't let myself feel the way I felt about you. Not back then. When things weren't quite right. When it was right for me to walk away. But I want to feel that way. I want to feel everything with you.'

'I think I agree with you . . .' she whispered back. She so wanted to dive right into the clear, clean blue waters of hope and be immersed. To see sunlight dappling on the surface of the ocean above them, but she wasn't ready to drown. He was too handsome, he had too many girls after him. His stepbrother said he always had one hand on the door, when he had once had his hand on *her* door, and she had believed his reasons and she knew her own, but still. She didn't quite trust him somehow, or she didn't trust how she might feel about him, and she didn't trust his world. She felt overwhelmed by it, to be honest. It was a world she had been on the edge of for so long, even with Stella and Annabel, but she had been accepted there, by their families, their parents. She had made herself at home. She couldn't ever see herself being accepted by Caroline and Isaac. Or Balth. Or Cressie. It all made her cautious. Sensible. Careful. 'Or in another world, that I would like to, but I really don't know. I think . . . I think I just want to be friends for a while.'

'You do?' He looked crestfallen. 'Why?'

She couldn't voice any of her reasons, but she simply knew she wanted a whole lot out of life and she didn't think he was the one to seize those things with. She didn't think he was her Perfect Love, as much as she had enjoyed the evening and Foxes, so she simply said, 'I think it would be better. Suit us more.'

'It would suit me to kiss you right here,' he said, and her stomach gave a flip but her mind was steady.

She couldn't deny how attracted she was to him, but she could be friends with a rich country boy with complicated parents, a cold stepbrother, and a girl who was just right for him and was in love with him, couldn't she? She could deny this overwhelming attraction, this urge to say 'sod it' and have him kiss her?

Couldn't she?

'No,' she said, shaking her head. 'No, I don't think so.'

'Oh.' He pulled a comical face. 'But I can take friends, I suppose.' He looked at her. Her heart started to quicken its pace. *Kiss me anyway, fool,* it said, but she couldn't let that happen. He narrowed his eyes. 'Well, then,' he said, 'how would you feel about being writing buddies?'

'Yes . . . ?' she replied. 'That's a nice idea. How would that work?'

'We send each other what we've written so far, then after that, a chapter at a time. We critique. We're not in competition, as we write different genres. We give feedback. We write the next chapter. And we spur each other on.'

She thought about it. 'So, we make each other accountable,' she said. 'Yes, I like that.' She needed to be spurred on. Her godmother had inspired her, her father had encouraged her in his own way, but they were both gone from her life. She needed some accountability. 'When do you want to start?'

'Well,' he said. 'If we have to be writing buddies and deny this undeniable electricity between us . . .' He revved up his Scalextric car on the track to prove his point '. . . then we might as well get on with it straight away. How about Monday?'

Chapter Twenty-Five

Leo dropped Olivia home the following lunchtime. As she walked back into the flat and deposited her bag on to the chenille sofa she had not yet been able to replace, Charlie's place looked small and a little sad after the grandeur of Foxes. But Olivia shouldn't compare, should she? It was pointless. Leo's life was held like a jewel inside a spinning, glittering satellite of fine things, old money and heritage; Olivia's was small and simple. She had no ancestry, all of that was gone. She had no fine things. She had no backup plan. But she still had the wedding photo of Charlie and Ann on the mantel. Their smiles as they came out of the church. The love that was perfect, just for them. And she knew she was right to turn down Leo Greene.

She unpacked her bag. She made herself some beans on toast. It was Sunday. She had no plans. Annabel had her parents over this weekend; Stella had gone away with Shoreditch Man to Bruges on an impromptu third 'date'. So Olivia had the rest of the day to prepare the first three chapters of her book, working title, *The Florist*, to be fit for Leo's eyes tomorrow.

After she'd cleared her lunch things away, she opened her laptop on the kitchen table and set to work, reading and editing what she'd written so far, swapping paragraphs around, inserting sentences, taking sentences out, fine-tuning her prose, honing her dialogue: re-writing and re-writing and re-writing. The book was about a florist who falls in love with a businessman who calls at her shop in Mayfair every morning to buy a single red rose, and Olivia had the whole plot all worked out. She'd made charts, word-flows, Venn diagrams – she'd used every colour in the highlighter rainbow. She knew exactly where she was going; she now just had to find the best way to get there.

She wrote chapter four, as she was in the zone. The words rattled out of her like a runaway train down a mountain track. When she finished, she read it back from the beginning, editing as she went along once again. Expanding the imagery, concentrating on making the dialogue sound natural. Then she left chapter four for the rest of the day, but got back to it at ten in the evening, bringing it up to the standard of the first three chapters. Finally, she returned to the first three chapters, and looked at them again. She didn't know if the quality was high enough, but she was willing to let Leo be the judge of that.

At eleven o'clock on Sunday evening, just as Olivia was about to shut the laptop, an email pinged into her inbox from leo.greene@gmail.com.

> *Chapters One & Two, 'Ben Chef Book' 1 (working title . . . sorry, I couldn't wait!!)*

She sat at the kitchen table and raced through Leo's chapters, devouring every word and wondering how he was digesting *hers*, for at two minutes past eleven, she had hastily emailed him the first four chapters of *The Florist*, email subject line *Neither could I . . .* before she changed her mind.

She grabbed a notebook and pen and started making notes. Then she made comments in the margin of Leo's Word document. She hesitated over the first comment she wanted to make. She wrote: *Your main character is a chef. This is very interesting! Isaac???*, then she deleted it. She was supposed to be critiquing Leo's chapters themselves, not the motive behind them. And she also remembered what she had overheard – Isaac's cruel words from the salon as she had listened from the hall – and she thought it better to stay silent.

When she had finished writing comments in the margin, going through the two chapters, she wrote a one-page Word document summing up her thoughts. She had seen something similar in a book she'd read a while back, detailing examples of editors' notes, and she hoped hers covered all the bases. She read it through again, checked there were no typos, but before she sent everything off to him, she re-wrote the first comment in the margin.

> *You made him a chef!*

And early the next morning, when Leo's feedback on *her* feedback came in, he had replied to her comment.

> *Yes, I did. As you know, I have quite a lot of insider knowledge. Does it work?*

He had answered all of her comments in the margin. Some with *Agree*, others with *Good point!* or *Hmm, I will think about this . . .* And there was a separate document where he thanked her for her *thoughtful and considered notes*, a phrase she had also read in that book.

You're very welcome! she emailed to him.

Thirty minutes later, his critique of her own work arrived. Leo had gone for a different approach: *all* his thoughts were comments in the margin, and there were a lot of them, and a lot of them were *long*.

She scanned the whole document quickly, wincing. Took a deep breath, read it again. Her immediate impulse was to fire back an email detailing a firm but polite defence against each and every one of his points, but he hadn't done that with her critique – he had been politeness itself – so she couldn't let him win. And she had to go to work.

Thank you, she wrote at lunchtime. It had been a quiet morning, and working on her and Leo's books was far more interesting than filing her boss's press releases. *These are very thoughtful and considered notes.* And by the time she wrote that, she knew that about ninety per cent of them were spot on.

She emailed Leo again that evening. *Are we going to re-write and re-submit to each other the chapters we've critiqued?*

No, he replied. *Let's crack on.*

A few days later, Leo's next chapter came in. A few days after *that*, she sent him her next one. It got easier, the note-making for Leo and receiving the notes from him. She decided to copy his method: everything in the margins, even if those margins did get rather crowded. She grew bolder. It was for his own good. She wrote, *Did you really mean to say that?* and *I see the 1950s are alive and well!* She suggested switching two paragraphs and writing a more cliffhanger of an ending.

This is great! Leo responded within the hour.

The writing continued to bounce between them. Olivia started printing off Leo's chapters at work, stapling them neatly together. She read them on the Tube home and on the way back in. He told her he did the same with hers, printing them off at *Money Talks,* folding them over at the corner and reading them on the bus, while waiting for the Tube, and in the bath. At Christmas, they took a short break. Leo went to Wiltshire; Olivia went to Annabel's. In January, they resumed.

The comments in the margins began to really stack up.

I agree, the chef is a little too overwrought at the end of that scene. I will amend. The part about the cat is not supposed to be funny!!!!!!!! Again, I will amend.

I'm really glad you love the bit about the skateboarding park and I will take on board what you said about what Jackson is wearing. Of course he would not be wearing a Simpsons sweatshirt when he is trying to impress Ali! I am going to deck him out in something completely different, in the pursuit of romance. Thank you.

Hmmm. I'm still mulling over the details of that character. You say info dump, I say vital character background! I'm going to step away for a few hours, take a walk and come back to it. But this is great food for thought, Livs.

Thank you for reading chapter eight. I love your suggestion about making Edward even more dashing, but I am wary of stretching incredulity too far, as surely no man can be that perfect – I mean, come on . . .

You really do write romance well, Olivia. I am blushing!!!!!!!

I love, love, love what Ben said about forgiving Claude, and at just the right time, too. I'm in awe, Leo.

I think you mean 'vicious' and not 'viscous' here?

Oxford comma??

In the springtime, Olivia suggested – gently – that Leo focused on his characterisation. She suggested he make lists of character traits, both physiological and psychological. He told her that was a great idea, and he did so, and began sending them to her. Then, he started sending her random lists of other things:

Considerations for the next chapter. I am thinking about:

A chess set

A severed finger

A double twist – jaw-dropping

Angela???

I am also thinking about:

My dinner tonight

Silent Witness

The morning we spent together in your single bed . . .

Olivia stared at her screen. Their time in the single bed in Pimlico? Why was Leo bringing that up again? But yes, she still thought about that, too, although she would never say so.

She fired a reply off immediately.

You need to stay focused on your work, or you will never finish that damn book. I agree, a severed finger and a bit more Angela would be marvellous in your next chapter . . .

By the summer, other bits of real life started creeping into their emails.

P.S. I had a terrible meal tonight – I bought a Tesco meal deal and I left the carbonara in the microwave for too long and it was horrible. Please tell me you've had a better day.

Yes, I'm in France! Just with a friend. A quick Friday to Sunday.

Nice, have a great time!

No, we are in Paris. 😉

P.S. What are your opinions about blue cheese, Olivia? If you were going to a birthday party of a man who had everything, would you take some? Like, a cheese wheel*?*

A cheese wheel *sounds extravagant, I hear those things are enormous. How about some Ferrero Rocher, or am I showing my class??*

Ugh. Awful Father's Day lunch today. I booked a table at Scott's for me, Mum and Isaac. Balth turned up with Cressie and Robert in tow. It was nice to see them but Balth behaved terribly and Isaac didn't even open my present. Someone was sitting on it and I had to hand it to him when we said goodbye, all flattened! My family have no idea what's going on with my book – such express disinterest. I bet your father would have given you more support, Liv. My lot are absolutely hopeless. Isaac may have had his face on a couple of cookery books, but he knows nothing about the publishing world. He's still referring to my writing as 'that little hobby' etc . . . xxx

Sorry your present got flattened. I do miss my dad a lot. I used to make a big fuss of him on Father's Day – Ferrero Rocher galore! I'm afraid to say I've spent the past two hours crying over his planing tool – the only tool of his that I kept – and his old West Ham scarf. Sorry you've had an awful day. x

I'm so sorry, Livs. And I'm also sorry for bringing Father's Day up. Want me to come over? Or to meet up somewhere?

She didn't. She thought it was safer that way. The emails and the critiquing had become so spirited, so enjoyable, she was afraid to see Leo in real life. She was frightened that seeing him would be a huge distraction. She had the job at the theatre. Her writing. She had also started an evening job, as she was struggling with the mortgage and the bills. A part-time cleaning job in the City, three nights a week, from 7 p.m. to 10 p.m., when she cleaned the offices of M. Gallagher and Sons, on the twenty-third floor of the Gherkin, for £9.50 an hour. She was busy; she was tired. And seeing Leo's handsome face would be an added complication in her life she simply couldn't fall prey to. An attraction that wouldn't serve her well.

No, thank you, I'm going out in a minute.

But she gave in. Leo wore her down. Two weeks later, they went for a drink – a little bar Leo chose in Mayfair, then afterwards they sat on a bench in a sunny spot in Hyde Park and read each other's printed-off chapters.

'This is nice,' Leo said.

'Shhh,' she replied, 'I've just got to a good bit.'

'Which bit's that?'

His thigh was a little close to hers. She wanted to shift hers away but she thought he might notice.

'The bit with the full moon and the back of the chip shop.'

'Ah. Yeah. I like that bit, too.' He turned another page. They continued reading. 'Could you ever imagine us lying in bed together, when we're old and grey, reading side by side like this?' he asked her after a while, his eyes not leaving the page.

She stopped reading. Her eyes didn't leave the page, either. 'No,' she retorted. 'Could you?'

'Maybe.'

She was surprised. 'Then you've got a very good imagination. Hey, maybe you should think about becoming a writer?' Her face broke into a sarcastic smile, but her heart briefly considered the vision. A double bed. Her and Leo. A bedside light, about to be switched off.

He had turned to her. He caught the smile. They carried on reading. Leo started reading her work aloud, which she begged him to stop doing at first, but then she started to tolerate it. Hearing him say her words out loud made her see them in a different way. It made her focus on the sentences she needed to re-write, the parts she needed to fix. It also made her feel that maybe one day she could do it; that she really could be an author.

'Thank you,' she said, when he'd finished.

'Thank *you*,' he replied. 'Oh, look. You've made a friend.'

A little bird had alighted on one arm of the bench – Olivia's end. It cocked its head at her, amused.

'*Hello*,' she said.

Leo had a half-eaten packet of chocolate biscuits in his bag. 'Stale,' he said, prising the top one out of the wrapper. 'Give her a bit.'

Olivia broke off a piece and placed it at the very end of the arm. The bird bobbed its head forward and pecked it into its mouth. Then it promptly flew off.

'Too full from lunch.' Leo laughed. 'What's your favourite chocolate bar?' he asked suddenly, a twinkle in his eye.

'Snickers,' she replied. 'What's yours?'

'Bounty,' he answered.

She turned to look at him. 'Oh, I thought you'd be more of a Mars Bar man,' she said. 'Something more everyman.'

'No,' he said. 'I'm not every man. And you're not every woman.'

'What am I, then?' She narrowed her eyes at him.

'You're Olivia. *Olivia, Olivia, Olivia*,' he said softly, and his words hung in the air like soft feathers. He was looking at her, really looking. They were sitting too close to one another. It was too warm, too springtime-sunny. They had read too many of each other's words.

'We're not people,' she said finally. 'We're *writers*. Now get back on with my work.'

Seven months to the day into their writer buddy cross-critiquing, when all the chapters had been read, and they had decided, after all, to carry on and re-read each other's edited chapters, Olivia got an email, no subject, and one single line in the email body.

I'm sending it off! x

Whaaat? she replied immediately. It was a warm June afternoon, a Saturday. She was at the kitchen table, at the laptop, the back door open to the yard and the sun sailing in. *You're ready? I thought you still weren't happy with chapter fifteen?*

Nah, but I'm going to send it off. A little impetuous, I know, but I can't tinker with it any more. I'm doing it in tranches. I'm going to send it to five agents, all who I've got from The Writers' and Artists' Yearbook. When I get the five rejections, I'm going to send it to five more, until I get a bite.

What about Royal Ben?

I thought about it, but no, I refuse to use nepotism! I'll make it on my own, kiddo.

Well, that's fantastic! Good luck, Leo.

Her book wasn't ready yet. She still had some work to do on the last three chapters and the epilogue. She kept working. Leo kept reading for her. In early July, he sent:

I got a bite!! Rowan Langford at The Langford Agency wants to have a call with me on Friday. Eek!!!!!!

That's amazing!

She waited for news.

Then a forwarded email, subject line, *Offer of Representation.*

Leo had got an agent. He went out on submission four weeks later, which meant, he told her, that his agent was going to send his book out to editors at publishing houses.

I know what that means!!!!!

You next! Get a move on. x

Soon, her book was ready. Olivia sent it off to a carefully selected cache of five agents and she waited, and she waited, and Leo waited with her, while *he* was still waiting to hear back from the list of editors.

Olivia got two immediate standard rejections, two complete and definitive silences and one eventually personal response. She forwarded it straight to Leo. It was from the agent, Janice Sullivan, at Becker and Stutt.

> *You are on the right lines. There was much here that I enjoyed. I did, however, feel that you are lacking some close first-person introspection, and some of the scenes could be a little bigger in execution and emotion. I'd be happy to see a re-write and a subsequent draft, though, if you are happy to work on one?*

Leo replied. *Congratulations! x*

Not really.

No, it's great. Do what she's asking and re-submit!!

But Leo was two steps ahead and at the end of September, his agent phoned him with the good news.

Jones Hill wanted to publish him.

Want to go out for a drink to celebrate? x

I can't. I'm working.

Working where?

Just doing something extra for the theatre. But I'm really happy for you, Leo. That's such brilliant news. And stop putting kisses on your emails. We are just friends!!!!!!

So, Leo signed his contract. He went for dinner with his agent and his brand-new, first-ever editor, Marjorie Petit of Jones Hill books. He ate Dover sole followed by raspberry roulade, and drank a kir royale. His book was coming out in summer 2009 and he had already begun working on book two of his two-book deal.

Olivia carried on working at the theatre and at the cleaning job. She continued sending her book out to agents, but she also began work on re-submitting her draft for Janice Sullivan.

Good luck with the next tranche of agents, Liv. The Florist *is really good and you've worked so hard on it. You've got this! You're right behind me and I know it will only be a matter of time. Drink? x*

Chapter Twenty-Six

London

Friday 12 February 2010

'There, there. To the left, no, a little more the right . . . a little more. That's it!'

The brown double doors to the library were wide open and two men were navigating a large whiteboard through them, directed by Tanya Brik, Leo's publicist, at the top of the steps.

'Morning, Olivia! Lovely day for it!' Tanya was partly visible behind a huge cardboard box. Olivia could spy an enormous fuchsia scarf and a camel coat.

Olivia, running a little late, was at the bottom of the steps. 'Morning, Tanya!'

It was cold; gently sleeting, with next to no wind. A chilled hush muffled the sounds of the city and rendered the Georgian buildings in St James's Square elegantly out of focus. Tanya was right; it was the perfect morning for readers to be cosily ensconced inside the London Library, watching Leo Greene present a workshop on 'Crime Writing and How to Absolutely Kill It'.

Olivia followed Tanya, the men and the whiteboard into the building and bypassed them at the lift to run up the flight of stairs to the first floor. In the Reading Room, Leo Greene, the bestselling author, was halfway up the metal ladder to the bookstacks that lined the upper walls – famous for their narrow, iron-grille walkways – and stringing up a huge banner with his name on it.

'There you are!' he called down. Leo was in his Author Clothes: charcoal chinos, striped chambray shirt, heather lambswool jumper and a jaunty paisley cravat that people who liked authors seemed to go wild for. 'I wasn't sure if you were going to make it.'

'Sorry.' Underneath her coat, Olivia was wearing her soft jersey dress with the peony print. Heeled Mary Janes. Smart, scholarly, supportive – that was how she wanted to appear.

Leo looked at her for a second too long, then said, 'Do you want a crime scene cupcake? We ordered way too many. They're over by the window.'

'Thanks!'

She walked past the elegant pillars and the reading tables with their Anglepoise lamps, to a desk set up by the large window at the back of the room, overlooking St James's Square. She recognised the errant scatter of Leo's workshop notes and materials. His random set of pens, his mobile phone. His coffee cup, and at least three lists on lined paper.

On a round table in the corner was a tray of cupcakes – Leo's book cover printed on edible paper toppers on each – and a Perspex box on the floor next to it stacked with three or four layers of spares. She extracted a cake from the tray.

'By the way, where do you keep the paper clips?' He was calling again from the ladder. She bit into the cupcake. 'We couldn't find them anywhere.'

'Hold on!' she called back. 'I'll pop down to the office.'

Olivia no longer worked at the theatre, which had closed down. She was assistant librarian, Monday to Thursday, 8.30 a.m. until 6 p.m., at the London Library, and she loved it. She adored working among the books, walking the 'stacks', assisting members and absorbing the muted atmosphere as people quietly studied at their desks under those nodding lamps. Virginia Woolf had been a member there, as had TS Eliot, EM Forster and Charles Dickens. Olivia felt she was following in the footsteps of great writers as she walked up the main staircase, where their portraits were displayed, or trailed her hand over first editions in the stacks – even if she was making none of her own.

She passed Tanya and the whiteboard being carried into the Reading Room, and made her way back down to the ground floor and the office, where she found the paper clips in the second drawer of the desk. On top, a big poster of Leo's event was unfurled, his smile bright and beaming at her. Officially, this was a day she had booked off, but unofficially, this morning she was helping out her friend.

'Should be quite the turnout.'

Chief librarian, Alistair Martin-Fox, was in the doorway. Grey hair, grey jumper, grey slouchy slacks, twinkle in his eye.

'Hello, Alastair. Yes, it will be.'

In half an hour, quite a crowd – mostly women, Olivia expected – would be pitching up for handsome Leo Greene and his workshop. She had seen the amounts of tickets sold; she knew how in demand he was. His debut novel, *Midnight Shadows,* had been a huge success almost overnight, making the top five of the *Sunday Times* Bestseller List only three weeks after publication, and staying there ever since. It had been reviewed in all the major newspapers; he had been a witty and adorable guest on Sara Jewson's *The Book Programme*; social media had eaten the book up; his sales were simply through the roof. Leo had reached the holy grail of publishing, and he was holding it in his hand and sipping its rich wine at steady intervals.

'I hope Mr Greene's taking you out for lunch after. The wind beneath his wings,' Alistair joked.

'I'm only his friend,' Olivia replied, with a frown. 'I'm just helping him out today. I'm not the wind beneath anyone's wings.'

She hadn't told anyone at the library that she was a writer, too, because she wasn't really, was she? She preferred Alastair and the rest of the kind, genial staff at the London Library not know that she had tried and failed; that, while she was friends with a best-seller whose glittering books shone under neon lights to widespread acclaim, her own novel flickered like a stubby candle, unnoticed, out on the wasteland.

'Do you think he'll sign my book for me?' There had been a hardback copy of *Midnight Shadows* on Alastair's desk for some time.

'Definitely. And there's loads of spare cupcakes if you fancy one. Over at the back of the Reading Room, just help yourself.'

'On a diet.' Alistair ruefully patted his stomach. 'Thanks, though. And thanks for coming in to help.' He smiled so sweetly she felt guilt at her terseness.

She took the small box of paper clips and was crossing the main entrance to the staircase when she spied Leo's friend, Billy Hastings, bounding up the steps two at a time.

Billy was new. A new writer friend of Leo's who Leo had met at a *Books! Books! Books!* event at Elephant and Castle two months ago. Introduced to each other as *wunderkinds*, apparently, both riding high in the charts, both raking in the accolades – Billy wrote fighter pilot WWII action adventures, selling 100,000 copies of his book, *Spitfire Skies,* after only five weeks – Leo and Billy had hit it off immediately. They went to bookish events together. They had meetings in pubs, Leo told her, where they discussed each other's work – different genres, no competition. Billy understood the heady heights, the thrill of immediate literary success. Billy *got it*, Leo told Olivia.

'Hi, Billy.' Olivia had met Billy at a couple of Leo's events.

'Hi, Olivia.'

Billy had dark spiky hair and a boyish nature. Up in the Reading Room, Leo was straight off the ladder and delighted to see his friend. They slapped each other on the back and beamed into each other's faces like they hadn't seen each other for weeks.

'Thanks for coming to support me, mate!'

'How could I not? It should be a great gig. The book's doing amazing. Want to go for a pint after?'

Olivia handed Leo the paper clips.

'Sure!' Leo's eyes flickered to Olivia. 'Would love to.'

'Great. We've got to toast your success.'

They slapped each other on the back again, then Billy started to pace around, hands in pockets, touring the library.

'Thanks again for today,' Leo said to Olivia. 'For coming in on your day off.'

'My pleasure.' She adjusted her dress. 'Like Billy said, it should be a great gig. And I'm always happy to help, you know that.'

'I do.'

Leo smiled at her. She'd been there for him his whole publishing journey; a bright shiny journey, in a fast car. She'd helped him edit his debut, not doing the work, but reading his amended drafts, continuing to give him notes. The big structural edit, the line edit, the copy edit. She'd even offered to do an extra proofread for him, when it had reached that stage, but he had said no, that was too much work, and she knew it was. She'd been to his big book launch at Parchment & Plots, recruiting Stella and Annabel as cupcake bearers; she'd held the new satchel he'd bought to carry his notebooks in and 'look the part' while he made a speech in front of a sizeable crowd, and read the opening chapter of his book. And she'd gone with him when he appeared on *The Book Programme*, along with Rowan, had waited in the green room for him, made him a cup of coffee in the break from filming.

'Are Isaac and Caroline coming?' she asked him.

'Those two? Of course not! They couldn't care less.'

'I thought Isaac might have read it by now. You know, the chef thing?'

'No. Listen, I would have preferred to take you out for lunch,' he said. 'Rather than go for a pint with Billy. But I know you probably wouldn't want to.'

'No,' she said. 'No, you should go and have your pint. Toast your success.'

He faced her steadily, his hazel eyes unblinking. 'You've been to my book things,' he said. 'Although not so much, recently. But I can never get you to go out for a drink or a meal with me. Why is that?'

She didn't answer straight away. While Olivia was passenger in Leo's fast, shiny car of success, she occupied it as Professional Friend. She had a role. If he accidentally touched her hand, or their fingers brushed by mistake, she could shrug off the spark of electricity *professionally*. If he looked at her for a moment too long, softness in his eyes, she could efficiently ask if he needed her to fetch him something. They were *working*; there was no place for any temptation. There was every need for her to deny his continued effect on her. But recently she hadn't wanted that role so much. She'd declined a few of his offers – was only here today with great reluctance, and because she worked at the library. Her disappointment in her own lacklustre publishing journey had made her want to get out of the car.

'I choose my battles,' she said at last, and she didn't know why she did, but before either of them could say anything else, there was a short cough from behind him. It was Tanya, in teal Vivienne Westwood, holding a clipboard.

'Positions, please,' she said. 'We're about to open the doors.'

'How do I look?' Leo asked his publicist, running a hand through his hair.

'Fantastic, of course!'

Olivia motioned to Billy, and they stepped to the side of the room. Leo took his place at the whiteboard. Tanya tested the microphone. And the ticket holders started trooping in.

They were women, and some men – some young, and plenty not so young – all smiling, all excited, unbuttoning their coats, freeing scarves and hats and gloves from their person. They beamed when they saw Leo, nudged each other, flashed him shy smiles. He smiled back at them all: handsome, adorable, clever, clever Leo Greene.

'So, how's it going with you?' Billy whispered to Olivia as Leo's fans gradually took their seats, opened notebooks and fished pens out of bags. Eyed up the cupcakes. Eyed up Leo Greene. 'The book? Leo told me about it. How's it all going?'

Olivia smiled blandly at him. 'How's it all going?' when something was going well was a welcome question. When something was *not*, it was the last thing an author with a book out in the world wanted to be asked. She wished Leo hadn't told him. *Why had he?*

'Well,' she said, 'it's going OK, thanks.'

'Good, good.' Billy's young face was earnest and eager. 'How are sales?'

'Erm . . . as well as to be expected,' she replied. 'I mean, there are *some* sales . . .'

This was not what she was supposed to say in answer to this question. She was supposed to say a suitably vague, 'My editor is very pleased with how things are going' – a line she had practised several times in front of the mirror, with a variety of sanguine facial expressions.

'Well, some sales is something,' said Billy, sympathetic.

'Yes, of course.'

Two months after Leo signed his publishing deal, Olivia signed her own. It had all happened astonishingly fast. She'd heard back from an agent, not the one she re-submitted to but a different one. Alice Jones at the Frederick Cole Agency. A week later, she signed with her and, three weeks after that, *The Florist* went out on submission, and – to Olivia's huge surprise and delight – an editor at Dawkins Wright, a small press who specialised in romance novels, said they wanted to buy it, offering Olivia a modest advance.

She accepted their offer, despite Alice's tempered caution that Dawkins Wright had a large roster of authors and an unquantified marketing budget. 'Don't expect huge things, but you never know. Or maybe we can see what else comes along?' But Olivia was impatient in the wake of Leo's success, and she accepted the offer.

Dawkins Wright had been lovely when her novel, now called *The Florist on Fenton Street*, was published – just a couple of weeks after Leo's. No, there had been no launch party, but her book had been sent out into the ether with heaps of best wishes and a bouquet of flowers, which arrived on the doorstep of the flat in Pimlico on publication day. Stella and Annabel – escaped from the country for the night – had turned up in the evening with their own bunch of flowers and a big bottle of Prosecco, Stella declaring this the most exciting day in her life bar none, and Annabel had brought a crayon-drawn celebratory scribble by her toddler, Jessica, to stick on Olivia's fridge.

'You've done it!' Stella had cried. 'You're a fully fledged and very clever author!' Annabel had fallen asleep by eight o'clock, declaring both that Olivia was a 'star' and that children were 'knackering and really bloody expensive'.

But sales had been disappointing. Olivia had only sold 220 books in six months and had recently attended a meeting with her editor and a marketing assistant, a meeting where there was croissants and fresh filter coffee and lots of encouraging noises, and pretty hopes that things would magically turn around somehow, but there had been no suggestion of Dawkins Wright signing her for a second book. It had been a one-book deal; Olivia wasn't sure there was ever going to be a publishable book two, although she was already well into writing one anyway, in a pique of stubbornness.

Olivia was disappointed, too. The advance had long been spent on bills, and low sales meant it was doubtful the book would ever earn out – cover the advance and then start earning her royalties. She had wanted to give up the cleaning job, but she couldn't afford to yet. And, actually, she enjoyed it. And mostly because of Melodi.

On Olivia's first ever shift, she'd been handed a tabard and a box of cleaning supplies and told to meet Melodi, a forty-year-old Albanian woman, fierce and funny, who had cleaned it *all*, apparently. They started with the bins, then wiped the desks, then hoovered, then set to in the little kitchen. Olivia would have quit on the second day if it hadn't been for Melodi. Not because the job was beneath her, but because it was so bloody hard.

Melodi was great fun. Melodi had a dry, caustic wit and a sense of mischief. Melodi had a day job working at a bookie's on the Old Kent Road, handing out betting slips and making polite conversation with drunks. She also cut hair for free, providing a mobile service for her neighbours on their housing estate. In some ways, Melodi reminded Olivia a lot of Charlie.

On Olivia's second shift, she'd followed Melodi into the kitchen to start on the washing up, where Melodi had immediately grabbed a half-empty bottle of champagne from the draining board and taken an enormous swig from it.

'Somebody's damn birthday!' she'd husked in her Eastern European accent. 'Still got its fizz, though. Want some?'

They had done the rest of that evening's cleaning moderately pissed and a friendship was born. Sometimes they went out after their shift to Burger King, where they would stuff down flame grillers and drink Diet Pepsi. Sometimes Melodi would tell Olivia about life back in Albania. Olivia told Melodi about Charlie and her working-class roots. About how she wanted to be a published author, and to write romance novels that sold well and readers loved. Melodi was fascinated. Melodi said it was amazing to have a talent, and Olivia must use hers to climb 'up on the ladder'. Melodi declared she would be her number-one fan and that she would come to all of the book parties and drink the fizz.

'Quite the turnout.' Billy was looking around the Reading Room appreciatively. A very pretty girl had just sat down with her mother. The mother was giving the daughter a bottle of water and the daughter was giving Leo a big sweeping smile under sweeping eyelashes. Then Olivia saw another pretty girl who was taking a seat at the back of the room. Long, honey-brown hair. A preppy striped scarf. A deep-plum velvet coat, and grey eyes the colour of huskies.

'You know her?' Billy must have caught her staring.

'Leo does.'

'Ex?'

'No . . .'

'Pretty,' he acknowledged.

'Yes.' Cressie looked lovelier that ever.

Tanya tapped the mic and began to introduce Leo, the book and the brilliance – and the wisdom Leo was about to impart. There was a loud round of applause, and Leo launched into the presentation Olivia knew he'd been rehearsing all week.

'Do you want to *kill* at writing crime?' he asked, and there was a murmured assent, one whoop and a 'Damn, yeah!' from a man dressed in black at the back, and everybody laughed. Leo was a rock star, and this was a captive audience of huge, devoted fans. 'Here's how I do it,' he said, and Olivia saw he had clocked Cressie at the back of the room, for he paused for a second, gave her a tiny wave with the tips of his fingers and continued confidently into his presentation, while Olivia's thoughts drifted on.

Something had happened at the cleaning job. A man had asked Olivia out. She wanted to think about that now, as she watched Leo gaining Cressie's full, doe-eyed attention. It was a couple of weeks ago. The man had still been at his desk when she and Melodi had come into the office one evening, with the hoover and the cleaning supplies. He was her age, about thirty, dark brown hair, tie off and over the back of his chair.

'Sorry,' he'd said, turning around, apologetic. 'I'll only be another ten minutes.'

'That's OK,' said Olivia. Melodi vaguely scowled at him.

They emptied the bins. There was a wastepaper basket right under the man's desk. He lifted it out for Olivia. 'Here you are,' he said. And then when she came back around to hoover, he theatrically lifted his shiny brown brogues.

'Thank you,' he'd mouthed to her.

She saw him again the next Friday evening. Melodi was off; sometimes her sister had to work, dancing for men in suits at Spearmint Rhino, the gentlemen's club ('They are no gentlemen,' Melodi would snarl), and the pay was better than Melodi's, so Melodi babysat.

'Sorry,' the man in the suit had said, as Olivia came in with the hoover and the box. 'It's me again.'

'That's OK.'

'I've already emptied my bin.'

'Thanks.'

His desk was tidy, too. A sheaf of papers neatly stacked; a brace of ballpoint pens lined up like sleeping soldiers next to his laptop. Olivia did the bins and the desks, and when she was in the kitchen, he popped his head around the door.

'I still had my mug, sorry.' He handed it to her.

'That's alright.' His face was tired, she thought, but handsome. The kind of handsome a man wasn't aware of. A man, she imagined – and she let her imagination take her to unknown places – who might be nervous to tell you he loved you, then never stop telling you.

He hesitated in the doorway. 'Have you been a cleaner long?' he asked.

'A while,' she said. It had been eighteen months. Then, she added, 'I work at the London Library during the day,' and she didn't know why she'd needed to tell him.

'Oh, interesting,' he said. 'St James's Square.'

'Yes.'

'That's a nice building.'

'It's gorgeous.'

'My name is James.'

'Oh, right. Mine's Olivia.'

'I'm very pleased to meet you, Olivia,' said James. 'Would you like to go for a drink?' he asked suddenly, and his wan cheeks suddenly pinked.

'Oh, no, thank you,' she said hurriedly. 'That's really nice of you, but . . . I'm very busy.'

'You have a boyfriend.'

'Yes, I do,' she lied. She couldn't go on a date with someone she cleaned for. *Could she?*

'That's a shame. You seem . . . lovely.'

'Thank you.' She'd appreciated this, tabard on, hair pinned up. 'Well, I should get on,' she'd said, and she had, but she'd seen him leave later, through two partitions of glass, a big coat over one shoulder and a briefcase in his hand, eyes down.

Leo was burning bright. He talked first about ideas, how he was on the lookout for them wherever he went. He talked about how he always went out with a notebook and scraps of paper, how he scribbled notes, lists on the backs of beer mats, CD sleeves, receipts. He held up one of his scrawly lists.

'*Green hat, long coat, tired, cynical, pipe smoker but no pipe – not any more – scuffed shoes, Racing Post* . . .' he read out. 'See?' he added triumphantly. 'That's already a character conjured up.' And his audience nodded, raptured. 'I got the idea from a friend of mine.'

He glanced over at Olivia and winked. She smiled weakly back. The wink, like the brushing of the fingers and the touch of the hand, was a signal of something more between them, if she let it become one. A reaching out that she sensed from Leo, sometimes. But hadn't there always been a sexual attraction, a connection? Something disastrous. Especially now. Because theirs was a connection and a friendship that had begun to turn sour.

There was an obvious imbalance. Leo's star was in ascension – gloriously, rambunctiously so; hers had appeared in the sky, twinkled slightly then petered out to nothing. Her book wasn't selling. Bookshops were making returns to her publisher. The great reading public was simply not interested. Since that meeting with her publisher, she had tried not to despair, tried not to want success so very badly, but sometimes the universe does not appreciate a trier.

Leo had started emailing her things like, *Great things will start to happen for you, too, I know they will*, or *Things will turn around*, and at first she would email back with her thanks and gratitude, then she began to be silent in the face of these words, or to throw them back at him and write that he was wrong, that it was alright for him, until he began to apologise for the good things that were happening to him, and there were so many of them.

She was increasingly despairing and jealous, and hating herself for it; Leo was bemused and often exasperated. She picked holes in the fabric of their friendship until the hole was bigger than what remained.

'Post-it notes, that's right!' Leo said – to a laugh. He was talking about plot points – beats, he called them – the Post-it notes he stuck on his office wall, dozens of them, in different colours. He was bouncing on the balls of his feet, excited. His audience was engaged – virtually *married* – laughing at his jokes, drinking him in, the commander of the room. 'So that's where you begin the second act,' he said. 'Check your pacing. Speed it up, slow things down, keep your reader guessing.'

He glanced over to Olivia again, gave her a quick, almost undetectable, smile. She returned one – always uncertain, these days.

Twenty minutes later, he announced a short break. He found her in the office, where she was hiding.

'What are you doing in here?'

'Just checking on something for next week.'

'Right.'

She didn't look up from the paperwork she was pretending to check. 'Cressie's here,' she said.

'I saw.'

'Did you invite her?'

'No. Yes. She saw the ad for it. I reserved her a ticket.'

'That was nice of you.'

'I hope so, she's my friend. Do you think it's going well?'

She finally looked up at him. 'Brilliantly.'

'I haven't seen you a lot lately. Are you still doing the cleaning job?'

'Why are you asking me that?'

Today of all days. Here they were, halfway through his wildly successful workshop, as a wildly successful bestselling author, while her silly little book was floundering and she was still working two jobs just to survive.

'I just wondered.'

She'd only told him about it – finally – to get out of a book reading he was doing at Waterstones a few weeks ago. 'Well, it's none of your business.' She returned to her papers, started shuffling them randomly. He looked at her, amazed.

'So, you're still working two jobs and burning yourself out.'

'I like the jobs that I have.'

'You *like* the cleaning job?'

'Yes, I like the cleaning job.' She glanced up. 'I wasn't born with a silver spoon in my mouth,' she said, 'unlike you.'

'It's not all it's cracked up to be,' he muttered, almost under his breath. 'And that *silver spoon*, as you so originally put it, has nothing to do with my writing career!' he protested. 'Anyone can make it as a writer!'

'You're a writer with a *cushion*,' she retorted. 'A very comfortable one. You have the luxury of time, and you've also been very lucky. *I'm* comfortable with the two jobs I'm doing and . . . and I'm comfortable being small and unsuccessful.'

'Since when? And you should never be comfortable feeling *small* . . .'

Since that meeting, she thought. 'But what if that's how I'm meant to be? What if that's all that's meant for me? I should just accept my life as it is and not hope it's going to get any bigger or better because it probably won't, and that's fine.'

'Now you're being defeatist!'

'Or *realistic*.'

'You're bitter.'

'You think I'm bitter?'

'I don't know. Yes. Perhaps I think you are, and I'm not sure it suits you. I don't think you've felt "comfortable" since your book was published.'

'It also doesn't *suit* me,' she cried, and she knew her eyes were blazing, 'to shrink and shrink while you grow and grow, to become dimmer and dimmer while you glow and glow and light up the skies, dazzling everyone. To be your friend, help out at your events, hold your bag, have people ask, "And what do you do, Olivia?" and for you to pipe up, "Oh, Olivia's a published author, too" – so sympathetic, so patronising. And, well, I think you're becoming a little arrogant.'

'*Arrogant?*'

'You think you deserve it, not just that you've been lucky. You with your private education and your rich parents. You're loving it just a bit too much!'

'What, you think I'm strutting around, boasting all the time? I've worked *hard*!' he shouted. 'I've worked bloody hard! And my parents are nothing to do with it! God knows they're not. And, you know what, you've got a chip on your shoulder about being working class. You always have.'

'Maybe I have!' she shouted, and she was almost crying now. 'Maybe it's sitting there every day, spurring me on.' She tapped at her right shoulder ferociously. 'You don't have that. You have everything. You've always had *everything*! But you've lost something, too. Recently. You've lost . . .' She inhaled. 'You've lost your vulnerability.'

'You want me to be *vulnerable*!' He shook his head in disbelief.

'I liked it when you were, just like you liked it when *I* was, when I lost my father. You liked my sadness, my bittersweet neediness – you slept with me because of it, didn't you? You used to have a softer, less self-important side—'

'Like a likeable flaw in one of your romantic heroes? Your *only* romantic hero, to date. Writing believable, successful characters . . . how's that working out for you?'

She winced. 'That's a low blow.'

And Leo shrugged, a shrug that told Olivia a lot of things but, mostly, that their friendship, or whatever this was, was over. He had said too much. *She* had said too much. She looked at her watch.

'It's time to go back up.'

'Wait,' he said, and he looked defeated. She had defeated him with her words, she realised. 'You know, I thought – recently – we might be able to start something up again, you and me. I hoped . . . well, we could maybe become more than friends again. I realise now that it was a very stupid idea. It's still not the right time for us, is it?'

'I don't think it'll ever be the right time for us, Leo.'

'No.'

'I need more than what you're offering.'

'I can see that.' He grimaced.

She was crushed, exhausted.

'I'm going to go back up.'

She was back in her place at the side of the room. Leo was nearing the end of his presentation. He was talking about clues, saying he scattered them throughout his books, that when Agatha Christie wrote her mysteries, she would reach the end and then go back and add them all in, and he did the same. He made a self-deprecating joke about comparing himself to Mrs Christie and his audience laughed.

Leo had finished. The congregation was rising from their seats and heading for the big desk, lining up, clutching copies of *Midnight Shadows*. Leo gathered and stacked his notes, got his signing pen ready, ran his hand through his wavy hair.

'Thanks so much, all of you, for coming. I really do have the best readers! If anyone wants a signed book, my pen is poised!'

He sat at the desk while his readers queued up. They laughed with him, watched with delight as he signed their books. Smiled adoringly into his face. Cressie reached the front of the line, and Leo broke into a broad grin. He touched Cressie on the wrist. Cressie bent over the desk, her small pale hand cupped at its edge, and gave him a kiss on the cheek. As the kiss landed, Leo glanced over at Olivia, his eyes blank.

◆ ◆ ◆

There was no one in the lobby of the library when Olivia left. Nobody to see her stand at the top of the steps outside the library and breathe in the cold, sharp air. She walked down into St James's Square and bumped straight into a man in a dark grey overcoat, the collar turned up.

'Oh, it's you,' he said – the handsome man who had stayed late at the office. 'St James's Square.'

'Hello,' she replied.

'Are you on your lunch break?'

'Sort of.'

He was smiling at her. His eyes roamed over her face, and he looked captured by it.

'Would you like to go for that drink?' he asked her shyly. 'Or do you still have a boyfriend?'

She smiled to push away her sadness. She smiled to paper over her broken heart. *His* smile was warm and exclusive, and seemed, if not the promise of something, then an escape from something else.

'I'd like to go for that drink.'

Chapter Twenty-Seven

Venice

Wednesday 10 January 2018

Libreria Acqua Alta ('bookstore of high water') was nestled at the base of a building on Campiello Testori and under the canopy of a spreading tree. Heralding its entrance were postcard stands, art books and posters and a table with a hand-drawn, water-washed poster taped at its end, declaring, *Welcome to the most beautiful bookshop in the world!*

Inside was a charming, chaotic tumble of books, cats and people: books stacked in gondolas; books in empty bathtubs, boats and barrels; new books and second-hand books scuffed at the edges or spineless; books piled high on shelves and tables; books bowed and squished and wedged together in concave towers. Narrow gondolas like quills were tethered high on the walls; there were cats everywhere: sitting on book stacks, winding nonchalant tails around them, lapping water out of bowls. And people: people looking at books, people buying books, people stroking cats, and people waiting for Leo Greene and Olivia Sackville.

'Oh, there you are!' Tanya was standing behind a gondola and a cat, in a cream cashmere sweater and a long silky skirt, her hair swept up into a fancy chignon. 'I was beginning to get worried about both of you. Fab hat, Leo!'

Leo grinned at her. Olivia smiled cautiously. 'We've just been for lunch,' she said.

'Oh, nice.'

Olivia was already regretting it, spending so much time with Leo today. The house, the hospice, the lunch. What had it achieved? Nothing except an uneasy alliance, she realised, and an acceptance they may never talk about the circumstances that had brought them to this point: civil non-friends, fellow book festival attendees with history, one-time lovers who could never quite make it to falling in love . . . And then there was the walk here. What he had said to her.

'Should be a good turnout,' said Tanya, bending to stroke the cat, who stared up at her and then shot off. 'I hope your wrists are limbered up for all the signing.'

Olivia looked for somewhere to hang her coat. Meryn appeared with a clipboard.

'We'll be ready to rock in about ten minutes,' she said. 'The authors will be sitting over there.' She pointed to a table wedged at the back of the bookstore, four chairs behind it. 'So, if you want to wander around for a bit . . . There's quite a few here for it already.' A couple of women had clearly recognised Leo. They were nudging each other and beaming in his direction. A young man waved shyly at Olivia. 'Oh, and here's Frances and Anthony!'

Anthony met Leo with great enthusiasm, immediately pulling him aside to divulge some choice piece of nonsense. Frances admired Olivia's coat.

The bookstore was filling up; plenty of people wandering in through the entrance. Tanya gathered all of their jackets, and Leo's ridiculous hat, and stowed them in the base of a wall-mounted gondola.

'Did you bring your special pen?' Leo asked Olivia.

She tapped her bag at her side, tried to appear sunny and not completely in her own head. 'Yes. Pen for box labelling, pen for signing . . .'

'Do you have another I can borrow? I've forgotten to bring one.'

'Sure.' They were playing at being buoyant. Olivia felt anything but. As she handed him a smart navy-blue ballpen, Valentina appeared in a pistachio tweed suit, her voice high and bright like a fork pinging a champagne flute.

'Good morning!' she cried. 'If the writers would like to take their seats!'

Felicity popped up behind her. 'The seats over there,' she echoed, pointing. 'Make your way, please.'

Olivia and Frances walked to the table at the back of the room, Anthony and Leo following, and, somehow, she and Leo ended up sitting next to each other again, in the two middle places, thighs wedged together on primary-school-like chairs.

'Cosy,' Leo remarked with a small sigh.

'Hmm,' Olivia replied. She didn't want to get cosy with him, to be this close. She needed some distance from him. He had said something else to her, as they'd walked to the bookshop from lunch. They had been ducking down an alleyway Leo was sure was part of the maze that would lead them here, but it hadn't. It had brought them to a dead end, an abrupt canal in shadow, a flaking wall rising behind it – a building that seemed to be almost creaking in its dilapidation.

'We need to go back,' Leo had said. And then he'd placed his hand on her arm. 'I do think we need to go back, Liv.'

'Save it for your therapist, Leo,' she'd replied flippantly, but he wasn't flippant. He was serious.

'I don't think anyone else knows me like you do.'

He was looking into her eyes, and she was worried he could see into her soul. It was almost as if he was going to kiss her.

'Isn't that the problem?' she replied, almost in a whisper. And, after an endless moment in that dank, shadowed space, he let go of her arm and released her soul. Mumbled something about really needing to get there on time, and after that he'd only talked of books and bookshops as they'd re-navigated the alleyways of Venice and peered up at any part of the skyline that might give them a clue where they were going.

It turned out that everyone currently in Libreria Acqua Alta wanted a book signed. They formed four orderly lines, pretty even in length. Leo's queue was mostly female, Olivia's was all female apart from a man in a cagoule, Anthony's was middle-aged people who all looked rather like him, and Frances's was a complete mixture – young and old, and everyone in between.

Leo was busy getting his pen ready, rolling up the sleeves of his jumper. *He loves this*, Olivia thought, the occasional theatre of being an author after being cooped up in a study for months. He liked the showmanship, the talking about it all. He always had. She enjoyed it to a point. She felt her best self was in her work and that her words, carefully chosen when she wrote, were not always the right ones when interacting with people in real life. Often, afterwards, she wished she had selected better.

They each had a pile of their books in front of them. Leo's, with that menacing city-at-night cover. Hers, coral and pink and classic font. Anthony's quirky and cartoonish, a man in tweed in a flat cap with a pheasant pitched over his shoulder. Frances's, green and orange and abstract, 1970s swirls and stylised bubble writing.

Olivia felt something soft at her leg. She reached down to pet a little black cat that had stolen under the table, tickle it behind the ears. For the first time, she noticed there was music playing in the bookstore – Peggy Lee, 'Emotions'. Gillian had liked Peggy Lee. Once upon a time, Olivia imagined Gillian had brought all her old albums with her to the house on the Lido; that Gillian would lie on a big sofa and listen to her favourite songs, or get up on a rug and dance, solo, to northern soul. And it was true that Olivia was certainly feeling a lot of different emotions here in Venice.

Her first book signee was the young man who had waved at her – a shy Venetian called Nicolas, in his early twenties, who wanted her to put three kisses. Then an English woman in a padded gilet and huge silk scarf. Beth was third in line.

'You didn't have to queue up,' Olivia chided her gently. 'I would have signed a book for you, anytime.'

'I know.' Beth placed her copy of *The Curator on Church Street* on the table.

'What would you like me to sign?' Olivia asked her.

'*Always believe in love, Olivia Sackville.*'

Olivia smiled. 'Sounds like a command.' A rather difficult one, she felt, but she signed the book and handed it back to Beth.

The signing went on for another thirty minutes. There was a lot of convivial chat, as there always was, people hanging around, wanting a little more.

Anthony rose from the table first.

'I need to stretch my legs.'

Frances got up, too, 'for a vape', and disappeared out of the fire exit, which was basically a door that led straight out on to the canal. Leo announced he had to make a call and headed for the front entrance. Olivia felt the absence of his thigh next to hers. She stayed in her seat, neatly stacking up the remainder of her books and re-packing her bag until they all returned.

Leo held out his hand for her and, as she stood up, she took it. She knew about electricity between two people: she had re-fashioned it hundreds of times in her books, between a hero and a heroine, trying to avoid cliché, trying to make it sound fresh, original, but there it was again, as familiar as an old coat on Guy Fawkes Night and as jolting as fifty volts.

She didn't want to feel this way. She couldn't. All evidence was to the contrary. She let go of Leo's hand.

'Where are we going?' Leo asked Tanya, briefly looking down at his empty hand, and up at Olivia, then turning to collect the three books he hadn't needed to sign.

'Just through there,' said Meryn. She gestured over to another door with her clipboard. 'The back porch. Tanya has arranged some refreshments.'

Olivia self-consciously put her hand in the pocket of her dress. They went to the gondola to fetch their coats and head outside.

'Oh, this is cute!' Olivia exclaimed.

'Isn't it?'

Before them was an uneven, unwieldy staircase made from an almost papier-mâché compression of old and no longer usable books, destroyed by floods, soaked by the *acqua alta* of Venice, but preserved as squelched-together stacks, in bled-out, melted colours – like piled-up skeins of fabric in a haberdasher's. Plastic mats marked each tread. At the top was a wall, and beyond, the canal. It was a living staircase of books and words, water and history, and Olivia found it utterly charming, as did Anthony and Frances, who appeared behind them with Tanya.

'Go on up,' Tanya said. 'And sit at the top. I'll bring you hot drinks and something to eat.'

'I'm not going up there!' Anthony looked horrified. 'As pretty as it is, I might do myself an injury. Who wants to go to that lovely trattoria I spotted across the square instead?'

Frances glanced down at her high heels. 'Me, I think,' she said. 'No one minds, do they? I don't think there's room for all of us up there, anyway.'

They disappeared back into the bookstore. Leo shrugged at Olivia and, tugging at the knees of his trousers, started walking up the right-hand side of the haphazard book steps, holding his hand out to her again.

'I can manage,' she said, but then she changed her mind, and she took his hand again.

The steps were surprisingly firm. The summit, a delight, with its view of the canal. Leo sat down and she sat next to him, their feet dangling over the smushed-together book steps. She could still feel the sensation of her hand in his.

'Well, this is different,' he said. 'You're not too cold?'

'No, I'm alright.'

'Did you enjoy the signing? Did you notice that man who joined all four queues?'

'I did.'

'Widely read,' Leo commented, and Olivia smiled. They looked around them politely, to the canal, and tried to peer at some of the books for any faded titles on their spines, until Tanya appeared with a tray hosting two mugs and a plate of biscuits.

'Hot chocolate,' she proclaimed, 'and biscotti.' She handed the tray up to Leo who bent to receive it. 'According to Beth, who gave me a hand, the hot chocolate is in your book, Olivia, and the biscotti is in yours, Leo.'

'Is it?' Olivia knew it was. She knew that in chapter four of *The Curator*, Kath and Justice sit in the little Italian café in Primrose Hill and drink hot chocolate, just after they bump into each other for the second time.

She had no idea about Leo's book, but clearly Beth was right as Leo said, 'Correct!' They watched Tanya go. Leo took the first sip. 'Very nice,' he commented. 'There's a place here called Inizio's. It's where all the old boys go for their coffee in the morning, and they do the most amazing hot chocolate. It's tiny. All the old men jostle at the bar, and chat and drink their espressos before heading off to begin their days. You'd love it. Whenever I'm in Venice I go there. I stand at the bar and wonder about the stories of some of those old boys, where they're on their way to, if they have wives, children, grandchildren . . .'

'I've been there,' Olivia admitted. 'Once. When I came to Venice that time. It was mentioned in a guidebook I had.'

'The time after us?'

She baulked. 'Yes. I didn't see my godmother but I stayed here a week anyway.'

'I didn't know that.'

'Why would you?'

They sipped their hot chocolates. Olivia could hear the gentle lapping at the edge of the canal below them.

'She seems a tricky character,' he said. 'Gillian.'

'Yeah, she is. Coming here was kind of a pilgrimage for me, I guess, in seeing her, but I don't think it's going to work out.'

'It still might.'

She shook her head. She thought about her planned visit to the hospice on Saturday. She still really couldn't see that happening.

'And this was all from the funeral? When you asked her if she resented you?'

'You remember that?'

'Of course.'

She nodded. 'That wasn't all,' she said. 'There was something else from the funeral.' Why was it sometimes so easy to talk to him, she thought, particularly when they were alone? Why could she just tell him things, straight from the heart? Was he right, and did he know her better than anyone else, too? 'My reading. The one I wrote, anyway. I couldn't read it, the celebrant did. What a disaster it was. How inadequate. It was so awful that Gillian had to take over.'

'Go on . . .' He was listening like he had in the Rivoli Bar, all those years before. That was why she could talk to him, she realised. It was how he listened.

'Well, I felt so wretched, so guilty I hadn't been there, so terrible that I'd never said the right words to him, that I couldn't write any true, meaningful words, either. What I wrote was too factual, too impersonal. I'd thought, what was the point, when it was too late? He had gone. So it was just a simple summing up of an entire, good life. No one laughed, no one even cried. I had not done him justice, and Gillian's face, when the celebrant had finished, said it all. I was supposed to be this budding writer, I was supposed to put into words what we both were feeling about him, but I didn't. And she took over. She was only meant to be reading a poem, that one about the ship, but instead she spoke about my dad. She spoke off the cuff about northern soul, about their school days, about what a lovely man Charlie was, how proud she was of him – as a single father, as a carpenter, everything. While I just sat there. I just sat there.'

Leo looked thoughtful. One vessel honked at another on the canal beneath them. A lone gull *caw-caw*ed above the skyline. Olivia waited for his response; his condemnation, maybe.

'Perhaps you could write something for your father now,' he said.

'How do you mean?'

'Well, have you ever thought of writing him into one of your books? To honour him in some way? To say all the things you didn't say at the funeral? To say all the things you wanted him to know?'

He had her attention. 'Have a character who's a carpenter, you mean?'

Leo nodded. 'Yes, something like that. A wonderful character, who's also your dad.'

Like *Ben Midnight*? she wondered. Leo's chef that Olivia knew he had written for Isaac, but Isaac wasn't wonderful. He was not a wonderful father. They'd had a row once, her and Leo, a big one, here in Italy – the one that had brought an end to them – and Isaac and Charlie had both been in it. But Charlie *had* been wonderful. Charlie could be honoured.

'And maybe he has a daughter, who has the right words.'

Something surged within Olivia. A hope. An opportunity. A chance to do something she knew would be really good for her. That hope swelled up in her like a wave approaching the shore, and she was grateful for it. 'That's a lovely idea,' she said. 'I like that a lot. Thank you, Leo.'

'You're very welcome.'

They held each other's gaze.

'And thank you for helping me at my godmother's house this morning, and for coming to the hospice. I really do appreciate it.'

'You're welcome,' he repeated. 'As long as I'm not being too saintly,' he added. 'I mean, I don't want to be accused of that again.'

She laughed. 'No, Leo *Nightingale*,' she said, 'not too saintly.'

There was a beat. 'I'm not planning to make any wrong moves here,' Leo said quietly. 'I want you to know that. I'm trying to be very careful here in Venice. With you.'

She didn't quite understand what he meant. 'OK . . .' she said, studiedly neutral.

'I'm trying,' he repeated. 'So, you're not going to run away?' he asked her, a gentle smile on his face, a tender look in his eyes.

'I thought about it, but no.' She smiled at him. 'I'll stay.'

They sat in silence for quite some time.

'Can I get you anything else?' he asked her eventually. 'More hot chocolate? More biscotti?'

'No, I'm OK, thank you,' she said.

'Shall we go back down? Find the others?'

'Alright.'

She had felt she could sit up here with him for hours, on this unwieldy, damp pile of books. She had felt comfortable with him. Calmed. Better. But it was time to go.

Leo stood up. Far too quickly. To steady himself, he shifted his left foot, and then his right, but the edge was there, and his foot was away from him, and he was grabbing at the air, limbs flailing, and he landed on the lower tier of books, flat on his back with his legs in the air, like an astonished ant.

'Are you alright?' she called down, and he was motionless for a second, his eyes closed, but then he opened his eyes and his mouth, and he absolutely howled with laughter. Tears ran down his face, and he said, 'Bloody clumsy idiot!' in such a sweet, funny way, she was laughing, too, and wiping her own eyes, and the sound of their laughter echoed around this small space and was carried down to the canal.

'Sorry,' she said. 'But that *was* really, really funny.'

'See, we *can* have fun! Reminds me of the peacock,' he added, still lying on his back. Still giggling.

'The peacock?'

'Yeah, the peacock in Tuscany. Do you remember?'

'Let me help you,' she said, and she wended her way down the wobbly staircase made of books, and she helped him to his feet, which he got to with an exaggerated groan.

'Are you really alright?' she asked him.

'I'm fine,' he responded, patting himself down. '*Don't* you remember the peacock?' he asked again.

'Of course I do.' She was still holding his hand. She liked how it felt. But the mischief of the peacock meant Tuscany, and Tuscany not only meant almost falling in love with him, but saying goodbye once again.

Chapter Twenty-Eight

Tuscany

Wednesday 5 August 2015

Henrietta Winters, the historical fiction writer, was tiddly already. It was only 10 a.m. and she'd drunk a bellini with her croissant, an elderflower martini with her eggs benedict and was moving on to a gin and tonic with 'a nice bit of toast'. The pool to her right glistened Hockney blue in a Gauguin sun. The begonias in their ceramic pots around its edge strained to hear the conversation on the terrace.

'Happy hour again,' commented the psychological thriller writer, a dry fellow called Martin Lang who was here to get away from his wife, or so he told everyone – daily, with a cheerful roll of the eyes – when everyone knew he was actually setting his next thriller right here in Arezzo, Tuscany.

'It's five o'clock somewhere,' defended Henrietta, writer of the Anne Boleyn series of time-slip novels, 'and who needs an excuse? We may be writing, but we're still on holiday.'

Some writers' retreats were alcohol-free zones; this one, at a beautiful Tuscan farmhouse on the rise of the Casentino Valley in

Arezzo, was definitely not. Henrietta had taken full advantage of the 'all drinks included' manifesto on the four days of the retreat so far. At breakfast, then at the late lunch the writers would break for at 4 p.m. – with white, red and rosé supplied along with huge salads and tomato-and-mozzarella tarts – then at dinner served at 9 p.m. Margo, their host, was an Irish woman who had moved to Tuscany in the mid-1970s and was now fluent in both the language and the cookery.

The company was Henrietta, Martin, Clemmie and Samantha – two giggling fifty-somethings who both wrote romantic comedies set in Cornwall – and Olivia Sackville, who had now joined the ranks of bestselling authors.

Their table on the terrace had a yellow tablecloth and a salt-shaker in the shape of a cockerel. Double doors flung wide open behind them led to the spacious living room of Villa Margo and the six bedrooms that lay off it. Beyond the pool and the boundary of the property were the sloping terraces of the vineyards that Olivia could see from her room with a view at the far end of the villa, and which they overlooked now: the combed neat lines of the vines, a red tractor rolling along a distant lane, a man in a cap sitting high on its seat.

All Olivia had wanted was sunshine, peace and quiet, a warm pool to swim in, a simple room with white bed linen and the breeze from an open window, and the quiet pressure of other writers. It was new to her, the communal writers' retreat – *company* – but her new novel was turning out to be an absolute pig. She had written three quarters of it but still didn't really know what it was *about,* so when her agent had told her of this retreat and encouraged her to go, after one of Olivia's epic brainstorming (read: moaning) sessions, she'd taken a deep breath and agreed. The other writers would spur her on. The other writers, slaving away, would inspire and motivate her. She would give it a try.

Between mealtimes, it was quiet when they all disappeared to their rooms, and if Olivia listened really carefully, she could hear the *tap-tap*ping of keyboards and coffee cups being set down on tiled tables, and Henrietta's snores.

For now, the air was filled with Martin's laments about the London Book Fair, Henrietta's slurps, and Clemmie and Samantha babbling like a stream through a brook about men and tropes and bestseller lists.

Clemmie nudged Samantha. 'Go on, ask her,' she said.

'Ask who, what?' Henrietta looked up from her drink.

'Olivia,' said Samantha, fixing her with an intense look. 'We've been really respectful around you for the past four days, respected your privacy and all that, but now we have questions.'

Olivia smiled. 'Go on.' She adjusted the strap of her pink sundress, one she'd bought from a designer boutique on the King's Road last year after a lunch with Stella and Annabel to celebrate her thirty-sixth birthday.

'OK, how does it feel to have a bestselling book?' said Samantha. 'Or rather, bestselling *books* – a handful of them. To be a great big success, a superstar author, like "one of the top one per cent" successful. I mean, we're floundering down at the bottom like minnows. We're doing OK . . .' She looked at Martin and Henrietta, clearly including them. 'We're enjoying it. It's a lovely life, writing – who wouldn't think so? We do make enough to come somewhere like this . . .' She wafted a hand around. 'But to know that everyone is waiting for your next book to come out, actually *waiting* for it, *bated breath* waiting for it, and that you're pretty much guaranteed every book is going to be a success. What is *that* like?'

Olivia considered her answer. 'It's really nice,' she admitted, 'and it *can* happen to anyone, I believe. You need a lot of luck and ideally a great marketing team, and you need constant hope, even when you feel you can't possibly have any left.'

In 2010, *The Florist on Fenton Street* had continued to flounder, and Olivia continued to work at the London Library by day and the cleaning job by night. She also continued working on her new book, *The Stylist on Sydney Square,* into which she poured more heart, and dug a little deeper emotionally. It was about a woman living in a women's refuge who preoccupies herself by cutting the hair of the other residents, then sets up a street salon for the homeless, and finally starts her own business – finding heart-stopping love along the way. It was published by Dawkins Wright in early 2011 and by word of mouth, osmosis or magic, rather than marketing, it became a massive bestseller. Readers said it was impossibly romantic, that it was bittersweet but uplifting, hopeful and inspirational, and the book flew all the way to the top of the *Sunday Times* Bestseller List and stayed there for several weeks.

Olivia's career took off – *whoosh!* – and she was soaring, releasing a book a year, each and every one a great success, to her delight. All the previous disappointment just fell away until she wondered if she would forget how it felt, the despair and the disenchantment of trying to make it as an author, but she knew she never would. That every ounce of it was compounded into her happiness to make it an infinitely more satisfying drug.

The money, too, was great. She was finally comfortable. She gave up the cleaning job, and her work at the London Library. She sold the flat in Pimlico, packing up her memories of her father – along with quite a few tears – and taking them with her to her new house in Marylebone. She had done it; she had achieved her dream, and she had done it all on her own.

'Do you always get a book launch?' asked Clemmie. 'Laid on by the publishers? We have to organise things ourselves, don't we, Sam?'

Sam nodded. Henrietta said she last did something at a brunch place, and had her own cake made, and Martin muttered something about a pub and three people turning up.

'Yes, I do usually,' Olivia admitted. 'They are nice things to have, I suppose . . .' For the book launch of *The Stylist on Sydney Square* at Parchment & Plots she had invited all of her friends, including Stella and Annabel, of course, ex-colleagues from the theatre, Alistair from the London Library, and Melodi, her partner-in-crime, who had drunk some of the fizz and had a great time. It had been a wonderful evening. 'Look, I've just been lucky, that's all. Really lucky. My first book was a complete flop, my second became a hit – it was all out of my hands! Now, I just have to keep writing and doing the best I can.'

'Must be lovely, though.' Clemmie sighed. 'Success and fame.'

'Well, I don't think I'm actually *famous* . . .'

Success, Olivia thought, as she stirred her coffee. It *was* lovely, but lovely things should be shared with others. She had shared it with Stella and Annabel, and with James, in fact, for almost two years, until that had come to its natural end. And now success kept a good part of her warm at night. Very warm. But, she thought, as she looked around the eager faces at the table, there was another part of her that success couldn't reach. Another part that was *lonely*. But, of course, she wouldn't be telling the present company that.

'But you've been on Oprah's Book Club! On the *television*. With *Oprah*. How on earth was that?'

'It was . . . terrifying. OK, can we please stop talking about me? Who would like more coffee? I can go and find Margo . . .'

Olivia was rising from her seat. Clemmie had started to nudge Samantha again, but this time she was not looking at Olivia but behind her, down the cobblestone driveway to the iron gate at the front of the villa, where the red tractor had pulled up with a trailer on the back, and there was a man and a suitcase sitting inside it.

The man had his knees up, one elbow across them, and he was wearing a floppy cream suit, a white fedora and dark sunglasses.

'Good Lord! Who's that man?' exclaimed Samantha.

Henrietta lowered her sunglasses and peered over the top of them. 'Well, I don't know,' she murmured appreciatively. The man climbed off the trailer and pulled his suitcase down after him, before brushing down the knees of his suit.

'Looks dapper,' said Martin, disconsolately considering his own Bruce Springsteen t-shirt and baggy shorts.

'Definitely!' said Clemmie admiringly.

Sam shielded her eyes and trained them on the figure who was now wheeling his case up the steep path. 'Wine salesman?' she suggested. 'Twenty bottles of red in the suitcase?'

'We are getting through rather a lot,' observed Henrietta absently, shunting her sunglasses back up.

'That's not a wine guy!' cried Clemmie, eyes like saucers. 'That's the crime writer, Leo Greene!'

Olivia sat back down. Leo Greene looked up, caught her eye and gave her a surprised half-wave. Henrietta was beaming. Martin looked excited. And Clemmie and Sam were simpering schoolgirls catching sight of that handsome lad from the school next door, the one they could never stand a chance with.

'Hello, everyone!' Leo said, as he approached the table on the terrace. Henrietta set down her martini; Olivia resisted the urge to pick it up. 'This *is* the writers' retreat? Villa Margo?' He stopped by the table, whipped out a handkerchief from the breast pocket of his jacket and mopped his brow under his hat. 'Blimey, it's hot,' he said beguilingly, 'and that pool looks very inviting – are we allowed in it?'

'Of course we are!' Henrietta cried. 'But wouldn't you want to take all your clothes off first?' She grinned at him above her expansive bosom. 'And yes, this is the Villa Margo. But we've all been here for four days. There's only one day left. You're late.'

He shrugged. Everyone except Olivia – who was frozen in the bright sunshine – smiled or giggled.

'Two days is enough,' said Leo. He placed his hanky back in his pocket. 'I've only got an epilogue to write, and I'm late because they've been shooting the movie of *Midnight Preys* in Perugia. I went along to see how it was all going.'

'How is it all going?' asked Martin.

'Really well, thanks.' Leo looked proud, as well he might. *Midnight Preys* had been a huge bestseller two years ago and was now being made into a movie starring Ryan Gosling and Cate Blanchett. Not that Olivia was following Leo's career with interest. Not that she was *always* following Leo Greene with interest, and from a more than respectable distance.

'How did you hear about this retreat?' Clemmie asked. She surreptitiously rolled on some lip balm.

'My agent told me about it. Ears to the ground and all that.' Leo looked directly at the frozen woman. 'It's been a while, Olivia,' he said. 'How did *you* hear about it?' he asked. 'I didn't think you'd be the writers' retreat type.'

'I'm not,' said Olivia, and the other writers looked at her. 'But it's been fabulous.'

'Great! Well, I'm dying of thirst.' Leo took off his jacket to reveal a rather crumpled white shirt, unbuttoned way too far. 'What do I need to do to get a cold drink around here?'

The others were only too willing to oblige, pulling out a chair for him, rustling him up a glass of cold sparkling water, and some pastries from the kitchen. Samantha even said, 'Ooh, you used to be a food critic – I hope this is good enough for you, sir,' when she plonked a bowl of segmented Seville oranges in front of him, causing Leo to laugh, his hazel eyes lighting up in mirth; his mouth, that warm surprise, as ever.

'I'm going back to my room,' Olivia said, standing up. 'I think I'll start early today, I'm on a tricky chapter. See you all at the usual time.'

They watched her leave, but she was only aware of Leo, his eyes fixed on her, suddenly serious. In her quiet room, she set up for the day: flinging open her window to bring in the woody scent of the vineyards below the villa and the sound of the tractor bumping once again over the distant fields. A glass of chilled water on her desk, an open laptop and a notepad and pencil were her only companions. She would write until lunch, but not sit with the others, instead sneaking out some bread and cheese from the kitchen. She would work on until supper, rising to shower and to dress determinedly in what she had planned to wear for tonight. She would not think about the last time she and Leo had spoken, five years ago, at the London Library. Her words of bitterness; his of exasperation and anger. She would not think about the last time she had seen him, when their taxis had passed in Knightsbridge traffic one summer evening last year. How his profile had made her want to cry.

At 7.30 p.m. she stepped on to the terrace, apprehensive in a navy-blue cotton tiered maxi dress. Leo was in the pool, doing lengths. Before she had time to walk away, he was at the coping.

'Hi,' he said, 'you look nice.' He slapped his elbows on the side of the pool and glanced up at her. Wet hair, a droplet of water hesitating on his bottom lip, two smooth brown shoulders.

'Thanks.' She didn't know what else to say. She barely wanted to look at him, he looked so good.

'It's been a long time,' he said.

'Five years,' she replied, then instantly regretted having that number to hand. 'More or less.'

'It's good to see you.'

Was he expecting her to say, 'You, too?' She didn't say anything.

'Are you OK with me being here?'

'I'm not sure *why* you're here, to be honest.'

'I told you, I was nearby for the movie. My agent suggested I come. How do you want to play this, me being around?'

She stared at him. The droplet of water left his lip and slipped down his chin. 'I don't want to "play" anything. I just want to get back to yesterday when you weren't here.'

He grinned. Then he bit at his bottom lip. 'Congratulations on all your success,' he said. 'I've been wanting to say that to you for a long while.'

'Congratulations on the continuation of yours.'

He nodded. 'I almost sent an email a couple of times.'

'That would have been very generous of you.'

He placed his palms flat on the edge of the pool and lifted himself out, water dripping from his sleek seal-body on to the slabs. He walked to fetch his towel, slung over the back of a wrought-iron pool chair, and started rubbing at his tanned shoulders with it.

'So, really I—' he started.

'I've forgotten something,' Olivia muttered. 'I just need to . . .' She flapped her hand in the direction of the villa and hurried inside. Back in her room, she sat down on the bed in relief and horror. She couldn't do this. She couldn't exist in the same space as Leo Greene. Why was he so unbothered about doing the same? Why was he *here*?

She sat on the bed for twenty-five minutes until there was a knock at the door. It was Clemmie, in a startling orange dress and far more make-up than usual.

'We're all going out,' she said, her lips a glossy coral. 'To that restaurant down the valley. We're giving poor Margo the night off from cooking. Are you coming?'

'Who's going?' Olivia asked.

'Well, all of us . . .'

'Is Leo Greene going?'

'Yes. Do you want to come?'

'No, I don't think so. Sorry. I'm going to stay at the villa. But thanks for knocking for me.'

She closed the door, lay down on the bed. She lay there for a long time, until, through her open window, she could hear faint strains of music, staccato hoots of laughter and the *plink-plink* of cutlery against china.

She got up and leaned through the window, twisting her head to spy the restaurant down the small hill to the right of the villa. She could only see its trellised roof, entwined with summer roses and fairy lights. She could only detect the delicious notes of wild garlic and rosemary and chargrilled vegetables.

She didn't want to go to a beautiful restaurant with Clemmie and Sam, and Henrietta and Martin, and Leo bloody Greene. She didn't want to change out of the dull navy dress and put on the one she had added to her case, last minute – the one with the 1950s shape, the full skirt, in baby pink. The dress she felt like a ballerina in. She didn't want to refresh her make-up, using that new nude lipstick she had bought on a whim at the airport and shoved in her travel bag. She didn't want to brush her hair and curl it into a pretty chignon at the nape of her neck . . .

But the perfect evening can change the most hardened, the most obstinate of minds. The perfect evening can entice with a wink of candlelight and the beckoning finger of fun and laughter. And a man you wanted to forget, but never could, can turn your life upside down once again . . .

Chapter Twenty-Nine

Olivia hadn't packed any shoes except flip-flops and trainers, but her toenails were painted fuchsia, and her heels were smooth, so she decided to go barefoot. As she walked down the cobbled slope to the restaurant, enjoying the feel of the warm stones beneath her toes, she told herself several things. That she was the same girl she'd always been, one to never miss a party. That her new writer friends were all there, and why would she not want to join in with them? And that she could handle Leo Greene – every last damned delicious molecule of him.

The restaurant was called Nico's and was in a pretty two-storey yellow building with blue shutters and window boxes tumbling with begonias and petunias. Out the front, it had a row of cast-iron tables and chairs under a striped awning, but these were all empty this evening, as was the ground floor of the restaurant. As she walked through it, Olivia could see everyone on the terrace out the back: laughing faces, flippy dresses, white shirts and dark trousers.

A waiter, chomping on a bread roll behind the bar, looked up at her.

'*Buona sera*,' she said, in bad Italian. 'I'm from Villa Margo, up the road. My friends are here. Can I?' She gestured to the terrace.

'Of course,' he said in very good English. 'It is a lively party already. You forgot your shoes?'

'No,' she replied with a smile.

At first, she couldn't see the gang from Villa Margo. The smiling faces before her were not ones she recognised. Then she saw Clemmie, behind the central enamel wood burner and framed by a pretty pergola, roaring with laughter at something Leo was saying. Henrietta, Sam and Martin, making up the circle, were also hanging off his every word.

'Olivia!' cried Leo, as she walked over. 'You came!'

'Yes,' she said, positioning herself between Sam and Henrietta. Henrietta was brandishing yet another martini. 'I saw the party from my window, and I thought I'd better see what was going on. Author curiosity wins every time, doesn't it?'

She attempted a tight kind of laugh, the kind she would need alcohol of some sort to loosen. Leo looked devastating: a white shirt, casual blue jeans, slip-on loafers and no socks, a look she normally hated but it manifested so well on him.

'Barefoot,' he observed with a smile. 'And a nice dress.' He narrowed his eyes at her admiringly. 'You look like a ballerina.'

'Thank you. You look like you're up to no good.'

'Just chatting. Having an enjoyable time.' His tanned face was glowing, his teeth gleaming, his eyes shining. He should have been on the cover of a magazine, but instead he was here. Life had been kind to Leo Greene. That silver spoon was now a whole cutlery set. But didn't she have the set now, too? She had once told him that she would shrink and shrink while he grew and grew, but now they stood together – in the publishing world, at least – as equals.

'Someone's got to keep morale up in such a dreadful place,' joked Henrietta. She slurped martini happily through her straw.

'Yes, it's *awful.*' Olivia played along, looking around her. Everyone looked happy, everyone had a smile on their face. It was August in Tuscany, and life was beautiful.

'What are you drinking?' Leo asked her. 'Would you like some wine?'

'Rosé, please.'

He reached out to touch the arm of a passing waiter, engaged him in friendly conversation, and the Villa Margo writers watched him hungrily. Olivia knew they were all enchanted by Leo Greene with his big brain and his movie-star looks. His smile, that came so readily and was so easily absorbed by all around him. How he walked down a street like sunlight did, his presence gradually sweeping over everything and everyone in its way. Their friendship had been ruined – mostly by her – five years ago, yet he was at ease. He was offering her wine. He was paying her compliments. She wondered how he did that.

A glass of wine appeared for her, and Olivia sipped it gratefully. 'Thank you.'

'Hey, Leo,' said Martin, reaching for his arm like Leo had the waiter. 'I want to hear all about this movie deal you've got. How long you were optioned before you got it. If they're changing it much for the screenplay . . .'

Olivia was relieved at the chance to turn away. She couldn't spend the entire evening trying not to stare at Leo's face and sitting with her regrets.

'How are you finding it overall?' she asked Sam. 'The retreat? Has it been useful for you?'

'It's heaven,' Sam replied, quickly checking the contents of her glass. 'And I'm getting so much done. I think it's the peace and quiet. I should get my two books finished this year after all.'

'That's good.'

Leo and Martin drifted away, Martin gesticulating wildly. He appeared to be leading Leo to the buffet table.

'I guess you don't have to be so prolific, as each one of your books is a guaranteed success,' Sam continued. 'You can take your time. You're not constantly rushing things out there, hoping one of the damn things sticks.'

'It's about one a year, and I do work hard.' Olivia felt the need to defend herself. She also remembered when Leo had done the same. Their awful row in the library.

'Of course you do.'

'I'm not lazy . . .'

'Well, of course you're not! You've had how many books out now? Four?'

'Five, actually.'

'The latest being *The Milliner* . . . ?'

'. . . *on Mild Court Road*, that's right.'

Olivia hated this, this competitiveness. They were all on the same side, weren't they? It wasn't as though if one book did well, then others had to fail.

'But I bet your advances are really great, and keep you going for a long time, and then there's all those foreign rights deals . . .'

'Oh, look, there's a band setting up!'

Olivia motioned to the far side of the terrace where four young men dressed in black were taking to a tiny stage: tuning up instruments, executing a tap and a shiver on the drums, revolving a double bass with a flourish. They were a swing band with a Frank Sinatra type crooner who launched, once they were ready, into 'Strangers in the Night'.

'Oh, how I love *Italy*!' sighed Sam.

'How are we paying for this, by the way?' Olivia asked. 'Surely this party is not free?'

'There will be a hat going around at the end,' Sam said. 'We all pay what we believe the party was worth. And by the look of some of the high rollers here, I'm sure the restaurant is going to more than make their money back.'

She smiled pointedly at Olivia. Olivia smiled vaguely back. She allowed her eyes to flit to the buffet table. Martin was no longer to be seen, and Leo was talking to a very attractive woman with one of those glamorous headscarves swept tight over her crown and flowing to a big knot over her shoulder.

'How do you feel about Leo being here?' Henrietta asked. 'You literally ran away from him this morning.'

'I did not run away!'

Henrietta scoffed. 'You didn't even finish your eggs Benedict and that's not like you.'

'I had a very tricky chapter to wrestle with.'

'So you said. You know . . .' Henrietta indulged in a dramatic pause. 'I think you two have history,' she said shrewdly.

'Why would you say that?'

Henrietta tucked a frizzy stack of hair behind her ear. 'Well, let's just say the crackle between you could rival any lightning I've ever seen, or have written about, probably. As soon as he arrived at the gate of the villa it was like, *pow*!'

Olivia shook her head. 'There's no *pow*!' she insisted.

'There *so* is! What went down with the two of you on the publishing circuit?' Henrietta tilted her head at Olivia like a bird, but before Olivia could laugh her off with a retort, Henrietta cried, 'Look! He's coming over!'

The woman with the headscarf was now talking to a gentleman in a blue suit, and Leo was walking their way.

'I'm going to the bar,' Henrietta whispered. 'Enjoy him. He's absolutely gorgeous!'

Leo was holding a drink of lurid green and shrugging above it apologetically. 'I've been given this,' he said. 'I'm not sure what it is. Some kind of cocktail.' He grinned and Olivia's heart peeled away from the inside of her body and became weightless, rising inside her like a Chinese lantern. Yes, he was gorgeous. Yes, his eyes were the colour of Swiss mountainsides. His skin velvety and delicious. His mouth amazing. *Get down,* she told her heart. *Get down before you hurt yourself. You've been here before, after all.*

'It looks . . . dangerous,' she said, but wasn't everything here tonight? Wasn't just standing this close to him really dangerous? She'd finished her glass of rosé and she could feel the alcohol doing its work. Lowering her resistance, making her forget everything they couldn't be to each other. She could feel it ebbing to her fingertips, her toes – her rudderless, foolish heart. She'd been lonely, and he was here.

'It's bloody strong.' He paused above it. 'So, how are things? Apart from the obvious,' he added. 'I mean, wow, Olivia, your career. It's just gone . . .' He scooped an open palm towards the trellis roof in a manner that indicated stratospheric.

'Thanks. Yes, it has,' Olivia admitted. 'It's just been unbelievable. And yours, Leo. The movie . . . it's such great news.'

'It is.' He looked thoughtful. 'It was one of those things that took an interminable time to get the green light – so long, you assume it's never going to happen, and suddenly it just did!' He clicked his fingers and flashed her a soul-collapsing smile. 'But things are good?' he repeated. 'Life is treating you kindly? I heard . . .well, I heard that things didn't work out with you and James.'

'Where did you hear that?'

'Royal Ben.' Leo looked sheepish. 'You know he and your agent get together for drinks once in a while. Essential agent knowledge sharing . . . and you know what gossips they both are. So, you're no longer together?'

'No. Not for a long time. My decision,' she added, so Leo wouldn't think she had been dumped. The truth was James had proposed to her and she had said no. She had been happy with him, for a while. She had loved him but not enough. When it came down to it, she couldn't see herself being married to him, or having babies, being with him for the rest of her life. He wasn't what she needed, although she still wasn't sure what that was.

'I'm sorry to hear that.'

'Thank you.'

She had heard nothing on the circuit about Leo – about his private life, rather, and she wasn't going to ask him.

'How did you end up on the writers' retreat?'

'Alice pretty much forced me,' Olivia admitted. 'She thought it might be good for me.'

'Ah. You're *tolerating* it, then?'

'You could say that.'

'You haven't all been reading each other's chapters, then, each evening?' He smiled gently at her and she felt a bolt of pain for those happy days, when they were friends who read each other's work.

'No,' she replied, and she wanted to say, 'That was only with you,' but she didn't.

'And you're flying home on Friday?' They were skirting round so much, she thought. There was so much they couldn't say.

'No, I'm going on to my godmother's, in Venice.'

It was a visit Olivia had forced upon Gillian, to be honest. It was coming up to the eleventh anniversary of Charlie's death, and she and Gillian had still not made a repair, fixed the tear in their relationship. She wanted to see Gillian at her house on the Lido. Olivia wanted to ask her, finally, how she could make things right.

He nodded. 'Is she well?'

'Yes, as far as I know.'

'Funnily enough, Isaac is over here too,' he said. 'I'm meeting him near Pisa on Friday. But first I'm going to Siena to check on another day's filming. A different scene,' he explained happily. 'A *fight*.'

'A fight in Siena, wonderful.' She grabbed another drink from a passing tray. 'What's Isaac up to in Italy?'

‘Cooking. A big night at a friend’s farmhouse.’

‘Your mum not with him?’

‘No, she’s at home with the dogs.’ He cocked his ear. ‘I think you like this one,’ he said. The band had struck up a strange, acoustic version of Oasis’s ‘Champagne Supernova’.

‘I do.’

He stared at her, his hazel eyes unblinking. ‘Shall we dance?’

‘God, no!’ she replied, but Leo laughed and playfully took her hand. He swayed, he tried to engage her in a slow, comical jive. She was reluctant, confused. They had spoken about nothing. They had not addressed what had happened to them in London, but she giggled foolishly and tried to go with it, and not to love the electric shock of her hand in his.

‘I have two left feet,’ he whispered, ‘I don’t expect you know that about me.’

Suddenly, Clemmie and Sam and Henrietta were in their orbit, and Leo’s hand left hers, and they were all in a circle – laughing, shouting inconsequential things to each other over the music, calling for Martin to come join them. He dance-walked over with a drink in his hand, and the group of writers danced on the terrace of the little hillside restaurant in Tuscany, to the band who became livelier with each song.

More cocktails came around. The buffet food all but disappeared. At half past ten, they were all whooping it up to an Italian-accented version of George Harrison’s ‘Got My Mind Set on You’ and Olivia was twirling, rather drunkenly, in her fifties dress, but by the end of the song it was just her and Leo again. The others had dispersed to another corner of the terrace, to the bathroom together, to who knew where. All Olivia knew was that she was drunk, and Leo had hold of her hand again and she was feeling something she hadn’t felt in a long time.

Happiness. Not just book-success happiness or friends-happiness or that dull kind of contentment that gripped you on an autumn evening when you walked home through the park and scuffed at the leaves with the toes of your shoes, but giddy, light-headed happiness – that feeling you're not only glad to be alive, but you're *participating*.

A kind of happiness, despite everything, but a happiness she knew was fleeting and short-lived. A happiness that was tinged with regret and a familiar kind of longing.

'Would you like to sit down?'

The song had finished; the band had announced a twenty-minute break. Leo was blowing air up into the waves of his hair to cool himself down.

'Where?' They both looked around them. There were a few seats around the edge of the terrace, but they were all taken.

'Up there?'

There was a gap where the trellis ended and the back of the building began, and they looked up at the yellow stonework, now cast a honey-grey in the dusk, to spy three windows with green shutters, each with an ironwork balcony, Juliette style, and flowers in pots. The middle window and its balcony were wider, and the balcony had two iron chairs and a small table.

Leo took her hand again and suddenly they were inside the empty restaurant, looking for the stairwell, and up those stairs, and stealing along the first floor, through a room with a dining table with a plastic floral cover and a television on a lacquered cabinet, to the window at the rear with gauzy curtains pulled back, and out on to the balcony. They took to the chairs and grinned at each other with the thrill of making it up and out here, overlooking the pretty trellised roof of the terrace – and no one knew they were there, for no one else was looking up through the gap.

'Well,' said Leo, 'this is nice. Hang on!' He dashed back into the Italian living room and returned with a dusty bottle of screw-top red wine and two glasses.

'Won't we get in trouble?'

'I'll replace it tomorrow.' He unscrewed the top and poured them both a glass. 'You know, this is the equivalent of two characters sitting on one of those fire escapes on the outside of a tall building in New York,' he said. 'During a wild party.'

'Those people are usually teenagers.' She took a sip of her wine. 'Smoking cigarettes and complaining that neither of them has hooked up with the person they wanted to.'

She was thirty-six. Leo was thirty-seven; they weren't teenagers any more.

'So, how about you?' he asked her, his gaze focused completely on her. 'Was there anyone here you wanted to hook up with?'

Her eyes fell to her glass.

'Of course not. What about you?'

He answered with a soft look she didn't dare read. They sat and sipped their wine. The chatter from the party smoked gently up to them. The dark of the mountains in the distance framed their horizon. The night air was warm and sweet.

'Why are you happy to spend time with me?' she finally ventured. 'I walked away from you. I was jealous and insecure. Why are you OK with me?'

He kept soft eyes upon her. 'Because a lot of water has gone under the bridge since then. Because I was no angel, myself. You were right, I was arrogant, self-important, all those things. I made you my minion. Made you assist at all those events, not considering how you were feeling about your own book career. At the same time, I had designs on you, but no wonder you didn't want to take me up on any of them. I was awful.'

'I was worse,' she said sadly. 'I'm so sorry for how I was that day. I was so bitter.'

'It's OK,' he said. 'The publishing business is not for the faint-hearted. I understood how you felt. I get how you couldn't be around me.' Although that wasn't the only reason. Leo had his designs and she had her desires. She had simply shut them away in a box, that was all. Trapped them in her despair and her loathing of his success. He tapped at the back of his hand. 'I have to admit something.'

'What?'

'I knew you were going to be here at the writers' retreat. Alice told Ben. Ben told me.'

'Oh! Right . . .' She tried unsuccessfully to hide her surprise.

'So I decided to squeeze in coming to find you. I wanted to see you,' he said simply. 'I've missed you.'

And once again, the cocky charmer, Leo Greene, was almost replaced by a man with a soft voice and sincere heart. The version of a man she once thought she might love, if the circumstances were right.

'Right,' she repeated. She didn't fully trust the version of that man. 'You have designs again?'

He laughed. 'I was curious about you. Is there anything wrong in that? Are you happy to see *me*?'

'Happy is not quite the word . . .'

'But you can bear it?'

'I'm not sure. I'll have to think about it.' She thought for more than a second. 'You know, you could have reached out to me in London,' she said. 'If you *missed* me.' She didn't believe that was true; she believed he was just saying it. 'It would be quite easy to do.'

'It was never the right time,' he replied. 'But Italy is perfect.'

'Italy *is* perfect,' she admitted. She had been lonely and he had sought her out. He was able to forgive her transgressions at the London Library. He had offered her the chance to forgive his. Maybe they could be friends again. She looked out over the Tuscan skyline. Felt the warmth of the sweet night on her arms and neck, the cool of the iron beneath her bare feet, the heady holiday escape of the night, this night. And Leo, Leo Greene, sitting right next to her after all this time. Close enough to reach out and touch.

'I like sitting here with you,' he said.

'Me, too.' A confession. It just slipped out.

She looked at him, but now he was gazing out over the skyline, his handsome, unreadable face lit by the lights below and the glow of the moon. Her equal. Her sometime friend. Her one-time lover, Leo Greene, and she wondered what the rest of the night might hold.

Chapter Thirty

'Shhh!'

'What is it? Oh, God, it's a bloody peacock! Did you know there was a bloody peacock?'

'I think Margo might have mentioned one . . .'

'It's stalking me!'

'I swear it's not, Leo. Peacocks don't stalk. They're far too aloof.'

'I don't like the way it's looking at me. What if it does its thing?'

'What thing?'

'That swooshing thing, when the feathers go up, like in *Jurassic Park*.'

'You're an idiot!'

Two rather half-cut people were attempting to walk up the cobbled stone driveway to Villa Margo, a large peacock standing on the grass to their right, watching them.

'I've just never cared that much for birds . . .' said Leo. They staggered past the peacock, Leo staring at him suspiciously. '. . . since a damned seagull stole a bag of *frites* from me on the Riviera in 1992.'

Olivia laughed. 'How continental! You never told me this.'

'I was ashamed,' said Leo, which for some reason made Olivia howl with laughter. 'Hush,' he admonished, 'or you'll make him do his thing.'

The peacock stayed tightly composed, his little crown like a tiny hang-gliders' hammock, but the two creeping past him did not, and Leo tripped somehow on something – a stone, a twig, his other foot – and before Olivia knew it, he was lying on his back on the grass to the right of the driveway, feet in the air like a startled beetle, laughing his head off.

'Shhh! You'll have Margo out here!' She had no idea where the other writers were. In bed, probably. They had not been on the terrace of Nico's when she and Leo had eventually come down from the hidden balcony at the party.

'Clumsy idiot!' Leo muttered through his laughter. 'What a bloody clumsy idiot!'

She flopped down next to him on the grass, tried to put a hand over his mouth before she collapsed in giggles, too, and there they both were, helpless on the grass.

'I do have fun with you, Olivia,' Leo said eventually, and they got to their feet and made their way to the terrace, and then to the side of the pool – Olivia shoeless, Leo with his tie slung over his shoulder. He flopped on to one of the loungers, his face half in shadow, half-lit gleefully by the pool room light.

'Sit down,' he said. 'Let me look at you.'

'You've been looking at me all night.'

Olivia fell on to the other lounger. They both lay there, their heads turned, staring at each other. She wanted him, she thought. Yes, she was a little drunk, but something about Italy and this night and her desire for a connection with somebody made her feel he had the answers to all of her questions. That he could be her salve, her stay, her succour. She didn't want to be flopped on loungers with Leo by the pool, as lovely as the night air was, and the sound of the cicadas in the bushes and the full, ripe moon overhead. She wanted to be in his room, his bed – or hers. She wanted to remember every small detail about him. She wanted to learn still more.

She didn't care about the past and she didn't care about the future. She only cared about now – this moment. And she wanted to spend it in his arms.

'I need water,' she said. 'And I don't mean getting in the pool. I have water in my room.' Neither of them moved. Leo's eyes were as languid as the pool. She could feel her blood, her heart rising and falling in her chest, the soft pulse at her neck, her wrists. 'You'll come to my room?' she asked him, the very heart of her loud and clear.

'OK.' Leo stood up and held out his hand. This time, it was not the soft touch of once-lovers, nostalgic and hesitant, but the urgent contact of the here and now, as he slid his fingers to interlock with hers and held on tight.

In the villa, in her room, when they were standing close together, he made a sound, almost a groan. It came from somewhere deep within him and, in her, it stirred something she had not felt since they were last together. The touch of him was like a small fire; the way she gave into him with such immediacy a revelation, although it wasn't a surprise, as she knew it would be like this should they ever come together again. That it had to be this way between them.

He was caressing her chin. Her hand was at the back of his head, in his hair. Her other hand was gently undoing the buttons of his shirt, from the top to the bottom, until it was at the concave scoop of his stomach above the waistband of his trousers, and now he was unzipping her dress slowly at the side – how did he know? – and fiddling for the tiny mother-of-pearl button that fastened the teardrop cut-out at the nape of her neck, careful not to break it for it was delicate, like she was. He abandoned it for a moment, to place his thumb within the drop and rub small circles on her skin. And then the mother-of-pearl button was dealt with, and the dress simply became a piece of fabric that disconnected from her and fell away to the floor, and she was in her underwear, and she was unzipping his trousers and it was time to have her heart try to catch his again, like a swinging trapeze artist reaching for another in the dark, with just the dim light from the auditorium below to guide them.

'Maybe we shouldn't,' he said. He was tracing his forefinger over her collarbone and down into the soft hollow beneath it.

'Maybe we shouldn't what?' she murmured.

'Sleep together.'

'No?' she murmured, then kissed him once more, deeply, longingly.

He groaned again. 'No,' he whispered. 'Maybe it's better if we don't. If I get into that bed with you, who knows if I'll ever get out again.'

'Would that be such a bad thing?'

'I don't know. I don't know.' He pulled away from her, and she was so surprised, so disappointed, she wanted to cry out. What was he doing?

'Leo?' He was frowning. He was running his hand through his hair. He was stepping back from her. 'Leo? What's happening?'

'I don't know if this is the right thing to do,' he said. 'I feel we're rushing into this. You're drunk, I'm drunk. I don't want to take liberties.'

'You're not taking liberties! I want this. I want this, Leo. Hey!'

His hair was all mussed up. He had taken another step back. 'No,' he said. 'No. Let's not do this. It's too . . . monumental. It's getting us in too deep.'

'Why? It can mean nothing. It can mean nothing at all.'

She didn't believe that, but let him do so if it would let them continue.

'It won't mean "nothing". I can't. I can't . . .'

She knew it was over.

'You want to see how we both feel in the morning?'

She stepped back, too, now. Rejected, accepting. She inadvertently gave a little hiccup and they both smiled bashfully. The moment was truly over, the mood gone. Maybe it was for the best. She was drunk, and so was he. Perhaps this was unwise. Perhaps in the morning everything would look clearer and she would see this for the mistake it was. Perhaps he was right. It was too monumental. It could only lead to trouble.

She tried to steady her breathing. She tried to be sensible. She walked over to her desk and started randomly ordering her pens.

'You'd better go,' she said. 'See you in the morning.'

Chapter Thirty-One

Olivia awoke the next morning, far too late, with a horrendous hangover – the kind she hadn't had for years. The early morning sun was a bright butter-yellow, a beam of it slicing through the curtains to form a wide canal on the bed. She'd never had that glass of water. And she was sure someone was knocking on the door.

'Morning, sleepyhead,' Leo said, standing in the doorway dressed in linen trousers and a navy-blue shirt, holding his fedora in his hand. 'I'm driving to Siena today. Want to come with me?'

'What?' She rubbed at her eyes. 'I thought you had an epilogue to write.'

'They've brought the shoot forward by a day,' he said. 'The filming and the film set is in Siena. Would you like to come? I've hired an Alfa Romeo Spider; we'll be like Audrey Hepburn and Albert Finney in Two for the Road.'

'Didn't Audrey and Albert drive to the French Riviera?'

'Well, I'm not going *there*. The seagull, remember?'

Olivia smiled. They were both pretending they hadn't left each other the way they had last night, with him slipping out of her door in the small hours and her leaning against it after he had gone, wondering what on earth just had and hadn't happened.

'I'm supposed to be here for the last day of the retreat,' she said. 'What time even is it?'

'Half eleven,' he replied. 'You've missed most of it. Surely this will be better – an Italian road trip for two? I mean, it's only an hour to Siena, but it should be fun. Actually.' He looked sheepish. 'I wondered if I could drive you all the way to Venice, to your god-mother's, spend some time together. Stop off at a couple of places along the way.'

There was no reason to say yes to him, and every reason to say no. Last night's temptation had almost been a disaster. She had the retreat to complete. She was in danger of liking him too much – again. What would Sam and Henrietta say? What possible point was there in resuming their friendship that, at this moment and in last night's moments, seemed tenuous at best? How would she explain to Alice she had bailed out early and not finished the chapter she was supposed to be working on? But then again, Alice was to blame for Leo turning up in the first place. And Leo was a very tempting man, and Olivia was a lonely author who seemed to be up for saying yes.

Hadn't she jumped in a car with him before, and driven to Wiltshire? Would it really be so bad to jump in with him again?

'I won't get in the way? At the film set?'

'No, of course not. There's always loads of people hanging around.' He grinned at her as if to say, *Don't take offence.* 'So will you come?'

'OK, then,' she agreed. She was being uncharacteristically spontaneous. She was happy to miss the last day of the workshop. She wanted to go to Siena with him. She had no idea what he was doing, but somehow she wanted to come along for the ride.

'That's the spirit. The car's being delivered in fifteen minutes.'

'Right, well, I'll pack my stuff. And I said I'd call Gillian this morning. Give me half an hour?'

'Perfect. You won't regret it.'

Olivia brought up Gillian's number on her phone. She had asked for it a couple of years ago by letter, for emergencies, she had said, and Gillian had sent it in a letter back to her, with not much else in it except some brisk business news about the Guggenheim and a photo of one of her dogs. The visit, pressed upon Gillian by her god-daughter, had also been arranged by letter.

Gillian sounded out of breath when she answered the phone.

'Oh, hi, Olivia!' It was strange to hear her voice again after all this time, Olivia thought. She wondered how Gillian felt hearing hers. 'I'm just heading off to the Guggenheim. There's a new exhibit going up today and I've got a ton of things to do.'

'Fantastic! Hope it goes really well. I'm just checking things are still OK for Friday.'

'Friday?' Gillian sounded distracted, half out the door.

'Yes, when I'm coming, remember?'

'Oh, yes, Friday. Yes, of course that's OK. If I'm not here, just let yourself in. The key will be under the blue pot by the front door. Right, must dash!'

And the call was over. Gillian didn't really want her to come. Gillian was suffering her. Gillian felt captive. But Olivia needed to see her godmother, so long estranged. They needed to talk.

Twenty minutes later, she was wheeling her little suitcase to the boot of a cute-looking vintage sports car – its roof down – that Leo was patting proudly like a dog.

'Let me help you with that.' He reached for the handle of her suitcase.

'No, I can do it.'

Olivia placed the suitcase in the boot, next to Leo's and a rolled-up picnic blanket. He was holding the passenger door open for her.

'You don't need to do that, either.'

'No, I know. But I want to,' he said, grinning, 'Siena awaits.'

He closed the door and started the car's throaty engine. They purred out of the drive, and, at the gate, Leo gave a jaunty wave to the writers on the terrace.

'See you, guys!' he called out. 'I'm whisking Ms Sackville off to Siena. She won't be back, I'm afraid, but she'll see you in England sometime!'

Olivia gave a small, embarrassed wave from the passenger seat, especially as Leo was talking like someone from some long-ago era, and Leo roared off, leaving open mouths on the terrace.

'On the road again,' he said to Olivia with a smile, once they were down the hill and on the picturesque road away from the villa. 'It's like we just can't help ourselves.'

Which is exactly what she worried about, that they weren't helping themselves at all – that *she* wasn't – but for now, what did that matter? She'd never expected to arrive at a villa in Tuscany for a writers' retreat and leave it on a road trip with Leo Greene in a vintage Italian sports car. She'd never expected to nearly sleep with him again, and how much she'd wanted to. But life was full of surprises.

'You OK?' he asked as she wound down the window and let the soft breeze tickle her hair. The scent of olive groves drifted in through the window, the sun a morning concerto on the fields and the lanes.

'Perfectly,' she replied with a smile so warm for him it almost brought tears to her own sunlit eyes. This was dangerous, she thought. Dangerous for her heart. But her heart wasn't giving her any other choice.

They were on the road. Their path was set. And she had no idea where the road was going to end, and with what words.

Chapter Thirty-Two

Venice

Thursday 11 January 2018

The water taxi to the Guggenheim was slow, its engine a spluttering spit that threatened to peter out at any second. Another taxi, passing it at speed, hosted a fresh bride and groom. The smiling bride held on to her veil in the wind and spray. Her diminutive groom saluted merrily to other canal-goers from the feather and fluff of her bell skirt as their vessel coursed through the water like a palette knife through royal icing.

A little cold for a wedding dress, thought Olivia, in their slow boat to the Grand Canal, but perhaps wedding days were like wool winter coats and kept a person warm. The driver of the happy couple's boat beeped his horn, and several other boats around it responded, including their own, in carnival spirit.

'How lovely.' Frances sighed. She was seated next to Anthony, with Tanya the other side. On the opposite seat were Olivia, Leo and Meryn. 'I wonder where they're going? I mean, where are the other guests?'

'Perhaps they eloped,' suggested Tanya. 'Perhaps they wanted it to be just the two of them.'

'That's what Hamish and I did,' Anthony recollected, with a smile. 'A Highland fling for two – whiskey and tartan. A dream. Neither of you have been married, have you?' he asked Olivia and Leo.

'Nope,' said Leo.

Olivia shook her head.

'Not even close?'

They looked at each other.

'No,' they said in unison.

'Shame,' said Anthony, and he turned to Frances to immediately regale her with more tales of his idyllic wedding day.

Olivia swivelled in her seat. The grand white frontage of the Guggenheim was in their sights, its wide and low vista a pristine pause in the courtly faded line of taller Venetian buildings. She and Leo took in its central entryway – with four arched windows spanning either side and its grand steps, the green hedged flat-top of its roof.

Leo had knocked for Olivia at midday. She had opened the door to him holding an almond croissant on a tea plate in one hand, and a large china mug of coffee in the other.

'I didn't see you at breakfast,' he'd said, 'so I stole this for you from the kitchens.'

She had overslept, not intentionally, waking at nine thirty, but had avoided breakfast deliberately, and Leo. After she had helped him up from his bookish crash mat at the back porch of the Libreria Acqua Alta yesterday, Tanya had returned, as had Anthony and Frances, clutching bulging paper bags from a nearby bakery, and the four authors had travelled back to the hotel together. She and Leo hadn't spoken on their own again. Olivia had declined requests of a group dinner. She had gone to her room, switched the television on, ordered room service, drank two miniature bottles of vodka mixed with Coke from the mini bar, and slumped into bed to toss and turn all night.

They shouldn't have laughed like that. They shouldn't have talked like that. *Clumsy idiot, peacocks* . . . Him telling her he wasn't going to make any kind of wrong moves. She needed time, and she needed space; things she'd had for a long time without him.

'Thank you,' she'd said, taking his breakfast offerings. 'I overslept. But I'll be at the meeting point in time this afternoon.'

She had smiled politely. Closed the door quietly on his bemused face. Marvelled that, for Leo, each encounter between them here in Venice could simply evaporate like the ankle-deep waters of St Mark's Square after the *acqua alta*, while for her, they remained absorbed, a seeping papier-mâché-sodden part of her, weighing her down.

'Did your godmother have a farewell party on the roof of the Guggenheim, too?' he asked her now.

'She did.'

Olivia stared up at the grassy terrace on the roof, getting nearer and nearer. Her godmother had sent her one last postcard, not long after she'd first become ill: a photo of the Guggenheim on the front, and some sentences on the back about a perfectly warm night with young interns drinking champagne in plastic cups, dancing to Roxy Music and twirling around and around the departing Gillian like fairies. Olivia wished she had been there for that bittersweet farewell. She wished she could have seen Gillian's face, clapping as the others danced, inside the piped hedge border of the Guggenheim's picturesque flat roof.

'Almost there!' Meryn stood up. The water taxi putted up to the jetty at the white steps of the Guggenheim and wriggled into place. Its passengers disembarked.

Beth was waiting outside with the Italian book bloggers, her anorak zipped up to her neck. Felicity and Valentina were heads-down over a lectern set up at one end of the main gallery, in front of which wood-and-metal classroom chairs were set in rows. The mayor of Venice, Armondo Alessandro, was expected.

'The public won't be in here for another twenty minutes,' Felicity said, looking up at the authors. 'You can have a mooch around if you like. Familiarise yourselves.'

Olivia was full of awe and sadness on entering the airy exhibition space and its sense of calm and serenity, that her godmother had walked these cool marble floors, carrying papers or art books; directing the interns, instructing them in the hushed gallery rooms housing Pollocks and Picassos, on how to put the covers on the exhibits at night; talking to the curator about upcoming exhibits – sculptures, jewellery collections – in her forthright way.

'Excuse me.'

A young woman was behind her, long dark hair in a middle parting and wearing an olive-green shift dress and flat silver sandals. 'Are you Olivia Sackville?' she said. 'I'm Claire Martell. I used to be an intern here. I'm now assistant curator. I know your godmother, Gillian.' The young woman had a French accent. Soft blue eyes.

'Oh, how lovely!' Olivia exclaimed. 'I believe my godmother was happy here.'

'She was very kind to me,' said Claire. 'She used to bring in little treats, sugared almonds and lemon drops. She used to tell me things about life in London, and of her famous author god-daughter.'

'Really?' Olivia was so surprised.

'Of course. Actually, we have some possessions here of hers. Some papers. They were discovered at the back of a drawer a couple of weeks ago when we replaced the desk, and, as we knew you were booked to come, thought perhaps you could give them to her? Let me show you.'

Claire led Olivia from the gallery to a small, pristine office which smelled of lavender and linen, furniture polish and art books old and new. It had simple white walls, the green of an occasional potted plant. A Hermès scarf swooned over the back of a cream upholstered chair.

'Here you are,' said Claire, pulling a scroll of papers, secured with an elastic band, from the top drawer of a filing cabinet.

Olivia turned the roll in her palm. 'Thank you. What kind of papers are they?'

'I'm not sure. Old receipts, typed notes . . . I'll leave you with them, for a moment? I must make sure everything's ready for the mayor.'

Olivia nodded, and Claire left. Olivia prised the elastic band off the scroll and unrolled the papers, fanning them on the desk in the office.

Two were what looked like invoices, both for dresses, as Olivia knew the word '*vestito*' was Italian for 'dress'. There was an old ticket for the Venetian opera, tea-stained in one corner. A flyer in English for a special show at the Guggenheim – an exhibition of Picasso in 2015. And a clipping from a Venice newspaper about the 2012 carnival, when a late *acqua alta* had disrupted events but not spirits, and Andrea Bocelli had come to the city to sing. There were also two A4 posters, both featuring events at the Guggenheim – an evening with the curator, and a Salvador Dali retrospective. And a third thin piece of A4, clinging to the bottom of one of the posters, a typed piece of writing Olivia happened to recognise.

'Oh!' she exclaimed, peeling it free. She read it twice.

I saw a father and baby today at a library. The baby was sitting on her father's lap, in the children's corner, a muslin square caught in her fist and her father's attention equally captured. Love and tenderness, and constant kisses on the cheek and the forehead and the top of the head abounded. A look of pure love, no conditions, no boundaries – between a father and a daughter. A relationship that would only grow as the seasons turned and the years marched by . . .

It was what Olivia had written during the workshop at the library in Islington, about the father and baby. The piece of writing she had once posted to her godmother, but Gillian had never acknowledged. Yet she had kept it with her possessions and her keepsakes. How strange.

Olivia carefully gathered the papers, rolled and secured them with the elastic band again, placed them in her tote bag and left the office. Back in the gallery, Beth was hovering, seemingly waiting for her. Her pink pinafore dress was made of felt, huge green buttons at the shoulders.

'I'm really looking forward to the readings,' she said, approaching.

'I would say, "Me too",' Olivia replied. 'But they always terrify me.'

'Oh, really? But you're so good at them!'

'It's all fake confidence,' Olivia admitted. She was still trying to process her godmother having kept that piece of writing. 'I hate reading my own words out loud.'

'Are you reading first or is Leo?' Beth adjusted her glasses. They were standing in front of a polished bronze statue of a round-bellied bird.

'I am. He's last, I think. After Frances then Anthony.'

'I hope he reads the bit about the bucket,' said Beth, looking wistful.

'Sounds gruesome . . .'

'No, it's just really clever. I actually read something about him and his family last night,' she added.

'Oh, like what?'

'Well, I know his father is Isaac Feu . . .'

'*Step*father.'

'Oh. I didn't know that . . . Anyway, I read that Isaac has just done some huge restaurant deal, something he's been planning for years. There was a big photo of him, and one of Leo. You should look it up online.'

'Oh, really?' Olivia had no desire to see Isaac's scowling face again.

'Yes. It's a great photo of Leo.'

She imagined that most were. Guests were arriving now. Seats were being taken. Olivia saw Leo was holding court. Shaking hands, doling out smiles, chatting everyone up – male and female. Everyone looked thrilled with him, as usual, including a man in elaborate mayoral robes.

Meryn caught Olivia's eye and walked over. 'Showtime,' she said. 'You ready?'

'Ready as I'll ever be.'

Olivia took her copy of *The Curator on Church Street* from her bag, then gave the bag carefully to Meryn, who hung it over her arm. Felicity and Valentina went to the lectern and introduced the event, thanking everyone for coming. The four authors gathered behind them, lambs to the slaughter – or at least, that was how Olivia saw it. When she was announced as the first reader, the two organisers stepped aside, and Olivia walked forward to place her book on the lectern, opening it at the page she had marked.

She took a deep breath. Looked out into the crowd, and the first face she saw was Leo's.

'You got this,' he mouthed and, a little surprised, she began.

'*When Kath arrived at the bus stop in the early hours of the morning, heading for the museum, Justice was waiting for her . . .*'

She finished the excerpt to appreciative applause, Leo clapping the loudest. Blushing, she exited the stage. Frances was next. She confidently read the lively prologue of her novel, *Streatham*, eliciting laughs and the occasional gasp from the audience, and ended to solemn admiration, when she spoke of her teenage character, Marie, and the father she cares for.

'*Marie locks up at night. She switches the dishwasher on, she turns off all the lights downstairs, she helps her father in the bathroom, and she draws the curtains across in her father's bedroom before tucking him in and giving him a kiss. There's a photograph of them on the windowsill. A photo of when Marie was a baby, and her father was well. Her father is holding her up to the camera, their faces together. And now Marie holds her father up. Now she tucks her father in, and kisses him on the cheek . . .*'

Olivia thought of the roll of papers in her bag. Her godmother's receipts and miscellany, the snippets of her life here in Venice, and Olivia's words among them. She joined in with the applause for Frances when her reading came to a close, but she was listening for her godmother's footsteps across the marble floors.

It was Anthony's turn. He had everyone in stitches with an excerpt on his absent-minded valet, Terrence, falling into the pond at Cliftonville Manor.

Then Leo stepped up to the lectern with his book, joy in the eyes of everyone in the crowd. *Handsome devil*, Olivia thought, and not for the first time. There was a tab marked in his paperback copy, but he bypassed it, turning the pages instead to a later chapter.

It started with a scene at a market. The checking out of an alibi. But then Leo read on.

'*Ben had loved Martha from almost the first time he saw her.* Almost, *because the first time he saw her she had been covered in engine oil and wearing a baseball cap that said,* Eat Shit! *She worked the radio for the cab office but sometimes she fixed cars, too. She had efficiently rolled out from under a Ford Mondeo on a dolly and Ben had been sunk.*

'He found her bewitching. Funny. Challenging. He had tried to fall back out of love with her three, maybe four times. He had tried to stitch up his heart inside the pocket of his army surplus coat and not let her get to it. But she already had . . .' The crowd was rapt as Leo continued reading, the rumble of his voice undulating over them. *'When he solved the crime on Lancaster Street, it was because of her. Her delicate silver bracelet, her skinny wrist, angled by the cab office mic stand, had triggered something in Ben's brain – something about the victim – and had finally led Ben to the culprit. He owed Martha, but he didn't know how to repay her, as he didn't know if she would ever forgive him. But he had learned about forgiveness now, or at least, the way to try for it. He could see the way ahead of him, if he made the right moves. Took the right advice. Became a better man. He hoped one day to be worthy of her, to have her look at his face and say, "You give me everything I need."'*

When he finished his reading, he closed the book and looked out across the crowd. Olivia expected his smile to be cocky, but it wasn't. It was a slow, sad smile which was appearing to melt many hearts, including that of the mayor, but then he turned his gaze upon her, and he raised his eyebrows, just a touch, his eyes a slow fire.

'Thank you very much, Leo,' said Valentina, stepping up to the lectern as Leo receded from it. 'And that completes our readings this evening. Let's give another big round of applause for Olivia Sackville, Frances Holland, Anthony Beau and Leo Greene.'

There was polite, art-gallery applause. The line of authors fell away. Anthony grabbed Frances's arm and started gabbling to her about her prologue. Valentina and Felicity began arguing about the configuration of the chairs. Olivia and Leo were left standing together.

'Very nice,' said Leo appreciatively.

'And yours. Maybe I *should* read another one of your books sometime.' She smiled shyly at him. He had spoken about love. About resisting falling in love. About seeking forgiveness.

'I take it your two get together at the end?' Leo's eyes were gentle, his mouth a work of art. The soft lighting of the gallery only made him look more handsome.

'Of course, the happy ever after and all that. Not yours?'

'I don't know yet.'

'Oh, I thought you said Ben loses Martha?'

'I've got several more books to go in the series. I may have changed my mind about their future. Can Ben prove himself to Martha?' he asked, his eyes suddenly soft and serious.

'Or can Martha prove herself to Ben . . . ?'

Leo gave her a look that made time stand still. 'I like the idea of a definite ending for them though. A lasting one. Wouldn't that be nice?'

'It would.'

'Why didn't you join us for dinner last night?'

'I was tired.'

'Tired of me?'

'Maybe.' She would never be tired of Leo Greene.

'It was fun. And I thought we had fun yesterday, at the bookstore.'

'We did. Maybe that was the problem—'

'Time to mingle!' Valentina was in front of them, clapping her hands. 'And then, later, it's upstairs to the roof terrace for a little party! We have heating,' she added.

'Oh, great!' said Leo.

'Oh, great,' echoed Olivia.

Valentina started talking to Leo about his reading, asking him about the cab office, what it meant, what was a 'dolly'? Olivia was approached by some people from the audience, eager to talk about the passage she had read, about happy ever afters, and her writing process. Some champagne was served. The space buzzed with literary conversation.

Eventually, the champagne flutes were drained, and the audience trickled away, but the authors were still in demand. Leo was commandeered by Valentina again. Anthony and Frances started talking to Claire. And Olivia found herself in front of Magritte's 'Empire of Light', the famous, paradoxical painting of a nocturnal house under a sunlit sky.

A party on the terrace . . . She wasn't sure she wanted to stay for it. A party with Leo Greene was always dangerous, for starters. And the roof terrace, where the interns had danced around her ailing godmother, light as air . . . Gillian's memories would be up there, memories Olivia wasn't a part of. The words 'too late' once again carried across the months and the years like a little boat on the sea of Olivia's mind.

'Just make your way up whenever you're ready,' said Felicity, tapping her on the shoulder. 'There's more champagne, and we have music.'

'Music, champagne, and great company,' said Leo, who had turned around from his conversation with Valentina. 'What more can a man ask for?' And Felicity actually blushed, but Leo was looking straight at Olivia.

Chapter Thirty-Three

Olivia made her way up to the roof. Led by Felicity and Valentina, the others had gone into the arcade wing to look at some other exhibits, while Olivia had gone to the bathroom, so she didn't think anyone would be up there yet. But as she emerged on to the roof – a high, flat lawn, bordered by those dwarf hedges, overlooking the city – there was Leo. He was perched on one of the low bordering walls and he was talking on his phone.

Olivia stood on the threshold for a while, watching. Leo was chatting animatedly. Smiling. The occasional laugh. His words were carried away on the breeze to the canal beyond, so she could not decipher them. Was he talking to the same woman as before? When the call was finished, he placed his phone in his jacket pocket, pulled his orange notebook from his satchel to his lap and started scribbling in it, the curl of the damaged spine resting on his thigh, the press of the loose sheets tucked inside, just visible.

'Hello.' She had walked over.

He looked up. 'Hello.'

'I thought you were still downstairs.'

'I came up.'

'What are you doing?'

The terrace had a blazing patio heater stationed in each corner and the one by Leo gifted a mellow glow to the side of his face, like he was in candlelight.

'Making a list,' he said. 'Ideas for a new book.'

'*Murder at the Guggenheim*?'

Above them, the grey clouds of hovering dusk were readying to make themselves disappear into the night. The rooftop was an amber glow against soft grey; a platform from which to enjoy the pretty lights of Venice, coming on one by one.

'Something like that,' Leo replied. 'A murder in a museum could be really interesting, I think.'

'What sort of things do you have on your list?' She sat now, as she wanted to see.

'Fish out of water, artsy people. A stolen sculpture,' he said, showing her his open page. 'White space. Cool marble. Moneyed accents. I'm thinking one, maybe *two*, murders,' he added. 'A beautiful stranger.'

'That's a great list,' she said. 'And always a good idea to have a beautiful stranger.'

'Yes, I think so. It's a starting point, at least – something to work from.' He frowned, scribbled something else at the bottom of the list: '*The local mayor*. Do you still write little scenes wherever you go?'

'Yes, I do.' She thought of the scene her godmother had discovered, now in her bag.

'Written any since you've been here?'

'Of course.'

'Do you show anyone these days what you're working on? Before anything goes to your agent, I mean?'

'No,' she said. 'I used to have someone who was really good at reading for me. But these days I just rely on myself.'

They stared at each other. She liked the play of shadow on his face. The light in his eyes, eyes staying on her for far too long. He looked like he was about to say something, but then voices sounded.

'Ah. Here they come,' he said.

The other authors and Meryn and Tanya were wandering out on to the terrace, Claire and the curator, Sofia, close behind, with three interns. Then the mayor, Beth and the Italian book bloggers. Between them, they were carrying small crates of champagne, wobbling trays of glasses. They wore jackets over dresses. Shawls wrapped over shirts. The mayor was wearing a mohair trench coat over his suit.

Tanya held a speaker; she set it up in one corner and attached it to her phone. The lull and lilt of Andy Williams singing 'Music to Watch Girls By' drifted over the roof and up into the sky. They talked in clusters in the glow of the patio heaters under a night sky, silver and gold.

The light was ambient, the music timeless: the sugar-crusted smoothness of the old crooners – Sammy Davis Jr, Burt Bacharach, Tony Bennett; the husk of Ella Fitzgerald and Billie Holiday. The interns disappeared and returned with a tray of bellinis and a picnic basket of mini savoury tarts: mozzarella and basil, smoked salmon and crème fraiche, prosciutto and honeydew melon. Then hot soup from a nearby trattoria – minestrone – in pretty bowls and huge soup spoons. And Meryn's wife, Junie, appeared, fresh from Milan, to much delight and hugs all round. She brought Disaronno and a bag with shot glasses in, releasing more delight. And Tanya started singing along to Billie Holiday in a startingly high voice, and everyone stopped to listen.

Always, Olivia was aware of Leo. Where he was, who he was talking to, what he might be thinking as he sipped his liqueur.

The music changed to something more up-tempo. The Mavericks – 'Dance the Night Away', and spirits were high enough, this Venice night, for shouts of 'I love this one!' and a spot of swaying to turn into a dancing circle of people with lit-up faces up there on the roof. And among them danced the living ghost of Gillian Goddard, lighter than air.

Leo was singing along, full of energy and gusto, his two left feet entertaining them all. Olivia tried not to recall another evening in Italy when they had danced, and she'd thought – mistakenly, once again – there might be another chance for them to be perfect.

'Hey, Leo!' Tanya was waving to him. 'Can you help me with something?'

'What's the trouble?' Leo's face was flushed. Olivia's heart was way too full.

'Sofia the curator needs a chair. A proper one, not just the edge of the roof. There's one down in the office – would you be OK to go and get it?'

'Sure,' said Leo. 'Give me a minute.' He turned to her. 'Want to come with me, Olivia?'

'Me?'

'Could you? I might need a hand.'

'OK,' she replied before she had even thought about it at all.

The gallery was now only dimly lit. The interns had placed the hessian covers on the paintings; the sculptures cast soft shadows on the floor. Inside the office, one small lamp in the corner illuminated the ordered space.

'This one?' Leo gestured to the only chair in the room. It was cream, and button back.

'I guess so,' Olivia said. She was not sure what she was doing down here. Why Leo had asked her. But now they were alone together, she knew her heart was beating faster and that all her senses were pricked up, watching, waiting.

Leo sat down on the chair. 'Harder than it looks,' he observed. The open door behind him was kissing the back of the chair so he pushed it gently and the door closed with a click. 'Oops,' he said, with a bashful smile.

'You don't need me,' Olivia said, walking towards it. She would deny her senses, not give them something to get excited about. 'I'm going to go back up.'

'Really? Could we not talk for a while?'

She paused at the door. 'We've talked a lot since we've been here.' And she didn't want to talk in a room with a closed door and dim lighting. She went to turn the handle, but the door wouldn't budge.

'I can't get the door open.'

'Really? Let me have a go.'

Leo got up. He tried the handle, pulled at the door – nothing.

'Oh no.' Olivia tried it again, and the door was stuck fast. 'What do we do?'

'Have you got your phone on you?'

Olivia shook her head.

'No, me neither. Well, there's no point yelling like maniacs. There's no one out there. So, I guess we just sit tight until they send a search party. Here, take the chair.' He gestured to it. She took off her coat, placed it on the desk, and sat down.

'You're right,' she said with a smile. 'This is singularly uncomfortable.'

Leo shrugged his coat off and laid it on top of the filing cabinet. He sat down on the floor, his back against the wall, and started undoing the lace of his left shoe.

'I bought them this morning in a chichi shoe shop just off St Mark's Square,' he said. 'They're killing my feet.' He eased off the shoe with relief, revealing purple socks, and set it on the floor. He started on the other one. 'Damn! I've done it too tight.' He stopped fiddling with his shoelace and looked up at her. She looked down at him. 'I need your nails,' he said.

She raised her eyebrows. The room was silent but for the soft hiss of the radiator and the beating of her heart, which surely he must hear? His eyes were hazel pools of light; hers couldn't be dragged from him. She saw a swallow pulse up and down his throat.

'Why don't you come down here?'

'I don't think so.'

But she slipped. She always slipped when it came to Leo Greene. She got off the chair and came and sat down on the floor next to him, folding her legs underneath her skirt. She leaned over and undid his lace, trying not to look at his face. Leo took the shoe off and placed it next to the other one.

'That's better,' he said softly. 'Now my dancing might improve.'

'Unlikely,' she replied, but her blood was bobsleighing around her body. He was too close; they were too alone. This wasn't right, but it was also really, really unbearably, confusingly, giddyingly wonderful. Why else was she down here?

'It's lonely in Venice, don't you think so?' he said, staring at her.

She laughed a nervous laugh. 'We're surrounded by people.'

'I know, but it's the romance here, isn't it? The architecture, the beauty. It makes me *feel* a little lonely.'

She couldn't bear to look at him, kept face-forward. *What about the woman you keep speaking to?* she thought. 'I can't imagine you ever feeling lonely.'

'Well, I do, sometimes, in a room full of people.' She made the mistake of turning her head towards his. 'You never made me feel like that.'

She sighed. 'You left me, then I left you – when we were friends. Then we left each other. A sad little three-act play we both would have walked out of halfway through if we'd gone to see it.'

'I liked being in that play with you.'

'Did you? When it was both a tragedy and a farce?'

'I liked it,' he repeated, and his gaze made her breathing feel exaggerated. 'I haven't seen another play I've been as interested in. And maybe we're only at the interval. Maybe the play's not over.'

She looked at him. His soft eyes, his eyelashes. 'What are we doing here, Leo?'

'Sitting on a floor in an office in a museum . . .'

'I know that, but . . .'

'You're still very, very pretty, you know that?'

'I'm nearly forty.'

'So? What's that got to do with anything? You're beautiful, and you'll always be beautiful to me, even if you live to be a hundred . . .'

'I won't live to be a hundred . . .'

'I'd like to be around to find out.'

'Stop it!' Her body felt like it didn't belong to her. It was a pulsing, charged thing, no longer under her control.

'What if I don't want to stop?' He tried to take her hand; she managed to pull hers back. 'Please don't tell me you don't feel it, too. Please don't tell me it's gone?'

She shook her head, trying not to reveal how much her body was shaking. 'It's Venice,' she whispered. 'It's what Beth said about our books. That we both wrote the same scene. It's what we've said tonight, about bringing our characters together again. A definite ending to a love story. It's making us overthink . . . it's making things . . . dangerous.'

'I like dangerous things with you.' He spoke in a whisper, too. A magnetic, magical, intoxicating whisper. 'I've tried not to admit that to myself, but it's true.'

'You said you were going to be careful here.' His face was close to hers. Her breathing was heavy. She swallowed.

'I might have lied. It's not natural for me to be careful. I'm spontaneous. You know that. It's my fatal flaw.'

'Please don't . . .' But she didn't move.

'Why not?' He brought his face even closer, and she felt her heart might explode right out of her.

'*Our books . . . can our characters prove themselves to one another?* Oh God, Leo, I don't know. In another world I could almost imagine . . .'

'That we could write our way back to one another . . . ?'

He leaned forward and placed his lips on hers. They were soft and warm. He tasted of honeydew melon. He kissed her and she kissed him back. He closed his eyes and she closed hers. He questioned with his tongue, and she answered. He placed a hand under her chin, a cupping motion – *just like he always did, just like he always did* – and she ran her hand into the soft waves at the back of his head. He murmured, and she sighed, or was it a moan? She didn't know. She didn't know anything any more. He pressed his body closer. She shifted hers so he could allow it to happen.

And then the door opened.

Through it came Claire, the assistant curator.

'Oh, sorry!'

They had pulled away from each other. Olivia had snatched her hands, both of which had been in Leo's hair, back down by her sides. She stood up, adjusting the waistband of her skirt. Leo grabbed one of his shoes and started casually putting it back on.

'Thank you for rescuing us,' Olivia said stiffly. 'Who knows how long we might have been stuck down here?'

'I'm sorry,' repeated Claire, looking highly flustered. 'This door does get jammed sometimes. I was just coming down to get some more napkins.'

'Does Sofia still need the chair?' uttered Leo, dealing with the other shoe.

'Oh, no, I think Sofia's gone home. I'll go and check . . .' And, pink-cheeked, Claire was gone.

‘That shouldn’t have happened.’ Olivia grabbed her coat and started putting it back on. She was still breathing hard.

‘Why not?’ Leo’s face was earnest and endearing. ‘It was really nice. Didn’t you think it was really nice?’

‘It still shouldn’t have happened. I don’t think it’s good for either of us.’

‘Kissing you in a locked room? Felt good to me.’ He took up his coat, too, but held on to it.

‘We’ve crossed the line.’

‘I don’t like the line. I *wanted* to cross it.’

She shook her head. ‘I can’t do this again, Leo,’ she said. ‘I can’t go there.’

He stared at her, a curious look in his eyes. ‘You’re really *very* beautiful,’ he said.

‘Leo . . .’

‘I’ve missed it, kissing you. I’ve missed *us*. I’ve missed that little mole on your neck you can only see if you get really, really close. Remember in Tuscany how we—’

‘I try to forget Tuscany!’ she cried. ‘I try to forget it every day!’

‘I think I’d like to *remember* it every day. Before it all went wrong—’

‘It couldn’t have gone more wrong, Leo! Can I forgive you? Can you forgive *me*? Can we really do that? Tuscany should have been where we left it. We should have left everything there, that night. The things that were said . . . everything . . . Didn’t it all just prove we weren’t right for each other? That we *aren’t* right for each other?’

‘If I could do that night again, I would,’ Leo said sadly. ‘Believe me, I’ve been through it so many times.’

‘But we *can’t*!’ she cried. ‘The same circumstances would have led us to exactly the same scenario, the same hurt – don’t you understand? We can’t change *anything*!’

'So you'll do the same as you did that night? You'll run away? Drive off into the sunset in the passenger seat of a Fiat 500?'

'No,' she replied. 'No, I'm not going to run. I'm going back upstairs, to the party, and I'm going to dance and chat to people and have a good time – but forgive me if I don't come over to talk to you. Forgive me if I try not to catch your eye. Forgive me if I can't *do* this, OK?'

Leo shook his head. He exhaled slowly. Messed up his hair above his right ear. 'I've gone wrong,' he said softly. 'I've jumped the gun. I haven't done this right. I'm sorry, Olivia.' He shook his head sadly. 'I hope we get another opportunity to talk, this trip,' he said to her. 'I want to make things right.'

'No,' she said to him. 'No. It's too late. It's always been too late. Make another phone call. Leave me alone.'

Olivia was true to her word. She didn't run. She walked up the stairs and back to the terrace and the party. She laughed and made conversation. She listened to anecdotes and to Fleetwood Mac. She sipped champagne and nibbled on the tiny tarts. She didn't catch his eye, but she could feel him. She could feel him everywhere – behind her, in front of her, over in the corner. She could still feel his lips on hers. And at about a quarter past midnight she felt he was leaving, and, with a heart full of sorrow, yet again, she turned to see Leo give Beth a quick kiss on the cheek and slip away.

Chapter Thirty-Four

Tuscany

Thursday 6 August 2015

The charmingly cracked, burgundy leather seats of the Spider were low. The retro radio in its black-and-cream dashboard crackled and cut out constantly. The car smelled beautifully of lemony furniture polish, old oil and aged rubber.

'You need leather driving gloves and some sort of cap,' remarked Olivia, as she and Leo purred down the winding valley lane from Villa Margo, intense yellow wheatfields to their left, green rolling hills to their right. Cicadas were humming in the hedgerows. A church bell was tolling from some distant village.

'Not in this heat,' Leo said with a smile, going straight over at a fragrant little junction.

It was scorching. The sun was behind them, a jolly friend. They picked up speed and soared through dreamlike Tuscan roads that wound through gold and green countryside studded with tall, thin cypress trees watching them like soldiers, past raked-straight lines of vineyards, under the fulsome bright blue of the sky. Olivia's hair was buffeting everywhere. She gave up on scooping it up with her hand and pulling it into a makeshift ponytail, and let it fly free.

'Are you hungover?' Leo asked her.

'Not now.'

'Do you want to find something else on the radio?'

She nodded, twiddling with the old-fashioned knobs until she came to a pop music station, and who should be playing but Phil Collins, fizzing and fading in and out with 'Two Hearts'.

They grinned at each other.

'Someone is always playing Phil Collins somewhere,' Leo said. 'Even in Italy.'

'I don't mind a bit of Phil now,' Olivia admitted. 'The older I get, the more he grows on me.'

'Quality will always be recognised eventually . . .' said Leo, looking pleased. 'Would you like a mint?' He was opening the glovebox, reaching for a green-and-white striped packet.

'Oh, they're spearmint,' she said, taking it out for him. 'I don't trust spearmint.'

'Try one, they're nice.' She shook her head and he grinned. 'Suit yourself. Get one out for me, though, please.'

She peeled off the silver paper at the end, eased out a green disc and placed it between Leo's lips, letting her fingers linger there for a couple of seconds, knowing she was crossing that line again, but there was something about Italy, something about Leo, that continued to stir things up for her. Continued to make her wonder if she was ready to fall. Not for a friend, not for someone from a different world, but for her equal, her lost chance, Leo Greene.

They streamed along, driving leisurely. Sometimes, Olivia grew drowsy and nodded off to the symphony of the engine and the cicadas. Sometimes, she stretched her arm beyond the window and fluttered her fingers in the rushing air. But not once did she question what she was doing here on this adventure. She was living in the moment – this moment – for as long as it lasted. The car, the sunshine, the radio, the being with him. A small slice of heaven.

Leo slowed the Spider and pulled into a small, stony lay-by, where the plummet of a green valley rolled out before them. He switched off the engine.

'Thought I'd stop. What a view!'

'Isn't it just? I feel like we're in a painting, it's so gorgeous. I bet you loved writing your scenes set in Tuscany.'

'I did.' The way he was looking at her set her heart off racing. 'And I'd like to write another one, right here with you, if that's alright.' And with her heart thumping in her chest, and with the Italian sun basking over the bonnet and that gorgeous view spread before them like a picnic blanket in an EM Forster novel, Leo kissed her through her half-closed eyes, until Olivia spied a butterfly had landed on the steering wheel, making them both laugh, before it skittered off again.

'That was a surprise,' she said. 'You ran away from me last night.'

'I know,' he replied. 'I'm sorry. But I had to. I had to run away from you last night, and I had to kiss you now. I'm sorry,' he repeated, and Olivia wondered why. 'We should be in Siena by twelve,' he added. 'And then tonight – would you like to drive to Bologna? It's a bit out of the way, but we can go via Pistoia, which is wonderful, and there's a little place in the city I know where we can stay tonight. An old townhouse, views of the piazza. And tomorrow afternoon, I'll drive you to Venice.'

'Sounds lovely.' She wondered, did he mean they would share a room? Why would they not? He had just kissed her, last night they had been close – so close – so surely he didn't mean to be only friends? Her question and his answer did not help her. 'What are we doing here? You and me?' she asked him. She couldn't help but ask; the words simply escaped her. 'What is this thing? This road trip?'

He started up the engine. 'I'd just like this opportunity to be with you,' he said, 'as long as you want that, too? Shouldn't we just seize it? Seize the moment?'

She nodded. She was already storing everything about this moment that she would cherish in memory. The stationary car overlooking the lush vineyard, its engine ticking and popping under the bonnet. The warm sunlight dappling through the trees of the valley. Leo's lips.

They pulled out of the lay-by, a frown of concentration on Leo's face, leaving that view in the rear mirror, but there were plenty more. A tiny church on a hillside, flanked by a nestle of cypress trees. A bird soaring through the stretch of a lacey, pulled-apart cloud. A lane winding to the distance like in a child's story book.

As they drove past a field of tall, nodding sunflowers, she asked him, 'What sort of scene is it? The film?' She had decided to move on to safer ground, for both of them.

His eyes remained on the road. 'It's a fight scene between Ben Midnight and the man he suspects of killing a woman in North London, but he doesn't have any proof. He tracks him down to Monteriggioni and confronts him in the piazza and they start brawling. That's the scene. We should be there in about twenty minutes, and you'll see it for yourself.'

'Monteriggioni? The walled town? I thought we were going to Siena?'

'Little surprise.' Leo smiled.

'Oh, fascinating!'

She'd seen it in a travel programme, but in real life it was even better. Atop a hill, Monteriggioni was an ancient medieval village encircled by a stone wall with fourteen imposing watchtowers and was the kind of enchanting place that made a curious author, arriving by road in a vintage sports car, gasp when it was first glimpsed, and sigh when it was driven into.

They parked in a small cobblestoned alleyway just behind Piazza Roma, and walked past Santa Maria Assunta church to a cordoned-off area of the square where there was a flurry of activity: people wearing headsets, people fussing around two actors – one with a prosthetic gash in his cheek, the other she knew to be a notorious womaniser. Leo was commandeered immediately; Olivia was gestured to a low wall overlooking the piazza where she could observe. She watched Leo take a canvas director-style chair and a big pair of headphones. She watched him leaning forward, engaged in the action as part of the scene was set up and shot. She watched as he concentrated – a frown, a laugh – take after take. He sat back in his chair while a shot was being blocked and caught her eye. He gave her a happy wave, and she was happy, too. Happy enough. To be in Italy with him, without direction.

Afterwards, they drank sparkling water and ate a lunch of figs, parma ham and goat's cheese in a trattoria at the edge of the square. They wandered the city in the sunshine, talking no more of past lovers, but of great loves – food and movies and books. They stopped again, for sodas and ice cream. They discussed Scorsese, Coppola, Fellini and Capra; they talked about *La Dolce Vita* and *It's a Wonderful Life*.

At 5 p.m., they returned to the Spider and set off for Bologna, arriving just before seven. Leo parked outside a tall, stone town-house that looked like it had been some kind of fortress in a former life: battlement windows, latticed and grilled; red bricks sooted by time; an imposing, panelled wooden door.

Inside, at reception, Leo booked two rooms, and Olivia said nothing. But on the stone stairs, going up to their rooms, she asked him, 'Do you have a girlfriend?'

'No,' he replied. 'Meet downstairs at nine?'

And at 9 p.m., as church bells tolled from Piazza Maggiore, they met in the lobby, showered and dressed for dinner.

'I'm taking you to the best undiscovered restaurant in the city,' Leo told Olivia. 'I like the dress. Very *Roman Holiday*.'

She was wearing something straight out of the wardrobe of Audrey Hepburn: a white short-sleeved blouse tucked into a belted full skirt, and kitten heels.

'You need to lint-roller your trousers,' she replied. 'They have fluff on them.'

She immediately pulled a roller out of her bag and handed it to him. Doing it herself seemed too intimate, and she didn't know where they stood on that.

'Can you do my shoulders?' he asked her, after the trousers were done.

He handed the roller back to her. She quickly did each shoulder of his shirt for him, not that they needed it, trying not to look at his lovely face, smiling at her.

'See. This is why I need you in my life,' Leo said, but she wasn't sure if that was true. Still, he took her hand as they left the hotel. Olivia didn't know *what* she wanted long-term, but tonight she only wanted Italian food, the night sky and Leo Greene, at whatever level he wanted her.

They walked along narrow streets, sallow moonlight peeking through gaps in the ancient buildings. There were a lot of people about: evening strollers, early diners who had already dined, babies in pushchairs kicking pudgy feet into the warm air as the wheels rumbled over the cobbles. Olivia tried not to stare into the pushchairs; she tried not to smile too much at the babies as they trundled past. For some time she had known she was ready, at last, to have a child, but time and fate was rolling on by, too fast, too transient, to stop and notice.

They found themselves on a short bridge over dark water.

'A canal?' Olivia stopped and looked into the glistening channel of water.

'I think so,' said Leo. 'The only one remaining here, and only glimpsed in places.' He nudged her onwards to a short, cobbled passageway, where an open door and a warm welcome was waiting for them.

Casa Angelo was a tiny wood-and-stone bar and restaurant full of dark mahogany tables, mallard-green ladder-back chairs, horizontal bottles of wine strapped to the walls on iron brackets and the background music of Vivaldi. The portly maître d' was charming and effusive and insisted they try the best pizza, pasta and burrata in the city.

'This place is wonderful.' Olivia set down the menu; she had chosen. 'How do you know about it?'

'Robert Defrey,' Leo said, unblinking. 'It's a restaurant he always bangs on about, whenever anyone mentions Italy.'

'Robert . . .' She remembered that name. Cressie, his daughter, at Foxes, and her doe eyes. 'Did he invest in Isaac in the end?'

'Close to,' Leo said. 'There's a deal in the works at the moment. What wine would you like?' He passed her the drinks menu.

'That was a long time coming. I thought it was going to happen years ago.'

'It didn't. The stars never aligned for it, but Isaac's latest incarnation of Confit has failed. It's been kept out of the press, but he's proved too flaky to get an investment with another bank, and his TV work has dried up as he's too volatile and difficult to work with. He's on the verge of bankruptcy but refuses to sell the house. Everything is resting on Robert lending him some cash and it's hopefully happening now.'

She was going to ask about Cressie, but she stopped herself. Why bring that ghost to the table? She conjured up a memory of her in the London Library, in the queue to get Leo's book signed, the look on her pale heart-shaped face.

'Balth never made his great fortune, then?' she asked Leo instead. Another spectre at the feast. 'What's he up to now?'

Leo pulled a face. 'He's coming tomorrow night to Isaac's meal at the farmhouse,' he said. 'Jetting up from the South of France where he's been running a bar. Which wine shall we go for? The Chianti or the Bolgheri?'

They ordered a bottle of Chianti and two courses. They talked to the waiter about where the burrata was made and how the pizzas were hand-stretched. The starters were brought to the table – as well as a burrata to share; they had both gone for the creamy garlic prawns. Olivia was hungry.

'Isaac makes something like this,' Leo said, forking up another prawn. 'Except he wraps each prawn in pastry and flambés it.'

'It's delicious.' Olivia tried another mouthful, stole another glance. 'Are you looking forward to seeing him tomorrow?'

'His Italian show meal? As much as I ever am.'

'Are things better now between you?'

'Better? How do you mean?'

'Well, is he nicer?' A member of the waiting staff swapped Vivaldi for Enrique Iglesias on the stereo.

He laughed. 'I don't think Isaac could ever be "nice".'

'No, I suppose not. It certainly wasn't when I knew him. I just wondered if he'd mellowed.'

'*Mellowed?*' Leo smiled carefully. 'Absolutely not. Did you hate him?' he asked seriously, staring at her curiously over his raised fork. 'When you met him?'

'No, I just didn't get him. I thought he was quite cruel to you.'

For the first time in a long time, she thought about it. She thought about what she had overheard that time, years ago, at Foxes. What Isaac had said about Leo. Isaac was cruel. Isaac didn't see Leo as his son, only Balth. Isaac was tolerating Leo for Caroline's sake.

'Cruel?' Leo's gaze narrowed a little.

'Or you could see it as *character building* . . .'

'Do you not like my character?' Leo was smiling, but something in his eyes told her he was combative, on the defence. He seemed angry.

'Yes, of course I do.'

They finished their starters. Drank more wine. A waiter arrived with a tray he set up on a stand, and started setting out plates of *bistecca alla Fiorentina*, sautéed cabbage, and anchovies in garlic and olive oil.

The steak was tender, the anchovies salty and tart, the wine rich and delicious. The doors were flung open to the hot and sweet night air; a car horn blared and a gaggle of teenagers walked past – boys in shorts and t-shirts, pulled-up white socks and sliders. One leaped forward and grabbed another by the shoulders, making him jump, then they dissolved into laughter.

Leo watched the group as they disappeared. He seemed on edge. Disjointed. Quiet. He picked up his phone. Checked it. Set it down again.

'Are you OK?' she asked him.

'I'm fine,' he said. There was a beat. Then, suddenly, he launched into something. Words she wasn't expecting. 'Isaac used to like to scare me,' he said. 'When I was a kid.'

'Oh? Did he? What do you mean?' Olivia set her fork down on her plate.

Leo's hazel eyes were intense on hers. 'Well, it was stupid things, like he would jump out on me when I came out of the bathroom.' He smiled ruefully. 'Or he would trip me up, stick his foot out as we were walking. Knock on my bedroom door but not be there when I opened it. Just stupid stuff. I would screech, then he would laugh and ruffle my hair. Tell me to "man up".'

'You've never mentioned this before.' She looked at him carefully, his beautiful hazel eyes reflecting the candlelight.

'No. He once did something at a canal,' Leo said, staring out of the open doors as though the canal they had crossed was in danger of rising up and crawling along the cobbles into the restaurant. 'It was ridiculous, really . . .'

'Tell me.'

He looked back at her.

'We were out on the canals, a barge holiday. In Wiltshire. The Avon and Kennet Canal, going through one of the locks. Isaac had just opened the lower lock and the water was starting to run out and the boat go down. I'd never experienced it before, and I didn't know what was happening. He grabbed me and started shouting, "We're going down! We're going down!", pretending it was never going to stop, and I was terrified because you believe an adult, don't you? – especially when you're seven – and I was crying and clinging on to him but of course we did stop eventually, and the gates were opened and we went through the lock and he started really laughing, proper belly laughing, as though it was the funniest thing he'd ever seen. So, I laughed, too, you know.' Leo's smile returned. 'He toughened me up, I suppose. Stopped me being a sensitive little drip. You might say it was cruel, but I don't.'

'Then why are you telling me?' she asked gently.

Leo's expression was blank. 'I really don't know. I've never told anybody else this. Nobody's ever really challenged me on Isaac before.'

'Is there anything else?' she asked him tenderly, her heart softened towards him. He looked boyish, unshielded. 'Anything else you want to say?'

Leo's face changed. His reply was snappy. 'What are you, my therapist suddenly?' he asked her.

'Do you have one?'

'Of course not! Don't believe in them! What, you think I need one?'

'You tell me.'

She couldn't read him. There had been many times on this trip so far when she couldn't read him. There was something behind the merry chat and the sunshine and the kisses. And if it was because of Isaac, she wanted to know.

'Well, how about this?' Leo said sullenly, and the words just fell out of him, like rocks tumbling down a well. 'He packed me off to boarding school and never wanted me to come back in the holidays. He put a lock on the fridge so I couldn't access anything between meals. He never said hello to me when I entered a room. He bought me lots of books so I would shut myself in my room, or the bathroom, and not bother him. But maybe that's just what busy dads do,' he added, with a terse smile.

'I think you're making excuses for him.'

'No.' He took a slug of his wine, tapped his fingers at the corner of the menu. 'So, what are you thinking for dessert?' His voice was now full of levity. He was smiling again, one eye creasing into a soft wink. He'd mentally moved on.

'Something chocolatey,' she said. But then she asked him, 'And your mother? Do you feel she never stood up for you enough?'

'Something chocolatey,' Leo repeated briskly, and he ordered them both chocolate gelato with an amaretti biscuit. She ordered a mini hot chocolate to go with it. He ordered a beer. They had returned to safer ground. They had climbed out of the ravine and they were now standing in the sun, blinking at the world around them.

Yet she continued to watch him very carefully. His face remained bright, open, and he never answered her question, but he had confessed something really important to her. He had shown his vulnerability and it had moved her. She knew she was falling, falling for him. For the man with the boy still inside him. For the writer she shared equal footing with. For the Leo Greene she had known for a long time.

'So? Venice tomorrow,' he said. 'What are you and godmother going to do together?'

'I don't really know,' Olivia replied. 'She seems tremendously busy.'

'I'm sure she'll find time for you.'

'I hope so.'

'You're great to spend time with, you know.' His eyes were fixed on her, but in them were reflected the candlelight and her uncertainty.

'Am I?'

'You still have the same effect on me. I wish you didn't, but you do.'

He leaned across the table and he kissed her. She welcomed it. She thought she would drown in it. She hoped it would last forever. But the waiter arrived with the ice cream. They pulled away from each other reluctantly. They ate the ice cream slowly, letting it melt in their mouths, savouring each bite. They hardly took their eyes off each other. Leo paid the bill. They moved outside into the dark streets.

He took her in his arms so quickly, she gasped. His lips were greedy now, searching, devouring. He pressed her up against a brick wall by the canal, and she loved it, the damp bricks at her back and Leo's hot mouth on hers. She clutched him closer to her. Drank him in. If their kiss in the car this morning had been a sweet, sunny interlude, and the kiss at the table had been a prelude, this was a black, hot night, intoxicating and sweet and dangerous. She never wanted to let him go. She wanted to gorge on him. Keep him hers forever. But forever can sometimes only last a moment. And even before they were interrupted by another laughing group of teenage boys in t-shirts and shorts, passing them by the canal, heckling them in Italian, and they broke away from each other, she knew that moment was gone.

Chapter Thirty-Five

It was just after 9 a.m. Her phone was ringing. It was shattering the quiet of her room on the third floor of the townhouse, the calm of the hazy stripe of sunlight pitching across the stone floor from beyond the gauzy drape at the window, the loneliness of her big white bed.

Olivia was alone. After their kiss, its interruption, a gathering of themselves she didn't particularly want but Leo seemed set on, they walked back from the restaurant quietly, and she and Leo had said their goodnights on the staircase. He had been friendly, almost businesslike, after the tumult of their evening: 'See you in the morning. We'll go to the Archiginnasio, maybe the La Piazzola market.' She had nodded her agreement as he had left her. She was stunned, overwhelmed, undone. She could never catch him, she thought. He was a moth in a moonlit sky and she had no net sturdy enough. *Why had he kissed her? Why had he kissed her like that?* It wasn't fair.

She answered the phone.

'Hi, Gillian. Everything OK?'

'Yes, hello. Yes, everything's fine.' That rushed, breathless voice came down the line again. 'Well, actually, there's a problem. I need to go into the Guggenheim today. A minor crisis with the new exhibit.'

'Oh, really? All day?'

'Yes, with a late finish, I should imagine. Unavoidable, I'm afraid . . .'

'Is there no one else who can deal with it?'

'Not really. They need me. Does that work for you? To come tomorrow instead?'

'I suppose so. I was—'

'Great! See you tomorrow, then. Come anytime. You know where the key is . . .' And the line went dead, and Gillian was gone.

Olivia got up, showered and dressed. She met Leo in the tiny breakfast room downstairs where they ordered custard-filled pastries and strong coffee. He was buoyant this morning, in sightseeing mode, talking on and on about the places they would visit, like they were a couple of interrailers. She found a moment to interject.

'My godmother called me,' she said. 'I'm going to Venice tomorrow now, not today, so can you please drop me at the station after breakfast? I'll get the train to Padua and have an evening there.'

'You don't want to sightsee with me this morning?' Leo looked disappointed, but no more than she was. That meal, that night, and now it was all over – again. 'Are you sure you want to take off? I was enjoying spending time with you. I don't want to let you go yet.'

But you've let me go so many times before, she thought. *You let me go last night. What's different about now?*

'I think it's for the best. That I go. It'll save you driving me to Venice this afternoon. You have Isaac's thing tonight, after all. It will give you more time. So, if you could drop me at the station . . .'

'Right. Well, maybe . . .' Leo hesitated. Rubbed at his nose with his thumb. 'Maybe you could come with me to the meal at Santa Luce tonight and I'll drive you to Venice in the morning?'

She stared at him. She had no idea what he wanted from her, no idea why he wouldn't just let her go.

'Do you really want me to? I mean, would you want another night?' *Of separate beds, of nothing but her escalating yearning for him? Her confusion?*

'Why wouldn't I?' Olivia again thought she caught a flicker of reservation flit across his eyes. 'Do! Come with me! There's going to be a great al fresco ten-course tasting menu, and lots of rich idiots will be turning up . . . We can manage Isaac,' he added, like Isaac was a bull who might not be tethered to its post when they got there.

'Well, if there's going to be rich idiots . . .' she said. She didn't know. She didn't know if she wanted to go with him. She didn't know if her heart could take more glorious Italian hours with him, or if he would come to regret pitching one too many spontaneous invitations her way. But she didn't want to leave him. She didn't want to say goodbye when there could be more of him, more of Italy with him, more chances for electricity and danger and love. 'OK,' she said finally, for she was a fool, and fools make the worst of bad decisions, all the time. 'If you're sure, I'll come with you.'

'Great,' said Leo merrily, and, giving her a wink, he tucked back into his pastry.

◆ ◆ ◆

'My godmother refuses to use maps. She would always say road signs and instinct are quite sufficient,' said Olivia. They were in the Spider on their way to Santa Luce, near Pisa. She had a huge paper map spreadeagled across her lap, and one of Leo's knees.

'And was she right?'

'Mostly, not.' Olivia giggled, letting a funny memory of Gillian and Charlie come to her. She and Charlie and Gillian had driven to Hastings once, in Gillian's Mini, for a small holiday. They had stayed in a guesthouse with a grumpy landlady near the front, had eaten fish and chips sitting on the sea wall, had played the penny arcades. And it had taken them way longer to get there and back than it should have done. 'Dad would yell stuff like "Turn now, Gillian, NOW!"' Olivia continued to tell Leo. 'Which she completely ignored, and then when we arrived somewhere three hours late, she blamed his "poor navigational skills" for putting her off!'

Leo laughed. He didn't offer an anecdote of his own featuring Isaac and Caroline, but Olivia remembered the one from last night. The canal. The crying little boy. And still Leo didn't truly acknowledge what a bully that man had been to him. 'Anyway,' she added, letting the happy memory of Charlie and Gillian melt away. 'Let's hope this one can help us.'

She traced her finger over the road she thought they were on. Obviously, there was no satnav in this vintage car, no internet connection for their phones; they'd already pitched up to two farms and an empty cattle-shed.

'Oh! I *think* it's a right turn just up here,' she said.

'Sure?'

'Not sure. But let's give it a go.'

Leo had been a little quiet on the journey. Olivia wondered if he regretted asking her along. After breakfast, they had put his sightseeing plan into action, walking the cobbled streets of Piazza Maggiore, visiting Archiginnasio and the market at La Piazzola. She wouldn't put any pressure on tonight, she thought. Or herself. No expectations. She would treat this last night as frivolous, Italian fun – outdoor dining, lavender fields (for she had already imagined them as a backdrop for the farmhouse that Leo had told her was called La Clementina), and a soft, glorious Tuscan sunset. She even had on a dress to match the aesthetic – a floaty white thing with lace panels. They would be friends. They would have one last, confusing, platonic night together. Tomorrow could be held at arm's length. Tomorrow was a painting she didn't want to imagine herself brushed into, not yet.

She didn't want that at all. She didn't want to be just friends, in a white dress. She wanted *him*. But would she be brave enough to tell him that?

Leo turned into a single-lane road, almost a track. They rumbled along it for a while, shrugging hopefully at each other, then there was a sharp bend to the right and there, etched into the side of an undulating slope, was the most beautiful stone farmhouse – the colour of speckled oatmeal, with duck-egg blue dollhouse shutters at its doors and windows, a flat terracotta roof and, laid out behind it, the long accordion keys of rolling lavender fields.

'It's beautiful!' she exclaimed, giving herself a delighted 'tick' for the lavender.

'Isn't it just?' Leo manoeuvred the Spider up the track narrowing by the second. 'I'd seen a photo, but it hardly did it justice.'

They parked on a patch of pearly gravel at the side of the farmhouse, next to a red Mazda and a mint-green Fiat 500, and stepped out to take in the hot and sweet air, the hazy horizon, and the greedy hum of plump bees in the distant lavender. They walked around the far corner of the building and saw on the gently sloping lawn behind, before it gave way to violet stripes, one very long, unmade trestle table and three stacks of charming farmhouse chairs.

'This will be wonderful,' Olivia said, impressed. 'Thank you for bringing me.' They wandered a way down the lawn, took in the view in its full magnificence. It was romantic, she thought. It was so bloody romantic. The farmhouse, the rolling fields of lavender. How could they just be friends? How could she deny how she was feeling?

'My pleasure,' Leo replied. He was so handsome. He was so close. He was a man who had shown her all sides of himself.

It rose up within her, her confession. It had to come out. All her resolve and her best-laid plans for this day disappeared on the fragrant air. 'Oh God,' she said, 'there's something I need to tell you.'

'What is it?' He glanced at her, concerned, his hazel eyes iridescent and questioning.

She gulped. 'Something that's bothering me. Quite a lot, actually.'

She had to say it. She had to tell him. She couldn't help it.

'What is it? You're worrying me.'

'I'm getting feelings for you,' she said, the words tumbling out of her. 'I'm sorry, but I am. I just needed to say it out loud. I'm so sorry.'

'Don't be sorry.' He went to touch her arm, his eyes full of warmth, of the beautiful countryside, of the realisation she must have made a terrible mistake; she took a step backwards.

'But I am, because it shouldn't be happening. I just needed to tell you. I . . . I don't know what—'

'It's OK,' he said. 'It's OK.'

'It's not!' she cried. 'I've just been feeling worse and worse since I've been on the road with you! You kiss me, *three* times, then it's been separate rooms. You confide in me, some of your deepest childhood memories, then it's goodnight on the staircase. You've made me fall back almost in love with you and it's not fair!' She was nearly crying, against the majesty of the backdrop and the beauty of him. He stepped towards her. 'Don't hug me!' she cried. 'Don't you dare *hug me* or I really don't stand a chance!'

He denied her request. He stepped forward and he hugged her. She resisted, her body rigid against his, her face turned to the side on his warm chest, trying not to breathe him in.

'It's OK,' he said, stroking her back. 'It's OK. You're right, I've not been fair. My mixed signals. Me not letting you go. I just wanted to be with you, Olivia, that's all,' he said, pulling back from her so she could see his face, and what she saw there gave her hope. His hazel eyes were soft and deep, his mouth was smiling, just for her. His words . . . *I just wanted to be with you, Olivia.* 'And what do you mean?' he added softly. 'Fall back almost in love—?'

'THE ARTICHOKES! WHAT'S THE STORY WITH THE DAMN ARTICHOKES?'

It was a furious shout from somewhere behind them. Through an open window. A voice Olivia recognised, even after all this time, as Isaac's. She and Leo looked at each other, the moment punctured.

'I really don't want to go in there.' Leo frowned. 'We'll talk about this later. *Olivia.*' He touched the side of her face. 'I promise we'll talk about this later.'

He took her hand. They walked along the front of the house, its stone soaking up the midday sun, to the shuttered front door. Inside was a cool, spacious hallway that opened to a large, open-plan sitting room with stone walls and curtainless windows, a small bar to the side. To the rear were stable doors Olivia supposed could be flung open to the lawn, and an archway to the right led to the kitchen.

As they entered the kitchen, Leo let go of her hand.

'Isaac!'

Isaac didn't look up. He was bending over a chopping board doing something taxing with a large slab of fish and a paring knife. The kitchen was in disarray: produce and herbs and half-opened paper parcels over every surface; copper saucepans sitting on a huge range, lids high-hatting in steam; leaning towers of plates and bowls on the floor; fridge door ajar, cupboard doors adrift.

'Isaac?' Leo walked over to him and patted him on the shoulder.

Isaac wasn't alone in the kitchen. There was a chef at the sink who turned around and rolled her eyes good-naturedly at Olivia.

'I'm here with my old friend, Olivia,' Leo said quickly to Isaac's bent head. 'We met at a writers' retreat and she's on her way to Venice, so I'm driving her there. Via here.'

'What?' Isaac finally looked up and wiped a meaty claw across his forehead. His face was red, his eyes bloodshot. 'Oh, it's *you*,' he said, staring at Olivia. 'Didn't you come to a dinner party once? Right, right. Fine, I suppose. Another bugger to upset with my heinous cooking.' He bent his head again and carried on operating on his fish.

'I'm sure it won't be heinous, Isaac.' Leo placed a placating hand on a sweaty arm. Olivia thought he seemed relieved at Isaac's begrudging acceptance of her.

'Humph.' Isaac shrugged him off. 'I'm not so certain about that. We've had a series of utterly impossible disasters.'

'Nothing that can't be rectified, Isaac. I'm Magdalena, the sous chef,' said the lady at the sink. She was elegant in a black jersey and clean navy-blue apron, her dark hair pinned off her neck. 'Your stepfather has been an absolute pain in the arse,' she said to Leo, her English impeccable. 'But he's a genius, as ever, so we indulge it.'

'Genius only gets you so far,' grunted Isaac. His apron was filthy. 'Without the right ingredients.' He stared now at Olivia like she was some alien species, and Leo didn't fare much better. *No pleasantries, then*, she thought. No 'How've you been?'

'And all the right ingredients are here,' soothed Magdalena. 'Including the artichokes, which are safely in the fridge, doing exactly what they're supposed to do. So far today, Isaac has objected to the wrong-size carrots, the texture of the pepper and the available quantity of saffron,' she explained to Leo and Olivia. 'But this is Tuscany. We use what is on our doorstep, or nothing at all.'

'I'm sure it will be delicious.' Olivia thought it definitely smelled so. There was something wonderfully garlicky and aromatic escaping from under the bouncing lid of at least one of the saucepans.

'Humph,' was Isaac's distracted reply. He didn't look up. 'By the time the fucking guests get here, I may have to retire to the cottage garden with a shotgun.'

Olivia laughed – well, it was funny – but no one else did. 'Would you like us to do anything?' she asked. 'Help . . . in any way . . .' Her voice trailed off.

'Just go and wait outside,' he said huffily. 'Or get a drink or something. Everyone will be arriving at six o'clock sharp. And God only *knows* if we'll manage to get anything decent out for anybody . . .' He grabbed a large stainless-steel bowl containing a batter-like gloop from the maelstrom of the counter he was standing at, and started whisking at it frantically. 'Oh, and your mother's here,' Isaac snapped at the bowl. 'She flew out yesterday. To support me, apparently, although all she's been, since she got here, is a ruddy nuisance.'

'Mum?' Leo turned a little white. 'Well, that's a surprise. Where is she? I can—'

'Leo!' There was an open door from the kitchen to what Olivia supposed to be the cottage garden and Caroline, in yellow floral sundress and white Birkenstocks, stepped through it, a wooden truckle with a slope of hammocked daisies crooked over her elbow. 'I'm so happy to see you! I got Patricia to take care of the dogs, and I caught the late flight from Bristol last night. You're looking wonderful, darling. I said to Isaac you'd have a nice healthy tan . . . Who's this?' She stopped. One of the daisies flopped over the side and to the floor.

'This is Olivia,' said Leo weakly. 'My old friend. You met her once, quite a long time ago, at Foxes.'

'*Hello*,' said Caroline suspiciously, turning back to Leo. 'You've not brought Cressie?'

Leo stepped forward and hugged his mother. Olivia couldn't see his face as it was in Caroline's shoulder. 'Hello, Caroline,' she said waveringly, to Caroline's face over his back.

Caroline didn't reply, and when Leo reluctantly finished the hug and turned around, Olivia raised her eyebrows at him in a question he didn't answer.

'I don't understand,' said Caroline. Her hair was a soft grey now, her eyes a little more lined. 'Why would you bring a friend here and not your fiancée?'

'*Fiancée?*' Olivia rounded on Leo.

'I can explain. Perhaps we could go out into the garden and—'

'Leo and Olivia are just here as author friends,' interrupted Isaac robotically, over the scurry of his whisking. 'They bumped into each other at a writers' retreat, and they've travelled here together before Olivia goes on to Venice. That's what I've been told. And that better be the case, or I don't think Cressie will be too happy about it!' he exclaimed loudly.

'What *is* going on?' Caroline asked. She stared at Olivia as though she were a phantom, which Olivia felt she was in this family, after all this time.

'I'll talk to you in a minute, Mum, I promise. Come with me,' Leo commanded to Olivia, and he grabbed her hand and pulled her through the open doorway.

The cottage garden was pretty. Lazing wildflowers turned their faces to the sun. A low wall of smooth round stones bordered the space. Beyond, the lavender fields were a purple haze.

'This better be good!'

'I'm sorry,' said Leo, a frantic look on his handsome face. 'I can explain . . .' He stepped over and pushed the kitchen window shut from the outside.

'*Cressie?*' Olivia was incredulous. 'You're with her? She's your *fiancée*?' Leo nodded miserably. 'I don't believe this!' She thought of the London Library again, Cressie's face, Leo's eyes. 'Why on earth didn't you tell me?'

'We got together,' said Leo, shamefaced, and she had never seen that look on him before. 'About a year ago. We've been together for a year. We got engaged.'

'How lovely!' she said with venom. 'I'm so pleased for you. What a great story. So what the hell am *I* doing here?' She opened her arms sarcastically to the beautiful scenery. She felt sick. Leo was engaged. He had brought her on this road trip and he was *engaged.*

'I've been a bloody idiot,' he said. 'But I just wanted to see you. I just wanted to spend some time with you.'

'I don't understand it!' she cried. 'Why would you *want* to, if you were marrying someone else?' *That would explain the no touching*, she thought. The separate rooms. How bloody noble of him! She was gripped by a lurching pain, a glancing blow to her stomach.

'I needed to see you.'

'Why? Because you found out I was at a writers' retreat just up the road? Because you thought it would be a laugh, after five whole years of not seeing each other?'

'It hasn't been a *laugh* . . .'

'No.' She shook her head. 'No, it hasn't.' She was furious. 'Why *her*?' she asked. 'Why did it have to be her?'

Leo looked crestfallen. 'Because she never made any secret of the fact that she liked me. Because she was around. She's always been around. And . . .' He looked rather sick himself. 'I was persuaded to get together with her because of the deal.'

'What deal?'

He spoke quietly. 'Because of the deal Isaac is hoping to do with Robert Defrey.'

Olivia took a sharp intake of breath. 'Wow!' she said. 'Wow. Now I've heard it all. So, at Isaac's bidding, you finally did the decent thing, the thing your old friend from home had been waiting for all this time, and asked Cressie out. And then, happily, you fell in love, and now you're going to get married. How long did it take, Leo, to fall in love with her, once you started dating? Two months? Three? Six?' When in *seventeen* years he wasn't able to fall in love with *her*?

Leo said nothing. Then he said, 'I'm not sure I *am* in love with her.'

'Oh, fabulous!' She threw her arms up in the air again. 'This gets better and better. When's the wedding?' she asked.

'At the end of next month.'

'And you're not sure if you're in love with her?'

'No.' He ran a hand through his hair.

'Then what sort of a coward are you?' He was about to speak, but she held her hand up to him. 'Don't say any more,' she said. 'I don't want to hear it! I want to get out of here. I want to go. You need to drive me to the nearest railway station.'

'If you want me to,' Leo muttered, but he didn't take his eyes from hers. 'But I don't want you to go.'

'Why? Because Caroline and Isaac would know something was up if I flounced off in a squeal of tyres after finding out you're *engaged*? That they might think there was something *more* to this? Me pitching up here with you?'

But there wasn't, was there? There was nothing more. They had only been 'friends' this trip, apart from one sunlit kiss and one fervent embrace in a back street, and that night when he'd honourably restrained himself in her room . . .

'And it's a really important night for Isaac,' Leo said quietly, and she laughed bitterly.

'Right,' she said. 'Right.' She shook her head at him ruefully. 'I tell you what we'll do,' she said. 'So *Isaac*'s not upset, and your mother, I'll stay and play nice,' she said. 'I'll stay and be *friends* with you, as that's all we've ever been, really. *If that*.' She was walking back to the door of the farmhouse now. She was kicking herself for saying she had been getting feelings for him, as her only feelings now were those of rage and disappointment. 'And then you can take me to the station at midnight like fucking Cinderella.'

In the kitchen, Olivia immediately approached Caroline, who was helping Magdalena top and tail some green beans.

'Leo hadn't told me about Cressie,' Olivia said sweetly. 'What a lovely surprise to find out they are together. We really are here just as author friends and *old* friends, Caroline.' She was speaking like someone in a play. 'There's nothing else going on.' And there wouldn't be, she thought. Not ever again. 'It's really nice to see you both,' she lied. 'And I hope the evening is a big success. Is there anything I can do to help?'

Caroline eyed her, still a little sceptically. 'You can help me set the table,' she said.

They worked together, laying the long trestle table, arranging little glass vases of wildflowers, and folding napkins. Polishing knives on their skirts. Setting up the chairs. There was minimum conversation, maximum discomfort.

At 6 p.m., there was the throaty sound of a luxury sports car pulling up at the front of the farmhouse. Then another. The *clack* of high heels, and the *slock* of designer flip-flops on the polished tiles of the sitting room. British and Italian voices, a moneyed symphony through the now pitched-open stable doors; handkerchief-hem dresses, swanky leather loafers, expensive handbags, slicked-back hair, bare shoulders and made-up faces. And Balth, dressed in jeans frayed at the bottom and a pink paisley shirt, swaggering across the lawn with a large bottle of whiskey dangling from his hand.

'Oh, shit,' said Leo. He was standing behind Olivia, but she had been ignoring him. 'I hoped he'd forget to come.'

Balth didn't seem to find it unusual, or to care, that Olivia was there. He shook hands absent-mindedly with Leo. 'Hello, there,' he said, after she was introduced, giving her a kiss on both cheeks and a pat on the waist, before leaning back to ruffle at his golden mop of hair, shifting it this way and that. 'I remember you. How are you?' he asked, rather mechanically. He was shit-faced, she decided. Whiskey breath. Totally unfazed.

Isaac stood in the double doorway like a battleship, his fleet of rich guests behind him.

'Time to take our places!' he announced.

Olivia and Caroline stood back and let the guests spill out on to the lawn, find their place cards – for Caroline had provided them, uncharacteristically – and sit down, Magdalena among them, changed from her chef's gear into a pea-green maxi dress.

There wasn't a card for Olivia, but Caroline told her a seat had been reserved for her next to Leo.

'Are you OK?' he asked her, as he dropped into his chair.

'Never better.' She flashed him a pleasant smile.

He looked at her. 'A wall's gone up,' he whispered, leaning his face a little too close to hers. 'A big one. I'm worried I won't be able to scale it.'

'Damn right.' She tried to avoid his eyes, those eyes that could undo her. 'And this is not a wall, it's a *war*.'

What he'd done could not be excused. Her bricks had thrown themselves up and sandwiched themselves in place so fast the Trojans wouldn't get through it, let alone Leo Greene.

She turned to Magdalena, sitting the other side of her and applying lipstick using the back of a knife as a mirror.

'I've been excused,' she explained to Olivia. 'Isaac wants to take all the glory at this stage.'

'Oh? Who will help him serve?'

'He's got a busload of teenagers turning up from the catering college at Lucca.' She checked her slender wristwatch. 'They're cutting it pretty fine.'

Indeed, a yellow school bus could be seen trundling slowly up the track to the farmhouse. It stopped with a belch, just short of a silver Aston Martin, and its doors opened to release a band of excitable teenagers – boys and girls – in black trousers of various lengths and white t-shirts, who were at the table within five minutes, pouring champagne ingratiatingly into flutes.

'Not for me.' Magdalena placed her hand over her glass. 'I'm driving back to Pisa at ten,' she told Olivia.

The young servers brought out the first plates: crostini with chicken liver pâté, capers and sage. As the guests ate, Isaac travelled up and down the table, taking questions and appreciation, both rumbunctious and needy. Then there was *panzanella*, followed by *pappa al pomodoro* – a hearty tomato and bread soup with garlic, basil and olive oil. *Pici cacio e pepe* – hand-rolled thick pasta with a rich sauce of pecorino cheese and black pepper. Course after course they came, each dish more delicious than the last.

Olivia kept her body turned from Leo's and talked to Magdalena and everyone in her left-hand orbit. She heard about Magdalena's sister, who lived in France and ran an artisan craft shop. She chatted with a man across from her who was a sommelier in Rome. She deflected nonsense from Balth, who was at the wrong end of the table for her to escape, droning on about the South of France, about his plane, his playboy lifestyle.

'And then, when I got to Biarritz, I had to land the plane on the bloody roof,' he droned, as the sun set amber and golden over the lavender fields behind them. 'Which was not what I expected, but, hey ho, magnificent men in their flying machines, and all that, ha ha. What are you actually *doing* here, Lydia?' he asked her, across the table.

She froze in her seat.

'It's *Olivia*, and I'm just passing through,' she told Balth sweetly. 'I'm here on a research trip.' *For heartbreak*, she thought. Thorough research.

'You're not banging Leo, then?' He said this far too loudly.

'Of course not!' she dished back, raising her glass to him sarcastically. 'I'm not a total idiot.'

But she had been, she had been the biggest kind of idiot of all. She had slipped back on to the road with Leo.

After course number nine – a lamb cutlet with a frilly cap and green beans in peppered butter – Isaac changed into a really loud shirt, white with big green leaves on it, and placed both palms face-up on the table to receive his benedictions, of which there were many. The sun was on its final descent, blinds up, trays stowed for landing. The waiting dusk was thick and sweet. The candles were lit by the teenagers.

After dessert – the zabaglione cake she remembered from the dinner party at Foxes – Isaac made everyone change places and, somehow, he decided to plonk himself next to Olivia, a meaty lump. He was drunk, his face red and ruddy. His solid frame backlit by the setting sun on its very last slip now, ripe and golden, a hazy yolk melting into the horizon.

'Alright?' he demanded of her.

'Perfectly,' she lied. She had done her duty, eaten the food, talked to the people, and now she just wanted to get to Venice to see her godmother.

'Balth, change places!'

Their short exchange had obviously been quite enough. Isaac slumped into Balth's chair and Balth dropped nimbly into Isaac's – the blue-eyed golden boy. He leaned in towards her, his breath alcohol-ripe.

'Be careful with Leo,' he whispered, his arm buttressing the underside of the table, his hand and its brush of blond hairs too close to her knee. 'The thing with Leo you need to understand is that he tends to go for what's right in front of him. Haven't you noticed?'

'It's no business of mine,' she said, but her brain was sparking, the neurons pinging against each other.

'Yeah,' he repeated. 'He's always been the same. Otherwise,' he shrugged innocently, eyes glazed, 'not a second thought.' He took a finger and pressed it to her clavicle to make his point. 'So if he tells you he's missed you, don't believe him.'

'Thank you for the tip,' she said. She silently removed his finger. He narrowed his eyes at her, concertinaing some of his freckles.

'Leo told me something about you once.'

'Did he?' She squeezed out a smile.

'It was a long time ago, after you came to something at Foxes, I think. He said you were a challenge, and he liked that.'

She raised her glass and took a sip from it. 'Did he? That's lovely. And I was *there*, I guess, so there was that. Excuse me.'

She got up from the table, rising into the heady smell of sweet evening and lavender, tinged with lingering summer herbs. She didn't know where she wanted to go, but she walked down to a solitary cypress tree at the edge of the first lavender stripe. She leaned against it, looking back to the table, and saw Leo chatting to a woman with a blonde chignon.

Leo Greene. Handsome, charismatic, casual. Grabbing those just passing by, or at a loose end, or wanting to escape. Looking around him all the time for another spontaneous encounter. Marrying the girl who had been right there waiting, all along. The understudy ready to take up the script and walk on stage, and all Leo had to do was to hold out his hand.

Olivia took a breath. Then another. She walked back up to the lawn and sat next to Magdalena. After a while, she got up again, approached Leo and tapped him on the arm.

'I want to go,' she told him. 'I'm going to get a lift with Magdalena to the station.'

'Don't you dare!' he said quickly. 'There's no way you're running out on me.'

'Yes, I am.'

'Come and talk to me, *please*. Come down to the lavender fields.'

She shook her head.

'Just five minutes.' She stared at him. His chestnut waves, his hazel eyes, his full and delicious bottom lip. The space of skin between the two edges of his shirt. All of him that she had almost loved. '*Please*.'

'Five minutes,' she echoed, and they walked down one full stripe of soil between the lavender batons, far from earshot of the guests at the table and those milling on the lawn. The lavender fields were a blur of purple Impressionism. The soft flow of the skirt of her dress fell behind her and scuffed through the grass. These were the brushstrokes she might think about tomorrow – when she was gone.

'I don't want to be here,' she repeated, when they had reached the end of the line. 'I need to go.'

'I made a mistake.' Leo tried to take her hand. 'Not telling you about Cressie. I should have told you. You were right, I was a coward. But my desire to see you just overtook all that, I suppose. My need to—'

'Your desire to see me, and make a complete fool of me, completely overrode the fact that you're about to get *married*,' she said coolly. 'Yes, that's great. You pulled me out of a writers' retreat, and brought me on a merry dance that would end with me telling you I was catching feelings for you, like a heroine in one of my own goddamn books! I think it's totally selfish, actually.'

He looked contrite. 'It *was* totally selfish. I'm sorry. But you're not the only one who's "caught" feelings,' he said.

'Don't make air quotes at me. I hate them.'

His hands went down. 'I've always had feelings for you.'

'I don't believe you.'

'Yes, I have.'

She scoffed. 'Right. And you've always missed me, too . . .'

'You don't believe me, but wasn't I trying to take things to a different level when we were last in each other's lives? Wasn't I always hoping? Always asking you out on a date? Always accidentally touching your hand, trying to get a response? But you were resistant. You didn't want it.'

'The "designs". You were an arse.'

'I know. And then you went off with James.'

'And you went off with Cressie. Eventually. Do you love her? You said you weren't sure, so now I'm asking you outright. Do you love her?'

'No.'

'But you're going to marry her?'

'Honestly? I don't know. I don't know if I can hurt her like that.'

'By marrying her or *not* marrying her?'

Leo didn't answer.

'Or is it just for the deal? You'll marry her, without love, to please Isaac?'

Leo looked down at his shoes.

'Alright, then. How about this? A challenge – I've been told you like those.' He looked up at her. She wasn't sure she wanted to do this, but if he said he had feelings for her, she wanted him to think carefully about what they were. She wanted him to know himself, when she felt she didn't know him at all. She was just going to say it. 'You can't marry Cressie,' she said. 'Because you love *me*.'

He stared at her. They were both breathing, that was all they were doing. Standing in the lavender fields, taking in the air and each other. She waited. She didn't particularly believe what she had just said, but she wanted – needed – to know if *he* did. Leo opened his mouth to speak.

'*Leo!*' There was a bellow. Isaac had reared up to stand at the head of the table, red-faced and bullish. Leo immediately glanced up at Isaac, reactive, alert.

'Don't go running,' she pleaded. 'Don't go running to him.' Leo looked torn. He hesitated in his spot. 'That bully doesn't deserve you. Please, please, don't go running!'

'It was for the deal,' Leo protested. 'Everything has been for the deal.' He glanced back to a pacing Isaac again, and Olivia pulled him beyond the lavender to behind the scruff of a hedge, and exploded.

'Leo, *please*! Why are you still trying to placate him, make him *love* you? He used to scare you, he made your childhood – and all the years since – horrible. You retreat to being a little boy in his presence, and now you're a grown man you're still trying to get his approval and I don't know why! You've even based your whole writing career around your main character being a *chef* and still he doesn't give you the attention you crave. Why are you still chasing him? I just don't understand it!'

'Because he's the only father I've ever known!' Leo shouted, his eyes wild. 'Because I want him to say *once* that he's proud of me!'

'He's not your father . . .'

'He *is* my father,' Leo repeated, through clenched teeth. 'You may not have one any more, but *I* do.'

She felt like she had been slapped. 'No, you haven't!' she roared. 'Not if you knew what he *says* about you! I overheard him. I overheard, all those years ago, when you took me to Foxes. He was talking to some chinless wonder in the salon, and Isaac told him you weren't his son, because *Balth* was, that he treats you the bare minimum, and only because of Caroline. That he only *tolerates* you, Leo!'

'Is that right?' Leo's top lip tried to curl into a snarl while his bottom lip began to tremble.

'Yes. He said you weren't his son, Leo. You need to stop giving him respect as your father because there's none coming from him to you! None whatsoever!'

The air chilled. Leo's blazing hazel eyes turned a cool silver. He spoke slowly. 'Thank you for telling me. That's good to know. You know, we've had such fun here in Tuscany. We really have. And now, yes, I believe you should go.'

'I shouldn't have told you that,' she said quickly, feeling sick and hollow. 'I'd kept it inside me for a very long time and I shouldn't have allowed it to come out.' She had gone too far. She had blurted out an awful truth, and not for his own good, but because she wanted to hurt him.

All the heat went from her. All the fire. She was left with herself, and that was worth nothing. She didn't deserve her own tears that sprung up now while she was furiously trying to defend herself from them. But she did deserve that look on Leo's face as she turned away.

She walked past the hedge and back up the groove between the rows of lavender, stumbling on the earth in her sandals. As she approached the courtyard, Magdalena was putting her bag in the boot of her car, her keys under her chin. Olivia glanced at her watch; it was ten o'clock.

'Are you ready?' Magdalena asked.

'Thank you, yes.'

Leo's boot was unlocked. Olivia took out her suitcase and placed it in the little trunk of Magdalena's Fiat 500, then she got into the passenger seat and closed the door.

How flat and irrevocable it was as they eased down the little track away from the farmhouse. How desolate it seemed when the Virgin Mary from the rearview mirror gently swung as they crunched along the gravel, and a bug on the inside of the windscreen struggled to be free.

Leo was framed in the farmhouse door, watching them go. Olivia saw him, his face expressionless, from her side window, then in the wing mirror, getting smaller and smaller. She knew it was right to leave. She knew the book needed to be closed. Theirs was a story that should never have been written. Theirs was a story that had ended too many times already, and it was finally time to set down the pen.

Chapter Thirty-Six

Venice

Friday 12 January 2018

The dress was pale yellow silk with long bell sleeves, a sweeping skirt, a high neck with tiny mother-of-pearl buttons, and a low cowl back. It was what Stella would call a showstopper, and when Olivia had packed it for the Final Dinner, she'd shaken her head at herself with a smile. This was not a 'get in, get out and get home' outfit. This dress was a *statement*.

Her hair was in a low side ponytail, her make-up subtle but with plenty of glow. Her reflection in the mirror surprised her, but she was Olivia Sackville and she deserved to look and feel like this. She deserved to be celebrated as an author tonight, and not to shy away in navy jersey just because Leo Greene was going to be there. She would get through the evening and then she would go home. She'd been playing with fire since she'd got here and soon it was time to walk away.

There was a knock at the door, and another glamorous woman, in a red sequinned number and a voluminous fur coat, was standing in the doorway.

'Well, it's safe to say I caused quite the stir in the water taxi,' Stella said with a smile, giving Olivia a quick and gentle hug so not to crush either of them. 'I thought I'd come ready. You look amazing!'

'So do you! I'm so glad you're here.'

Stella threw her suitcase in the corner of the room, then flung open the curtain at the large window, revealing the night lights of the Venice skyline.

'Bloody hell, it's beautiful here!' she exclaimed. 'Tell me again why I've never been?'

'Because you prefer Verona, or Capri, with some fleeting, irresistible man or another.'

'Ah, Capri . . .' Stella looked wistful. 'My *belle epoque*, even though I know that's the wrong language – and "fleeting" is the best policy.' Stella had recently returned to her original philosophy of fun and freedom. 'Can I borrow some lip gloss?'

They sat side by side on the dressing table stool, facing the mirror.

'How's Gillian?' Stella asked. 'Did you get to see her?'

Olivia pulled a face at her own reflection. 'Yes,' she said. 'Once. We didn't talk much. I mean, I tried to, but she wasn't very receptive. I might go to the hospice again in the morning, or I might not. I haven't decided yet.' The only reason she might, she thought, was the piece of writing she had found in Gillian's papers. A possible white flag.

Stella nodded. 'I'm sorry,' she said. 'You know I'm always sorry about your godmother. How's Leo?'

Olivia had sent her friends several SOS text messages about Leo. Annabel had told her to be careful; Stella had told her, very unwisely, to go for it.

'He's . . . well, he's still here. He's going to be there tonight. Last night, we kissed at the Guggenheim.' Her words were flat.

'Kissed at the Guggenheim? How bloody romantic!'

Olivia shook her head. 'No, it was downright disastrous.'

'How did it happen?'

'We got locked in an office. We got too close. It happened – it shouldn't have done.'

'But was it good?'

'Of course it was good!' But Olivia could not allow herself a smile in the mirror.

'And now . . . ?'

'Now, nothing. There *is* nothing. Nothing to go on. Everything to try to forget.'

'Oh, Liv.' Stella touched up her left eyebrow with a stubby pencil. 'I'm so sorry. You haven't talked?'

Olivia blotted her top lip with her finger. 'No. Well, we've talked, but we haven't got anywhere near the truth of us. We've kissed, but where has kissing ever got anyone? There's too much history. Too much of everything.' Olivia shook her head. 'So, I'll see him tonight, I'll say goodbye and I'll go home and try to forget about him, all over again.'

'That seems eminently sensible, which is very *you*, of course. But tell me something.' Stella pulled the scrunchie from her hair and Olivia watched it cascade down in waves. 'How do you feel when you look at him?'

Olivia fixed her eyes on her friend's in the mirror and gave her a rueful smile. 'Like I want to cry! Like I'm all lit up inside . . . Damn, you're really not helping! You're supposed to be my reality turning up,' she complained. 'Giving my head a wobble, helping me to see clearly.'

'You know me, I think reality is overrated.' Stella flashed that familiar, much-loved smile. 'Now, shall we go and paint the town?'

Olivia stood up and let her dress swish to the floor. 'Let's do it,' she replied. Her last night in Venice. She would get through it all and then she would go home.

Chapter Thirty-Seven

The Final Dinner was at the Palazzo Venetis, on the Grand Canal, in a waterside restaurant. Floor-to-ceiling windows overlooked ripples studded with the gleam of refracted lights. Two grand fireplaces with fires roaring in their grates bookended a frescoed room decked with miniature winter trees and fairy-light arches. Down its centre, a long mahogany table hosted towering candelabras, white lilies floating in silver bowls, and tableware that blinked in the candlelight.

'Bloody hell, I'm blown away!' Stella was shrugging off her coat and letting one of the attendants take it from her. 'This is gorgeous!'

'It really is,' agreed Olivia. Admiring the decor was not the only reason she was looking all around the room; locating Leo Greene was the other. 'Shall we get a drink?'

The bar was in a small anteroom with the soft red glow of bordello lighting, gilt cornicing and sensuous portraits on the walls of naked people drinking from brass goblets. Another magnificent fireplace was chucking out heat, and behind an onyx bar with a marble top a pair of young bartenders giggled until they were asked to serve Olivia and Stella a glass of Prosecco.

'Where is everyone, then?' Stella asked. 'All the other authors? I'm dying to meet Frances Holland.'

'Yes, she's great.' Olivia kept her eye on the archway from the restaurant. 'You'll love her.'

They sipped at their Prosecco, wandered back out of the bar to the room that was filling by the second with the elegantly dressed bookish people of Venice. Olivia noted velvet and silk, taffeta and lace, the low-level murmur of rarefied chat, the golden clink of toasts to herald in the evening. Waiting staff glided round with trays of canapés – miniature salami on brioche, bite-size burrata on a thin springboard of bruschetta. Tanya and Meryn arrived together, then Valentina and Felicity – both startled to be in red dresses – with Beth, in a long eighties-style puffball gown.

'There she is!'

Frances had entered the room in a green satin dress and a mink stole. Olivia allowed Stella a full ten minutes before she let her rush over. She saw Stella touch Frances lightly on the arm, her face lit up, and Frances turn to her in pleasure.

Stella was lost to Frances, and Olivia was lost to herself and to Leo. He was standing by one of the fireplaces, in a tuxedo and a gold bow tie, a glass of whiskey in hand and chatting to a dour-looking man in a grey suit. The handsomest man in the room and the only one with the power to break her heart. She made her way back into the bar, where they were now serving pale frothy concoctions with sugar-crusted rims; dozens were lined up.

'What are these?' she asked the aquiline bar boy.

'Limoncello cocktails.'

Of course, she thought. She took one and sipped it slowly, savouring the lemon, the punch of alcohol, the tartness and the sweetness. Then a hand was on her arm.

'There you are. Come and say hello.'

It was Beth. At the window were Leo, Anthony and Valentina.

'Aren't you a sight for sore eyes?' said a smiling Anthony, at Olivia's reluctant arrival. 'Am I allowed to say that these days?'

'You can still say that.' Leo spoke softly. 'Especially if it's true. You look beautiful.'

'Thank you,' she replied, not daring to look at him. 'I think we've all scrubbed up well, haven't we? The occasion certainly demands it, and the setting.'

'It's so stunning,' agreed Beth. The room was full now. Olivia could barely make out Frances, Felicity, and her traitor, Stella, at the other side. 'And the view . . . Look!' Down on the canal, the lit-up buildings were grand and solemn, toppling over each other to be reflected in the water. A gondola transporting a young couple wrapped in blankets was meeting one coming the opposite way, hosting an older couple swaddled in furry coats. Both men raised their hand in a genial salute, and Olivia could make out the older man nodding at the younger one as if to say, 'This is what it means to go the distance.'

'Only in Venice,' Anthony observed. 'What a truly miraculous city this is!'

'Valentina, can you take a photo of me and Anthony?' Beth asked, pulling her phone from her clutch bag. 'My sister's a really big fan.'

Valentina nodded. Beth threaded her arm through Anthony's, grinning at his pudgy face stuffed into a stiff collar and the three of them peeled away, leaving Olivia and Leo on their own.

'How was your day?' Leo asked her.

Olivia answered without looking at him, her eyes still trained on the evening lull of the canal. 'Good, thanks. Quiet.' She'd spent the entire day in her room.

'I went to Murano this afternoon, distracted myself with a glass factory.'

Distracted? 'Was it good?'

'Yes, very interesting. It would have been nice if you'd gone with me.'

'I couldn't have done that.'

'Why not?'

Another wan smile. 'I'm trying to avoid you.'

'Yeah, I noticed that. I *am* noticing that.'

His hazel eyes were unblinking, and her heart was suddenly beating in her throat.

'I hope I'm not sitting next to you at dinner,' she said truthfully. 'To be honest, I'd rather say goodbye now, be done with it. I wish you weren't here.' She wished she wasn't there, either. She wished to be home in Marylebone. She wished she'd never come to Venice.

'I'm glad that you are,' he said, his gaze piercing right through to her soul. 'We need to talk.'

'I think we're done with all that.'

'Do you? Let's see how we go, shall we?'

'I know how we *went*,' Olivia retorted. 'And it's always been in the wrong direction.'

He shook his head. 'Maybe before a man in a red jacket announces that dinner is served, we could—'

'Dinner is served!' They both turned their heads and a man in a red jacket, with a bushy moustache, was theatrically banging a bronze gong with a felted mallet. 'So, if you'd all like to take your seats . . .'

The murmuring crowd gravitated towards the table, finding their places, setting their drinks down in a buzz of anticipation. Olivia saw with dismay that she was seated next to Leo and there was no chance to swap the place cards without him seeing.

'I know you were thinking about it,' he whispered, gesturing at the cards as they took their seats.

'Mind reader!' she whispered back, her face burning.

'Good evening.' Philip Jackson-Wright, who Olivia recognised from the internet as the director of the festival committee, was at the head of the table. 'Welcome, everyone. It's lovely to see everybody here looking so elegant for our Final Dinner.' He beamed at all the faces around the table. 'I think we can definitely say this has been a marvellous week. And I'd like to thank the authors from the UK who have come to Venice and made this book festival so enjoyable.' There was a smattering of applause. 'We hope you enjoy tonight's Final Dinner, and we wish our authors safe homeward or onward travels. So, let's raise a toast.' He lifted his glass. 'To books! And to Venice!'

'To Venice!' the diners echoed.

Dinner was served. First, a spicy tomato soup with toasted ciabatta. Next, a fish course, with Parmentier potatoes and the finest of green beans. Leo became quickly preoccupied by the chatty lady to his left; Olivia, by the man on her right – a book blogger called Nigel who had travelled to Venice from Birmingham via Berlin, arriving tonight with his winning ticket from an online competition to meet four British authors at a swanky dinner. He was on an Interrail trip, next stop: Greece. Olivia pretended to be fascinated by his tales of youth hostels and train stations, by the books he had read and what he planned to read next. He hadn't read *her* books, he told her, but he had read all of Leo Greene's. The man was a genius as far as he was concerned, couldn't be bettered . . .

But she was hyper-aware of Leo Greene next to her. Of the warmth of his body, the timbre of his laugh – shared with the woman to his left – of all the times she had kissed him, or nearly loved him. Whatever Nigel said, she had one ear on Leo's words, trying to catch them. Her body was tilted slightly towards him; her left shoulder angled to his, her left hand flat on the tablecloth by his water glass. She hated her body for its betrayal, for how it wanted him.

Stella winked at Olivia from across the table. Ensconced next to Frances, she *had* swapped place cards.

'Alright?' Stella mouthed.

Olivia nodded. 'Fine,' she mouthed back.

'Could you please pass me the black pepper?'

Leo's warm voice. Leo's eyes shining in the candlelight. His throat blushed by the flickering flames at the centre of the table.

'Of course.'

Their wrists brushed lightly as he took the pepper mill.

'Thank you,' he said.

'You're welcome.'

'Great food,' he added.

'Yes, absolutely.'

She had barely touched hers, apart from the soup. The fish, although flaky and tender, she had found hard to chew. He smiled at her, and her mouth reciprocated, easy and yielding. How very easy it was to smile at him, to look at his face, to be with him. How very difficult it was to be anywhere near him again.

The lady to Leo's left commandeered his attention once more and Nigel, to her right, started telling her that his fillet was very similar to one he'd had in Lucerne. Olivia and Leo didn't speak again until after the dessert of tiramisu, and coffee and petits fours, when Leo's inquisitive lady got up from the table.

'OK?' he asked Olivia, far too kindly.

'Yes, thank you.' She could barely look at him.

'I want you to pass the pepper, the sugar, the whatever, so I can brush my hand against yours again, but the meal is over.'

'Yes, it is.' What was he saying to her? Her blood started to fizz around her body. She had to grab at the edge of the table to anchor herself.

'I loved our kiss last night.' His voice had dropped to a whisper.

Dismayed, she found herself responding, 'So did I.'

'I've loved every moment here in Venice with you. I've loved seeing you again.'

She almost couldn't breathe. She remembered Stella's question, back at the hotel, and her answer. She remembered every moment she and Leo had ever shared.

Leo scraped back his chair and stood up. 'Would you like to go outside? To the balcony? For a chat?' he asked her.

'Yes.' Her chair was already back, too. 'Yes, please.'

Leo pulled open the door. The balcony was wider and more ornate than the one at Palazzo Tesoro and softly lit by struggling hurricane lamps. There was a brocade armchair there, too, as though someone had pushed it out and then forgotten about it, with two capes draped over its back – both dark velvet with faux fur trims.

'Would you like one of those?' Leo asked her.

She nodded. 'I feel like I'm in *The Phantom of the Opera*,' she tried to joke, as he placed one gently over her shoulders, but her smile died away when she saw how he was looking at her.

'Don't you want the other one?' she asked, her voice quiet and her body shivering in spite of the heavy garment.

'No,' he said. A phone started ringing. Leo pulled his phone from his inside jacket pocket and declined the call.

'Is that your girlfriend?' Olivia asked. 'The person you keep speaking to?' Why had he brought her out here if his girlfriend was going to be phoning him? she thought. What was she *doing* out here?

Leo shook his head. 'No, it's not my girlfriend,' he said. 'It's my therapist.'

'Your *therapist*?'

'Yes, I've finished the official sessions, but we've been having catch-up calls. Every so often. I arranged for some calls between us while I was in Venice. I needed a little extra help, a little coaching.'

'In?' She was curious.

'In how to deal with *you*.'

'Oh.' Olivia was taken aback. The call he'd taken at Harry's Bar, and the one he went out to make at the bookstore. The one she'd caught him during on the rooftop of the Guggenheim. Leo was talking about *her*? 'And what did he say?'

'*She*,' Leo corrected. 'She's called Catherine. She said to take it easy, to not scare you off. Go gentle. Historically, I've been a little spontaneous. I've rushed in. I didn't want to do that this week.'

'And have you stuck with it, Catherine's advice? Have you dealt with me well?' Olivia was still shaking. She wished she could stop.

'Not all of the time. I was all over the place on the first day here, to be honest. And not last night.' Leo grimaced. 'As wildly enjoyable as that kiss was. But tonight I want to do it right. I want to say the right things. I'm ready. Although maybe I do need that call with her first . . .' He grinned. 'Are you OK?' Now he was looking at her, concerned and tender. The Leo she had almost loved. 'Do you want to do this?'

'I'm OK,' she replied. 'I'm really OK. You can say a few things.'

They were standing close to each other. She could see the restaurant's sumptuous lights in his eyes; she noted the breeze playing at the edges of his hair, the set of his mouth.

'You're really ready?'

'Yes,' she replied. She had pushed back her chair, and she had come out on to the balcony with him. It was the Final Dinner. Last chance. She was ready to hear what he had to say.

'Well, we've talked a lot since we've been here, but we haven't talked about the things that really matter.' Leo put one hand in a trouser pocket, then took it out again. He ran his other hand through his hair. 'But I need to now, because we can't get anywhere, we can't move on, not without us getting into all of this.' He took a deep breath. 'I knew you were going to be here,' he said. 'I mean, I didn't know until I was booked, but then I did. And I was curious about seeing you, about seeing how you were these days.' She nodded, bit her lip, tried to keep her eyes on his, which were shining, earnest. 'And then that book blogger, Beth, said we'd written the same scene in our books, which was crazy. So crazy, it just made me all the *more* curious . . . And I'd missed you.'

She shook her head. 'You hadn't missed me.'

'I *had*, and I need to apologise to you. I really need to apologise to you. I couldn't just bulldoze you with it, when we first met again. I had to take my time. I had to take counsel. But I can't wait around any longer.'

'Go on.' He was so close she could almost touch him.

'I want to apologise to you, Livs, for Tuscany, for Cressie, for not telling you about her, or the engagement. For taking you on a *road trip* without telling you. I'm sorry I said something awful about you not having a father any more. I'm sorry for everything. I behaved so badly in Tuscany. I truly was making such a big mess of my life at that time. And it was after that trip I went into therapy—'

'Because of what I said about Isaac . . .' Olivia interrupted.

'No. No,' he said. 'I mean, yes, I needed to hear that. I really needed to hear that. It was the truth – a truth I had been blind to, and I really ought to thank you for that, because things have changed now, after therapy. I see him for who he is. I'm not constantly seeking his approval. I'm not *running* to him.' Olivia almost winced at the memory. 'And that little kid inside me came all the way out, and he was heard, and he was validated at last, which I so needed. Isaac can't affect me now. I can stand up to him. I have the tools to deal with him. In fact, you'll be surprised, but I've just bailed him out. Given him the final money for the investment. It's for *Mum*, really,' he added. 'But it's a nice bonus to have him sucking up to me for a change.' He grinned. 'But that wasn't what made me call someone.'

'So what was it?'

Leo sighed. Tugged at his hair. 'What kind of man calls off their wedding at the eleventh hour?' he cried. 'A week before? Good God! What kind of man does that? What kind of man gets himself in that situation in the first place, about to marry a woman he doesn't love? Of course, it was all tied up with Isaac, and I went through all of that with Catherine – I *really* went through it, as I said – but Isaac wasn't the catalyst for therapy, and neither were you. It was me. I needed to find out what kind of man I really was, and what kind of man I wanted to be, and now I know. Well, at least I know how to try to be a better man. I'm taking the steps. I'm trying to be a grown-up. And you were right.' He stepped closer towards her and placed his hands gently on her wrists. 'You were right to challenge me. I couldn't marry Cressie because I loved *you*. It's always been you, Livs. I haven't stopped thinking about you in three years. It did affect me seeing you at that party at the V&A. It was like a . . . thunderbolt. A thunderbolt I tried to pretend hadn't just annihilated me.' He smiled. 'I've missed you. I always miss you when you're not around. I just feel that we belong together, you and me. That we need to be together. And I'm here now to tell you that I love you, Liv. I love you.'

Olivia stared at him. She vaguely registered the night-time slop of the canal below them. The low hum from the restaurant behind them. The night sky above them.

'I appreciate that,' she said quietly. 'I really do.'

'And I haven't just thought about you since we last met here in Italy. I've thought about you for the past twenty years.'

'Hasn't all twenty years proved is that we *shouldn't* be together?' She loosened the cape at her neck and let it fall from her. The urge to flee, to run, had overtaken her. She couldn't do this, she thought. They had too much history. Too many stories. Too many chapters, too many scenes. They had been down roads together and the roads had gone nowhere. They had been spontaneous, and careful, and hopeful, and sad. And none of it had worked out. She didn't trust this. She didn't trust his words. Words could be cheap and they could be wonderful, and they could save you, or they could destroy you.

'You've always been on my list, Olivia Sackville!' Leo cried. 'I've always been grateful you've been out there in the world.' But she was laying the cape over the back of the armchair, smoothing its velvet flank quickly with her hand. 'Please don't tell me you're running out on me again!' he cried, eyes flashing.

'I am,' she said. 'I have nowhere to go, but I am.' Her hand was already on the glass door of the balcony. 'I need time,' she said. 'I need space to think. I always believed, each time with you, at the close of each chapter, that we *were* at the end, and that we *should* have been at the end, but now I'm wondering something else. That we've simply had too many beginnings.'

She didn't trust what he was saying to her. She didn't know if she could unstitch her heart and lay it open to him again.

'Olivia!' He walked towards her.

'Please give me time, Leo. A little time.'

'*Olivia!*'

But she was already pulling open the door.

Chapter Thirty-Eight

There was a hurried goodbye to Stella, who Olivia insisted stay – to drink the drinks and talk to the people and dance if dancing was required – and Olivia would see her back at the hotel. There was a speedy exit from the lobby. A hastened jolt down the steps to the jetty. Then, a mobile phone that started ringing in a bag, the number on the screen telling Olivia it was the Hospice Calma Bianca. It was Piera's voice she heard as she reached the jetty and the nurse's words stopped her in her tracks. They were the words no one ever wanted to hear, about someone they had once had in their lives.

'I'm afraid your godmother is really not well, and I think you should come at once.'

The water taxi was not fast enough. Olivia's feet did not carry her swiftly enough to the oak door of the hospice, which was locked and had to be banged on several times until Olivia heard a voice behind it, and the shift of a key in the lock and it was Damonte, quiet-faced, pulling the door open for her, and she was afraid she was rather noisy, in her high heels and the swish of her dress, crossing the empty lobby and through the glass door and over the herringbone of the courtyard, under the Americana awning and up the staircase where Leo had tugged at the knees of his jeans – and her phone began to ring again.

Gillian's door was closed. Olivia knocked softly but then, scared, burst in, to the dimmest of dimly lit rooms, the nodding lamp on the bedside table bent so low there was merely an inch between its domed head and the circle of light on the melamine. A hush, that was like the hush of a thousand stars, looking down silently on the earth. And her godmother motionless in the bed. Her hair softly combed. Her arms down by her sides.

'Is she gone?'

Olivia's voice was frantic. Piera was at the far side of the room. Her face was pale and it crumpled a little when she turned and saw Olivia.

'Yes. I'm so very sorry.' Piera spoke softly, concern and compassion flooding her round face. 'There was an increase in the infection. A sharp, unmanageable rise in temperature. Her organs shut down and it was all very, very sudden. I'm so sorry.'

'Oh no!' Olivia approached the bed, sank down on to the chair. Felt despair at the sight of her godmother's face, silent and peaceful.

'I'm so sorry,' Piera repeated.

Olivia nodded. Dropped her head in sadness, the past flooding back to her. Charlie waving goodbye from the stage inside the theatre. His funeral, with Gillian's true and good words up at the lectern, and Olivia's ineffective ones. Gillian's face, and how she couldn't ever look at her god-daughter. The years and the distance between them, never bridged.

'You can say goodbye to her,' Piera said. 'I will go, but I will return soon. To make sure you're OK.'

'Thank you, Piera,' Olivia mumbled, among tears that were now free-falling.

Piera walked to the door, but hesitated in the doorway. 'And I think maybe she knew this was coming. This morning, Damonte said she wrote something for you. It's on the nightstand. I cannot make head nor tail of it, but maybe you can,' she added, and after smiling sadly at Olivia, she left the room.

Olivia sat with Gillan for a few moments, weeping silently, and then she rose from the chair. Gillian's notepad was next to the water beaker, the notepad on which she had played Hangman and Dots and Boxes with Damonte, had written her instructions and her thoughts. At the very top of the open page, in familiar handwriting, was a note: *Damonte, I feel . . .* but this had been crossed out. And underneath it were more words, that Olivia read quickly, her heart pulsing in her chest.

Dear Olivia, if there is no more time, I'm writing this now, so you will know.

I couldn't bear to see you. That's the truth. After your dad had gone. You look so much like him and I couldn't bear to see your face, as every time I did, instead of making me remember him with love, it made me remember how it ended for him, outside that theatre. How he fell, and I wasn't able to catch him. I wasn't able to save him. I'm so grateful that you weren't there that night to see it. That you had already said goodbye. Please be grateful, too, Olivia. He wouldn't have wanted that for you. He was so proud of you, and I know you were proud of him, too. And I'm so sorry. I'm sorry I was cruel. And distant.

I've been so, so foolish.

And I hope these words are enough. x

Olivia read this note several times, this letter to her that told her so much, and after the fifth reading, her heart a little lighter, she flicked to the page behind, her eyes taking in a completed game of Dots and Boxes, and a line, right at the bottom, in a different familiar handwriting.

Leo Greene's.

If time doesn't heal, words can.

Leo, she thought.

Leo had written Gillian a note and it wasn't about food at the hospice, like he had said. It was advice, suggestion, salvation. His words had meant Gillian had written to her, bringing peace, an explanation, a redemption. *Yes*, her godmother's words were enough, for they meant Gillian had not been angry with her; she had just not wanted to be reminded. And Charlie knew his daughter had been proud of him after all.

Olivia closed the notebook, placed it quietly back on the bedside table and re-took her place at the bedside.

'Thank you,' she whispered to Gillian. 'Thank you.' And then she whispered into the room, into the night, into the forever, 'I'm going to write about my father in my next book. I'm going to have a wonderful character – a dad, who's a carpenter. I'm going to do my father justice. And he can have a best friend just like you. A loyal and lovely best friend. I hope you're together again. I hope that girl who played Mary and the boy who played Joseph are dancing on a stage somewhere. And if I could write that, I would.'

And, as the darkness and the lights of Venice courted the window and the world continued to turn, Olivia held her godmother's hand and whispered the words she would honour for the rest of her life, while knowing that Leo's had been everything.

Chapter Thirty-Nine

The birds of Figo were noisy at 7 a.m., letting the Venetians know they were awake and ready to play by gathering in the winter trees and scattering across the pale porcelain sky like gunshot. Olivia was also awake, as she had not slept at all. Returning from the hospice at 3 a.m., she had sat on the bed and waited for Stella, who returned at four, and they'd talked, and Olivia had told her everything – everything she never had. Olivia had cried, and Stella had held her in her arms until she'd left at six for her train to Verona.

'I can stay,' Stella had insisted in a muffled voice. 'I don't have to go.'

'No, go,' said Olivia, releasing herself from their hug. 'I'll be OK.'

'I'll call you,' Stella had whispered, propping open the door and reaching for the handle of her suitcase. 'And you call me if you need me, day or night. Promise?'

'I promise.'

'What are you going to do about Leo?'

'Honestly, I still don't know. But I will. I promise you that, too.'

Olivia got out of bed, her body like lead, her heart like a stone. She quicky showered and eased on jersey joggers, a sweatshirt, her big coat and her beanie hat. She would go to the lobby to book a few more days at the hotel so she could do what she needed to for her godmother. She would head for the hotel grounds afterwards, maybe; walk around, and send a large, sad piece of her heart up to the Venice sky, for both Gillian and her father.

Grabbing her bag and her keycard as she left the room, she glanced briefly at the pale yellow dress, hanging on the front of the wardrobe, then let the door close behind her.

The lift to the ground floor was empty. Her reflection in the mirror best ignored. She was experiencing a light-headed circle of emotions. Great sadness about Gillian. Great *relief* about Gillian. And the greatest indecision about Leo Greene. He had done a wonderful thing in prompting Gillian's note. He had given her the lovely idea of writing her father into a book. He had become a better man, he had told her so. He had taken all the right steps, eventually. He had learned how to forgive and be forgiven, and how to express that to her. It made up for so much. It made her wonder if they could move on from the past, and into the light. It made her wonder, was it enough?

Olivia turned the corner to head to reception and, clumsily wiping her eyes, bumped straight into Tanya.

'Oh, God – sorry, Olivia!'

'No, *I'm* sorry!'

Tanya had dropped her handbag, scattering make-up, a purse and other expensive-looking detritus all over the floor. Olivia saw she'd also dropped Leo's A4 notebook, the one with the matt orange cover. A sheaf of papers had slipped from it and fanned themselves rather prettily over the marble.

'Oh, dear!' Tanya cried. 'I've only just had reception tape up the spine for him . . . Are you alright?' she asked, looking at Olivia with some surprise.

'Of course, I am. Let me help you . . .'

Tanya was on the floor, retrieving her make-up. Olivia bent to pick up Leo's notebook, its spine indeed repaired with Sellotape, then the papers. The first had Leo's unmistakable handwriting and an underlined heading: *Gratitude List*. Then a sub-heading: *Things I Appreciate in the World.*

It was dated Monday 9 October 2017, and Olivia couldn't help have her eyes skim down the page.

Lemon butter

A good whiskey

Clouds

Freshly mown grass

Badgers

Umbrellas

Sunshine on a rainy day

Hyde Park in the springtime

Olivia Sackville

She picked up another sheet. It was dated 12 July 2016.

Apples

Rainbows

The morning mist when it clears

Steak and chips

Garlic

Robins

Seals

Olivia Sackville

And a third. 2 December 2015.

Butter chicken

Bounty bars

Cherry blossom

Cats

Coldplay

Olivia Sackville

Crouching down, Olivia quickly flicked through the remaining pages and there, at the bottom of each and every page – and there were more than a dozen of them – was her name. The very last sheet she picked up was dated yesterday, 12 January, with the time added – 11.45 p.m., and Leo's gratitude list only had three entries:

Olivia

Olivia

Olivia

'Where's Leo?' Olivia stood up. 'Is he in his room?'

'No,' said Tanya, dropping the last lipstick back in her bag with a soft click. 'He's gone to Inizio's, where the old boys go. For coffee.'

'Can I take his notebook to him?'

'Sure.' Tanya looked bemused. She watched as Olivia stacked the lists together, slotted them back inside the notebook with the orange cover, slid it into her bag and hitched the bag over her shoulder.

'You look like you're on a mission,' Tanya commented. 'Are you sure you're OK?'

'I hope to be wonderful!' Olivia replied. 'If wonderful will still have me.' And, blinking back fresh tears, she started to run.

Chapter Forty

Mid-note in the bustling dawn chorus of the city, the streets and alleyways of Venice were an absolute maze, but Olivia – somehow – while on the water taxi she had run for, had conjured up the directions for Inizio's from when she'd been there before: through St Mark's Square and then turn right, left, then right again, a final right at the little *tabaccheria* and head past the fruit stand.

Right, left, then right again. Past merchants setting out street displays and sweeping front steps. Past early-bird tourists walking aimlessly alongside the Grand Canal, soaking up the pale cool of the morning. She almost knocked into an elderly Venetian with a cart full of oranges. She startled a young couple about to embrace. Her bag slipped from her shoulder, her plimsolls were too tight to be running in, but she was running.

There was the tobacconist's. There was the fruit stand. And here was Inizio's. It had the tiniest of entrances. Inside was a narrow galley of a bar, a glass-fronted counter, hosting row upon row of pastries and filled rolls. Men, three or four deep, in coats and woollen hats, queuing at the counter, talking animatedly to each other. Those in the front row rested their elbows on the glass, waiting, or were already drinking from small brown cups on small brown saucers. Three generations of men were serving, constantly moving to and from the counter. To and from the coffee machines. Plonking down steaming espresso cups. Taking the white saucer of coins slid to them. Ringing cash in at the till.

Inizio's had its own cheerful symphony: the chime of the cash register, the clink of cups in saucers, the morning babble. Venetian men, fuelling up for the day. And there he was, standing at the end of the bar, front row, squished between two gents in woolly beanies, hunting in his coat pocket for coins to put in the dish, an empty cup in its little brown saucer on the counter in front of him.

She squeezed past the old boys, who paid her no mind. And she was already close to Leo, in his big coat and his furry trapper hat, when he turned.

'I hope you're not following me,' he said, his face warm and surprised.

'Well, I kind of am,' she replied, but her voice had gone at the sight of him, and she was crying, crying right here in the coffee bar among all the old boys. 'Gillian died.'

'Oh, Livs.' His arms were already around her, he was already holding her up, stopping her from falling to the tiled floor below. She let him take her weight, allowed herself to sink into him, permitted him to catch her. She let him hug her. 'When?'

'Last night.'

'Oh, I'm so, so sorry.'

She nodded. Gave a sob. 'I got there too late. She had already passed away. But she left me a note. She said that all these years she'd been distant because she couldn't bear to see me, because I'd reminded her too much of my dad. And the night he collapsed.' She could barely get the words out. 'She said he knew I was proud of him. But she'd already gone.' She buried her face in his coat and she cried into it for a long time, in the hubbub of the coffee bar, for her godmother, for her father, for the lost years . . . then she finally lifted her face to his.

'Sorry about that,' she whispered, tears still in her eyes.

'That's perfectly alright.' Leo's voice was tender. His arms were still tight around her. 'I'm so glad you got that,' he said. 'That closure. I know you really needed that, Livs.'

'I did.' Her voice was small. 'Please don't set me off again,' she pleaded at the look on his face, 'I might never stop. You wrote on her notepad,' she added. 'In the hospice. Thank you for that, Leo.'

He shrugged gently. 'It was only a few words,' he said. 'But it was worth a try. Words are always worth a try.' He held her for a few moments. 'What do you need me to do?' he asked her, looking into her eyes. 'I can be in Venice for as long as you need me. I can come with you, whatever you need to do or arrange. I'll be here to support you.'

'I believe that,' she said.

'You do?'

She nodded. 'Can we talk about *us* for a little while?' she asked.

'If you want to.' He was hesitant. He stroked her back.

'I need to.'

He released her, but he didn't let her go. He kept hold of her hands, the space between their bodies narrow, the space around them small in this tiny bar. 'OK,' he said.

'I believe a lot of things – now,' she said, her eyes steady on his. Her heart was pounding. She was grieving. She was resolute. She was ready. 'I believe you,' she said. 'I believe that I'm on your list. That you have thought about me. That you still put me on your list after everything. I just needed time.' She smiled gently and tapped at her bag, at her side. 'And I have your Gratitude Lists. I wasn't snooping, I promise. Tanya dropped your notebook, and I picked them up. It's been mended, by the way.'

Leo nodded, his gaze fast, his eyes not leaving her face. 'Glad to hear it.'

'*Scusi?*' A man in a flat cap pushed past from behind Olivia, and got himself up to the bar, elbows landing, fingers clicking for the server.

'Have you really thought about me for twenty years?' she asked Leo.

'Yes, I have,' he said. 'From the moment I first saw you, I wondered what your story was, and whether I could ever be a part of it. And I've been happy that you're in the world, whether you've been in *my* world or not. I've just liked to think of you out there somewhere.'

'And now I'm here,' she continued, 'in Venice, with you. And forty old boys getting coffee. I've been reading the wrong words for a long time,' she said. 'I've been unable to turn the right pages. But now I want to make it to the end of the story. *Our* story.'

'Your godmother has just died,' he said gently. 'So, in the kindest possible way, are you sure you know what you want?'

'Yes, I do, and I know what I *need*, too,' she said, the tears in her eyes sparkling. 'I've never been surer.'

Another man, standing next to her, was staring at them, his rheumy old eyes unblinking. He said something to Olivia, and she replied in clumsy Italian, 'I'm just getting my morning coffee and the man I love – hopefully.' And he smiled at her, a perfect Italian toothy grin.

'*Bella,*' he said. '*Buona fortuna.*'

'You speak Italian?' Leo looked surprised. 'You never told me that.'

'You never asked. I took a class, that week in Venice. I went to Italian school every day.'

'And what did you say to our friend here?'

'I said I liked his hat. *Leo.*' She turned back to him as the clamour of the coffee bar percolated around them: the clink, the froth, the steam. She looked into his beautiful hazel eyes with all their fire and all their strength and all their vulnerability, and, with all of hers, she chose her words carefully. 'Nobody else makes me feel like you do. Nobody else comes close. You're the only one I want to go on a road trip with. The only one I want sitting in my bathroom, while I have a bath. The only one to tell me I can do this, when I really feel like I can't. And you're the only person I want to listen to me saying these words, right now. *I love you. I love you.*'

Leo smiled. A slow succulent smile that spread across his lovely face and lit up his eyes. He pulled her into him again.

'I love you, too, Olivia,' he whispered into her neck. 'I'm pretty sure I always have.' He stroked her back. He took one hand and cupped the side of her face, drinking her in. The row behind them was jostling for coffee. A man in a green coat was gabbling at them in Italian, equally amused and exasperated.

'I think we need to move on,' she mumbled.

'I agree,' Leo replied. 'How about getting married and making a baby with me?'

'That would be quite some move.' She looked up at him, eyes wide. 'Is there time?'

'We can *make* time. We can write it into the book of us.'

'I've got a busy few days,' she said, biting her lip and trying to quieten another rising swirl of emotion.

'*We've* got a busy few days,' Leo reiterated. 'We're going to get through this together.'

Olivia nodded, wiping away the tears she knew would come again, but, with Leo by her side, she could let heal her.

'And then we're going to create something wonderful.'

Her aching heart soared to the ceiling along with the steam of the coffee.

'Can I kiss you now, please? I've spent thirty-six hours thinking about doing it again, and most of those believing I'd never get another chance.'

'Do you think the "old boys" will mind?' she asked him tenderly.

'Let's try them . . .'

He kissed her, and the old boys stopped chattering to each other and raising their morning coffee cups to their lips; they whistled through their teeth and clapped and cheered, and the steam rose, and the change clinked in the saucer, and the coffee machine hissed and spluttered, and the pale winter sunshine nodded through the steamed-up window, and another wonderful day in the beautiful city of Venice was about to be written, in a perfect story of love.

ACKNOWLEDGEMENTS

Huge thanks to my wonderful editor, Victoria Pepe, for continuing to believe in my work and publishing my stories. And to Caroline Hogg, the editorial team and all at Lake Union for their invaluable help on this book.

Thanks also go to my agent, Diana Beaumont, for her hard work and passion.

And to you, the reader, thank you! I just love writing, and to be read is still a dream come true.

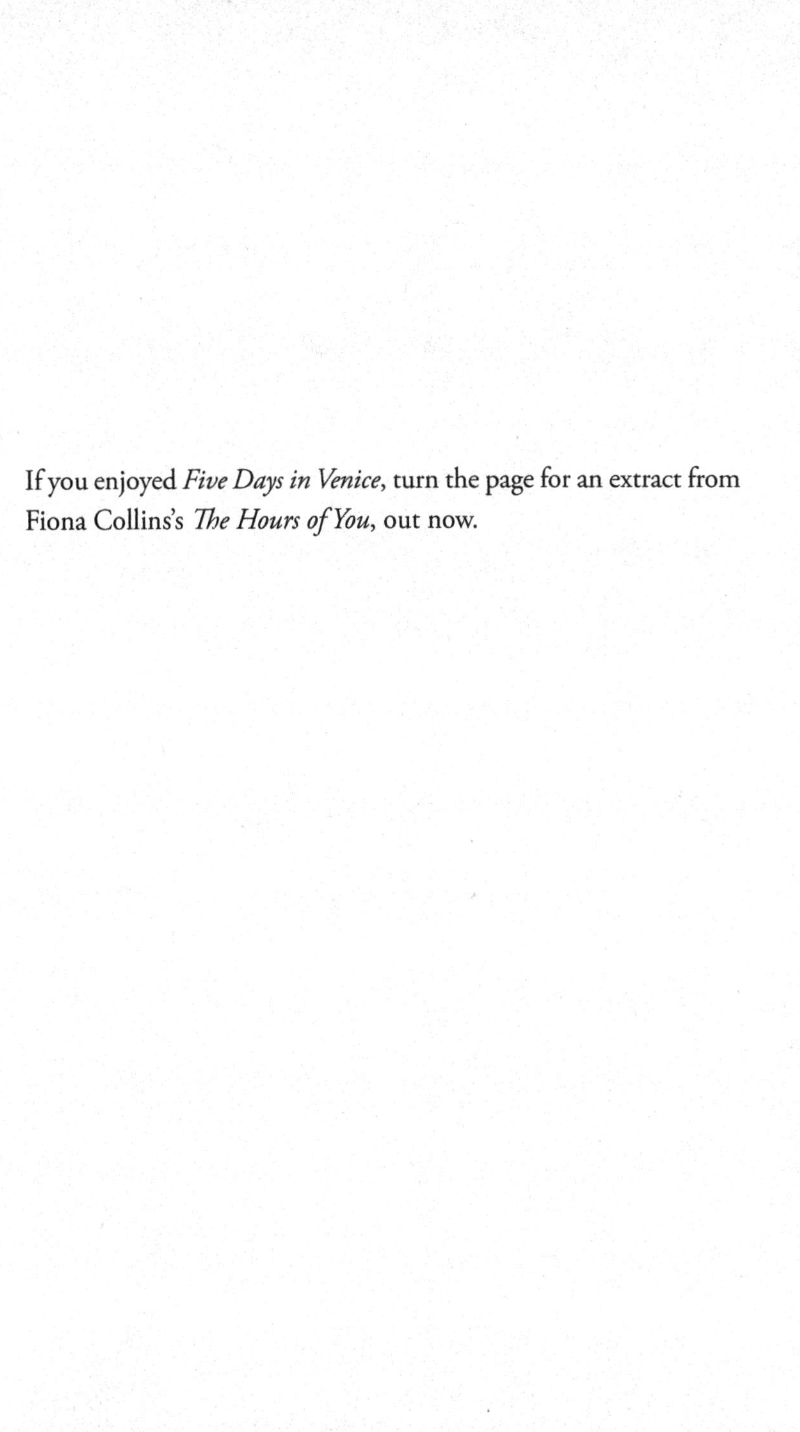

If you enjoyed *Five Days in Venice,* turn the page for an extract from Fiona Collins's *The Hours of You*, out now.

Prologue

When they were in love, it seemed the sun shone on them every day. When they were in love, when day became night, dark skies blanketed them in a velvet warmth and drew them closer together. Every hour they knew was succulent and miraculous. Every moment they shared was a kind of paradise.

Sometimes she caught him looking at her, entwined in sloping grass on a seasidey summer's day, or in the pearly milk of a winter's morning as they lay plaited and half-awake in bed. She drank in the trace of his lopsided smile and his green eyes steady and true and full of love for her – for her! – and almost believed it could be forever, this love. That they would always be this way, lying in each other's arms and summoning their combined future to be both certain and endless.

Maggie and Ed. Ed and Maggie. How could it be any other way? When they were young and in love it appeared they had a lifetime, but they were wrong. Lifetimes were long enough roads to see them stumble, or lose their way, or take each other far from reach. They were roads that led where she least expected: a wintry pier on a blustery December afternoon where an icy wind, whipped from a grey sea, did nothing to dry her bitter tears.

That day, she had cried until she felt her heart was all wrung out, like a useless rag. She had just lost him forever and he had not even said goodbye – that word was hers – and she knew she would not see him again. There was no road that might lead her back to him now. No rising and falling sea that would carry her his way again.

He was lost, and so was she.

Chapter One

5 P.M., ON THE ISLAND

The sun was too bright, the sea was too blue, but the hand of the young man waiting to help Maggie Martin step off the rocking wooden fishing boat into the azure shallows, bathwater warm on her calves, was reassuringly steady.

'Welcome to Mémoire,' the young man said. 'I will be escorting you to your accommodation. I am Amine.'

'Thank you, Amine,' Maggie said. She didn't expect Amine welcomed many lone female travellers – aged sixty-one, in shorts and a *Hotel California* vest top, with a camera slung around their neck and a boat boy's Man United bucket hat – to Mémoire Island. She clung on to Amine's hand like she never wanted to let it go.

'Where is your luggage?' he asked her.

'Here!' called out Salou from the boat, the mischievous barefoot boy who had pelted her with unanswerable questions about Premiership football all the way from Le Digue and had laughingly plonked his hat on her head as the boat first loped into the miraculously clear waters of the port there.

'Don't burn your head, my lady!' he had exclaimed before coiling up the mooring rope, and she had laughed too, but she was more worried about getting her fingers burnt here on the island.

Salou reached over the idling and silent driver at the boat's stern, hooked up her orange rucksack by his thumb – the rucksack that made her feel like an overgrown, over-aged backpacker, but had been a practical choice – and swung it to Amine.

'Travelling light,' Amine commented with a smile, as he caught it.

'Hardly,' muttered Maggie. She felt the baggage of her past permanently slacking off her like a deflated lifebelt.

'See you tomorrow, my lady!' Salou shouted. Maggie took off his hat and threw it back to him, squinting now behind the sunglasses she had bought at London City airport. They were not dark enough for the dazzling butter-yellow sun glancing off the turquoise Indian Ocean. They didn't provide enough protection. She wanted to get back on the boat. Then the other boat. The ferry to Praslin. The smaller aeroplane. The big aeroplane. She wanted to be back in London, in her neat little flat with its heavy furniture, its worn brown leather sofa with the folded green blanket at one end, her record collection and her books; the rain drumming on the dirty window that looked blankly down on the street below.

Instead, still holding Amine's hand, Maggie scooped through the water to the shore, her espadrilles in her hand and the undulating sand cool and silky beneath her toes.

'Bungalow Marguerite is over there,' said Amine, as they emerged from the gentle surf and her toes became buried now in the dry sand, almost pearlescent pink, of a never-ending beach. 'See?' Amine released his hand from hers and pointed along the verdant slip of palm trees and vegetation flanking the beach. She could just make out, at the furthest point, a jutting elbow lipped by golden sand and scattered with pale cottages.

'Wonderful,' she said, repeating what Simone, her editor at *Supernova* magazine, had said after uncharacteristically booking Maggie's accommodation herself, so intrigued had her friend been by the tiny island of Mémoire.

'Quaintly beautiful, my dear, if a little basic,' Simone had added as she handed Maggie a printout with a photo of a crumbling yellow cube of a bungalow, topped with a pitched thatched roof and fronted by a veranda hitched together by bamboo canes. 'And from what I read online, you'll probably be the only tourist, apart from *you know who*. Whoever would have thought,' the younger woman had concluded, shaking her silky black bob prettily at Maggie before gliding back to her office, 'you'd wind up on a remote desert island like Mémoire for your last ever job?'

An island like Mémoire . . . It certainly was remote. It had taken Maggie twenty hours to get here. And it was definitely beautiful. Maggie was in a picture postcard scene: the sea, the sand, the palm trees, the sun . . . and the heat was miraculous to her for January, when in London she'd be shivering her socks off. But her last Where Are They Now? profile for *Supernova* was going to be memorable for all sorts of reasons, and the remote and beautiful setting would be the least of them.

Amine set off up the beach, Maggie's limp rucksack slung over his shoulder. Maggie followed, squinting. The sand was deep and scalding hot. She wanted to put her espadrilles back on, but Amine was striding ahead. He and the rucksack disappeared into the pretty mesh of palm trees and tropical foliage, and she had to trot inelegantly to catch up with him on the canopied scrubby path. It wound between the scaly trunks of palm trees and the smoothly viscous tangle of roots.

'Mind yourself, Miss Marty,' said Amine, as, espadrilles back on, she navigated a low-hanging branch camouflaged by palm leaves the size of small cars.

It was too late for that, she thought. She was already here. She wanted to get on and off Mémoire as quickly as possible. She wanted to get what she had come for and run.

They walked. They avoided low-hanging branches. Finally, the dense grove of giant green leaves and dappled, sandy earth opened out and the path morphed into something more pedestrian – and recently and resolutely brushed. There was a rusty sprinkler keeping idle and near-silent time on a spiky teardrop of grass. Five rough-hewn bungalows nestled in a cluster. On the veranda of one leant an old bicycle. In the doorway of another, a small girl was poised on one foot, like a crane, in a faded red sundress.

'These homes belong to islanders,' said Amine, 'but Pa Zayan is happy to move out of his to accommodate the occasional visitor . . .' He led her past the first two bungalows and to the third, whose veranda looked like it had just been doused with water.

'Welcome,' he said, as he stepped on to the veranda and opened the door for her. 'I hope you like Bungalow Marguerite.'

'Oh, it's lovely,' Maggie exclaimed, and she immediately felt bad for Pa Zayan, who she hoped had temporarily moved in with a kindly daughter not too far away. The bungalow was cute. There was a small bed with pale blue bedding, tepee-d by a gauzy mosquito net. A bamboo bedside table with an upside-down book on the top (*fiction?* she wondered. She didn't read fiction any more. She'd devoured slim volumes of Fran Leibowitz and Joan Didion essays on the plane). A table and two wooden chairs tucked into each other on a swept terracotta floor. And to the rear was a white bathroom, simply tiled.

'Only cold water,' said Amine apologetically, showing it to her. 'But it's very warm on the island so . . .'

'Cold water is fine,' said Maggie.

Amine placed her rucksack carefully in the corner of the room. She could imagine the letter at the bottom, nestling under her make-up bag whose edge was bulging against the canvas. She was strangely reminded of being pregnant with Eloise: a foot jutting from under a rib, an elbow attempting to stretch out of what had once been her waist. That letter at the bottom of her rucksack was a message in a bottle she had been asked to deliver – if the hours and the man allowed.

'Thank you, Amine,' Maggie said. Amine looked surprised and delighted to be tipped. As he turned to leave, she asked him, 'Do you happen to know where I might find a man called Ed Cavanagh on the island? At this hour?' she added, amused at sounding like a stilted Jane Austen character in an Eagles vest top.

'*Mr Ed?* Sure.' Amine grinned. 'He'll be down on the beach, west of where your boat came in,' he said.

'West, as in, to the right?' she clarified. *Mr Ed?*

'To the right, yes. He'll be there with his boat. Just past the little jetty. Blue boat, yellow mast.'

'He has a *boat*?'

'Yes. Goes out in it every morning.' Amine nodded his head. 'Enjoy your stay, Miss Marty.'

She still didn't bother to correct him. 'Thank you, Amine.'

Once Amine had gone, Maggie showered in cold water, unrolled a raspberry batik maxi dress and retrieved flat leather flip flops from her rucksack, then made herself up to look decent but not as though she had made a great effort. She headed out of the bungalow, walked back through the shaded grove and down to the beach, where the sun was low in the sky but still fiercely hot.

Setting off to the right, she slipped off her flipflops to walk barefoot in the cooler-now sand. Soft waves were breaking lackadaisically on the shore. A gull, swooping on the horizon, took off towards the sun, and lone clouds drifted with no particular place to be. She passed a small jetty, two young boys at the end, fishing lines and dangling bare legs in the water. There was a boat, in the distance, bobbing on the turquoise water. It looked like a blue boat with a yellow mast.

Maggie stood and watched it for a while, her heart an anxious prisoner behind her ribs, her nerves a jailor's jangle of keys. Finally, she saw him, a figure who came to stand at the mast. *Was* it him? Her missing person? She raised an arm, wondering if he could even spot this stick figure on the beach, waving hello.

They were so far apart, she thought. She was sixty-one, worn around the edges, voluntarily detached from life. A woman who needed to work on both her posture and her regrets. He was *Ed Cavanagh*, and likely to turn the boat around and sail away once he saw her.

They had known each other for so long, but now didn't know each other at all. They had first met a stone's throw from another coastline, one that couldn't be more different, where the sea was a grey-green sludge flanked by a pebble beach and a host of glaring seaside attractions, and where nothing much ever happened – not to her, anyway – until the hot August afternoon when she finally spoke to Edward Neville Craddock.

ABOUT THE AUTHOR

Photo © Siobhan Johns Photography

Fiona Collins grew up in an Essex village and, after stints in Hong Kong and London, returned to the Essex countryside where she lives with her husband and three children. She has a degree in film and literature and has had many former careers including TV presenting in Hong Kong, being a traffic and weather presenter for BBC local radio and as a film and TV extra.

Follow the Author on Amazon

If you enjoyed this book, follow Fiona Collins on Amazon to be notified when the author releases a new book!
To do this, please follow these instructions:

Desktop:

1) Search for the author's name on Amazon or in the Amazon App.
2) Click on the author's name to arrive on their Amazon page.
3) Click the 'Follow' button.

Mobile and Tablet:

1) Search for the author's name on Amazon or in the Amazon App.
2) Click on one of the author's books.
3) Click on the author's name to arrive on their Amazon page.
4) Click the 'Follow' button.

Kindle eReader and Kindle App:

If you enjoyed this book on a Kindle eReader or in the Kindle App, you will find the author 'Follow' button after the last page.